Going for Two

A NOVEL

CAMELLIA BOOK TWO

MARIE VEILLON

HOMEGROWN PUBLISHING LLC

First edition February 2024

ISBN 979-8-9889657-2-5 (ebook)

ISBN 979-8-9889657-4-9 (paperback)

ISBN 979-8-9889657-9-4 (hardcover)

Cover design by @cindyras_draws

marievwrites.com

 Formatted with Vellum

Author's Note

This novel could be categorized as a "minty rom-com" or a closed-door romance with the door cracked open. It incorporates Christian themes, especially Catholic views on prayer, marriage and family, and chastity.

It includes heavy innuendo and discussions of sex, chastity, NFP, and fertility awareness, as well as semi-steamy and fade-to-black scenes, implied nudity, crude humor, and mild language; however, any explicit spice happens off-page. If it were a movie, it would probably be rated PG-13.

Additionally, please be aware of the following content and depictions, which some readers may find triggering: women's health; pregnancy and childbirth, especially high-risk and premature delivery, breastfeeding, and postpartum health; mental health; alcoholism and substance abuse; child neglect; family loss; legal guardianship and child custodianship; and body consciousness. It is my intent to treat these topics with the sensitivity they deserve, and I promise to deliver a HEA in the end.

On a lighter note, the writing style of this book purposefully reflects the grammatical and syntactical quirks more common to those who speak and think in a Cajun accent. In other words, it sounds weird on purpose.

GOING FOR TWO

—See also, *Two-Point Conversion*; in football, after a team scores a touchdown, it may opt to kick a routine extra point or try for two points by lining up to run a play from scrimmage in the same manner as a touchdown attempt. Two-point conversions are risky and less often successful; however, the additional point, whether lost or scored, often changes the outcome of a game.

For Kait

And to all of the JD critics:
If you thought he was either too spicy
or too Catholic, stop reading now.
You won't like Blake.

Going for Two

Prologue
SEVENTEEN YEARS AGO

LOREN

I CROSS MY ARMS AND GLARE AT THE BACK OF MY brother's head. There's no way any of these boys are making a move on me with him lurking around tonight.

I lean back against the brick wall, watching as Tenley gazes up at Landry with a look of pure adoration. Of course, he just *had* to come to my first boy-girl birthday party, even though he's a grade ahead of everyone here, and now he's ruined everything by asking *my* best friend to dance. Tenley's been crushing on Landry for what seems like forever, and while I want to be happy for her, since there's a good chance she's about to get that first kiss she's been dreaming about, she *did* leave me all alone on the loser wall ... for my brother.

Hoobastank's "The Reason" blares over the speakers in the backyard, and I huff as I watch the couples swaying awkwardly around the pool, the lights twinkling and reflecting off the water. It's totally unromantic, and that song is stupid anyway. I tell myself I'm better off waiting for a more magical moment to get kissed for the first time.

My eyes dart around until I notice the empty pool house. There's no hope of getting asked to dance since everyone seems to have already paired up, and I can't bear being the lone wallflower any longer. I resign myself to settling for the sanctuary of the empty building until the party is over. It's not exactly the grand evening I imagined, but I've had enough mortification for one night.

As soon as I can tell no one is looking, I scramble over to the pool house and slip inside. There's a futon and a few other furnishings, including a small bookshelf. I sift through the titles, settling on a Nicholas Sparks novel. Just as I make myself comfy on the lumpy futon, I hear the door creak open.

"Oh, sorry." I glance up to find one of my classmates, Blake Bourgeois, standing in the open doorway. "I didn't realize anyone was in here. But I can go if you want to be alone." He hitches his thumb over his shoulder.

I shrug, already embarrassed about being found hiding out. "It's fine. I just came in here because the party was so boring."

He nods. "Totally lame."

But he looks slightly dejected, and I can't help it as a smile spreads across my face. It's somewhat reassuring to see one of the most popular guys in my class striking out, too. "You're welcome to hang out here if you want. It's not like I own the place or anything."

He stuffs his hands in his pockets and glances down at his feet. "Okay. I'll just ..." He looks around the room for another seating option, but it seems as though the futon is it.

"It's okay to sit. I won't bite," I offer with a smirk. He nods and blushes slightly before reluctantly taking a seat next to me. "Although I suppose you're more worried about being seen with me," I add softly.

He huffs out a short laugh as he turns to face me. "I'm not afraid of Landry Reed," he says, raising his chin defiantly.

I roll my eyes. "Well, you might be the only boy here who isn't. And if that's not true, then I'm literally the least desirable girl at this party."

"What makes you think that?" he asks, furrowing his brow.

"It's not like any of you were lining up to fill my dance card tonight," I mumble.

"Your what?"

I shake my head, reminding myself that most kids my age aren't exactly fans of Regency era romance. "No one's asked me to dance." I feel dumb as soon as the words leave my mouth. "I'm also pretty sure my best friend is making out with my brother by now."

He cringes. "If you mean Tenley Robin, then yeah. She and Landry were ..." He clicks his tongue.

"Ugh, of course," I groan. "He ruins *everything*."

"I know the feeling," Blake says, sighing heavily. "My parents made me bring JD with me tonight. I think they wanted the free babysitter. But it's so unfair. He's two years younger, and they still let him tag along."

"He's only eleven? Wow, I kind of thought ..."

"Yeah, yeah, I know. He's already taller than me. Everyone thinks he's older."

I can tell I've hit a nerve when he looks away and his ears turn red. "So, um, I guess your brother salted your game tonight too?"

He laughs. "Yeah, I guess."

"Is he really out there dancing with someone?" I ask, my eyes growing wide. He nods, and I climb up on my knees to peer out of the window. Sure enough, the younger Bourgeois is locked in with an eighth-grade girl. "How?"

He shrugs. "It's always like that for him."

We're both quiet for a minute before I speak again. "Is that why you left the party?"

"Maybe."

"Does it bother you? You know, having your brother around all the time?"

He glares at me, surprised at my line of questioning. "Doesn't it bother you?"

"Of course it does. Everyone treats me like a baby when Landry's around. Plus, we have absolutely nothing in common." I lean back and cross my arms again.

"Yeah. And I just—I couldn't bear to stick around and watch him get his first kiss before I do," he admits quietly.

My brow shoots up in disbelief. Blake is generically cute with his blond hair and blue eyes, one of the smartest kids in our class, and a great athlete. He's also known for being a smooth talker, and his parents are loaded, at least by Camellia standards. I can't fathom that he could be as inexperienced with the opposite sex as I am. "Wait, *you've* never kissed a girl?"

He keeps his eyes trained down and stares at his lap. "No."

"Well, why not?"

He chokes out a laugh. "Lack of opportunity, I guess."

"Oh." I sit there and ponder his predicament. "You do know that most of the girls in our class think you're hot, right? All you'd have to do is—"

"Find one who isn't already dancing with my little brother?" he asks, cutting me off.

"Oh, I see. I'm sorry."

He shrugs again, absently picking at the hem of his shirt. I put my book down before springing up to my knees for some more recon.

"There's still time," I announce from the window. "They're only dancing."

"What do you mean?"

"Why don't you cut in? Steal your first kiss back," I suggest as I turn to face him again.

He smirks at me, apparently amused. "You think I still want to kiss the same girl who's willing to get with my eleven-year-old brother? No, thanks."

I grin back at him. "Good for you, Blake Bourgeois."

"Well, why aren't you going back out there, *Loren Reed*?" he asks, his eyes suddenly looking bluer and more sparkly than I remember. "Are you going to let something as silly as your best friend swapping spit with your brother ruin your night?"

"Yeah, I think I am," I say, though I'm still smiling. "Besides, no one is going to dare to swap spit with me as long as big brother is watching, even if they were interested in a dork like me."

He furrows his brow. "Maybe you just need a little more confidence. Plenty of guys think you're cute."

"They do?" I squeak.

"Uh, sure—I mean, I guess," he replies awkwardly, his cheeks turning pink. "And you have a really nice ... brain."

"Too bad no one cares whether I'm smart. Most of the time I feel invisible, between having Landry for a brother, a coach for a dad, and the first girl in our grade to get boobs for a best friend. I'm starting to doubt I'll ever get kissed."

I expect him to laugh, but he only looks up at me, his eyelids heavy, and my stomach flips. "Well, I see you," he says, his voice deeper than it has been up to this point.

Maybe I'm crazy for reading this much into the first romantic interaction I've had with a boy, but this feels like my only opportunity. I swallow hard, and my heart thumps in my chest.

"Blake?"

"Hmm?"

"Would *you* kiss me?"

~

BLAKE

My eyes widen. "Would I—what?"

Loren lifts a shoulder and shoots me an apologetic look. "It's just, I'd kind of like to get it over with, you know? We're already here, and if you still want to beat JD to it, you probably don't have much time."

I can't believe I'm actually getting propositioned, although it feels more like a business arrangement than a date. Or maybe she's making a pity offer after hearing me accidentally blurt out that I've never kissed a girl.

Regardless, I'm *down*.

I wasn't lying when I said I thought Loren was cute, though I've never admitted that to any of my friends before because she's kind of ... different. Not to mention, her older brother is a total douchebag. But I still like that she's not afraid to be herself and that she's smarter and funnier than most girls our age.

"So, should I kiss you, like, right now?"

"Only if you want to." She looks down at her hands. "And don't worry, no one has to know, even if we don't go through with it. I won't tell anyone."

It's getting harder to hide my nerves, and I'm almost struggling to breathe. "Are you sure?"

She rolls her eyes. "It's just a kiss, Blake. It doesn't have to mean anything."

"Okay." I gulp.

Loren nods and turns her body so our knees are touching, but she's so petite that I have to lean down to meet her. I clear my throat and reach over to cup her face gently, and her eyes flutter closed. She rests her hand on my arm as she waits patiently for me to close in the space between us. Then I inhale deeply as if I'm preparing to go underwater, unsure of whether I'm supposed to hold my breath the whole time or what, and I brush my lips against hers.

They're soft—*really* soft. In fact, her lips feel nicer than I imagined.

I lean in, pressing against her a little more firmly, and my head gets all fuzzy. But she pulls away abruptly, leaving me there with my chest heaving and my lips still puckered.

"Well," she mumbles, her fingertips drifting to her mouth. "That wasn't so bad. Right?"

I blink, suddenly feeling the urge to run my thumb along her bottom lip, too. "No. It wasn't." My voice cracks awkwardly, and I die a little on the inside. "Uh, thanks, I guess?"

She nods. "I'm glad we could help one another."

"Yeah," I agree, still staring at her mouth. "But, um, aren't you worried about ..." I swallow hard again and cringe. "You know, tongue?"

"You mean, how to use it and stuff?" she asks quietly, and I nod entirely too eagerly. "Sure, I suppose. But I already kind of forced you to do this, so I didn't want to—"

"I don't mind," I say quickly, and the corner of her mouth turns up. "I mean, we might as well, right? So that we'll know what to do the next time, when it really counts."

"Okay," she breathes, already leaning in.

I hold back a groan as our lips meet again, cradling the back of her head in one hand and sliding the other down to her lower back. I'm running purely on instinct as I open my mouth, but she follows my lead. I use about all of the self-control I can muster to slowly trace the inner edge of her bottom lip with my tongue. Her fingers rake through my hair as I do it again, this time venturing farther into her mouth. And *man*, is this not the best thing I've ever done.

She lets out a small sigh, and it registers somewhere in my brain that she's enjoying it, too. And I really like the idea of being responsible for making her feel good enough to emit a sound like that. I am officially hooked on this whole kissing thing.

I push my luck by inching my hand down her back to cup her butt, and when she doesn't seem to mind, I grasp a handful of her to pull her even closer as I deepen my exploration of her mouth. She clutches at my hair more tightly in response, then slips her tongue between my lips and does some kind of maneuver in which it curls against mine. I can't help myself as a strange growl rumbles through my chest, and I swear in that moment this must be why people get married, because I would be perfectly content to continue on with her like this for the rest of my life.

I'm plotting on how I can slide her over and into my lap when she backs away again, our lips making a smacking sound as she breaks the seal between us.

"Did you hear that?" she asks, both of us breathing hard.

"Huh?" It's all I can get out. My head is still foggy, reminding me of the time when my friend Jase had stolen a bottle from his parents' liquor cabinet. But Loren tastes so much sweeter and warms my chest better than that whiskey had.

"I thought I heard my brother calling me," she explains, rising to look out of the window again.

"Oh, maybe he's looking for you?" I offer as I wipe my mouth with the back of my hand. It's obvious I haven't recovered as quickly as she has.

"I should probably …" She bites her lip and gestures toward the door hesitantly.

"Yeah, uh, same." But leaving her is the absolute last thing I want to do.

"Thanks again for the practice," she says with a coy smirk.

I grin back shyly. "Yeah. You, too. It made me feel better."

Her cheeks darken, and I hold back an audible reaction. I have no idea what's happening inside of me, but my body and my brain are definitely not on the same wavelength. And every little thing she says or does is garnering a reaction from one or the other.

"And, hey, a promise is a promise, right?"

"What?" I ask, confused.

"This stays between us, no matter what?" she clarifies, her expression hopeful.

"Oh, yeah, right. Of course."

She nods and stands, so I follow suit. "Well, good luck with your brother problems, Blake Bourgeois."

I laugh shortly. "You, too, Loren Reed."

She smiles again and turns to walk out, and I trail behind her.

"Oh, great, you found her," I hear Landry's voice as soon as we step out of the pool house. "Lo, I've been looking for you everywhere."

Her brow goes up sharply. "You have?"

"Yeah, I hadn't noticed you disappeared at first."

She ducks her head. "And just like that, I'm back to being invisible," she mutters.

I clear my throat, stepping forward. "I noticed her," I say to Landry, my eyes flashing to Loren's. "In fact, she's been here with me the whole time."

Don't ask me what the hell I'm doing picking a fight with her brother, especially since she just made me swear not to tell a soul what we did. Maybe I just want him to pay for making her feel bad all the time.

"Is that right?" He closes in the space between us.

I glare at him as we stand toe-to-toe. We're pretty evenly matched, size-wise. But unlike him, I grew up with a brother, which means I'm a more practiced fighter. "It's what I said, isn't it?"

"Landry, don't," Loren pleads beside us. "Nothing happened, all right," she adds quietly, to my disappointment. But I can tell she hates this kind of attention, and the last thing I want to do is hurt her.

"Is that true?" he asks me without looking away. I'm vaguely aware of the crowd gathering around us. "Or were you messing around with my sister?"

I huff, lifting my chin and glaring at him with disdain. "Of course not."

And then I hear the rumble of laughter as it makes its way around, and I glance over to see Loren's face flushing. They've apparently taken it to mean that I wouldn't stoop to her level, and although my intention was to save her from further embarrassment, I'm afraid I've accidentally made her the butt of a cruel joke.

I clear my throat. "I mean, no, I would never ..."

But even Landry is biting back a smile now. I only wanted to convey that I'm not desperate enough to take advantage of a girl or force myself on someone who doesn't want me, yet I'm only making things worse.

"Right, because who would?" Loren mutters sarcastically, her arms crossed and her watery eyes trained on the ground. Her friend Tenley comes over to drag her away.

"That's not—it's not what I meant," I stutter, too little too late. I watch helplessly as Loren and Tenley walk off, just as my brother makes his way to the scene of the crime. He bumps Landry's shoulder as he approaches, and the two of them exchange heated looks.

I groan and push JD back. "Come on, man, we're leaving." But, of course, JD has to make a show of shoving Landry out of our way, and I'm torn between chasing after Loren and stopping an impending throw down. I sigh as I take one last look at her retreating form before turning to land a right hook directly on Landry's jaw, throwing as much of my weight into the punch as I can. Then I grab my brother and walk away.

CHAPTER 1
Loren

My head pounds, and I keep my eyes shut as I push away from whatever firm surface I've been using as a pillow, leaving behind a small puddle of drool. I groan and wipe my mouth with the sheets, trying like hell to wake my brain.

The bed shifts beside me just as a large, masculine hand snakes its way over my bare stomach. Then a half-moan, half-sigh emanates from what must have been my human pillow a second before.

My eyes pop open as the realization hits me.

I'm in bed ... *with a man?*

Oh, fudge.

"Mm, closer," my sleepy companion murmurs, and his fingers curl around my hip.

Slowly, carefully, I turn my head to the left, the movement triggering a wave of dizziness. I blink in disbelief.

"Blake?" I whisper.

His eyes remain closed, but his lips form a smile as he lies beside me on his stomach. At least he won't have my drool on his chest anymore.

But, um, WHAT ON GOD'S GREEN EARTH AM I DOING IN BLAKE BOURGEOIS' BED?

Ouch, my brain whines. *Stop yelling, would you?*

I roll my eyes at my inner monologue as I continue the silent screaming match in my head. Then I lift the sheets and glance down, realizing I'm completely naked. I've never slept in the nude in my life, yet here I am, lying next to my one-and-only rival in my birthday suit. I allow my eyes to travel over to verify that Blake is also undressed for the occasion. At least he's lying parts-down.

What ... when ... how ... why?

The only question I have the answer to at this point is *who*.

I shield my eyes from the light streaming in through the blinds and attempt to replay the night before, looking for clues that might explain how the heck I ended up here and whether the obvious occurred.

Okay, think, Loren.

What's the last thing I remember from yesterday?

Tenley and JD's wedding—I was a MOH/witness for their short but oh-so-sweet ceremony in church. We were all supposed to go to dinner to celebrate afterward, but JD pulled out and basically promised a slow, painful death to anyone who interrupted their makeshift honeymoon for the next day or so.

I bet he hadn't pulled out of anything else for the rest of the day.

I snort to myself.

And then I realize the current evidence suggests I tried to recreate a wedding-night scenario of my own with JD's brother last night. A shudder of panic overtakes me as I wrap my mind around the idea that I absolutely, most definitely did more than sleep in this bed with Blake.

I *really* did the deed with Blake flipping Bourgeois.

A montage of blurry memories floods my brain, beginning with an interaction immediately following the wedding in which I offered an olive branch by comforting an uncharacteristically emotional Blake, to grabbing takeout together and going back to his house for a few drinks, to toasting the happy newlyweds, and eventually to the events leading to my current predicament.

Heat flashes in my core as I recall the feeling of Blake undressing me and kissing nearly every inch of my skin, the firmness of his defined body under my hands, and even the reverent look in his eyes while we ... yeah. He'd been a surprisingly tender lover.

Lover? Ew, I hate that word. It's almost as cringy as *moist.*

I bite my lip. Even though Blake and I are the complete opposite of attached, I remember feeling cherished, maybe even adored during our encounter last night. It was totally unexpected, and now I'm left questioning whether the past seventeen years or so of teasing and animosity have only been a front for some other deeply rooted sentiments for either of us.

Blake shifts beside me again, bringing me back from my thoughts. I turn my head to watch him for a second, and his expression changes. He scrunches his face and grasps at my hip, pulling me in slightly.

"Don't go," I think I hear him mumbling, but it's hard to decipher. His face softens again, and I stare for a minute longer, admiring how his eyelashes fan over his cheeks and the way a light stubble has started to form a shadow over his sharp jawline. I fight the urge to reach up and run a finger over the planes of his face, because like it or not—and I definitely do *not*—Blake's body is absolute perfection. He's always looked more like a statue of a Greek god than a real human, carefully chiseled out of some precious stone, created just to tease the rest of us mere mortals. I learned long ago that it's much easier to dislike him than to try to avoid staring directly at him for too long.

He swallows hard and sighs again, and I do the same as I watch his throat working. Then I indulge once more and allow my eyes to follow the muscular trail that begins between his shoulders and leads to a dip in the center of his back, the sheets resting there. Just for good measure, I lift the blankets again to complete the visual journey down to the point of his lower back that's just above where his (shocking—I know) amazing butt begins. I've never seen this much of him before, but Blake is seriously and unnaturally gorgeous.

It's not even fair. No weird birthmarks, no repulsive patches of lower-back hair, just ... perfection. He's Mr. Golden Ratio.

My stomach flutters as I replace the covers, wondering what the hell a man this flawless is doing here with a hot mess like me. While I can vaguely recall him telling me "I've always wanted to do this with you" and "you're so beautiful" during the course of events last night, I can't help but feel like the way he practically worshiped my body with his was enough evidence of his attraction. However, since this *is* Blake Bourgeois, modern-day rake and accomplished seducer of women, it's more likely that he simply employed a few of his proven lines and his many years of experience in bed to create that very illusion.

And on that note, I realize I need to get out of here as soon as possible before I look too pathetic. I imagine he'll be waking soon and wondering why I'm still in his bed, and I'm pretty sure Blake isn't the type to invite his conquests to stay for brunch.

There's only one problem: I'm stuck here on foot. Who can I possibly get to pick me up and bring me back to my car, which is ... at Tenley's mom's house, I think?

Shit.

I begin the slow process of inching toward the edge of the bed like an awkward starfish, desperately hoping to avoid waking him up. I've almost made it out from under his hand when Blake lets out a deep growl and reinforces his hold on me. Then he rolls to his side and uses his forearm to pull me in until my back rests against his chest.

I panic and accidentally squeak as he curls his warm body around mine, pressing himself against me. My breathing quickens, and heat swirls inside as I try to convince myself that relaxing into him would be a terrible idea. Truly horrible. Self-destruction at its finest.

His lips find the back of my neck, and my limbs get all tingly. And my resolve is melting away faster than the One Ring in the fires of Mount Doom.

My hips have started moving on their own accord when I spot our clothes lying on the floor. How many women have been exactly where I am now? I bet none of them have entire arguments with themselves and make *LOTR* references in his bed. But I'm not like the others. I don't belong here.

This was obviously a mistake. In fact, I'm sure I'll laugh about it later. Maybe Blake and I will even laugh about it together.

Despite the allusions to Mordor, I am a rational adult, I remind myself. I summon the courage to speak up before he attempts anything else sexy enough to cloud my judgment again.

"Um, Blake?"

"Hmm?" he replies in a sleepy voice. Then he freezes, probably having just realized the identity of his newest cuddle buddy, and lifts the arm holding me against him before he scoots back, putting some space between us. And although I try not to take his reaction personally, because I am seriously okay with the fact that we're never going to be a couple or even normal friends, it still stings, just a little.

"Loren," he rasps as I twist around to face him. "I'm sorry."

"Yep," I say, a bit too heavy on the *P* at the end. Because I'm the most awkward human on the planet. "It's me. Loren. Loren Reed."

He exhales. "I've known you since we were five. I haven't forgotten your full name or what you look like, especially since last night, *Agnes*."

"Right," I cringe at his mention of my middle name. "Because now I suppose you *really* know me. In the Biblical sense."

He snorts but doesn't say anything for a minute as he rolls onto his back, rubbing his hands over his face in disbelief.

I know the feeling, dude.

Then he clears his throat. "Are you, um, all right?"

My heart melts a little as he glances over at me with a look of genuine concern. "Oh, yeah. I'm fine. Just peachy."

His eyes dart down to the outline of my backside under the covers as the corner of his mouth turns up in a mischievous smirk. "Peachy, huh?"

"Sorry. Too soon?" My face heats up in embarrassment. I have to get out of here, STAT. "Look, I hate to ask, but the only other people I'd trust to find me here and not blab about this to all of Camellia are most likely in a similar predicament, though they are not to be interrupted under any circumstances. Would you mind bringing me back to my car?"

A frown overtakes his features. "Yeah. Of course." Then he gazes up at the ceiling, seemingly in deep thought. "I'll give you some privacy," he says after a while.

He sits up in bed, and I can't help but stare when the sheets pool around his waist, his pristine abs on full display. He glares at me expectantly until I get the hint and avert my eyes. The bed shifts as he stands, and there's a light snap from an elastic waistband as he presumably slips on his underwear. I pretend to inspect my fingernails until he sets my clothes down in front of me.

"There should be a fresh toothbrush under the bathroom sink. Take your time," he says, his tone dry as he walks out of the room and shuts the door behind him.

I scurry over to the immaculately clean en suite, stopping to admire the amazing bathtub sitting under the window. I bet it goes unused. Blake's definitely a shower kind of guy.

After finding an unopened toothbrush in the cabinet, I do my best to freshen up and redress, even though I can't get the zipper of my bridesmaid dress all the way up on my own. I venture out to find my host sipping a cup of coffee in the kitchen. He's giving broody male-model vibes in jeans and a hoodie.

"Wow. That smells amazing right now," I accidentally blurt out.

"Help yourself." He points to the coffeemaker and the rack of pods. "Cups are in the cabinet on top."

I turn toward the counter when I remember my dress is still unzipped. "Oh, um, would you mind?" I ask, pointing to the back of my dress.

He sets his mug down before he walks over silently. Then he pushes my hair to the side and drags the zipper up, his touch making me shiver.

"Thanks," I mumble, turning to face him again.

But he avoids my eyes and reaches over me to open the cabinet door, inadvertently pinning me against the counter, and he brings a mug down for me.

"Thank you," I repeat quietly, unsure whether I'm flattered or offended by the gesture. The shelf is admittedly high for someone of my stature, after all.

He glares at me for a full second before he steps away and returns to his previous spot.

"Would you happen to know where my phone ended up?" I ask as I clamp the lid down over the pod.

"I'll call it." He slips his phone from his back pocket, and I'm surprised he even has my number saved. But then I remember the text messages we've been exchanging over the past week while helping JD and Tenley piece together their impromptu wedding.

My purse begins ringing nearby, bringing me back from my thoughts. Apparently, I never even bothered to take my phone out last night. I turn away from the coffee to retrieve it while Blake reaches into the fridge. He sets a carton of heavy cream and a small container of low-calorie sugar substitute down in front of me.

"Sorry, this is all I have," he says quietly, going around to sit on the other side of the island.

"You *would* drink boring coffee," I reply without thinking, and his lips turn up slightly.

I stir as I make a quick scan of the missed notifications. There's a text from Tenley, apologizing for bailing on our celebration dinner. Well, it's more of a "sorry, not sorry" and a promise to talk later. I chuckle to myself before I look up to find Blake staring at me again.

"Your sister-in-law asked for a raincheck on the family wedding dinner," I explain as I take a sip, the caffeine instantly soothing my throbbing head. "I'm surprised JD allowed her to make contact with the outside," I add with a smirk.

He nods knowingly before bringing his mug up. "Never seen a man more infatuated than my brother."

"But Tenley's totally crazy about him, too. It's sweet. And romantic." The conversation feels a little too familiar, and I wonder how much of this we talked about last night.

"Yeah, I guess. If you're into that stuff."

"Should we place bets on due dates yet?" I joke.

He snorts. "I'd put money on an announcement within the month."

Our eyes meet, and it doesn't feel like either of us are talking about JD and Tenley anymore. We're just tiptoeing around a discussion of our current situation.

Blake clears his throat, as if he's read my mind. "Loren, I'm sorry about last night. I shouldn't have initiated anything in the state we were both in."

I shrug. "We can share the blame. I'm sure I made a fool of myself, since I rarely drink that much and never enough to warrant a walk of shame the next morning."

He smiles at me again, and my cheeks flush slightly. "Then you're being remarkably cool for having just awakened in the bed of your sworn enemy," he says, a tinge of humor coloring his voice.

"Aw, are we not enemies anymore?" I stick out my bottom lip in a playful pout.

"You didn't seem to hate me so much last night," he reminds me with a cocked eyebrow.

"What can I say? I'd forgotten how good you were with your tongue," I deadpan over my mug, making him laugh loudly.

"I was hoping you'd update my customer review. My skills should have improved over the past seventeen years or so." He stares at me for a minute, his blue eyes sparkling.

I swallow hard before I answer, because the more I remember about last night, the more stars I could add to my verified review of the "Blake Bourgeois Experience."

"Maybe a smidge," I finally allow. "But I think you've had a lot more practice since then."

His smile fades. "I had to pass the time somehow," he remarks, his tone more serious.

I furrow my brow and take another sip as I consider what he's implying before self-preservation takes over again. "Look, Blake. We don't have to do this. I'm a big girl. I don't need your pity."

"My pity?"

"I don't need you to pretend last night meant anything to you just because you figure I don't usually do this random-hookup thing."

Okay, maybe that was an oversell. I'm not a casual-sex kind of girl, and I don't think I ever will be. But I'd rather deal with the overwhelming sense of guilt and regret later, away from Blake and his flawless abs and his five-star rating.

He nods slowly, actually having the audacity to look hurt by my words. "Right. Well, that's a relief, I guess." He turns and dumps his cup in the sink. "Ready to go get your car?"

Wow. He's kicking me out now? That escalated quickly.

"Sure."

He disappears for a second as I add my empty mug to the sink, then he meets me again at the door. "Here," he offers in a low voice, holding out another hoodie. "It's much cooler out today."

"Oh, thanks." I pull it down over my dress, and I'm instantly enveloped by his clean, masculine smell. He opens the door and gestures for me to go ahead, neither of us saying a word as we leave his house and head across town.

The drive gives me too much time to read into his current mood in conjunction with some of the things I'm just remembering he confided in me last night. Maybe it was insensitive of me to imply our conversation about his feelings of inadequacy and abandonment after spending so many years in his younger brother's shadow wasn't at least meaningful. But I also can't imagine anything I say or do actually matters to him.

I sigh inwardly as we pull up next to my old Toyota. She looks pretty worse for the wear next to Blake's newer, luxury model truck.

"Thanks for the ride," I say as I unbuckle my seat belt. "And for dinner."

And for the five-star—

"No problem," he mutters, thankfully interrupting my thoughts before I blurt out something else embarrassing.

I hold out my hand, and he glares at me as if he can't believe I'm actually this lame. "Frenemies?" I offer.

He mulls it over for a second before finally clasping his large hand over mine, lingering while his thumb softly rubs the inside of my wrist. I pull back before the rest of my body has a chance to react to his touch, barely catching the way he flexes his empty hand.

I look down shyly and realize I'm still wearing his jacket. "Almost forgot," I murmur, shifting my position so I can remove it.

He reaches over and stills me. "Keep it for now. I'll get it from you later."

"I could always send it back to you through JD or Ethan if you want."

He puffs up his cheeks and blows out a breath. "I was thinking it probably wouldn't be a good idea if my brother found out about this. He'd never let us live it down, don't you think?"

I cringe. "You're right. I suppose the same goes for Tenley now, you know, that whole 'two become one' thing. I get the feeling there won't be too many secrets between Mr. and Mrs. Bourgeois."

He laughs quietly, and I realize how awkward it sounds since that's Blake's last name, too.

"Same pact as before? It stays between us?" I ask.

"Yeah."

"Okay, well, I'll see you around, Blake."

"See you around, Loren." Surprised that he hadn't called me by my last name for once, I climb down from his truck, waving shortly for him to go. Then I notice a small note on the windshield of my car.

Blake Bourgeois? Not bad, Loren Reed. Not bad at all. You deserve a good man like Blake.

—Mrs. T

CHAPTER 2

Blake

"Flying solo tonight, Blake?"

I force a polite smile at my business partner's wife. "Yes, ma'am. I guess I need to step up my game. I couldn't seem to find a date."

My coworkers all laugh at that one. Stuff like this used to be a confidence booster for me, the jokes about my dating history and my reputation as a playboy. But lately, it just serves as another reminder that I'm likely to die alone.

Okay, so that's a little dramatic, even for me. I'm not dying, as far as I know. I've just come to the conclusion that I'm not "love-marriage-family" material. Hell, I don't even know if I'm fourth-date material at this point. And I guess I've finally gotten sick of going out with women who can't hold my attention, even if it's just to keep up with appearances.

"Oh, I can't imagine that," Mrs. Guillory remarks, although she says it low enough to imply she didn't mean for anyone to hear it.

My smile transforms into a cocky smirk. I'm used to garnering this kind of attention based on my looks, but I don't mind. If checking me out gives her joy, then who am I to deny the woman a small slice of happiness? And I happen to think blurted-out compliments that were never intended to be said aloud are the highest form of flattery.

"I'd have been a poor date, anyway. Look at all these distractingly beautiful women at our table," I offer, aiming a wink at Mrs. Guillory and making the other men roll their eyes.

Jada, our receptionist, gently nudges my ribs with her elbow. She doesn't mind telling me when she thinks I'm full of it, probably because she's even better than I am at using her customer-service flirt to get what she wants out of a client.

"Speaking of beautiful women, isn't she a friend of yours?" I hear Jada whisper. She gestures with her eyes, and I glance up in time to catch Loren Reed walking by in a short, flowy dress and heels. My heart immediately begins thumping against my ribs, and my lungs struggle to keep working. Then I notice the man beside her, matching her stride and tilting his head down to listen as they make their way to a table.

I blink and remind myself to breathe as I continue watching. Her companion pulls out her chair, and she smiles up at him when she sits. It's the first I've seen of Loren since the night we spent together a couple of weeks ago, and I hadn't thought I'd need to prepare myself for this—having to witness her on a date with someone else. Maybe a small part of me has been secretly hoping she wasn't telling the truth when she said our hookup didn't mean anything to her. But she's clearly moved on. Meanwhile, I'm sitting here dateless, tracking her movements like a desperate creep.

Jada's not wrong, either. Loren looks amazing. I've always thought she was beautiful in her own right, as if it were just a matter of fact. She's also one of those big personalities in a small package, with her own distinct style and a natural confidence that allows her to pull off nearly anything she wears. Some of her fashion choices seem a bit quirky at times, but she's definitively cute, dare I say appealing in a sexy-librarian kind of way.

It also turns out that she looks just as good in nothing at all. And that our bodies complement each other extremely well.

Like, *really, really* well.

Shit.

Now I'm thinking about things I absolutely shouldn't be thinking ... again.

I clear my throat and bring my attention back to the table. "Uh, yeah, she was Tenley's maid of honor the other day. And we graduated together," I finally reply to Jada.

"Hmm," she hums thoughtfully in response. Then she turns to her husband. "Pretty girl, isn't she?"

Aaron shrugs and looks back and forth between us. "Sure. She doesn't seem like Blake's type, though."

"She's not," I reply too quickly, and Jada lifts an eyebrow.

"You don't think she's attractive, then?"

I sniff indignantly. "I didn't say that."

"Oh, good. Because I've never seen you look at anyone the way you just looked at her," Jada says plainly.

"I wasn't looking at her any differently than I look at all the other women around here," I lie, actively fighting the urge to turn my attention back to Loren. "If anything, I was just trying to recognize the guy she walked in with."

"Uh-huh," Aaron starts. "And that's not bothering you, either?"

I swallow hard, my eyes skirting over to them again. I'm not jealous. But seeing Loren with another man *is* a blow to my ego, especially when I've already been struggling to mend the cracks she left by walking out on me that morning.

Unlike most of my experiences with women, it hadn't just been physical with us. I divulged more to her that night than I had to anyone in my life, mostly because she made me feel so comfortable, so understood. For the first time in as long as I can remember, I didn't need to pretend to be someone I wasn't. So I let my guard down, most likely setting the stage for the intense connection I thought we'd shared.

Waking up the next morning with Loren in my arms had me thinking all sorts of crazy ideas, like maybe all that teasing and taunting we'd done over the years had actually been flirting. Maybe my lingering attraction to her hadn't been one-sided after all, and this could be my chance to turn over a new leaf and give a real relationship a try. It's not like I was ready for a serious commitment after a single night together, but I couldn't ask for a better opportunity to prove I was capable of more than serial dating and casual sex. And the idea of making that transition with Loren was even more appealing because she's always been able to keep me on my toes.

I'd been wrong, though. The way she flinched and curled away from me when I attempted to hold her was like a punch to the gut. She immediately ruled out the possibility of me having any real interest or romantic feelings for her, probably because I've only ever been good at objectifying women, and reminded me that I'd never be worthy of love or a family of my own. And I still haven't come to terms with her accusing me of only sleeping with her out of pity, then rubbing it in by implying she was the one who felt sorry for me.

Poor Blake the Snake, right?

It wasn't the first time I'd made a fool of myself by assuming Loren was the one person who saw me as anything more than my reputation afforded, but I've learned my lesson. I'm sure as hell not setting myself up for it to happen again—with any woman.

I furrow my brow as I glance back to her table. Loren's eyes meet mine, and her lips part in shock before she looks down.

Her date reaches over and brushes his hand over her shoulder, making me feel something deep in the pit of my stomach. Then the waiter approaches, and Mr. Touchy-Feely continues holding her arm while they speak. But I can't stop staring at the spot where he's rubbing his thumb over her silky-looking skin. I'm doing my best to look as unaffected as possible when he says something that triggers a head tilt and a laugh from her, but my best isn't all that great right now.

She leans in closer to him, and I can't take it anymore. I stand abruptly, mumbling an apology before I basically storm over to the table without a clue as to what I'm doing or why I'm stopping to stand directly behind her. Maybe I'm worried that this guy might make a real move on her, or maybe the urge to touch her is just too strong. At least her date has the sense to drop his arm when he sees me rest my hands on the back of Loren's chair. Though, now I'm stuck having to avoid ogling her nearly bare shoulders and leaning in to check whether she still smells like roses.

"Hey," I say, clearing my throat.

Wow. Smooth.

Loren stares up at me with a blank look. "What are you doing here, Blake?"

"Celebrating my partner Mark's birthday," I reply dumbly.

"I mean, why are you *here*, at my table?" she whispers harshly.

I blink a few times, unsure of my answer. "I guess I thought it would be rude not to come over and say hello," I spit out after a while. "We are friends now, aren't we?"

She swallows hard and nods, then turns to her date and forces a polite smile. "Rowan, this is Blake Bourgeois. Blake, Dr. Rowan LaFleur."

He stands and reaches out to shake my hand, and I can't help but squeeze a little more firmly than proper. "Nice to meet you, man," Rowan declares with a wary smile. "You're that football player's brother, aren't you?"

Loren snorts quietly as I let go of his hand and return to my place behind her. "Yeah, that's me, The Other Bourgeois."

"Rowan is a good friend of Landry's," Loren adds quickly, I presume as a distraction.

"I guess he set this up, then?"

She looks down at the table. "Yeah."

"Nice. Well, I guess I'd call myself a family friend, too," I explain.

Rowan smiles widely. "Sounds like everyone knows everyone around here."

"That's fair, since Camellia's so small. Although, Loren and I happen to know one another more intimately than most."

She presses her lips together, clearly displeased with my response. "It does seem like I've never been able to avoid you for long," she mutters.

I lean in slightly, catching a hit of roses and wondering whether her signature scent originates from her perfume or her shampoo.

"Then you might as well quit pretending you're so surprised and unhappy to see me," I reply with a flirty smirk.

"Maybe I'm not pretending," she says through her teeth.

I shouldn't enjoy riling her up as much as I do, but I can't help myself. I glance down and see that her legs are crossed. There's a small tattoo on her ankle that I vaguely remember seeing before, a green leaf, and it's killing me not to reach down and touch it.

An ankle? Seriously, man? You're losing it.

I shake my head quickly. This is ridiculous. I'm not *that* attracted to Loren Reed. And she was right before—casual sex has never been a big deal to me. There's no reason to get all worked up over a random hookup now, especially one involving a woman I've known most of my life.

"You guys have dated before, I presume?" Rowan ventures after a while. He glances back and forth between us with that forced smile again.

"Not exactly," Loren answers, just as I reply with, "You could say that."

He raises a brow, but he looks more amused than intimidated. "I see."

Loren fidgets nervously in her chair during the awkward silence that follows.

"So, what's your specialty, Doc?" I begin again.

"Maternal and fetal medicine, mostly high-risk pregnancies."

I nod approvingly, and Loren volunteers that I'm a lawyer. Rowan pretends to be impressed, but not very well.

"I suppose you and Dr. Reed work together?"

"We do. I'm very happy to refer my newest patients to him," he affirms proudly.

He seems like a genuinely good guy. *Dammit.*

"And this date with his little sister is just a kick-back?" I pose.

Loren clears her throat harshly, but Rowan chuckles. "Landry and I have been friends for years, so I wouldn't exactly call it a kick-back. Although, I'm pretty sure I'd be coming out ahead, if that were the case."

He glances over at her, and she rewards his compliment with a shy smile. And I grip the chair back so hard that I'm afraid I might actually break it.

"I agree, Doc. You're a lucky man, but you should be forewarned. The lady reads a lot of romance novels. Her expectations are ..." I let out a whistle while gesturing over my head with my hand.

Loren scoffs and jerks an elbow back into my thigh, making me wince and grin stupidly.

"That's okay," Rowan returns, giving her *the look*. "I have a lot of practice with women."

I roll my eyes this time, but I notice the way Loren blushes. She can't really like this kind of crap, can she?

Because if she did, she'd be with me.

And maybe I'm not exactly relationship material, but what makes this guy more qualified to date Loren than I am, especially if he lives a couple of hours away?

If she'd have bothered to stick around long enough for me to explain myself the other day, I would have told her I was tired of wasting my time with women who couldn't offer me anything more than physical gratification. Yet, Loren assumed I'd gotten all I wanted from her and figured a stranger would be more interested in the rest. After all, she's got to be pretty damned desperate if she's calling on Landry to set her up.

Not that I necessarily wanted her to give me a shot. It's really the principle of it all that upsets me.

"Blake?" Loren's voice calls me back.

"Yeah?"

"You're still here."

I purse my lips, slightly embarrassed. "Right. I should get back to my own table. Pleasure to meet you, Doc. Enjoy your dinner."

And only dinner.

"Yeah, have a great night," Rowan replies before turning his attention back to Loren.

But I'm a glutton for punishment, so I reach out and graze my fingertips over the back of her shoulder, just low enough to stay out of sight. Satisfaction flares inside me when she gasps quietly and her eyelashes flutter. I lean down again, catching one more hit of roses—it's got to be her hair—and whisper, "See you around, Reed." Then I turn and make my way back to my own table.

Jada's grinning widely when I return to my seat with my tail between my legs. "Not a word," I mutter under my breath.

"You struck out, didn't you?"

"You're using words, Jada."

"You. Like. Her." She stretches each of the words out, and I grunt in response. "Have you dated before?"

"You'd remember if I had, wouldn't you?" I retort before I take a sip of my drink.

Jada's our go-to for nearly everything in the law office, from making dinner reservations to reminding us about doctor appointments. The other men count on her to send their wives the right color bouquets on their birthdays and to pick out jewelry for their anniversaries. She also keeps me in line, reprimanding me when I go too far with my sarcasm or make too many poor choices in succession.

"I haven't been taking care of you forever. I'm sure I don't know about every local who shares a history with you," she replies knowingly. "And I feel like I'd remember hearing about you and Coach Reed's daughter, especially if it had happened back in high school."

I glare at her. "So you do know who she is."

"Of course I do, Blake. This is Camellia. In fact, I'm pretty sure I waited in line behind her at the grocery store yesterday."

I let my gaze travel over to Loren again. She's smiling as she plucks a French fry from Rowan's plate. She pops it into her mouth and does an adorable happy shimmy, and I watch her lick her lips while the memory of our first kiss replays in my mind.

Then she turns, her eyes instantly locking onto mine from across the restaurant, and my heart does something funny in my chest. And I don't like it.

Or maybe I do?

I'm not sure yet, because I can't remember it happening before, at least not in my adult life.

She forces herself to look away, and I do the same.

"I'm not jealous, if that's what you're implying. I just wanted to vet the guy," I say after a while. "Her brother set this up. And Landry's always been a dick to her, so I'm not sure I trust his judgment."

"That's all though, right?"

I let out a measured exhale, trying to turn on the charm again. "Of course. You know me. Women like me too much for me to like only one woman."

She rolls her eyes. "Sometimes I wish you liked yourself a little more, Blake."

"Come on. I take great care of this temple," I reply, tapping my chest before taking a long draught of my drink and making her hum disapprovingly.

"What happened, man?" Aaron leans over from the other side of Jada. "Couldn't lure your girl away?"

I shake my head and put my glass down. "I guess I'm off my game tonight."

Then Aaron laughs and starts to tell us a joke, and I attempt to push Loren out of mind. But I can't help glancing over intermittently and noticing how well she and Rowan seem to be getting along. After about thirty minutes of struggling to redirect my attention, I give up and pull out my phone.

BLAKE

> I hate to be the one to break it to you, Reed. But you don't like that guy. He seems nice, but he's not your type.

I watch as she lifts her phone and frowns. Then she sets it down and ignores it.

So I send her another message.

BLAKE

> I'm serious. Your brother basically set you up with my brother. And we both know golden retrievers bore you.

> Hell, I bet the guy has his favorite jorts and a pair of white New Balances set aside for your second date.

She looks visibly frustrated while she reads, but she does take a second to respond.

LOREN R

> Leave me alone, Blake.

Now I'm the one frowning at my phone.

BLAKE

> I didn't want to be the one to say this, but there's no such thing as a nice doctor who's still single at his age. Wth is wrong with this guy if he has to drive two hours to get laid?

> Promise me you won't leave with him? I'll bring you back myself before I let you go home alone with Dr. Red Flag.

LOREN R

> Do you really think Landry would set me up with someone dangerous?

> And I'm not that stupid. I drive myself to first dates, and I never invite strange men into my home.

> But thanks, your concern is endearing.

I smile. I can't deny that I'm slightly relieved. But it's only because I care about Loren's well-being in general, and not because I'm jealous or anything.

Probably.

Maybe.

BLAKE

> You're welcome. After all, what are frenemies for?

She doesn't reply that time, but I think I see her smirking down at the phone. And I could swear her body language changes after that and she keeps a little more distance between them.

Our server brings out some brownie and peanut butter concoction while my table mates sing happy birthday to Mark, and it gives me an idea. I call the waiter over and ask him to bring the same dessert to my friends. As a gesture of goodwill.

A few minutes later, I watch as Loren's eyes light up when the dessert gets delivered. That is, until Rowan says something that has them all looking upset, and the server whisks it away. She smiles apologetically at her date, I assume because he sent the peanut butter brownie back after figuring out it came from me. While it pisses me off that he's denying her this small pleasure, I can respect the fact that I've crossed a boundary. In fact, I might think less of him if he hadn't refused it.

It's not long after when my table starts to clear out, just as Loren and her date pass on their way to the door. Rowan and I trade polite nods before I impulsively reach out and grab Loren by the arm. He stands by, looking concerned, but he stays silent.

"Hey, thanks for trusting me," I lean in to whisper near her ear.

She blinks a few times, seemingly surprised. "Sure," she replies, glancing down at my hand.

I reluctantly let go, noticing a slow smile spreading across her face. "It wasn't happening, either way. He's got a peanut allergy," she admits quietly, lifting the container in her hand. I can see the peanut butter brownie through the transparent lid.

I grin back at her, and she turns to let Rowan lead her out. Even though Jada teases me for it, I move closer to the door so I can watch him walk her to her car.

I'm just making sure she's safe, after all.

And then I drive home, alone, and go to bed, alone. Which is fine, except that I don't end up alone in the very steamy, very realistic dreams that haunt me for the rest of the night and into the next morning.

CHAPTER 3

Loren

My phone vibrates beneath the ever-constant pile of ungraded essays that graces the middle of my desk. I shuffle through the stack to check the message, which happens to be a dinner invitation from Tenley. It sounds like the results of today's hearing are worth celebrating, since she and JD were able to secure custody of her nephew, Ethan, despite his absentee biological father's attempts to break up their newly formed family.

I grin down at my phone, until I remember their legal representation.

As much as I'd like to join my friends, I'm equally unnerved by the prospect of having to face Blake again. I thought we'd managed a pretty good job of dodging one another for the past few weeks, until he ended up at the same restaurant as my last blind date—the date he basically sabotaged. And the mere fact that I let Blake get to me is enough to warrant avoiding him for the foreseeable future.

Maybe I could tell them I can't make it because I'm sick? I have been feeling a touch of indigestion with my coffee for the past few mornings.

One of my students walks up to my desk, his camouflage jacket reeking of campfire, body odor, and Axe spray. My stomach turns, and for a second, I think I might actually have a valid excuse for skipping out on everyone tonight. I cover my face with my hand, pretending to give careful consideration to his request to go to the restroom. Thankfully, the nausea subsides once he backs away and takes his offensive odor with him.

I answer Tenley, telling her that I'm happy to join them before I lose my nerve, then I get back to grading essays. About thirty minutes later, I receive another message from her.

TENLEY

I'm glad you'll be there tonight. It seems we have a lot to celebrate. 🙂

image of positive pregnancy test

I smirk down at my phone. Well, that didn't take long. I vaguely remember Blake predicting this exact scenario within the month. Looks like they've proven him right with a week to spare.

LOREN

gif of shocked Pikachu

WHAT A SURPRISE. I'M SHOOK.

Jk. Congratulations, my friend! 🐼🎉

TENLEY

Thanks!

Even though I knew the odds of this happening, that was literally mfw my bil figured out why I couldn't stop barfing in court all morning. 😆

I gulp audibly at her mention of Blake. And then my stomach flutters again once I remind myself that he and I also engaged in a bit of some potentially pregnancy-inducing acts on Tenley's wedding night. (Okay, it was more than a bit. The more I remember since then, the more fodder I have for writing my own spicy romance memoir.)

My heart rate quickens as I scan the calendar on my desk and count the days since my last period.

Holy moly. I'm almost a week late.

"Ms. Reed, are you okay?" I hear one of my students calling out from her seat.

At some point, I must have let my forehead drop to my desk and stopped responding to the rest of the class. My chest heaves as I struggle to stop hyperventilating.

"I'm fine," I lie, my voice cracking.

Then smelly-jacket kid, Myles, returns to place his paper on my desk, his sleeve bumping my elbow and stirring up that stale, musty scent again.

And that's how I end up hurling my cookies in a trash can in front of my Honors English II class.

One of the students is kind enough to let the office know over the intercom that I'm sick, and the principal comes in to give me a minute to collect myself in the restroom. At least JD is out for the hearing today, otherwise he'd have been the one showing up to relieve me in his new role as the assistant principal.

I stare at my reflection in the bathroom mirror for a second, willing myself to handle this situation like the reasonable adult that I am. It's probably just a coincidence that I feel sick today. Or this could simply be a fun, new PMS symptom. There's no use stressing until I know for sure, right?

Right.

I take a deep breath and resolve to continue my day, texting Tenley back on my way out of the bathroom.

LOREN

Yeah, I'm pretty sure any of us could have predicted this one.

How excited is your husband?

TENLEY

Oh man. He's unbearably giddy, though I'm not sure whether he's more pumped about having a baby or getting to prove to the football team that he finally got into my pants.

It's borderline annoying and absolutely adorable at the same time.

LOREN

I think that's the most accurate description of JD I've ever heard. 😊

So you really didn't know until getting sick in court earlier today?

TENLEY

Yeah, I guess I've been ironically ignoring the symptoms. But once I vomited and fainted in the judge's chambers, I realized the sore boobs and misty eyes weren't just PMS. Then I got a bfp as soon as I grabbed a test at work.

LOREN

BFP?

TENLEY

Big Fat Positive.

LOREN

Gotcha. I didn't realize you could get a positive test result that quickly. Unless it *was* a shotgun wedding after all?

TENLEY

Lol. No, this is definitely a "honeymoon baby."

But to answer your first question, yes. Depending on when fertilization actually occurs, it's possible to get a positive reading as early as eight dpo.

LOREN

DPO = Days Past Ovulation?

TENLEY

Right

LOREN

You're like the fertility awareness encyclopedia. We need to finish my FAM training.

> For argument's sake, is there a more accurate kind of pee stick? Like, the ones with lines vs the ones with words?

TENLEY

> Definitely Pink Dye > Blue Dye

> But the digital ones are pretty accurate, too.

LOREN

> *'The More You Know' gif*

I take a short detour before returning to my class, stopping in the counselor's office. "Hey Emma, mind if I swipe something from the girls' supply closet?"

"Of course, take what you need," she replies.

"Thanks! You're a lifesaver."

I slip into the storage area housing extra toiletries, scanning the rows of tampons and pads until I come across a case of pregnancy tests. I grab a pink-dye box and tuck it inside my jacket pocket before scampering back to class.

I manage to survive the rest of the day without getting sick again, though it's only after I force myself to have a snack. Once my students are gone, I stuff the pregnancy test into my bag along with that perpetual stack of essays. It's going to be an interesting night.

CHAPTER 4
Loren
THREE WEEKS AGO

My eyes water as I watch JD bring Tenley's hand up to his mouth. He kisses the inside of her wrist tenderly, and her shoulders rise and fall as if she's having to work harder to breathe. I'd never imagined an impromptu wedding could be this romantic, but I guess it's all about the main-character energy. And the way this man is staring at my best friend so intensely that he has to be reminded they're supposed to be here for an actual wedding and not just to adore one another in front of a live audience is just—*ugh*—chef's kiss.

My view starts to get blurry, so I fish out a tissue from the bodice of my dress. Then I glance over and notice Blake watching the bride and groom with a serious expression. His chin is still trembling when he catches me studying him. I expect him to turn away after his eyes meet mine, but he holds my gaze for a while as he blinks back his tears.

My heart speeds up as I continue staring at Blake. There's something different about him today, something resembling sadness and regret in his eyes. I smile softly, and he does the same before turning back to hand JD the rings. Their interactions always warm my heart, and today is no different as Blake tries to hide his emotions in front of his brother, even though JD is obviously touched by his sentimentality.

I'm not even supposed to be thinking about Blake, but here I am, concerning myself with his emotional state instead of witnessing the wedding I've been called in for. I figure he must be going through the full spectrum today, from happiness and pride to abandonment and loneliness. Since they lost their parents a few years back, Blake and JD have been all that's left of their family, and now JD is moving on with his new instafam. And with Tenley and JD's relationship having progressed so quickly, I imagine Blake hasn't gotten enough time to adjust to the idea of being left behind.

Father Conrad brings me back from my thoughts when he calls us over to sign the marriage license. My girl's hand trembles as she signs her name first, JD following her and scribbling a quick "III" at the end of his name. I step forward to sign on one of the witness lines, turning to hand the pen to Blake once I'm done. He shoots me a friendly smirk before scratching out some elaborate signature that nearly overlaps mine.

"Did you really have to one-up the rest of us with your fancy, lawyerly penmanship?" I whisper as we turn to walk back to the front, bumping his shoulder with mine.

He nudges me back softly. "I've gotta do something to make up for the lack of roman numerals at the end of my name, don't I?" he asks quietly, his tone amused.

We all take our places in front of the altar again, and Father Conrad gives the couple their final blessing before announcing them as Mr. and Mrs. Bourgeois for the first time. As predicted, JD pulls Tenley in for a borderline inappropriate kiss. Eventually, Blake has to call them back and remind them that Ethan's still around, though they don't seem to care. It's obvious that they only have eyes for one another.

Like I said, this is that top-shelf, chef's-kiss-level romance.

"That's not exactly church tongue," I scold them, though JD disregards my warning and pulls me in for a hug.

After congratulating the newlyweds and attempting to take a few pictures in which I repeatedly have to tell JD to quit staring at Tenley long enough to face the camera, we all walk out of the church together.

Well, the rest of us *walk* while JD practically *runs*, dragging Tenley along with him at a pace that makes everyone laugh again. The guy has a one-track mind, though I doubt Tenley is any less eager to get home after the conversations we've shared lately.

I watch as Blake stops to talk to JD, who's only response is to issue a warning for anyone who dares to interrupt them as he lifts Tenley and nearly tosses her into the truck.

"Come on, Blake," I say, trying to pull him away. "I think Little Brother can take it from here."

He surprises me by sliding his hand over mine so that I'm forced to keep it there over his arm. I swallow hard as his muscles flex beneath my fingers.

Ethan passes on the way to his own truck, staring at us carefully as he says goodbye. He doesn't seem thrilled about spending the night at his biological dad's, though I can't imagine he wants to go home with his aunt and uncle tonight, either.

"So, what now, right?" I ask, hoping to break the ice as Blake and I walk on.

"What now, indeed," Blake replies dryly. We reach Mrs. Therese's car, which is parked a couple of spots down from his truck, and he finally drops his hand so I can remove mine. It's probably the most physical contact Blake and I have had in years, and for some reason, it doesn't feel as awkward as it should.

"I suppose we're not going to get that dinner we were promised, are we?" I pose with a light laugh, and he shakes his head and smiles.

"Yeah, I just got a death threat, so you can probably go back to your regularly scheduled plans for this Saturday night."

"Oh, yes. I can just hear my stack of unread books calling me from home," I add with a playful eye roll.

He narrows his eyes at me. "That exciting, huh?"

I cross my arms. "I'll have you know that some of those stories can get pretty tense."

"Do they, now?" He cocks a brow, and I swear his voice deepens a couple of octaves.

My face heats up. "Well, not like *that*. But they can be suspenseful."

"Sure, sure. I'll bet you read that stuff for the riveting plot twists."

I bite my lip and shove him. "And what are you going to do now? Don't you have a date lined up for later?"

He cringes. "I don't know. A stack of books doesn't sound half-bad, to be honest."

My chin lowers, and I blink my eyes quickly in surprise.

Blake Bourgeois is a reader? And a crier? And maybe even a secret romantic?

"What, you think I'm illiterate?" he retorts after assessing my reaction. "I managed to get through law school without you, Reed. Though I did miss the competition from my favorite academic rival."

Tenley's mom returns and ends our conversation abruptly, saving me from having to continue responding to his flirting. Because although Blake's never hesitated to flirt with me in public, this feels different, and I don't think I have the heart to brush him off the way I always do.

"Still need a lift, Loren?" Mrs. T offers.

"If you don't mind." Blake hasn't moved yet, so I turn to him and explain that I left my car back at Mrs. T's house.

He clears his throat and looks away, suddenly seeming more awkward than usual. "Oh, well, you should have mentioned that before. I could have given you a ride."

I smile politely. "Thanks, but I figured Mrs. T would be going home, anyway, right?"

She smirks at me. "Since you mentioned it, I was thinking about stopping at the cemetery to visit Jude before I head back. I'm feeling a little sentimental, I suppose. But only if Blake's not too busy to drop you off?"

"Uh, no, not at all," he replies quickly, then sticks his hands in his pockets and shuffles his feet.

I glance back at Mrs. T. "Okay, then."

"Perfect," she returns, pursing her lips at me and bouncing her eyebrows suggestively.

I shake my head and roll my eyes, trying not to laugh at her as I walk away.

"Thanks for offering to bring me back," I say as we approach Blake's truck.

"No worries. I've got nothing but time."

I climb into the passenger seat, pondering his strange demeanor. "Blake," I begin. "Don't take this the wrong way. But, um ... are you *okay*?"

He stiffens and hesitates with his finger on the ignition button. "Yeah. I'm good. It's just been a long week."

"Right. I'm sorry for putting you on the spot, but you seem a little less 'Blake' than usual."

He huffs, a sardonic smile on his face. "I'm not sure what that even means, but I guess it's nice of you to ask, all the same."

"Even though we're not exactly friends, given our history and the fact that you've been abnormally bearable lately, the least I can do is offer a listening ear."

His expression changes, and he twists his lips to the side as he seems to consider my proposition. "I can't imagine you don't have anything better to do than listen to me gripe about my privileged life."

I laugh shortly. "Sadly, I do not," I mumble, more to myself than anything.

We're both quiet for a while before he speaks up. "Loren, would you want to grab dinner or something?"

"Dinner? With you? Like, right now?"

He lifts a shoulder. "We're already dressed, and we both have to eat, right?"

I think about his offer and where it might be coming from. I'm not dumb enough to think that he's asking me out on a date, but I'm still wary of his motives.

"Unless you're not comfortable hanging out, just the two of us," he adds.

I glance over at him. He's watching the road, but his expression says that he's nervous, that he's actually hopeful I'll say yes. I assume he's just feeling extra lonely, especially today, and in that case, I don't have the heart to refuse him.

"What did you have in mind?"

CHAPTER 5

Blake

THREE WEEKS AGO (CONTINUED)

"Anything you want. We could grab some takeout and go back to my place."

I cough awkwardly, hoping my offer hasn't scared her away. I'm so desperate for her company that I'd do just about anything to convince her to stay around, at least for the next few hours.

"And you don't think that would be weird?" she ventures after a second. "The two of us just hanging out and breaking bread after all these years of being enemies?" But she's smiling as she says it. In fact, she's so cute that my stomach flutters a little, and I'm not used to a woman giving me anything close to butterflies. I chalk it up to the emotional rollercoaster this day has been after watching my baby brother sign his life away.

Okay, that's not exactly what I mean. I know JD has always wanted this, and I'm genuinely happy for him. I just can't help but worry, especially since this whole chain of events began only a few months ago. It's been crazy watching him fall for Tenley and take on the role of Ethan's foster father/uncle, except for the fact that it's so on-brand for JD. Of course he'd declare that he's ready to settle down one day, and a perfect, pre-made family falls into his lap a week later.

I clear my throat, trying to bring myself back. "It's only weird if

43

you point it out, Reed," I answer her, unable to resist glancing back to measure her reaction.

She's still smirking at me. "Making things weird *is* my specialty."

"Then it's a good thing I like weird."

What? What am I even saying?

She chuckles lightly. "Is that so?"

I sigh, trying to recover. "Do you want to pick up your car now or later?" We're sitting at the one traffic light in town, and I need her to decide which way to turn in the next few seconds, even though I don't want to let her out of my truck just yet.

"I guess we can come back for it after dinner, although Mrs. T might suspect something when she comes home to find my car's still parked in her driveway," she replies with a raised eyebrow.

I shrug. "I think my reputation can handle a little bit of gossip if yours can."

"Hmm. I'm not sure I even have a reputation to damage at this point."

I frown. I don't like the way she talks down on herself. The light turns green, and I continue to the nearest town with any decent fast-food options. I change the subject by starting a debate about what to get for dinner, and eventually we settle on Chinese takeout. Loren places the order on an app on her phone, and I fish my wallet out of the center console to hand over to her.

"Here, use one of my credit cards."

She eyes me suspiciously. "We can split it. I'll pay, and you can Venmo me the difference."

"It's my treat. I am the one who suggested dinner." She reaches for the wallet hesitantly. "Stop making it weird, Reed. Just let me buy dinner. It's not like I'm going to expect you to pay me back with a night of hot—" I stop abruptly, realizing that I'm definitely the one making things uncomfortable now.

"No, what were you going to say, Blake?"

I press my lips together. "Nothing."

"Were you going to ask me to help you with your laundry while it was fresh from the dryer?" she asks, tapping her chin in mock consideration. "You know, some good warm-towel folding? Or perhaps you need someone to proofread one of your legal documents. Do you require my hot copyediting services?"

I snort, trying to ignore the improper thoughts I instantly concoct of Loren wearing glasses and not much else as she sits on my couch with a red pen and a stack of contracts. "As if I'd ever need you to check my grammar."

She rolls her eyes and smiles as she finally concedes and slips one of the cards out of my wallet. Then she begins rambling about work and having to return from her Christmas break until we stop to pick up our takeout order. On the way home, we trade funny stories about a few of her students, the ones I know from coaching.

I grab our bags, and she follows me inside after I unlock the front door. "Make yourself at home," I mumble, aware for the first time that, while my house is nice, it isn't exactly *cozy*.

"Wow, do you even live here?" she asks, stealing the words directly from my brain.

"I like things tidy," I return as I unpack our food, a bit embarrassed. "Let me guess, your place is a mess?"

"Maaay-be," she intones as she joins me at the kitchen island. "It's definitely well lived-in."

I think back to when we were kids. I can still see our work next to one another's on the class bulletin board, mine minimalistic and neat while hers was covered with scribbles and words going in every direction, though we'd still earned the same grade.

I smile as I begin setting out dishes and utensils, thinking that she hasn't changed much since then. She still seems to be the same witty, quirky, down-to-earth person, and she's definitely just as cute. It's actually kind of sad that we weren't at least friends all this time, now that I consider it. I've always liked Loren and thought she was pretty. It's just that the older we got, the more glaring our differences became, especially regarding our social lives.

Although my subconscious apparently finds her more along the lines of sexy these days, judging from my reaction to her helping JD get Tenley's attention with some staged flirting a while back.

I shake my head quickly, turning to the fridge. "What do you want to drink?" I already have my hand on a bottle of wine, and she glares at me suspiciously when I hold it up for her approval. "A glass or two won't hurt. We *are* supposed to be celebrating the fact that my brother has reached the next level in his quest for human perfection, aren't we? It's why I always keep a bottle of champagne in the fridge, just in case JD does something else magical on any given day."

She narrows her eyes. "Fine, I'll have a glass, but only if you promise to drink enough to spill your guts about this brother complex you keep not-so-subtly hinting at."

I flinch. "I don't have a brother complex." She stares me down, crossing her arms. "I guess that means I'm not as good at being passive-aggressive as I thought."

Her expression softens, and she chuckles. I sigh, realizing how much I like the sound of her laughter.

I open the bottle and turn to find a glass for each of us. "Why do you care so much about some deep-seated resentment I may or may not have been harboring for the past few decades anyway?" I ask from the cabinets.

"Because I've got nothing but time," she returns, mimicking my earlier reply and making me smile again.

Then she scoffs when I place the empty glasses on the counter. "Damn, Gus Gus. I agreed to a glass, not a fishbowl."

To be fair, the glasses *are* pretty big. But that isn't what catches my attention.

"Gus Gus?"

Her face reddens slightly. "It's what I used to call you behind your back in school. You know, like the mouse from *Cinderella*?"

I pour the wine, nearly emptying out the bottle between the two glasses. Oh well, I have plenty more, including the bottle of champagne. "But where in the hell did you get—oh. Augustine."

"Blake *Augustine* Bourgeois." The way she carefully enunciates each syllable of my full name makes me shiver.

"Fine, Loren *Agnes* Reed," I fire back, eager to move past the urge to ask her to say my name again so I can watch her mouth more carefully. "And all this time I thought *I* was the bully." I slide her glass across the counter, and she takes a seat before bringing it to her lips. I try not to watch and distract myself by taking a big gulp from my own glass.

She leans over to grab one of the takeout boxes, and my eyes dart down to the skin she inadvertently exposes when the neckline of her fitted bridesmaid's dress dips a couple of inches. I already had to stop myself from staring a few times throughout the ceremony, especially once I realized I'd been leaning around the priest to get a better look at her.

"Look, I had to save face somehow, Gus Gus. I needed to make the best of every opportunity I got to take you down a few pegs," she explains before she sits back and stuffs a forkful of noodles into her mouth.

I smirk as I watch her chew. "Right. Because I led such a charmed life and all."

"Didn't you?" She stares at me expectantly.

I shrug. "I guess. Though it's never enough for a perfectionist."

"Which is why you've always loathed me and my GPA?"

I let out an exhale and look down at my glass. "I never hated you, Loren. Only myself. But I'm sorry for making you feel like I did." She's quiet for a second, so I take another long swallow.

"After all this time, I really appreciate hearing that from you," she says softly. But then she adds, "And I am genuinely sorry for being smarter than you," as the corners of her mouth turn up in a cocky sneer.

I laugh and grab a fortune cookie to toss at her, making her giggle again. "At least you can say that you're still the same old intolerable smartass."

"I am what I am." She shrugs unapologetically and uses both hands to pick up her huge glass. "To JD and Tenley," she begins, and I lift mine curiously. "May their marriage continue to be the stuff of cheesy romance novels with a happily ever after and all that."

I nod once and take a drink, still wondering what inspired her sudden toast.

"And to Augustine and Agnes, may we move forward as tolerable frenemies. As the closest friends of the happy couple, this is only the first of many awkward family events we'll be forced to attend together. Hopefully we're able to entertain one another for the next few years' worth of baptisms and birthday parties, since I'm pretty sure they're literally working on making a shit-ton of babies, like, as we speak."

I snicker and clink my glass against hers this time. "To Augustine and Agnes."

The conversation shifts as we eat, and we begin reminiscing on some of the times we'd bested one another in high school. I'm pouring out the last of the champagne, which I'd opened after we finished off the second bottle of wine, when she brings up our first kiss.

"I still can't believe you punched Landry in the face that night," she says, slurring a little. "There I was, thinking you were setting me up as the butt of a joke, then I found out later that you were only trying to defend my honor."

I smirk, noticing how her eyes look glossy and wondering if mine are just as bad. I probably should have cut us off by now.

"It was the least I could do after you volunteered to be my test dummy."

The truth is that as far as first kisses go, mine had been pretty amazing. It's likely that Loren hadn't enjoyed it as much as I had, but it only took one try for me to realize that making women feel good was an instant dopamine hit, and so began my serial dating habits.

And, speaking of women staying over ...

"Oh, shit," I mumble to myself.

"What?"

"I forgot I was supposed to drive you back to your car later." I hold up the empty champagne bottle and glance at her, and we both laugh obnoxiously. "Looks like you might be stuck here overnight, Reed."

She groans but still has a smile on her face. Frankly, I'm shocked she's not freaking out or at least calling someone to give her a ride home. "Fine, but I'm not putting out until you hold up your end of the deal."

My eyebrows go up sharply. She's got my full attention now. "Which was ..."

She gets up and walks around with her wine glass, settling down in the chair beside me. "You promised to tell me how your bro complex has developed over the years, remember?"

"Oh, that. That's nothing."

"A deal's a deal, Gus Gus," she declares, leaning over to poke me in the chest. My skin burns where she touches me, even through the fabric of my shirt, and I have to take a second to compose myself before I do something embarrassing with her so close.

"There's nothing to tell. It's the same as it was when we were kids. My brother's still perfect, and I'm not, but I wish I were. End of story."

She scoffs. "No one's perfect."

"No, but he's still the Golden Boy. I was the first born, but he's 'Joseph Drake the Third.' I was the quarterback, but he got the football scholarship. I graduated from law school, just like my dad and his dad, and JD became the town favorite because he gave up playing in the pros to coach freaking high school football." I clear my throat as my voice gets thick. "Not that there's anything wrong with that," I add.

I look up to find her staring at me intently, not with pity, but with empathy. Then I wipe my hand over my face when I feel my eyes getting watery. "I'm sorry, please forget I said any of that."

"No," she says quickly, stopping me by placing a hand on my forearm. "I get it."

"Do you?"

She smirks. "You *have* met my older siblings before, right?"

I roll my eyes, remembering that they're both doctors now. "Fair enough."

"I'm sure you remember Landry being especially insufferable," she adds with a light laugh.

"But you still love him, right?"

"I do."

"I love my brother, too. He's genuinely the best human on the planet. I know Tenley makes him happy, and I'm extremely proud of the way he's stepped up for Ethan. JD deserves everything he's ever gotten and more." I sigh before I begin again. "But none of that means it's not hard to watch him move on while I'm still ... stuck."

She nods knowingly, reaching over to slide her hand over mine now.

"And then I feel guilty for being jealous of him, especially about something as stupid as a name, something out of his control. It feels like I'll never do anything as well as he does. And this is just another example of him one-upping me, because I know he's going to be the best husband and father ever, and I'm never going to be either of those." I pull my hand away and rub the back of my neck, overcome with embarrassment. "God, I'm so pathetic. Complaining about living in my brother's shadow on his wedding day? Geez."

"Blake," she begins, her voice soft, "you're allowed to have feelings. And I'm sure growing up with JD wasn't easy. Don't get me wrong, he's great, but he can be a lot."

Then I remember that, despite getting along so well, neither of them seemed to have felt any chemistry. For once, I've managed something JD hasn't. Because Loren and I have had chemistry before, and there's definitely something happening right now.

"And *you* are great for completely different reasons. I hear you're a fantastic lawyer, and I know for a fact you're an amazing coach in your own right. You're smart and funny. I mean, women flock to you, right? You have such great hair, and I'm willing to bet you're hiding a very spicy set of abs under your shirt right now." Her voice quiets, and she gulps as if she's embarrassed.

Our eyes meet, and a current of electricity crackles between us. My breathing quickens as I stare back at her. "There's an easy way to find out, if you're really curious," I murmur, my fingers already finding their way to the buttons of my shirt.

But she throws her head back and laughs, breaking the connection.

Shit.

I should have known that line wouldn't work on her.

"Oh, man," she says, wiping her eyes as her laughter dies down. "I'm sorry about that. I didn't mean to get so heavy-handed with the compliments."

I lick my lips. "I don't mind."

"I was just trying to lift your spirits, at least for now."

"You have. Thank you." But I can sense the way she's purposefully ignoring the flirty quality I've added to my tone. "Loren, can I tell you something else?"

"Sure," she agrees, her brow furrowed.

"I know we've always given each other a hard time, but I was serious before when I said it was all just a front for me. The truth is … I've always admired you and thought you were beautiful." I stop for a second before continuing. "I still do."

She blinks and looks away, as if she doesn't believe me. "You don't have to compliment me just because I said those nice things about you. I meant it, regardless of what you think of me."

"I meant what I said, too." I slide my hand over to rest on her thigh. "What if I told you that you've been on my mind since you helped my brother?" She bites her lip, and I can see her chest heaving as I move my hand up to her hip. "I've already admitted that you made me jealous, so don't you dare start thinking I'm only saying all this because you called me sexy first."

"I never used the term *sexy*," she replies, her voice trembling. "Only *spicy*."

I grin at her, letting my hand continue up her side. "Regardless, I should probably do something to ensure you believe me."

She tilts her head back slightly as I bring my left thumb up to graze over her parted lips. "And what do you plan to do?" she whispers against the pad of my finger, making me groan with desire.

I answer her wordlessly as I cradle her cheek in my hand and lean down to brush my lips against hers. Or, at least, I'd only intended to start out that way, but the instant our mouths meet, I know there's no way I'll be able to control myself with her. I've waited years for this, and having Loren in my arms feels every bit as good as I imagined.

She kisses me back for a while before she places both of her hands on my chest and pushes lightly, putting some space between us. "Blake," she breathes, her eyes still on my mouth. "I don't know if this is a good idea."

"And I think it's the best idea I've ever had," I say, my lips returning to hers immediately.

But she pulls away again, even though she seems reluctant. "We're both a little drunk, and you're in a vulnerable place. It's a recipe for disaster."

I shake my head softly, trying to draw her back in with my eyes. "You don't understand, Lo. I've wanted to do this with you for so long."

She closes her eyes for a second, as if she's trying to steady her breathing, then she finally nods. "So have I."

As soon as the words leave her lips, I'm kissing her again. Then I stand tall and scoop her up from the stool, urging her to wrap her legs around my waist. Her arms fold behind my neck, and I move my mouth down to her shoulder as I walk us to my bedroom.

"Loren," I say her name again, still holding her up. "Look at me." She obeys, exciting me even more. "I want this so badly, but I also don't want to push you too far. Promise you'll stop me if you change your mind."

She nods quickly, shifting her hips over me and eliciting a growl. Maybe it's a result of my profession, but I'm very big on consent.

"You are so beautiful," I whisper while I still have her attention. "I mean it."

Her brow furrows, as if she still isn't sure whether to believe me, so I set out to prove I'm telling the truth.

CHAPTER 6

Blake

"That was great, Blake," says one of the other
lawyers in the district attorney's office. David chuckles and pats my
arm as he adds, "You know the rest of us all love a good takedown of
Ryan Jameson."

I grin proudly, because he's right. None of us care for Ethan's
father, and winning a case against one of my least likable peers only
makes helping my family taste that much sweeter. "Hey, he made it
personal. I couldn't back down after that."

I may have my fair share of insecurities, but I don't lack confidence in my outward appearance or my abilities as a lawyer. I'd also
like to think I've done a decent job of prioritizing morality over
money. Practicing law in a town as small as Camellia means I've got to
take on most of the cases that walk through the door if I want to
make a decent living, but the majority of my work deals in family law,
custody arrangements like Ethan's, and divorces. And although some
of it can be disheartening, I like helping my clients see their way
through these unfortunate situations. I've also been known to take
the odd pro-bono public defense case, especially when a juvenile's
involved. Working with kids as an assistant football coach has given
me a little more insight into teenage boys in particular, so I've been
offering my services more and more over the years.

"You know, it's too bad you aren't throwing your hat in the ring for Assistant DA. None of us are looking forward to Jameson sliding into the position once Moreau finally retires."

"Who said I wasn't interested?" I straighten my shoulders and stuff my hands in my pockets. Truthfully, I *have* been considering the opportunity. I could help a lot of people in that position, and it's not like I have a whole lot of distractions to keep me from doing the job well.

"Come on, Blake. You know how these things are," David reminds me.

I lift my chin. "What's that supposed to mean?"

He scoffs. "The people in this parish are still too conservative and traditionally minded to accept a guy like you."

"A guy like me, huh?"

"Hey, we all know the good work you do around here," he begins, placing his hand on my shoulder. "But 'wholesome' and 'trustworthy' aren't the words people associate with the name Blake Bourgeois."

"Yeah." I nod. "Well, at least I get laid more often than the rest of you married guys."

This whole reputation thing is getting exhausting. My comebacks aren't even as clever as they used to be.

David huffs out a laugh. "Keep telling yourself that, man." He claps his hand over my shoulder one more time before he walks off, and I go on to pick up the rest of Ethan's files in the front before I run home to freshen up before dinner.

I check my watch and notice I don't have time for a shower, so I settle for ditching my tie and jacket before I meet JD and the others. I must be the last to arrive at the restaurant, because they're all standing near the door when I walk inside.

My heart immediately begins thumping harder as soon as I spot Loren among the group. I wasn't thinking she'd be here tonight, but now that she is, I'm not disappointed. Just nervous. And she's definitely avoiding eye contact.

I hold my breath as we crowd around the table, trying to decide whether I should make an attempt to sit next to her. To my surprise, she bolts over to the empty chair beside me, despite having ignored me since I walked in.

She finally glances up at me when I pull the chair out for her, and her huge, chocolate-brown eyes lock onto mine for a few seconds, making my chest feel tight. "Thanks," she whispers before she sits.

"So, uh, how are you?" I ask awkwardly once we're all seated and scanning the menus. Well, I'm pretending to scan the menu, but my eyes keep darting down to her ankle tattoo.

I may have Googled it since the last time I saw her and discovered it's a nod to *The Lord of the Rings*. I assume the connection is from her name, since it's called a Leaf of Lórien, or something like that.

It's cute.

She turns her mouth to the side and slips a hand over the tattoo as she considers, oblivious to my staring. "Fine. You?"

"I'm great."

"Good."

Okay, so, if this is how things are going to be, why did she purposefully sit next to me?

She clears her throat. "Blake, um, can we talk? Later?"

"About what?"

Her hand flies up to her neck as she tugs absent mindedly on a necklace, forcing my attention to the contrast of her creamy skin behind the dark, wavy hair framing her shoulders. "I was actually hoping I could explain in private, if that's okay?" Then there's a slight flush in her cheeks, the only color in her flawless complexion, and I find myself feeling smug because she seems nervous, too.

"All right."

She probably wants to apologize for the way she brushed me off a while back or to thank me for saving her from that bad date the other day. I raise my brow and shoot her a flirty smirk when some of the confidence I've been missing for the past few weeks eases its way back in. Even though her rejection still stings more than I care to admit, if she's willing to admit she was wrong to dismiss me, I can be the bigger person and at least hear her out.

"Your place or mine?" I whisper to her from behind my menu.

She glares at me. "Excuse me?" Of course she'd assume the worst. To be fair, I usually am the worst.

"You said you wanted to talk in private."

"Oh, right." She chews on her plump bottom lip for a second, and it's hard not to stare. "Can you just follow me home later?"

I nod and attempt to forget about our plans for the rest of dinner, but even the slightest chance of hooking up with Loren again—which I have no intention of doing—is enough to keep me distracted.

After taking the last few bites of my food, I glance across the table to find Tenley's mom looking back and forth between Loren and me expectantly. I smile politely, wondering whether Mrs. T ever noticed the way Loren's car stayed parked overnight at her house after JD's wedding.

Then I turn my gaze to my brother, his arm curling protectively around the back of his wife's chair, and I'm reminded of when JD recruited Loren to help him make Tenley jealous. Loren had been a great sport, coaching JD throughout the day and putting him at ease by making him laugh, mostly at my expense. But that's how Loren and I have always operated, teasing one another or competing for the last word.

"Hmm. You've been uncharacteristically quiet tonight, Blake," remarks Tenley, bringing me back from my thoughts.

I shrug. "Sorry. It's been a long day. Believe it or not, even the best in the business get nervous when they're tasked with bringing home their own nephew." I reach over to muss Ethan's hair from his spot on the other side of me.

He protests at first, pushing my hand away playfully, but then he turns to me and delivers an earnest, "Thanks for everything."

I glance around the table to find Tenley, JD, and Mrs. T all looking choked up. "What? No, not again, guys," I begin, hoping that my smile might lend some levity to the conversation.

"I'm the only one with a valid excuse to cry at the drop of a hat, for the record," Tenley announces, using her napkin to dab at her eyes. But JD exhales and shakes his head as well.

I hear a short sniffle beside me, where Loren is trying to hide her own red-rimmed eyes. "Not you, too, Reed. I thought your constitution was stronger than the rest of these crybabies, at least."

She rolls her eyes, but I can't help myself as I slip my hand under the table to rest on her knee.

We say our goodbyes after dinner, and I make sure I pull my sister-in-law in for a hug so I can whisper, "Congratulations," and "Thank you for letting him have this," in her ear. I'm not known for my sentimentality, but I've always tried to show my brother how I really feel when it matters. And I figure Tenley's an extension of him now. She's biting her lip and tearing up again when I pull away, so I spin her around and steer her back into JD's arms. He's happy to oblige.

"See you later, Reed," I say to Loren as I walk out to my truck. Then I take a deep breath as soon as I close the door behind me, finally free to let my emotions run amok in the privacy of my own driver's seat.

Bam, bam, bam!

I nearly jump out of my skin when I hear Loren's small fist hitting the glass, then I wipe my eyes quickly before rolling down the window.

"Shit, Reed, you scared the hell out of me."

"I just wanted to ... wait, are you *crying*?" she asks incredulously.

"No," I lie.

She raises an eyebrow. "Did you really hold it in all throughout dinner just so you could *pleurer* like a baby in your truck?"

"Why would I be crying?"

She purses her lips, but her haughty expression is nearly ruined by the fact that she barely clears the edge window and has to look up at me. "Because you're grateful that you got the chance to help JD secure his happiness. And you secretly love your new in-laws."

"What do you want, Loren?" I narrow my watery eyes, hoping to distract her from the way my voice cracks.

"To tell you to let yourself in when you get there. I figured you'd want to hold off a few minutes on following me home."

"Sure, whatever. I'll be right behind you." I raise my window as soon as she's gone so that I can finish collecting myself. My phone chimes, so I check it while I wait for Loren to drive off.

ETHAN R

hey "uncle blake"

what's up with you and ms reed

BLAKE

Idk what you're talking about.

ETHAN R

caidence saw you holding hands under the table

and mawmaw kept staring at you like she thinks something's going on

wanna tell me why was she just talking to you at your truck?

BLAKE

Caidence was mistaken. And ftr, Loren and I can't stand each other. It's been that way since we were kids.

ETHAN R

so you're saying you tease her bc you're into her?

BLAKE

I tease her because she needs to be reminded that I'm the smarter one.

ETHAN R

are you though?

BLAKE

Okay, I tease her because it makes me feel like I'm the smarter one.

ETHAN R

it's okay man

just admit you like her

your secret is safe with me

BLAKE

That crap might have worked with JD and Tenley, kid, but I'm not that gullible. Nice try.

ETHAN R

i'm onto you 👀

I curse and smile down at my phone. Then I wait for Ethan's truck to leave the parking lot before I turn in the direction of Loren's house.

CHAPTER 7

Blake

I KNOCK SHORTLY BEFORE I WALK INTO THE SMALL, shotgun-style cottage and call out for Loren when I don't see her right away.

"Hey, Blake, in here," she returns. I follow the sound of her voice through the narrow living room and into the kitchen.

"Want anything to drink?" she offers once I approach. She's digging in a large tote bag covered with what looks like various Shakespearean quotes.

"I'm fine, thanks." I cross my arms and attempt to look aloof. Then I spot my hoodie hanging off the back of a chair, the one I loaned her a few weeks ago, and I nearly blow my cover. "You, uh ... you said we needed to talk?"

She turns and tries to conceal a small box behind her back once she sees how close I'm standing. Her widened doe-eyes meet mine, and she takes a deep breath before she blurts out, "Blake, I don't know how else to say this, so I'm just going to put it out there—I'm late."

I furrow my brow, still distracted by the box she's hiding. I reach back and pull her arm forward, realizing what she means when I see the words "home pregnancy test" scrawled across the package, then I drop her hand and take a step back.

"As in … *late*-late?" I venture, my eyes now wider than hers.

She bites her lip and nods reluctantly. "Yeah, *late*-late. I haven't confirmed it, but I'm pretty sure something's up."

"Why are you telling me this before you've even taken a test?" My brain isn't processing as quickly as I need it to tonight, but that's probably due to the lack of oxygen since I'm holding my breath.

She shrugs and looks apologetic. "You're the only other person who knows about our night together. Well, I guess Tenley's mom has her suspicions, but we agreed not to tell anyone else, and I was too scared to take a test on my own. So here we are."

"Oh."

I'm surprised, since I've been thinking there's no way Loren wouldn't confide in Tenley, who'd undoubtedly tell JD, who would eventually threaten to kick my ass. But the fact that she kept our hookup quiet just further proves it didn't mean anything to her.

Or maybe she's too embarrassed to own up to it because she still thinks I only see her as another one-night stand. I haven't done anything to help my case in either scenario, since I've been too busy feeling sorry for myself to correct her misconceptions, especially the one about me wanting her out of my bed so early the next morning.

She interrupts my brooding when she wordlessly hands me the box so she can grab a bottle of juice from the fridge.

"Loren, not that I mind being here right now, but what happened to the whole 'I'm a big girl, we don't have to do this' spiel you gave me the morning after?"

Is it weird that I'm more focused on figuring out why she wants me around than finding out whether she's actually pregnant?

She stops chugging and pauses to catch her breath. "I'm not asking you to be here as a potential father, and I'm certainly not trying to trap you. I just need another living, breathing human to help me get through this part, and you're literally my only option."

And this time my stomach dips when she mentions the very real possibility of fatherhood in my future, and I start panicking, just a little.

"So, ah, you weren't on birth control or anything?" I venture, my voice unsteady.

She cringes. "No. A certain women's healthcare professional convinced me that it was better if I let my body do its own thing, especially since I hadn't been sexually active in a while."

I curse my dear sister-in-law and her philanthropic fertility-awareness efforts under my breath. "I guess I'd sort of assumed you were."

"I couldn't recall you taking any precautions, either. At least, not at first. Though, my memory is still a little hazy."

"I'm sorry." I shake my head slowly, trying not to dwell on the implications of my carelessness. "But I always have before, and Jada makes me get tested regularly. So you shouldn't have to worry about any other positives."

I'm sure my oversight was a combination of our lowered inhibitions and all those years of built-up sexual tension.

That's all, right?

"Jada?" Her eyebrows lift.

"My secretary."

"Right. Well, you can start opening that thing up if you want. I'm just about locked and loaded," she says before she returns to her hydration efforts, inadvertently making me laugh.

A minute later, I hand her the test stick, directing her on how to conduct her business. She makes a quip about never thinking she'd need my help to pass a test before she scampers off to the back of the house. Then she returns and gingerly places the stick down on the paper towel I've laid out for her.

"Now, we wait five minutes for the results," I announce.

"Okay," she replies, her voice thick. "Blake, are you scared?"

It's funny, actually. I've been so careful with other women over the years that I never thought I'd find myself in this predicament. I should be freaking out right now. Instead, I think I'm just relieved to be doing this with Loren instead of someone else. And those feelings are too important to unpack at the moment. I need to focus on making sure she's okay for now.

"Yeah, a little. But what's done is done, right?" I return. She nods and presses her lips together as her eyes begin to water, and I instinctively pull her in for a hug.

She allows me to hold her while she sniffles into my chest. "There's no way I can wait five whole minutes to look at that thing," she declares, pushing herself back.

I chuckle. "Same."

So we step forward together just as a second pink line materializes on the test stick. And my entire world changes in a single moment.

"Welp," she chokes out.

I exhale through my lips as my heartbeat throbs in my ears. "Yep. There it is."

"There. It. Is."

"It's freaking dark as hell, too, Reed. I must have gotten you, like, *super* pregnant," I blurt out before glancing down at her. She's wringing her petite hands, so I reach out and grab one of them to stop her. "I'm sorry. Are you okay?"

"Nope," she replies with extra emphasis on the *P*, making me smile.

And then I begin moving involuntarily again, turning her body to face mine and lifting her chin before I lean down for a short kiss.

Man, I could get used to this—

"What was that for?" she asks immediately, her eyelashes fluttering after I pull away.

"I, uh … just felt like you needed it," I explain, trying to sound as unaffected as possible.

"Oh, okay. Um, hold onto that thought. I'll be right back."

She spins on her heels and hurries off again. I'm unsure whether I should follow her at first, but then I hear her coughing. I knock gently before I open the bathroom door and let myself in. She's hunched over the toilet, so I grab a hair clip from the counter and use it to gather her long, brown locks and secure them behind her head. She heaves a couple more times while I find a clean washcloth for her, then she takes it gratefully.

I step out to give her some space, sitting on the edge of her bed and allowing my eyes to roam around the room, making note of the random clutter and the stacks of books dotting every surface. I could have guessed that Loren's a junk collector.

I'm reaching over to pick up the book on her nightstand when she walks in.

"Sorry about that," she apologizes as she sits beside me.

"No, no—it was the only fitting ending to that moment." I bump her shoulder playfully. "In fact, I almost joined you."

She huffs out a laugh. "I'm sure you're not used to garnering this kind of reaction from women."

I frown, because I can't help but feel embarrassed or even ashamed at my behavior every time someone uses it to make me the butt of a joke lately, especially when it's Loren.

"No, I guess not. But that seems to be a recurring theme when I'm with you."

She sighs before she speaks again, ignoring my last comment. "Blake, I don't expect you to respond to any of this now. But you should know that I plan to go through with this pregnancy. The alternative is not even a consideration, at least not for me."

I can't help but smile at the protective air in her tone. "I'm actually very relieved to hear that."

"And this probably goes without saying, but you're the only possible candidate, you know, as the father."

A sense of relief washes over me, which manifests as a cocky smirk. "So, you and Doc—"

"Blake," she cuts me off, pinning me with a sharp glare.

"Sorry. It's not my place to make any assumptions or judgments about your life, so I appreciate your honesty," I say, hoping she can sense my sincerity. "Thank you for telling me that."

She looks down at her hands again. "I'm sure all of this sounds incredibly cliché, but I really don't want you to feel like you're stuck. You don't owe me anything."

"Hey, hey," I interrupt her when her eyes begin watering again. I reach over and grab one of her hands to hold onto. "I thought we weren't doing this stuff tonight, hmm? I'm only supposed to be here as a supportive frenemy, not as the guy who put a baby in you, right?"

She smiles at me, despite my voice cracking at the end. "You're handling this way better than I expected, for the record."

I shrug. "Don't give me too much credit yet. I'm sure there's an early mid-life crisis looming on the horizon."

"I bet you'd mid-life crisis really well, too."

"Oh, definitely. I've already made a list of must haves: douchey sports car, tanning bed, new hunting camp, girlfriend who needs a sponsorship for fake boobs ..." I let go of her hand to check each item off on my fingers, hoping to make her laugh.

I'm rewarded with a giggle, and she surprises me by reaching up to run her hand through my hair, giving me the chills. "At least you're doing it before you need hair plugs."

I smile once I remember she said I had nice hair before. "Hmm. I like it when you touch me."

I didn't mean to say it out loud. Hell, I didn't even mean to think it. But I can't help how weird I'm becoming lately, and I don't foresee it getting any better after tonight. I'm afraid the realization that Loren and I are now linked for the rest of our lives may have already activated something on a subconscious level.

She gulps and slowly brings her hand back to her lap, her eyes locked onto mine the whole time. "And just like that, you keep surprising me, Blake Bourgeois."

"I think I'm surprised at myself, too."

She turns away quickly and stifles a yawn. "I'm sorry. Is it just me or has this been the longest day ever?"

"Oh, I wholeheartedly agree," I say on an exhale. "*Long day* is an understatement."

"Thank you again for being here with me."

I lift a shoulder. "I'm glad you asked."

She stands and offers a hand. "Walk you out?"

My head begins buzzing when I take her hand in mine, so I instinctively tug her back toward me. "Loren, would it be okay if I crashed here?"

"What?" Her eyes widen.

"I thought maybe you'd want the company tonight," I mumble,

suddenly feeling shy. And I'm never shy in front of women. "I could sleep on the couch," I add quickly.

She purses her lips while she thinks. "I'd really like that. But I'm afraid you won't fit on my couch."

"Oh." At just over six feet in height, I find most sofas too short for comfortable overnight stays. Regardless, if this is Loren inviting me to share a bed with her, I'm not about to turn her down.

"No funny business?"

I grin at her. "It's a little late for that, isn't it?"

"I mean it," she says sternly, but she's smiling back at me.

"Just sleep, I promise." I hold up my right hand and make a show of crossing my fingers behind my back with my left.

"I'm going to change," she declares, rolling her eyes. "Make yourself comfortable."

I watch as she finds her pajamas in the dresser before she disappears into the bathroom. "Do you need to shower?" she calls from behind the closed door.

"I'll get one at home in the morning," I answer as I unbutton my shirt. I unbuckle my belt, lingering for a second to consider how Loren might feel about me sleeping in my underwear.

Wait, since when do I worry about this kind of stuff? I've always considered my body to be my greatest asset, but now I'm second guessing whether I'd be offending her by stripping down. I dismiss the thought and bend over to remove my pants, just as Loren returns.

"You're not going to try and convince me that you're a bedtime nudist, are you?"

I shrug apologetically. "Sorry. I didn't think to pack my Ninja Turtle jammies."

She shoves me playfully when I walk around to the bathroom, so I surmise she's okay with me sleeping in my boxers. She certainly doesn't protest once I join her beneath the covers a few minutes later.

"Blake," she begins meekly. "Don't take this the wrong way, but could you please hold me for a while?"

I stretch out my arm, inviting her in, and she curls up beside me before we drift off to sleep.

CHAPTER 8

Blake

"Blake?" I hear a hint of panic in Loren's voice, though I can't quite bring myself to wake up fully.

"Mm," I hum. I can feel her warmth against my bare chest as I finally come to, and I take in a deep breath of her signature scent—roses. "You smell really nice," I mutter, pulling her in closer and burying my nose in her hair.

I get the sense that we've done this before, though, and my eyes pop open when her body stiffens uncomfortably against mine.

What the hell am I even doing? I've definitely crossed over into creepy territory with the hair sniffing. I'm not a sniffer—I'm not even a morning cuddler, unless it's foreplay.

But this feels so damned *good*. I sigh contentedly.

"I know I'm small and everything, but I'm not a teddy bear."

I reluctantly loosen my grip, stealing one more lungful before clearing my throat and backing away. "Sorry."

"It's just that ... I wasn't sure if you were aware, but, um ..." She gives up and shifts her position against me, and I inhale sharply through my teeth at the contact.

Seriously, *why* does she feel so good? What is happening to me?

"It seems that some of you wakes up before the rest."

I bite my lip and cringe behind her. "Right. Well, I'd apologize, but I can't exactly help it."

She giggles. "I understand. I just figured you'd want to know, since you promised no funny business and all."

"Did I?" I grind against her again, making myself groan. I really am a glutton for punishment when it comes to her.

"Yep, pretty sure you did," she replies, her voice squeaky.

"Then you'd better scoot, little spoon," I murmur near her ear. "Because I'm about to get real funny."

One more second and I'll quit, I tell myself. But when she lets out a soft moan, I just about lose it.

"Loren," I breathe, my hand creeping around her stomach and inching up beneath the hem of her tank top. "I mean it." Then I press my lips to the smooth skin at the back of her neck.

She arches her back slightly, and I curse under my breath. "As a newly established hormone factory, I'm pretty sure I cannot be trusted as the voice of reason anymore," she finally returns as she reaches around and clutches at me, urging me to push back again.

"Do you even understand what you do to me, Reed?" My voice is deep and husky, and she digs her fingertips into my backside in response. "This is your last warning," I tell her, pulling her earlobe in between my lips and dragging my hands away. Then I force my hips to retreat for a second until I can make sure she's a willing participant.

"We probably shouldn't," she whispers, but she sounds very unconvinced.

"I'm trying my best to restrain myself here, but I *really* need a clear yes or no answer in the next few seconds." My thumb is hooked beneath the elastic of my boxers, ready for the starting gun. I don't know whether I've built up our last time together in my mind or if the pregnancy thing is an unexpected turn on, but I've never felt a desire this strong. The rubber band holding me back is stretching beyond its breaking point, and I'm about to snap.

"I ... I, uh ..." she stutters for a second, and I hold my breath.

Beep–beep–beep

Both of our phones begin blaring out an alarm at the same time, and she rolls away from me to silence hers.

"Ugh," I groan loudly, shifting to lie on my back and rubbing a hand over my face. Then I reach over to snooze the alarm on my side.

I turn to find her sitting up now, her eyes wide and her chest heaving. "You. Stay over there," she demands.

I throw my head back against the pillow and laugh. "I'm sorry," I say after a while. "Maybe you should be the big spoon from now on."

"Maybe we shouldn't be spooning at all," she suggests, and my face falls. The last thing I want is a repeat of the last time we woke up together.

"Frenemies can share a bed, can't they?"

"I don't think that's the normal protocol."

"What about when they're already having a baby together?" The words slip out before I can help it.

She blinks a few times. "Are we?"

I sit up and scoot close enough for her shoulder to rest against my arm, because I can't shake the need to touch her. "I thought we both saw the evidence last night."

"I mean, together. Are we doing this *together*?"

I mull her question over in my mind. "If by together you mean that you're going to grow and give birth to our baby while I drive you to doctor's appointments and hang around in case you have a late-night craving, then, yeah. I'd like to, anyway."

"But not like, as a couple, right?"

My heart races again. "I didn't know that option was on the table."

"I didn't say it was," she counters quickly. "I just wanted clarification."

My lips twitch as I try not to smile. "Frenemies with benefits?"

She rolls her eyes. "No way. That's literally the worst romance trope of all."

"What do you mean?" I protest.

"I'm obviously too well read to fall for that one." She gestures toward some of the books stacked around the room. "I'm not entering any with-benefits agreements with you. No couple in history has ever come out of that arrangement unscathed." She crosses her arms and leans back against the headboard.

"But we've already established that the benefits are amazing. Those other couples must have been missing that element," I point out.

Her subsequent silence wounds my pride more deeply than it should.

"Or maybe it wasn't all that amazing for both of us. Okay, then," I say quietly, looking down at my lap. Well, that explains a lot.

"I actually meant the part about them falling in love, you know, because it's impossible not to form an emotional connection after a while," she explains. "And I'm pleading the fifth regarding the physical stuff."

I feel myself frowning—no, pouting.

"Wow, that bad, huh?"

She sighs in frustration. "Stop *bouder-ing*. It was the opposite of terrible, okay? I'm just trying to throw a wet blanket on this ... well, whatever that was just now."

I should be embarrassed by the combination of relief and heat that floods my chest. "Chemistry?" I supply, my smile growing wider by the second.

"Sure. Let's call it that. Just don't get cocky on me."

I pull up the sheets and pretend to check beneath as I snicker quietly.

"Ugh. Aren't you like, thirty?" She's trying not to smile.

"Thirty-one," I return. "But my sense of humor just turned sixteen."

She rolls her eyes, but the corner of her mouth turns up before she continues. "If we're really going to have a baby together—as friends—then we'll need to set some boundaries."

I narrow my eyes at her. "Isn't laying down the ground rules another one of those stupid romance tropes, or whatever you call them?"

"How would you know that?" she asks, rearing back in surprise.

"JD makes me watch too many rom coms."

She snorts. "That tracks. But we're just going to have to risk the ground rules, anyway."

"Fine. But this is a negotiation." *And I am well-equipped for negotiation.* I gesture with my hand. "Ladies first."

She lifts her chin haughtily as she begins, ticking the first one off on her index finger. "No unnecessary touching."

"Touching is necessary for sex," I remind her. She looks unamused. "All right, here's my counter: no sex—unless you ask explicitly—but I want unlimited rated-PG kissing and cuddling rights."

"Really?"

I shrug. "I told you, I like touching you. Is that so hard to believe?" She doesn't answer, so I continue pleading my case. "Besides, maybe you'll need a totally platonic foot rub one day. And I'm going to want to feel the baby moving."

"Okay, then why kissing?"

"I have my reasons. It'll make more sense later," I maintain, though I have no defense.

"All right. I'll raise you no nudity, and you've got a deal."

"Does that mean I have to wear a shirt around you?"

"And pants."

"Amended to allow fully clothed sleepovers, and we're on to item number two."

"Okay. Lay off the overly flirty talk."

But I'm not even sure I can, especially around her. Flirting is my default, the main component of my persona.

"Elaborate, please."

"I don't need to hear how good it makes you feel when I touch you, especially in the heat of the moment. It's confusing."

I furrow my brow. "I'll try, but I can't promise something won't slip out." I debate admitting this next part. "To be honest, I very rarely flirt with sincerity. But it's always been different with you. I accidentally blurt out that kind of stuff, then I'm embarrassed because

I actually meant it." I pause to check her expression. She's looking down, but her cheeks are flushed. "Besides, flirty banter is our thing. Without that, we'd just be bullying one another." I wait for her to acknowledge my confession, but besides a small widening of her eyes, she brushes right over it.

"Fair enough. We'll scratch that one because it's too subjective and hard to police. Next point, no one can know about the baby until after I tell my family, which won't be until after my first doctor's appointment."

"But what about—"

"*Especially* not JD. The last thing I want is to upstage their moment."

I huff. "As if I could do anything to upstage the Golden Boy."

"Let's put a pin in *that* conversation," she says, eyeing me suspiciously. "But I'm holding the line on this one. There's a huge difference between a married couple announcing their pregnancy and their best man knocking up the maid of honor after a drunken one-night stand."

"Whatever," I mutter. She glares at me until I speak again. "But I'm prohibiting the term 'one-night stand' from all future descriptions or mentions of our baby's conception date."

"Okay. And I don't want you constantly fawning and fussing over me as if I'm incapable of taking care of myself."

"Agreed," I say, still salty from the last one. I love my brother, and I've never seen him as excited for anything as he is about fatherhood. So I'm not sure why Loren's words bother me so much when I know she's right, but they do.

"That's all I've got. What about you?" she asks.

"Hmm?"

"Don't you have any other demands?"

"Oh. Yeah." I try to think quickly. "I defer all important pregnancy and baby related decisions to you, though I want informed consent and due consideration whenever possible."

"I can work with that. Anything else?"

"I promise not to overdo it, but I want first refusal when you need help with anything. And I'd like to be around for appointments and in the delivery room, if it's not too awkward."

"You can stand behind me. You don't need a front row seat for that show."

"Good. And I think it goes without saying that I want us to figure out some kind of co-parenting arrangement that works for everyone after the baby arrives."

"Okay."

My phone buzzes on the nightstand, but I ignore it and clear my throat. "I want to revisit one of the previous points. We'll wait until you're ready to make the announcement to everyone, including our families, but no one needs to know about the drunken-hookup part. I'd rather we tell people that we dated for a while but decided we were better off as friends."

"But it's not exactly true, is it?"

"Loren, I brought you back to my place where we talked over dinner and drinks. We laughed, we cried, we kissed ..." She fidgets uncomfortably when I trail off. "If that wasn't a date, then I don't know what is."

"And you expect everyone to believe we're secretly an item when they don't even think we're friends?"

"Of course not. We'll have to sell it, make a few public appearances as a happy couple and fool them into thinking we really tried." My mind races ahead. "This is where the kissing comes in, you know, in case we need to look more convincing."

She bites her lip. "Now we're adding 'fake relationship' and 'staged PDA' to the plot? Oof, I don't know."

I smirk. "Come on, Reed. What's the worst that could happen? You afraid of falling for me?"

"Ha! More like, what will *you* do on a date if you have to stay fully clothed?"

"Wouldn't you like to know?"

She rolls her eyes playfully and nudges me again. "You should check that," she offers, effectively changing the subject when my phone vibrates a second time. I pick it up and sigh before showing the group text to Loren.

ETHAN R

so uncle blake

wanna tell us about your new gf

"Ethan knows something's up. He and Caidence saw us, um, interacting last night," I explain.

"Oh. Well, why don't you have some fun with it, since we want them to think I've seduced you anyway, right?" she offers with a laugh, but her expression falls when she sees my face.

"I think you underestimate the unkind things people will say once they find out about us, even if we convince them we're a real couple."

She stares for a second before she brushes her hand over mine, and her lips curl up into a sad smile. "You know I couldn't care less about what everyone thinks, right?"

"Still, I wish I could save you from all that. I guess I never thought my reputation would hurt anyone else, but now I'm afraid I was wrong."

"All right, I get it. You're worried some of your exes might come after me," she says and lets out an exaggerated groan.

I can't help but smile, even as I roll my eyes. "I'm much more concerned about the Camellia rumor mill."

"Hey, I'm not afraid of a little gossip, all right? I can handle myself. And we're equally culpable in this situation."

I nod. "You're right. You knew what you were getting yourself into when you practically begged me to show you my spicy abs," I say, flexing for her.

She cackles out loud. "Your *what*, now?"

"You don't remember?" I ask, and she shrugs. "Right before we kissed, you paid me a whole list of compliments. According to you, my best qualities include my hair and my 'spicy abs.' "

Loren's jaw lowers. "I said no such thing! I would *never*."

I flash her a cocky smirk. "Oh, honey, but you did. You *definitely* did."

"Okay, but I hadn't seen you shirtless since, what, high school? How would I have rated your abs before I even knew they existed? I don't believe you."

"First of all, why would you bother to remember something like that from high school?" She doesn't answer, but her face flushes. "Secondly, you said, and I quote, 'I bet you're hiding a set of spicy abs under that shirt.' So it's even worse—you basically admitted to thinking about what I might look like topless, dare I say fantasizing about it."

She covers her face with her palms. "Look, as the coach's daughter, I was often stuck at football practice against my wishes. And it's not my fault that teenage boys love being topless."

"Why do you think I was so eager to walk around without a shirt at practice?" She groans from behind her hands, and I chuckle. "Do you really not remember our conversation from that night, though?"

She sighs and brings her hands down. "I can recall some bits and pieces. But stop pretending you noticed anything about me in high school besides my GPA."

I cock an eyebrow at her. "You used to sit and wait for your dad and Landry in that shady spot under the press box. But you were always too distracted by a book to notice me parading around with my baby abs out," I tell her, and she blushes again. "And I'm forgoing the opportunity to comment on what I recall about your 'bits and pieces' to apologize again for initiating something while you weren't sober enough to remember it. Although I'd be lying if I said I had any regrets, given the outcome."

"Stop apologizing, Blake. I'm a grown woman. I remember enough to know you didn't take advantage of me. And regardless of our history, I know there's no way you ever would have. I trust you. I'm just choosing to believe that I would never use the term *spicy abs*. At least, not to your face." She presses her lips together and suppresses a smile as my phone buzzes again.

JD

Uh, WUT?

TENLEY B

👀

"Go ahead," Loren offers. "Messing with JD will be good practice for dealing with Landry later."

I laugh softly and go back to my phone, still wary of what my family might have to say.

BLAKE

Nah, not really interested in sharing. I'd rather keep her all to myself, thanks.

JD

I repeat … Blake? GIRLFRIEND? Uh, WUT?

TENLEY B

NOW WAIT A DARN MINUTE.

ETHAN R

but i think we already know her

don't we

BLAKE

I'd call it casual dating. It's still early.

ETHAN R

liar

liar

🔥

BLAKE

Can I make him run extra laps when spring training starts?

JD

Of course you can.

Ay, E, tell me who it is and I'll make sure you don't have to run those laps.

BLAKE

Big E, my dude, my BOY, my favorite nephew … maybe we can come to a mutually beneficial agreement?

How about a literal get out of jail free card?

ETHAN R

gif of "Did we just become best friends? Yep" from StepBrothers

TENLEY B

You know what's funny?

I was having coffee with my mom the other day when she shared a nice bit of tea that definitely seems significant now.

Where's my bribe, bro?

BLAKE

At this time, I'd like to officially invoke my "Please Help Me Win Ethan Back" and "Give Me Your Blessing to Marry JD" favors.

TENLEY B

DAMMIT.

JD

But … but …

BLAKE

GREAT TALK GOTTA GO HAVE A LOVELY DAY YOU GUYS

"Looks like they took the bait, at least," I say aloud, trying not to acknowledge how much I like the way this feels, the two of us sitting so close and Loren giggling as she reads with her chin on my shoulder.

I'm already having too much fun tricking my family into thinking she's my girlfriend. It's all giving me … butterflies?

When's the last time a woman made my stomach flutter?

Only Loren's face comes to mind.

"Okay, but after we come out, I want in on the Robin-Bourgeois group chat," she says, bringing me back from my thoughts and making me smile again.

Yep. I like all of this way more than I should.

CHAPTER 9
Loren

"I'll text you later?" Blake offers when I walk him to the front door.

I shrug, trying to seem aloof while my heart is beating out of my chest. "Okay."

His eyes dart down to my mouth, but he leans in and kisses my cheek instead. I press my lips together when he pulls away, praying he can't detect the way he's making my insides melt.

It took everything I had not to give in to Blake's offer this morning—the frenemies-with-benefits one. As much as it pains me to admit, I am *really* interested in the benefits his friendship has to offer. But I know it's the worst idea ever, and I'm not that kind of girl.

Although, I could—

"Have a good day at school, Ms. Reed," Blake turns to say over his shoulder as he walks out.

No, that's a lie. Blake never simply *walks*. He saunters, he strides, he even struts. The man probably gives good promenade.

I blink away my inner monologue before I start casting him in the next season of *Bridgerton*. "You, too, Counselor," I reply, cursing my flirty tone.

He would have made a great Anthony, I think as I shut the door behind him.

I stretch onto my toes to watch from the small window as he does that sexy-stride thing all the way to his truck, and I sigh when I notice the way he's smiling to himself. He looks pleased with our latest developments.

I, on the other hand, still need to wrap my mind around the idea of being pregnant, especially the part about Blake Bourgeois being a doting father and fake boyfriend.

He drives away, and I stumble back to bed and lie face-down. (He struts, I stumble. That's how this goes.) I'm going to be late for work, but I need a minute to collect my thoughts.

Because I'm pregnant. Me—Loren Agnes Reed—with child. Knocked up. Pregananant. *Preganté.*

I am literally growing a whole-ass baby inside of me, as we speak.

It's already both the most terrifying and exciting thing I've ever experienced. I'm responsible for another human forever, and at the same time, I don't have to be alone anymore. I'm pretty sure I already love him or her more than anything in the world, too. It's the strangest feeling, to love someone I don't even know yet to such a great extent, but it's absolutely real.

I roll over and wipe the tears from my cheeks, then I allow my hands to travel down and cup my stomach. Thoughts of buying maternity clothes and going on leave from work flood my mind, not to mention all of the other expenses, like diapers and car seats and medical bills. But I suppose I'm lucky Blake will want to help financially.

I shake off the overwhelming stuff and go back to the fun parts. "Are you a little prince or a little princess?" I whisper, cradling my belly again. My face softens as I picture a toddler version of myself, and then a blond-haired, blue-eyed miniature Blake pops into my mind.

My chest constricts. At least there's a good chance that my baby will be gorgeous, given that half of the gene pool. Not to mention smart, talented, and athletically inclined.

"Blake. Freaking. Bourgeois. Let that sink in," I murmur to myself.

Never, not in a million-billion years, could I have imagined this reality. There are so many layers to this scenario that seem impossible: Blake and I hooking up, me getting pregnant, Blake reacting calmly and supportively, and, finally, Blake hinting around that he wants more from me than just an address for a child-support check.

Am I crazy for thinking he sounded disappointed about us not being an actual couple this morning?

The memory of his attempt to convey he'd wanted more than a single night in bed had been hazy at first. But I felt like the world's biggest jerk once I finally remembered the moment he turned to me with his chest still heaving and hope in his eyes to ask, "Now what? Where do we go from here?" And when I'd brushed him off, he made me promise we would talk about it in the morning. But I'd broken that promise by asking to leave as soon as we woke up and telling him he didn't have to pretend he had any feelings for me.

I cringe as I revisit the expression on his face while I failed miserably to be self-deprecating and funny that next morning. But it's not like I could believe Blake's been harboring some long-term crush on me or that physical intimacy means anything to him, not with his track record. And even if either of those were true, he's had every opportunity to prove me wrong since then. Besides, we're too old for silly crushes, making each other jealous, or thinking about first kisses.

None of that even matters anymore, because now we're having a freaking baby together.

And I know the ground rules are stupid, but I panicked. I need *some* form of protection. The man is ridiculously gorgeous, intelligent, funny, *and* now the father of my child. Plus, he's secretly sensitive, sweet, and wants to take care of me?

My face falls again when I realize what this all means. I've doomed myself to a lifetime of being stuck in don't-fall-for-him mode. And as daunting as single motherhood seems, I can't imagine it'll be as difficult as not getting my heart broken by Mr. Golden Ratio.

That's why I decided this morning: I cannot allow myself to enjoy any "benefits" with Blake. I'll have to keep my distance, because pining over him at our kid's birthday parties and when we meet up to swap custody for the weekend would be the worst way for this to end, aside from guilting him into a relationship and eventually growing to detest one another once he gets bored with me.

I'm not going to let us turn into my parents, who were coerced into a trip to the altar while they were still in high school when my mom got pregnant with Lilley, only to become trapped in a marriage filled with more resentment than love. Years later, by the time they got around to having Landry and me, they'd already started blaming one another for their unhappiness, my mom self-medicating with alcohol and my dad living vicariously through whichever one of his football players showed the most promise at the time. I'd rather live alone than risk raising my own child in that environment.

I think back on the first time I asked my mother why she drank so much. I was ten. She'd told me she was sad about all the mistakes she had made and that the drinking helped her sleep better at night. I'd walked away, thinking about what she meant and eventually settling on the notion that I was one of those mistakes.

One day I asked her again, this time in the middle of an angry rant. Well, actually, I'd screamed a rhetorical, "Why can't you just stop being a freaking drunk and be normal for once?" as I helped her to bed after a particularly bad binge. In hindsight, I think she'd started adding prescription meds to her cocktails by then.

"Because I can't make him love me," she'd murmured before passing out. My dad hadn't even come home that night. I bet he'd slept in his office at school.

I just wish she could have seen that I felt the same way, that I only needed her to be present to feel loved.

I sniffle and turn to dry my face on the blankets, and for the first time, I have an inkling of understanding and even sympathy for my mother. It's also a bittersweet confirmation that keeping things platonic with Blake is my only option. Now, as a mother, I recognize that my greatest obligation is to be there for my kid. I'm not willing to jeopardize my ability to be a supportive parent, no matter the cost. And there's nothing I won't sacrifice to be among the crowd, cheering on my son on the day of his graduation, or to be the one holding my daughter's hand when she finds out she's pregnant.

If that means I'm relegating myself to spend the second half of my life as lonely as the first, so be it. At least I'll have one kid, which is more than I expected. And I'll have a friend in Blake.

CHAPTER 10

Loren

THIRTEEN YEARS AGO

"Hey, Reed," I hear a deep voice drawl when I open the front door.

I groan at the way Blake Bourgeois' large form takes up most of the opening. He's wearing a pair of athletic shorts and a Camellia High football T-shirt that's just tight enough to show off his muscles. His dirty blond hair is still damp as if he's come straight from the shower. He smirks, revealing just a sliver of his perfect teeth, and I want to slam the door in his face for being so darn attractive.

It's so unfair. How does one kid get a double helping of good looks, brains, talent, and money, while the rest of us are left struggling for a few measly crumbs?

"Come on, let's get this over with, Gus Gus," I mutter.

"Who?" he asks, cocking an eyebrow at me.

"No one."

I turn and lead him into the kitchen, since I figure it'll be the easiest place to start. We're going to be working with straws, after all —thousands of straws—but I stop abruptly when I notice Landry and my mom are already occupying the space. It looks like he's trying to convince her to put down her liquid dinner and eat something solid for once, so I backpedal and opt for Plan B.

"Let's work in my room instead. I don't want Landry to bother us," I half-lie.

"You don't need to make up an excuse to get me into your bedroom, Reed. All you have to do is ask."

I roll my eyes and suppress a gag as he snickers at his own joke. "In your dreams, Blake."

"What's your brother still doing around here, anyway? Isn't he supposed to be off at college by now?"

"He backed out of going straight to LSU. He's starting at community college now, so I'm stuck with him for a few more months, at least."

He nods and follows me across the threshold of my sanctuary, my bedroom, the one place I never thought I'd have to worry about guys like Blake Bourgeois trespassing. I cross my arms and glare as he saunters in, stopping to examine some of the random trinkets and books strewn around the room.

"Cute," he says in a condescending tone. "Love what you've done with the place."

"Funny, I don't remember asking for your thoughts," I fire back.

He laughs again. "So, are we doing this, or did I come over for nothing?"

I glare at him and wonder whether he meant to sound so suggestive, but he continues running a finger over the cover of a well-loved copy of *Pride and Prejudice*, and for some reason, I shiver.

"Yeah, I suppose." I pick up the pile of clothes hanging over the back of my desk chair and gesture for him to take a seat, but when I turn, he's already helping himself to the edge of my bed. I huff and plop down in the chair instead, keeping my distance.

I watch carefully as he begins unpacking his book sack, pulling out a few packs of straws, a notebook, and a grocery store bag. "I figured we could model our bridge off of the one we know best—the I-10 bridge in Baton Rouge. Now, I've already found the measurements and started converting them down to scale. I also mapped out a design—"

"Hold on," I interrupt him. "Who said I'd be willing to go along with your ideas?"

He furrows his brow. "I thought since I'd volunteered us to be partners that I'd take the liberty of getting us started on the first project."

"Yeah, and about that—what the heck were you thinking? Why'd you tell Mr. Soileau that we were partnering up for the entire school year without even asking me?"

He shrugs, and I can't believe he has the nerve to look disappointed by my reaction. "I'm sorry about not talking to you first, but when he called on me and asked for a name, I kind of panicked. My instincts took over, and I figured teaming up with you would give me the best chance of getting an A in this class."

"Oh," I say, secretly flattered, though I'd never admit it. "So you just expected that I'd do all the work for the both of us, and that you'd reap the benefits? You know I'm still a tenth of a point ahead of you, GPA-wise, right?"

He sighs. "Why would I bother showing up with a game plan if I were only trying to get out of doing the work, Loren?" Then he presses his lips together before reaching around to pull something out of the plastic bag. He tosses a pack of my favorite candy at me. I barely catch it, bobbling it around like an idiot. "I even came prepared with a peace offering."

I stare down at the bag of Reese's Peanut Butter Pumpkins, the ones that only come out around Halloween. "How did you know?"

"I have my ways," he replies cryptically.

"Thank you. But you didn't need to resort to bribery. You could have just asked me to be your partner," I say quietly. "I would have agreed if you'd have explained yourself ahead of time."

"Would you really?" he asks, smirking at me again.

I can't help but smile. "Eh, probably not." Then I rip the bag open and shove an entire peanut butter pumpkin into my mouth, groaning at the taste. "There's just something about these, you know," I begin, probably grossing him out. "The peanut butter to chocolate ratio is absolute perfection, as if da Vinci himself formulated it."

I mime a chef's kiss, and he chuckles, seemingly pleased that I'm enjoying my gift.

"And you really thought I'd leave my physics grade to someone who thinks they use the Golden Ratio to produce a pumpkin-shaped candy? There's too much at stake here."

I sigh as I unwrap the second pumpkin. "You're right. I guess we have a better chance of coming out of this alive if we put our heads together for once. What kind of evil villain comes up with this crap, anyway? A bridge made of nothing but straws and straight pins?"

"Seriously. That dude needs a freaking life," he mumbles, flipping through his notebook. "Or at least to get laid."

"I'd never expect my students to do something this dumb and irrelevant for a grade if I were a teacher," I remark, digging around for the box of straight pins I'd purchased earlier.

"You mean to tell me you don't plan to torture your students just for the fun of it, Reed?"

I glare at him, surprised that he knows about my career aspirations. "Well, at least not in the beginning. But we'll see how bitter and bored I get by the second half of my career."

He laughs at that. "You know, I forget how funny you are."

"And I forget you're just a nerd disguised as a jock, Mr. Golden Ratio." He probably thinks I'm poking fun at him for knowing that term a minute before, but I'd be lying if I said he isn't ideally proportioned in every manner.

Well, there are still a couple of his proportions I haven't been exposed to, even after being forced to spend my summers and afternoons at the football field house for the past few years, though I figure Blake's incredibly defined abs and perfectly symmetrical face are a decent representation of the rest of him.

Or maybe that's his fatal flaw?

I stifle a giggle and look over at him. He's staring at me with a curious expression. "Did you just call me perfect?"

My face flushes slightly. "I called you a dork for recognizing the reference in the first place."

"Hmm. You brought up da Vinci first. Wait, hang on, you left a little bit of chocolate …" He reaches out and pulls my chair closer. Then he lightly brushes his knuckle over the corner of my mouth, leaving behind a trail of heat. I blink a few times and try to pretend like a current of electricity didn't just pass between us, and Blake clears his throat before wiping the back of his hand over his thigh.

"Thanks," I mumble as I struggle to open the box of pins to no avail, eventually handing it to him. He takes it wordlessly and opens it with little effort before giving it back, making me roll my eyes again. "Anyway, in regards to your point, I have never portrayed myself as anything other than a dork. I am what I am. You, on the other hand, have tried to bridge the gap between jock and homecoming king and valedictorian, and those don't really—ouch!"

I shake my hand out before looking down at my fingertip, and a small bit of blood bubbles up from where I punctured myself on a straight pin. "Shit, that hurt," I curse. "This doesn't bode well for the rest of the project." I move to bring my finger up to my mouth to stop the bleeding, but Blake reaches over and grabs my hand first.

He tugs on his T-shirt and wraps the hem around my fingertip, applying pressure. "There, is that better?" He looks up, concern etched on his face.

I nod, trying to remember how to breathe, and another awkward silence fills the room while he continues cradling my hand and squeezing my finger. I force my gaze away from the strip of skin he's exposed by lifting his shirt, and I jerk my arm back after a minute, instinctively shoving my injured finger between my lips this time.

And then I meet his widened eyes with mine and see that his pupils are dilated. I slowly remove my finger, watching his chest heave as he shifts his gaze to my mouth.

"There's … you, uh, still have some chocolate right there," he mumbles, wiping the corner of my bottom lip again, this time with his thumb. Then he shoves it into his mouth, audibly sucking his finger to clean it off and making a smacking sound when he pulls it out.

I swallow, licking my lips and noting the lingering taste of his skin, a salty contrast to the sweet peanut butter, and his brow furrows as if he's in pain. Then I watch as his eyelids get visibly heavier, just as he lets out something resembling a growl from deep in his throat. I bite my lip at the sound, and he inches his body closer.

Holy shit.

Is he making a move on me? Have I managed to turn him on?

Okay, so I may be one of the last virgins left in our class, but I've read enough romance novels to see where this is going. By now I'm breathing hard, too, and my eyes dart down to his lap.

Oh, fudge.

He's definitely into this. The shorts he's wearing leave very little to the imagination, and that's saying a lot, since I have a pretty wild imagination.

I involuntarily lean into him, his face so close now that I feel his breath fanning over me, and he chokes out a hoarse, "Gah, Loren," as he reaches up and cups my cheek. "You're so ... can I please—"

And, of course, that's the moment that my bedroom door flings open. "All right, Mom's passed out in her bed, but—"

Landry grimaces as his eyes bounce back and forth between Blake and me. To be fair, we are sitting close enough for our knees to touch, not to mention the fact that it probably looks like he was just seconds away from kissing me.

It certainly felt that way, too.

"What in the actual hell is going on in here?" Landry booms.

Blake jolts upright and looks at Landry. "A physics project," he replies, the husky tone of his voice betraying our innocence.

"Looks a lot more like biology," Landry retorts.

Then Blake's hands dart out to pull the nearest pillow into his lap, presumably in an attempt to cover up the evidence of our chemistry. Landry's eyes widen at the same time his nostrils flare, and I swear the next move he makes will be an attempt on Blake's life.

"It's not what it looks like, I swear," Blake says, shifting his position and lifting his hands innocently.

"Oh, so you weren't just making a move on my sister? In her *bed*?"

"She stuck her finger with a pin, and I was just trying to help." He shakes his head and exhales loudly. "You know what, forget this. I'm out." He turns to grab his backpack and begins stuffing his things into it while I glare at him angrily.

"Hold on, you're not thinking you're just going to leave me to do this project alone, are you?" I pose with my hands on my hips.

"I'll start working on it tonight and hand it over to you to finish it off."

"Finish what off, now?" Landry demands, but we ignore him.

"Okay, but you still can't abandon me to deal with this asshat on my own. I didn't initiate any of that just now," I say, fuming.

"Hey, first of all, you should be thanking this asshat for pulling Mom-duty tonight," Landry begins. "I'm supposed to be out with Carli Mayeaux, doing whatever the hell it was you two were about to do, yet I ended up having to keep Mom from washing down her prescription cocktail with a fifth of vodka again," Landry yells. "Then I got stuck putting her to bed. Meanwhile, you have the nerve to bring a freaking *Bourgeois* in here to screw around!"

"Ugh, Landry, just—get OUT!" I scream and throw the nearest thing I can find—a copy of *Twilight*—at his head. It flutters around before it hits him, lessening the dramatic effect. Then I snatch the pillow Blake was holding before and toss that, too.

Landry simply bats the pillow down. "I'll leave once *he* leaves."

"You're not my daddy, you know. I can take care of myself and ward off any unwanted advances on my own." I turn back to Blake, who's frozen, half-hunched over with one strap of his bag slung over his shoulder. Then I fling the back of my hand at his groin, and he lets out a strangled cry and doubles over at the contact.

Holy moly, THAT is obviously NOT his fatal flaw.

Ugh, shut up, stupid hormonal teenage brain.

"That'll teach you to keep your hands to yourself, Gus Gus," I say as he sinks down onto my bed, his eyes crossing. Then I turn back to Landry to make my point. "See, I'm fine. Perfectly capable of fending off any creeps. Now, get the hell out."

"Yeah, thanks, I don't think I'll ever be able to use my guy again after this," Blake mumbles in the background, and I jab an elbow back at his ribs, eliciting another grunt. "You're going to pay for that one, Reed," he whispers angrily, and I feel the corner of my mouth tilt up.

"This door stays open," Landry grunts. "And this isn't over, Bourgeois." He steps back, tapping his chest.

Blake straightens and nods haughtily at Landry. "You know exactly where to find me if you ever want to make good on all those empty threats."

Landry huffs. "Yeah, yeah, still up my dad's crack like the little kiss-ass you are?"

Blake shrugs then bounces a few times from his seat at the edge of the mattress. "Nah, man, I'm a little busy hanging out in your sister's bed these days."

"Lo, you'd better get a handle on your freaking boyfriend before I kill him," I hear Landry say through his teeth.

"What the hell, dude?" I turn to Blake, expecting to see him just as ready to fight, but instead he's smirking at me.

Then he leans over and whispers next to my ear, and I curse myself for shivering again. "That's what you get for hitting me in the junk. Although we could have come up with another one of your arrangements if you were that desperate for an excuse to feel me up."

I scoff and shove a bag of straws at his chest. "Get out, Blake," I order. "I mean it."

He presses his lips together, looking slightly remorseful. "Fine."

How Blake manages to bypass my brother on the way out the door, I'll never know. He glances back at me from over his shoulder, and I curse the fluttering I feel in my stomach as he shakes his head and walks away.

CHAPTER 11

Blake

"You are so freaking mid, dude," Ethan yells as he hops out of JD's truck, slinging his gun over his shoulder.

JD follows, laughing loudly as he comes around the side with his own shotgun. "The thing is, your aunt has what I like to call *high quality H20*," he says, morphing into a *Waterboy* impression by the end of it.

"Ugh," Ethan groans.

"Come on, Bobby Boucher," I call out as they approach. I offer a small pot of camouflage makeup, and they both dip their fingers and spread it over their faces. "What are you torturing the kid this early in the morning for, anyway?"

"He won't stop bragging about getting Tenley pregnant," Ethan retorts, pointing to the creepy Joker grin JD's sporting through the face paint. "We get it, bruh. It's not, like, this huge accomplishment you need to share with everyone we run into at the grocery store or the gas station."

I'm glad my own cheeks are covered by camo paint when Ethan so kindly reminds me of my current situation.

I'm still not sure how to feel after finding out I'm going to be a father. I think it's going to take some time for it to really sink in, but I've been doing my best to hold it together for Loren. Keeping it a secret from JD has been the hardest part so far, especially with everyone congratulating him and complimenting his baby-making skills. Even though I'm excited and happy for him, I'm already a little bitter about accomplishing the same feat and having to stand by while he gets to soak up all the praise just because he's married.

"Give 'em a break, E," I begin, hoping to redirect the conversation before I accidentally incriminate myself. "The man's had to jump through more than a few hoops to get that—"

"—marriage certificate!" JD yells loudly in an attempt to drown me out. "He was going to say 'marriage certificate.' "

I guffaw loudly, and Ethan turns to JD with his eyebrow cocked, a reminder that he isn't that naive.

"All right, enough beating around the bush. We're all men here, and I thought you guys had one of those open-dialogue relationships?"

"We do," JD says with a sigh. "At least, I hope we do." Then he nudges Ethan, whose expression softens. "Part of the reason I've been bragging so much is to teach him that sex isn't inherently wrong or dirty. It's an important part of a relationship, but it's also not something to be taken lightly. And it's my job to prove to him that waiting for the right person and a marriage certificate makes it that much more amazing and fulfilling, despite what the rest of the world will tell him."

Then JD reaches out and rests a hand on Ethan's shoulder before he continues. "Even though your grandparents did a great job raising you, you know what it's like to grow up without your biological parents. I want you to think about what kind of life you might be giving your own kids one day before you go on and make some. It only takes one time."

I swallow the lump of guilt lodged in my throat, and Ethan nods, staring thoughtfully into the distance.

"Oh, so it was just the one time, then?" he asks, turning back to JD with a grin.

JD narrows his eyes. "You sure you want me to answer that?"

I snort out a laugh, and Ethan turns to glare at me. "You're supposed to be helping, bruh. Whose side are you on here?"

"Sorry, Big E. I figured I'd let him have his moment, since he had to wait so long to trade in that marriage certificate for one measly ride at the fair. I bet it was over faster than he hoped, too. Did Tenley even get a chance to get buckled in before it finished?"

I may be projecting a little here.

Ethan stifles a laugh while my brother grunts and shoots me a dangerous glare. "You always have to take it too far, don't you?" Then JD turns to Ethan and hitches his thumb in my direction. "When I mentioned ignoring the rest of the world's take on things, he's who I meant."

I can't help the frown that takes over my features. He's right, though. I've always been the douchey foil to my brother's wholesome role model. Maybe he needs a reminder that people only think he's so perfect because I'm so terrible in comparison. Lucky for him, my latest screw-up will undoubtedly reinforce his Golden Boy status.

"But that's only because he hasn't found the right person yet," JD continues. "Sooner or later, he'll realize all that sleeping around has left him feeling empty, and he'll end up falling so hard for some poor, unsuspecting woman that he'll trample his own ego on the way to the altar. By the way, you still dating the same girl you were last week? If so, that's a new record. It's probably time to bring her around to meet the family."

Ethan turns his widened eyes to me, gauging my reaction, and JD sniffs before he aims a cocky smirk my way.

"You know I have a loaded gun in my hands, right?" I reply dryly, staring him down, even though my chest still feels tight.

JD puckers his lips and mimes a kiss at me, and I have to blink back the red that flashes in front of my eyes. "Eh, you love me. Besides, you don't have the heart to fake a hunting accident, bro."

I turn to Ethan. "Did I really fight to get you back from Ryan, only to hand you over to this clown?"

And then I remember that the kid misses nothing, and he lifts his chin, glaring haughtily. "Yeah, but now that you have a girlfriend, I'm glad I get to hang around and watch you turn into this guy," Ethan declares, nodding his head toward JD. I gulp as he continues, silently pleading with him. "What, no argument? I think you're already losing your rizz, Coach Blake."

I run my tongue over my teeth. "A few weeks doesn't mean anything. And there's no way I'd ever let myself go, not like he has."

"I'll have you both know that my wife loves me just the way I am. The only complaints I've gotten so far are related to forgetting to put the toilet seat down at night," JD replies, just as my phone vibrates in my pocket.

I pull it out to check the message, pressing my lips together to avoid the smile that threatens to overtake my face as soon as I see Loren's name on the screen. I ignore the way my stomach flutters when I read her suggestion that I accompany her to a faculty party this weekend.

LOREN R

It's the perfect opportunity to get the ball rolling on the fake-dating scheme, right?

I mean, unless you're busy.

It's cool if you already have a date planned.

The last thing I want to do is interfere with your life.

Just lmk either way, nbd.

But also, don't feel obligated to tell me if you are seeing someone else.

Shit.

I'm sorry. I'm going to turn off my phone now.

"You could probably stand to tone down the gas, man. It is a bit much," Ethan volunteers in the background.

That's actually a good idea. I force myself to think about my brother's excessive flatulence to keep myself from grinning down at my phone while I type out a reply.

BLAKE

Let me check my calendar and get back to you.

Oh, look at that. Turns out I'm free. I'll pencil you in.

"Hey, I held it in for months," JD answers, his tone more defensive now. "And I can't help what happens in my sleep."

I snort, half-amused by his reply and half-annoyed by my response to Loren. I'm starting to worry there's some truth to Ethan's claim just now. I didn't expect to get this lame this fast, but Loren's so freaking *cute*.

LOREN R

Cool. And thanks for ignoring my awkward.

Meet me at my house Friday night, around 7?

BLAKE

Come on, Reed. You know how much I like it when you make it weird.

And I'll see you tonight. I'm bringing home takeout and you're coming over for a LOTR binge and chill, remember?

"The theatrical versions are just the tip. Only the full extended editions count."

Unless you're too busy now?

You're not ditching me for someone else already, are you?

If so, he'd better be hot.

Oh, no ... it's not Dr. Red Flag, is it?

LOREN R

I bite my lip, smirking to myself as I slip my phone back into my pocket.

"If nothing else, Tenley's got to regret letting you watch *Ted Lasso*," I add, hoping to continue diverting their attention. With the way my face must look right now, I'm probably a dead giveaway.

Technically, this *is* the opportune moment for me to announce that Loren and I are dating. But I don't think I could pull off the lie in front of JD, not without Loren by my side, anyway. I might get away with stretching the truth most of the time, but he's always been able to sniff out my tell.

"Relax, guys. I was smart enough to marry a woman who thinks puns and fart jokes are funny. And Tenley already said she doesn't mind the gas, so long as I continue to make up for it in arm circumference," he declares with a flex.

"Good, I'm glad," I reply without thinking. "I mean, I don't have time to draw up annulment papers."

He stares at me strangely. "You sure?"

I huff. "Yeah, but if you keep making it weird, I'll take it all back."

"Does that mean you're finally going to rethink your lifestyle and consider settling down, starting by introducing us to your new girlfriend?" he ventures with a hopeful smile, and Ethan stifles a laugh.

"Let's not get ahead of ourselves," I mumble, just as a small flock of ducks lands in front of us.

We leave the duck blind about an hour later, JD directing Ethan to take care of our spoils in Ag class. It's one of the benefits of living in Sportsman's Paradise, I suppose.

I drive home for a quick shower, thinking about what kind of takeout I'm going to bring back for Loren tonight. Then I get dressed in a button-down and slacks, skipping the tie since I don't have court today. I head into work, and Jada briefs me on what needs to be done as soon as I sit at my desk.

She squints at me before she leaves. "Something's different about you lately."

I blink and sit up straighter in my chair. "What do you mean?"

"You seem …" She taps her chin. "Happy … smitten. You've got a girlfriend, don't you?"

I scoff. "Are you implying that I'd need a relationship to be happy?"

"No, but I can recognize that look on you when I see it, especially since I've never seen it on you before," she replies.

"I don't know what you're talking about," I mutter, waving her off and pretending to dig into the pile of work on my desk. But a smile creeps across my face again.

She gasps. "It's her, isn't it?" Then she plops down on the chair across from my desk. "Loren Reed?"

My eyes dart around nervously as I instinctively move to deny it. But I won't be able to pull off lying to Jada, either. There's also a part of me who wants to give her the wrong impression, just to see what it feels like to claim Loren as mine. And since I'll have to tell Jada about the baby, I could use this as a trial run.

"How did you know?" I ask, narrowing my eyes at her. My phone vibrates in my pocket, and I find myself hoping it's Loren again.

She squeals excitedly. "I *knew* you had a thing for her," Jada proclaims as I check the text that just came through. It's from my old, recently divorced buddy, Jase. He's trying to get me to go out with him on Friday night, but I don't even bother to read the whole thing before I tell him I'm busy.

"So, this is really a thing?" she continues as I put my phone away.

I shrug and smile shyly. "I don't know. Maybe."

"An actual-relationship thing?" She bites her lip and stares hopefully.

I roll my eyes, reminding myself not to oversell it. Loren and I will eventually have to stage a breakup, so I figure I should keep it vague. "I'm not sure yet, Jada."

I wait for the punchline, fully expecting her to deliver one of those jokes about my reputation that I haven't actually found all that funny in years. She'll at least want to question my motives.

Instead, Jada leans over and pats my hand. "I'm happy for you,

Blake. You're a good man, and you deserve this. And I'm not just saying that because you sign my very generous paychecks."

My chest expands as I study her more carefully. I was right. I like this feeling entirely too much.

"You really think I'm a good man?" I don't mean to ask the question aloud, and I hate the way my voice cracks even more.

Her expression softens, and she nods. "Of course I do. Why do you think I'm always begging you to take better care of yourself?"

"It's not like I'm unhealthy or reckless or anything."

"I'm not talking about the exterior stuff."

"So, you *do* think I need a relationship to be happy," I reply, cocking an eyebrow.

"No, but I wish you'd cut yourself some slack. You're too hard on yourself most of the time, probably because you're busy trying to be someone you're not," she says, pointing an accusatory finger. "I think Loren has known you long enough to see you for who you really are, and *that* is what you need."

I purse my lips and look away, and another text alert comes through. I sigh as I look at the screen again, figuring it's Jase's unwillingness to take no for an answer, but I swallow hard when I see Loren's name.

LOREN R

Keep in mind my current predicament and ignore how crazy these next couple of messages are going to sound.

Do you have peanut butter at your house? Or should I bring my own?

Jada clicks her tongue, bringing me back. "Look at you. You are a smitten kitten, Blake Bourgeois."

I tap on the text thread with Jase and flip the screen to face her. "See how much you know. I was replying to an invitation for Friday night. Jase needs me to be his wingman."

But another message pops up before I have the wherewithal to turn my phone around.

LOREN R

Do you keep it in stock regularly, or do you run a
BYOPB household?

I need to know these things if we're going to be
an item.

"Right, right. And what is it that I'm adding to your shopping list
to keep your girlfriend happy?"

I sigh. "Peanut butter. And other sandwich paraphernalia, I
guess."

"Is Loren a strawberry or grape girl?"

"Strawberry, I think. I'll let you know if I'm wrong," I say,
resigned.

"I know you will, my little smitty-kitty," Jada says with a wink on
her way out of my office.

CHAPTER 12

Loren

"THIS FEELS LIKE A TERRIBLE IDEA NOW," I SAY AS WE PULL up to the home of one of my coworkers.

Her husband's family was from a long line of farmers, which is the equivalent of "old money" around here. They have a huge home and an even bigger outdoor kitchen and patio area, and since Mrs. Julie loves entertaining, she ends up hosting most of our faculty gatherings. This time, it's a retirement party for our former assistant principal, Mr. Vidrine.

Blake shrugs. "It won't be so bad. We'll go in, shock the hell out of everyone, rip off that Band-Aid, then interject a little PDA for good measure," he says, bouncing his eyebrows suggestively.

"Fine," I reply with a grin. "Let's do it." I'm not sure why or how, but he's managed to earn my trust pretty quickly. Well, I probably trust him with my life, but my heart is another story.

He comes around to help me out of the passenger seat, which is fortunate since my legs aren't quite long enough to make that hop gracefully. Then he reaches down and laces his fingers between mine as he leads me toward the backyard.

The sounds of country music and laughter ring out as we approach the party, and the first thing I see when I round the corner is a huge "Happy Retirement James" sign. There's also another, smaller poster beneath that reads, "Good Luck Sucker," with a line drawn through the word "sucker" and "JD" scrawled above it.

I'm snickering to myself when I look away and realize everyone's eyes are on me—well, on *us*. I swallow the lump in my throat, and it takes all I have not to pull my hand back, but Blake holds on firmly, grounding me.

How am I already becoming so codependent on him? This is a recipe for disaster.

I mean, *more* disaster.

I don't see JD or Tenley around, so I drag Blake over to greet our hosts and the guest of honor before finding my principal and his wife. I notice a slight quirk in Mr. Soileau's smile when he watches as Blake untangles his hand from mine, only to move it to the small of my back.

I have to admit, I'm lucky to be getting away with not having to introduce my date and inadvertently provide our relationship status, since the staff already know him as an assistant football coach. Not to mention, we live in a town small enough for me to work with some of our former teachers, including my boss. So far, most of them only dart their eyes down to the point of contact between us, probably taking note of Blake's ease as he maintains some form of physical touch, and we simply allow them to make their own assumptions.

Mr. Soileau continues our conversation until Blake leans down and whispers an offer to fetch drinks for both of us. I reply with a smile and a nod, and he places an unexpected kiss below my ear before promising to return soon. My face heats up, and I swallow hard as I try my darndest to pretend there's nothing to see here, folks. Blake's lips making contact with my skin is just a regular, everyday occurrence, and certainly not one worth getting all flustered and bothered over.

"So, you and Blake Bourgeois, huh?" Mr. Soileau's grin widens, and I force a smile in return.

"Well, yeah. Kind of."

"I should call in an old teachers' lounge bet, then. Pretty sure I predicted this before the end of the straw-bridge project. Opposites attract and all," he says, nodding his approval and turning to his wife for reinforcement. "Right, Mona?"

"Definitely," she agrees with a wink, wrapping her arm around her husband's wide waist.

"I guess they do," I reply, my smile more genuine this time. I attempt to focus on my admiration of the perfect example of true romance in front of me and purposefully ignore the way my old physics teacher shipped Blake and me back in high school. But I end up glancing over at Blake anyway, only to find him already staring at me, making my face flush again. He tilts his head in a gesture for me to join him, and I excuse myself.

I'm about five steps away when I hear JD's voice booming from the side. "Hey, bruh, what the heck are you doing here?"

I freeze, unsure of what to do next. I survey my surroundings quickly, noticing Tenley at his side—hanging off his arm, naturally. I smile once we make eye contact, and my eyes dart back to Blake, hoping he'll take the reins on this one.

"I was invited," Blake says, his voice even.

"Wow, Ms. Sam called up the volunteer coaches too?" JD asks, referring to our secretary.

"Not exactly," Blake replies, one side of his mouth curling up as he turns to me and shoots me a smoldering look. "I'm a plus one." Then he holds out a bottle of water and gives me a short nod of reassurance.

I inhale deeply, trying to muster up the courage to take those last few steps to meet him, both literally and metaphorically. I'm finally willing my feet forward when I recognize that look of mischief in Blake's eyes, and he hands my drink to me and uses his free arm to pull me in closer. He winks at me before he tugs my body against his, pressing his lips to mine for a short kiss.

Then he backs up just as quickly as he went in, leaving me with my head in a fog. I blink and glance over at Tenley and JD. She's biting her lip nervously and watching her husband stare daggers at his brother.

"What the hell is this?" JD grunts. Tenley coughs and nudges him gently.

I look away as I bring my water up for a sip like the big old chicken that I am, but Blake's hand returns to my lower back as he scoots in closer beside me.

"What the hell does it look like?" he replies, amused. "I told you I was here on a date, didn't I?"

JD glares at him incredulously. "I can't believe you, man."

I furrow my brow. I hadn't exactly expected this reaction from him. "What's that supposed to mean?" I add my own rhetorical question into the mix.

"Well, he's been ..." JD turns his head away, seemingly embarrassed.

"No, go ahead and finish that," Blake demands, his voice curt.

"I didn't realize it was Loren. I'm sorry."

"You assumed I was seeing someone else, didn't you? Because I couldn't have been exclusively dating Loren for the past few weeks, since I'm only capable of messing around."

He shakes his head quickly. "No, that's not what I—"

"And why couldn't it have been me?" I interject, equally offended. "I guess if none of the other women were enough to keep him interested, then I certainly wouldn't be able to hold his attention for this long, right?"

"Don't you dare answer that," Tenley whispers harshly, glaring at JD. "It's a trap." She stops abruptly, then shuts her eyes, gulps, and exhales slowly.

"Oh, no." JD's tone immediately softens, and he turns to fawn over her. "Do you need anything? Do you want to sit down? Should I find the bathroom?"

She pushes him away as she shakes her head quickly. "No. I'm fine. The nausea is passing," she says, taking a few measured breaths. I hand her my water, and she takes a sip before shooting me a look of gratitude. Then she turns to Blake. "But I don't care who started this. If you don't kiss and make up, I'll puke on both of you."

My own stomach churns. I hope she doesn't have to make good on that threat, because then I'll probably be joining in.

JD sighs. "We'll behave, babe. I promise," he vows, rubbing her back softly.

"That's right, worry about your wife, kid," Blake says, lifting the beer bottle to his lips and taking a swallow. "And let me worry about Loren." I elbow him and shoot him a look. He's lucky I've been able to temper my morning sickness by keeping my stomach full.

"I'm sorry," JD grumbles in return. "Of course I think the world of both of you, and I'd have pushed you together myself if I thought you wouldn't kill one another within the first hour." Then he looks directly at Blake. "And you can't blame me for jumping to conclusions, especially after what you said about her before."

Blake smirks. "I was obviously lying. Well, not about her being a smartass, but about the 'intolerable' part. If I'm being honest, the smartass thing has always been a huge turn on."

Despite my better judgment, my breath hitches in my throat, not only because of his confession, but also because he's grasping me tighter from behind, physically confirming his attachment even though no one else can see.

"There are a lot of things I like about Loren," he says, lowering his voice as he stares down at me and fists the back of my dress.

I don't know if a man has ever made me weak in the knees before, but I finally understand the expression.

Then I remember that it's all part of our plot, that he's only playing along and misleading his brother to make our unintended pregnancy appear slightly less indecent later. It's just that Blake is so good at making me feel desired that I keep forgetting it's an act. And since we're only in Act One: Scene Three, I realize I am undoubtedly going to get my heart broken by Act Four, if I make it that far.

JD narrows his eyes at us. "I'm not surprised you like *her*, especially after our stunt a while back left you looking more jealous than Tenley, and you were in on it. I'm just shocked she's willing to bother with *you*."

"Well, it's not like I have a line of suitors at my door," I retort once I finally find my voice again, making them laugh and lightening the mood. "I'm thirty years old and have no prospects. I can't afford to be picky now that I'm nearing Charlotte Lucas territory. Because I'm an old maid with nothing to lose," I clarify, not expecting any of them to get the reference.

"Oh, then you're only dating Blake because he's the last available man in town?" Tenley catches me off guard, and her expression looks smug as she continues. "Or do you also have an intolerable-smartass kink?"

"I might," I say with a coy shrug. Then I cup my hand around my mouth as I whisper loudly, "Don't tell him I said this, but he's also kind of hot."

She chuckles, and Blake turns to wiggle his eyebrows suggestively at me. At least my attempt at humor seems to be diffusing the situation.

"But what about Dr. Rowan?" Tenley asks, bringing me back down again.

"Oh, um, the long-distance thing was ... it just wouldn't have worked out," I reply awkwardly.

"Especially since something was already going on between the two of you," Tenley says, pursing her lips and glaring shrewdly.

"Seriously though, if he does anything at all to hurt you, I'll kick his ass," JD interrupts her, looking at me and ignoring Blake. "Just say the word, Lo."

"You might try," Blake mumbles under his breath.

I snort. "While I appreciate the offer, I can handle myself."

Liar.

"Besides, I already have an overbearing big brother, and one's more than enough," I continue, ignoring my conscience.

"Yeah, he doesn't bother me either," Blake remarks, and my stomach swoops.

Then Tenley pulls JD away in search of refreshments, and Blake and I are left alone again. My phone sounds, and I pull it out to read Tenley's scolding for not fessing up sooner.

I smile to myself, relieved to have survived at least one of the interactions I'd been dreading, until I feel Blake's warm breath on my neck and his lips grazing my ear.

"You've got some explaining to do, Reed," he whispers.

"Hmm?" I squeak.

"Exactly when did you start thinking I'm so hot? Was this before or after you saw me naked?" he continues, making me shiver against my will. Thankfully, he backs away after a second.

"I thought we were supposed to be faking it for the cameras," I reply, keeping my eyes down.

"Were we?"

I look up at him from beneath my lashes. "We were."

He tilts his head to the side. "Hmm. I guess I forgot."

My stomach feels like it's attempting an actual somersault as I contemplate whether he's teasing me or trying to tell me he meant it when he admitted to liking me before. The trouble with this arrangement is that I suspect both are at least partially true.

"I love it when you wear that dress," he says, his eyes running over my body. "Have I told you that you look beautiful tonight? Because you do."

I sigh and roll my eyes. Now he's definitely messing with me. "You're violating the ground rules. 'No nudity' includes referencing nudity. And this is exactly what I meant before about excessive flirting."

He licks his lips and turns away. "I'm sorry," he says after a while. "I guess I got caught up in the moment again. Old habits die hard."

"Yeah, whatever. Look, I know we have to make it look real in front of everyone. But don't patronize me when it's just the two of us, okay?"

I glance up to find him frowning, his eyes narrowed. "Do you still think so little of me, Loren? Tell me you don't really believe every compliment I pay you is insincere or meant to bait you."

"The problem is I've never been able to tell when you're being sincere and when you're not," I admit. "And I'm not sure you know either."

He nods slowly, and his mouth gradually turns up in a sardonic smile. "Yeah. Well, sometimes I forget that you're smarter than me, too, but you always manage to remind me."

He stares at me a minute longer, and I don't like the way it's making me feel so vulnerable.

"I think I'm ready to go home," I begin, crossing my arms, but I stop short when I notice the way we've garnered the attention of a few partygoers.

"Hold on. Everyone's watching," Blake says when he sees them, too.

"They must think we're arguing."

He reaches out to grab my arm, loosening my stance and pulling me in closer. "We probably ought to keep this going for more than one date, though. Right?" He forces a smile before wrapping me up in an embrace.

I clear my throat and look up at him. "Right."

"Should we make up, then?"

I blink a few times. "Make up?"

He nods as his eyes dart down to my mouth. Then he closes the last couple of inches between us. I bring my hands up to his chest as he kisses me, and even though I can tell he's holding back, it doesn't stop my insides from turning to mush.

Dammit.

Why does he have to be so good at this too? Couldn't he at least be a bad kisser? Take a wide angle, miss the mark, use too much tongue, something? Anything?

He pulls away slightly, just enough to whisper, "Think they'll believe I'm taking you home for a different reason yet?"

"We should make sure they get the wrong idea," I reply, fisting my hands in his shirt and rising to my toes to crush my lips against his again.

I should feel embarrassed by the rumble of laughter in his chest. And I do—just not enough to stop. This is the biggest PDA stunt I've ever pulled, and I'm acting entirely too thirsty for someone who knows this is all fake. But when Blake slides his hand into my hair and cradles the back of my head, deepening the kiss, I practically forget about everything else.

Then both of our phones chime at once, and I flinch, breaking the spell. I turn my wrist to read the text message from Tenley on my watch. "I think it worked. Your sister-in-law just asked me if I needed to have 'the talk.' "

"Don't tell her, but I think it's a little late," he says, chuckling softly. He takes a step back to check his phone, snorting when he reads a message, I presume from JD.

I look up at him questioningly, but he shakes his head and presses his lips together. "I'll spare you. I had it coming after the way I've been roasting him for the past six months."

I roll my eyes, and he surprises me with one last kiss on the lips. "I guess we'd better give the people what they want, Agnes. I'll bring you home, now."

I bite my lip and nod, and he turns to lead me out. I can feel everyone's eyes on us again, as well as Blake's hand resting dangerously low on my back.

Okay, so I walk out of the party with my fake boyfriend's hand on my butt. But it's necessary, right?

He does leave it there until we get to his truck, though. And, stupid me, I let him.

CHAPTER 13

Blake

TWELVE YEARS AGO

"Well, that's it, our last physics project ... ever," Loren announces as we put the finishing touches on our latest assignment.

"Seems like they got easier as we went," I comment. "This one only took us a couple of afternoons."

"Yep. Less time you have to spend with me." She smirks, sitting cross-legged on the floor in my room.

"Aw, Reed. I guess you're not so bad. At least not when you're helping me get an A." I lower myself to join her.

She chuckles. "As much as I hate to admit it, partnering up might have been a decent idea."

I raise my eyebrows, surprised at her confession. It's a promising sign. "Maybe we make a good team."

"As much as I hate to admit that, too, I think you're right. When it comes to physics, anyway. Still, I'll be glad to get this class over with."

"No physics for you in college?" I ask, although I know the answer to that question.

"Heck no. Give me all the British Lit. I'd rather write a dozen essays in exchange for a single math problem."

"And now I know who to call to write my essays when I'm too

110

busy partying at LSU," I remark, putting my hands behind my head and leaning back against the bed.

She huffs and tries to sabotage me by pulling one of my arms out from behind me, causing me to lose my balance and fall over her, and my head lands on her thighs. Our eyes meet for a second before she tries to wiggle out from beneath me.

"Dude, why are you so heavy?" she asks as she struggles to shove me out of her lap.

"It's my huge brain," I retort, trying to keep a straight face.

"Sure, your brain, not all of these useless muscles," she says, punching me in the arm and immediately cringing and shaking her hand out.

"Hey, they come in handy ... with football, baseball, girls," I defend myself.

"Unlike your big brain." She rolls her eyes, but not before they dart over to check out my useless muscles again.

"Yeah, since you're the only girl around here interested in me for my intellect," I say, testing her.

"Perhaps, and now that I've used you all up, they can go back to fighting over your body." She clears her throat after a minute and moves to push herself up from the floor. "I should get going. No reason to stick around."

It's always like this with her. One of us makes a suggestive joke, the other may offer some witty rebuttal and a hint of innuendo, and just when things start to get good, she pulls away. It's probably a defense mechanism, but I wonder whether she has any idea that I'm so into it, that back-and-forth thing we do. It seemed pretty obvious after the first time we met to work together. I hadn't exactly done a good job of hiding my attraction to her that day, and it nearly cost me a physics partner. But I apologized afterward, and she reluctantly agreed to continue working together, under the condition that we do everything at my house.

I'm still not sure why she's so keen on keeping me away from her place. She claims she's trying to avoid any more conflict between Landry and me, though he and I have always been able to get along when required. I figure she's trying to protect us both from an uncomfortable situation brought on by her mom's addiction, but I've known about that for years, despite their family's attempts to keep it quiet. I also suspect that she doesn't like having me in her bedroom, for whatever reason. Maybe it's just too much exposure for her, or maybe I broke her trust when I made that regrettable comment about hanging out in her bed. It was supposed to be one of those times when I made her happy by making Landry mad, but it backfired on me.

I grab her arm, instinctively pulling her back down. "Loren, before you go, there's something I want to say."

"Okay." She stares at me expectantly.

"Do you remember Trent Manuel's thirteenth birthday party?"

"Duh."

"I've always felt like I needed to clear the air about what happened."

She presses her lips together in a hard line. "Clear the air? Or apologize?"

I laugh shortly. "Both?"

"I'm listening," she says, almost smiling now.

"I'm sorry about what I said to Landry and for embarrassing you in front of everyone. But I want you to know I wasn't trying to set you up for a joke or anything like that. I only meant to mess with your brother, because I hate the way he always makes you feel bad, and things came out wrong."

She looks down at her hands. "Oh. Thank you for that."

"For the record, I wasn't ashamed of being with you, and I wasn't just trying to brag about what we'd done in the pool house."

She nods quietly, and I continue.

"The truth is … I was actually really into it, and not just because I was anxious to get my first kiss over with. I kind of had a small crush on you after that night."

"You … liked me?" She blinks at me in surprise.

I shrug and smile coyly. "Well, yeah. You're different. How many thirteen-year-old girls would have taken charge the way you did? Not only did you make me an offer I couldn't refuse, but you also helped me one-up my little brother for once."

"Most people don't exactly see being different as a good thing, so I always figured you regretted wasting your first kiss on me."

This time I'm the one reeling back. "You thought I *wasted* my first kiss on you? Loren, you couldn't be more wrong."

Her cheeks darken. "I wasn't sure you'd even enjoyed it."

I snort. "Seriously? I'm pretty sure I was thinking of asking you to marry me after you did that thing with your tongue in my mouth."

Her face turns even redder, which makes my heart speed up. "Is that all it takes to get a ring from you?" she says, shoving me with her shoulder and making me laugh.

"At thirteen, it was more than enough."

"I guess a girl would have to do a little better than a spit swap to get a commitment out of you these days," she remarks.

"Hey, I've had a couple of girlfriends since then, thank you very much."

She glares at me. "Not that I keep tabs on your love life, but you don't exactly project long-term relationship vibes, Blake."

I frown. "Maybe I didn't think it was fair to get into anything serious knowing that I'm leaving for college in a few months. And maybe I just haven't found the right person." She doesn't say anything after that. "As far as I know, you don't have a boyfriend either. I assume you've been waiting to dip your toes into the UL dating pool?"

"I don't know if you remember this about me, but, uh, scary football coach for a dad and overprotective big brother?" She raises her arm and points down at herself. "So, no, not many guys have been willing to bother with little old Loren Reed."

"Oh."

I wonder whether that meant she was still relatively inexperienced. A scenario in which I returned her favor by making her a friendly first-time offer flashes in my brain, but I quickly force the inappropriate thoughts out of my head.

"Yep," she says, emphasizing the *P*. Then she looks down again and speaks softly. "And you've been to my house before. You know things aren't easy with my mom, especially since my sister left for college."

Until now, I hadn't realized just how difficult her home life must have been all these years. I slide one of my hands over hers where it rests on the floor, and she stiffens beside me. "I'm sorry you've had to deal with all that. I imagine it must be a lot harder than you've made it look, taking care of your own parents when they're supposed to be raising you."

She sniffles quietly, then pulls her hand back to wipe her cheeks. "Thank you," she whispers, her voice thick. She glances down at her watch. "It's getting late. I really should go home."

"What's wrong, Reed? Conversation too deep for you?" I ask, not even bothering to hide the disappointment in my voice.

"As a matter of fact, it is," she agrees without looking at me. "And now that this project is finished, I can get out of your hair and head back to my place to watch my mom pass out on the couch while my dad continues avoiding us by going out of his way to help every other kid in town. And you can get back to your perfect life."

"Loren, wait," I begin. "Don't go."

"Why? What do you want from me, Blake?" she asks. "Because for the life of me, I can't figure it out. Am I your physics partner, your friend, or just the competition?"

"I thought we were at least friends."

She snorts. "But only when the door is closed, right?"

"Well, no, but ..." I grimace. She has a point. Even though we seem to enjoy one another's company and have been hanging out more than necessary for these projects, it's not like we interact much at school, and we don't really have any friends in common.

"So which is it?" She throws her hands up in desperation. "Because my instincts tell me you've only been nice to me so you can get your A. Why do you want to be the valedictorian so badly anyway? It's not like you need the extra scholarship money like I do."

I open my mouth to answer her but can't quite find the words.

"Or do you just get a kick out of messing with me? Maybe that's it, since I know how much you enjoy pissing off my brother. It would make sense that you're only pretending to care so you can distract me long enough to pass me up—"

"Loren," I interrupt, reaching up to stop her by gently yanking her arm. "Would you just shut up for a minute? I'm trying to ask you out."

She trips over her feet, probably in shock, and I catch her in my lap this time. "You what?" she spits out, her eyes wide.

I lick my lips and try to breathe regularly, even though her petite frame fits so perfectly between my thighs. "I, uh ... I just ..."

Dude, why am I so freaking nervous right now?

She frowns, waiting for me to get it together.

"I thought maybe, since we're both single, that we could go to the prom together. But, like, only if you wanted to."

She blinks at me in disbelief. "You're actually serious?"

I slip my hand around her hip. For some reason, touching her this way calms me. "Why wouldn't I be serious?"

"Because you're ... you. And I'm *me*. I'm so *me* that I didn't even bother to buy a dress, because I knew no one would ask, and because I don't have a functioning mother to take me dress shopping."

"There's still time, though, right? My mom could help you find something to wear. She loves you, and she loves shopping. And she doesn't have any daughters, so it would actually be perfect," I offer.

But she continues staring at me incredulously. "It's a pity offer, then. Did your mom put you up to this?"

My shoulders drop in frustration. "It's not a freaking pity offer. I mean, yeah, my mom did encourage me to ask you, but it wasn't her idea. I went to her for advice because I wasn't sure what you'd say, and, well, here we are."

She looks down quietly.

"So, I guess that's a *no*, then," I mumble after a while.

Loren extricates herself from my lap. "I don't know, Blake. I just don't understand why you couldn't find anyone else to take to the prom, of all places."

I tilt my head back and groan. "I haven't asked anyone else, because I want to go with you. Because I like you, and I think you're cute. And I thought we'd have a good time together and that maybe a small part of you would be willing to admit you like me, too. That I'm not crazy and that you feel this ... chemistry or whatever it is that happens between us when we're alone together. But, shit, Reed, for such a smart girl, you're making this so much more difficult than it should be."

She frowns at me. "No. I get it now." I notice her eyes watering again. "I've been such an idiot. It's Landry, right? That's what this whole thing is about? Do you really hate my brother so much that you'd stoop to this level?"

My jaw drops for a second. "I seriously have no idea what you're talking about."

"Let me guess. You were just waiting until prom night to make the actual proposition, weren't you? You've tried being charming and cute, but I wouldn't bite, so you've been saving your 'I'll pay you back and be your first' offer for something like this. And you figured I'd be so flattered that you asked me to the prom that I'd happily go along with your plan. Then you could tell everyone you hooked up with Coach Reed's daughter or that you slept with Landry's baby sister."

"What?" I squeal. "You think I'm only trying to get into your pants so I can brag about it?"

She narrows her eyes at me. "You wanna rephrase that while you can?"

I scoff. "You just accused me of using you to get to your brother, when I really don't have any reason to hate him except for the way he treats you. I don't know how else to convey how messed up that would be."

"No, I'm talking about the 'only' part of that question, which implies there are other reasons you're trying to get into my pants."

"I mean, if you really wanted to get your first time out of the way, I certainly wouldn't turn you down," I retort. Then I cringe internally once I realize that makes me sound exactly like the kind of jerk Loren's accusing me of being.

"And you just assumed I'd be interested, that I'd be grateful, even? Was I supposed to throw myself at you after you called me *cute*?"

"Well, not exactly."

"What makes you so sure I'm even attracted to you, anyway?"

I feel my face heating up, but I'm not sure if it's from anger or embarrassment, especially since Loren's one of the only people I've ever felt comfortable being myself around. Hearing that she doesn't think much of the real Blake is a new low.

I clear my throat. "I guess I misread the situation. Sorry for hoping I'd found someone interested in my big brain for once."

"Yeah, well, I'm sure you'll be fine, since you still have all those useless muscles to fall back on," she murmurs, crossing her arms over her chest.

I huff incredulously as I stand up beside her. "Wait, that's your problem, isn't it? You *do* think I'm hot, and you hate yourself for it." Her eyes widen when I take a step closer. "It makes you feel shallow, doesn't it? So you'd rather pretend you don't like me at all than fess up and see what happens."

She swallows hard as I move in so that we're standing toe to toe. "You're wrong," she chokes out, but I can tell I've struck a nerve.

"Are you sure? Because it certainly feels like I'm right. I can take my shirt off if you think it'll help you make up your mind, Lo. In fact, you can have whatever you want from me."

"You're so full of yourself," she breathes, though her eyes roam over my torso, as if she's already picturing it.

I smirk as I reach out to cup my hand around her hip and pull her in closer. "I'd rather have you full of me though," I mumble, regretting the line as soon as her expression falls.

She pushes off against my chest. "I'd never be desperate enough for that," she declares, her lip curling and voice uneven. "You disgust me."

Then she turns to grab her things and stomps out of my bedroom, and I curse under my breath.

"Wait, Loren, I'm sorry. I shouldn't have said that!" I yell after her as she scrambles down the stairs with her petite legs.

"You're right, you shouldn't have!"

I groan as I start after her. "Get back here and let me apologize, Reed! You're not completely innocent in this, either. Stop acting like you weren't into it before I put my foot in my mouth!"

"Sure, and here's my answer to your invitation to the prom," she calls, turning to walk backward long enough to flip me off. Then she bumps into my mom and changes her tone. "Oh, hey, Mrs. Monica. Sorry your firstborn's such a jerk, but thanks for having me over again."

"Yeah, well, she's officially uninvited—forever," I boom as I bolt down the stairs, ignoring the look my mom is giving me.

Loren stops and turns at the front door. "Don't worry, I wasn't planning on coming back. After we turn in this last project, I don't want to see you until graduation. And I'm not even planning to see you then, because you'll be stuck behind me, in second place."

"You're sadly mistaken if you think this is over. You'll regret giving me the motivation to make sure I'm the one delivering that valedictory address next month," I fire back, standing over her now.

She scowls at me, but not before her eyes flash down to my mouth. "Don't ever talk to me again," she says quietly, tilting her chin up in defiance.

And dammit if I'm not fighting the urge to lean down and kiss her so hard that she sees stars. Her chest heaves beneath me as I step closer, and I gulp when her eyelashes flutter. Because I still miss the feeling of her lips against mine, and I'm dying to press my mouth to hers right now.

But I refuse to give in. If there were ever something between the two of us, it would have to be more than just physical, and kissing her now would only prove her right, regardless of my intentions. Instead, I reach behind her to turn the doorknob.

"My pleasure." I gesture toward the open door.

Then she huffs and turns on her heels, and I sigh as I watch her get into her car and drive away.

CHAPTER 14

Loren

I reread the card I plucked from the flower bouquet I received earlier today before slipping it back into my purse. After all these years, I can still recognize Blake's handwriting, and he's evidently gone through the trouble of stopping at the florist's and filling out the card himself.

I know this isn't a real date. I know this is all part of the show. But, dammit, the naive romance lover in me wants to squeal and pretend that the handsome, charming lawyer really wants to whisk me away to a formal ball where I'll wear a fancy, sparkly dress and super high heels, we'll sip fancy, expensive champagne all night, and he'll twirl me around on the dance floor in front of all his fancy, lawyerly friends, because I'm just so darn enchanting.

But that's totally unrealistic, since Blake isn't really my boyfriend.

Being pregnant and unable to walk in stilettos doesn't exactly help my chances either.

Tenley gets my attention when she clears her throat from the driver's seat. She generously offered to drive when I texted her earlier to request an emergency dress-shopping trip.

"Truth be told, I'm really glad you asked me to come with you this afternoon. There's something I wanted to talk to you about."

"Oh?"

She glances over shyly. "It doesn't compare to the expensive bouquet from your boyfriend, but that little bag in the back seat is yours."

I smile and turn in my seat to find the gift bag in question. "What's this?"

"Somewhat of an apology. You know I'm terrible at this girly stuff, but I still feel bad about not giving you a proper bridesmaid experience."

"Ten, why would you think you owe me anything? It was your wedding. I was just glad to be a part of it."

She shrugs. "Just open it."

"Okay," I agree, hesitantly reaching in to pull out a gorgeously decorated copy of Jane Austen's *Persuasion*. There's a bookmark sticking out, and I open the book to find what looks like a folded-up ultrasound image with writing on the back. "Will you be my godmother?" I read it aloud, then I gasp and turn in my seat to face Tenley. "Really?" I ask eagerly.

"I know it's a lot to ask, but JD and I both agree that you're the best *tante* for the job."

I press my lips together to stop my chin from trembling, but my voice still cracks when I give her my answer. "Of course, Ten. Nothing would make me happier."

"Thank you, Lo," she tells me, and her eyes look watery when she glances my way again. "For everything. I owe you more than you know."

I nod and swallow the lump in my throat. "Thank you for letting me play a role in your story. And I'm totally hugging you about this later, like it or not."

She sniffles through a laugh before she clears her throat again, her cue that she's done with the mushy part of this conversation for now.

"So, not that I'm complaining, because this is actually one of my favorite books, but I'm not sure I get the reference," I say once we've both managed to pull ourselves back together.

"Oh, um, sorry. I told you I was terrible at this stuff. I looked up 'Jane Austen books with a cool aunt,' and this is what I found. The mom's best friend basically becomes the main character's favorite aunt, right?"

I smirk. "You're right, she totally does. This is perfect. I love it," I declare, replacing the bookmark and hugging the book against my chest. I decide against bursting her bubble by explaining that Anne's surrogate aunt and mother figure, Lady Russell, nearly ruins Anne's life by talking her out of marrying her one true love. It's the thought that counts, right?

"Speaking of godparents ... How are things going with you and my charming brother-in-law?" she transitions.

I gulp. "They're—it's ... good."

"Good?"

"Mm-hmm," I squeak.

"Seriously? That's all I get?" she demands. "I still don't even know how this developed. And what ever happened to the cute MFM specialist, anyway?"

My heart beats loudly. "Uh, well, Blake and I sort of ... we have a little more history than you probably think."

She laughs. "I always wondered, especially after that party when we found the two of you alone in a pool house."

"He gave me my first kiss that night. And I gave him his," I admit with a smirk.

"Your first kiss must have been better than mine," she teases. "Wait, have you guys dated before? Like, in secret?"

"Not officially, but I guess you could say there's always been a little something between us. Sometimes it feels like chemistry, sometimes animosity. It changes day by day, from one year to the next."

"And lately it's been feeling like chemistry?" she offers.

I shrug shyly. "Yeah."

"What made you decide to actually get together this time?"

"I guess ... *you*." She looks confused, so I continue. "In helping JD get your attention, I suppose we also made Blake a little jealous. And watching him go out on a limb to bring you and JD together sort of made me rethink my vow to hate him forever."

"That and the way he wears a suit, right?"

I groan when a vision of Blake unbuttoning his cuffs and loosening his tie flashes in my mind. "Gah, *yes*. A whole lot of that."

She chuckles. "Have you guys had the DTR discussion yet?" she asks as she pulls into the parking lot.

"Sounds like you're finally speaking Gen Z. Ethan's been rubbing off on you."

Tenley glares at me when she catches on to the way I'm dodging her questions, and I'm pretty sure her spidey-senses are tingling by now. I need to steer the conversation away from Blake and me if I don't want her figuring things out. The woman is basically a walking pregnancy test with all of her experience as a midwife, and I'm terrible at keeping secrets about myself as it is. I scramble out of the car, cringing internally when she catches up to me at the boutique door and mumbles something about continuing our conversation later.

"Hey, there. Tenley, right?" asks the saleswoman from the last time we were here.

Tenley smiles and nods. "Hey, Nicole. You remember my friend Loren? She needs a Mardi Gras ball dress for this weekend."

"Oh, sounds like fun." Nicole eyes me up and down, presumably to check out my body type for the best dress style. "How did the wedding go?" she inquires as she leads us over to a rack of brightly colored gowns.

"It was perfect," Tenley answers with a grin. "We're expecting our first baby in October."

Nicole smirks. "I guess you were right about that dress, then," she says to me with a snicker, referring to the way I teased Tenley about her super modest wedding dress being too sexy. "So, tell me, what style are you looking for? And what's your date like?"

I show her a few dresses that catch my eye, and she pulls a couple of her recommendations for me to try on, including one with a cropped, high-neck top and fitted skirt.

"I do love that one, and the separate top and skirt might help with the length, but I don't have the goods to pull it off," I say as I run my hands over the beading at the top. Although it technically covers most of the chest, it relies on a good bit of that illusion-type material and strategically placed beading to remain somewhat modest.

She eyes me. "I don't know, girl, I think you might. And if not, we'll stick some on."

I glance over at Tenley, who chuckles. "Don't look at me," she begins. "I don't have any experience with stick-on or push-up bras. I'd never even fit my left nipple in a dress like that. But it is gorgeous, and it can't hurt to try it on, right?"

I shrug and resolve to take her advice. I enter the dressing room, starting with the two-piece dress. Nicole comes in to zip me up, and I'm pleasantly surprised when it fits like a glove. Even the length is good, which *never* happens. I glare at myself in the mirror. Besides my butt, I've never had much in the way of curves—until now.

Whose boobs are these, anyway?

Oh, yeah—the baby's. Perhaps there are a few benefits to getting knocked up, right?

I continue turning and smooth my hand over my stomach. The tiny pooch forming beneath my belly button is probably only noticeable to me. But even if it's technically just bloating, there's definitely something there.

"And you thought you weren't going to have the boobs for it. Honey, your knockers look great," Nicole says, ushering me out of the dressing room.

Tenley's eyes widen when she sees me. "Wow, Lo, you look amazing. Green is totally your color." She shakes her head and blinks a few times when I turn in a circle, and the salesgirl gushes over me. "Who's finding a dress on the first try, now, hmm?"

I blush a little, because she's right. I do feel pretty hot. I just wonder if Blake would agree.

No—wait. His opinion shouldn't matter, right? I don't care whether he thinks I look sexy. I only want to feel sexy when I let him take me on a romantic night out.

I sigh.

"Here, just let me fix this. One of your girls looks a little higher than the other," Tenley interrupts my thoughts when she comes over to adjust my top.

"Ow," I whimper when she tugs too hard and inadvertently pushes on my boob.

"Oh, sorry, I didn't realize I was being rough."

"You're not, my boobs have just been super sore since ..." I dart my eyes to the side when I realize what I've let slip.

Tenley clears her throat. "PMS?"

"Oh, uh, yeah, probably," I lie.

"Lo, did you get back on your birth control pills?" she asks carefully.

I force a smile. "You caught me."

She turns her body so Nicole can't hear us. "Is it because you and Blake are sleeping together?" she whispers, then she cringes. "Wait—don't answer that. I only wanted to remind you that we never got to finish your fertility awareness training."

I bite my lip and shrug shyly. "I, um, we ..." I'm afraid that no matter how I respond, she's going to see right through my lies. I sigh. "Blake and I—"

"Whoa, did you say Blake? As in, Blake Bourgeois, *the* Blake Bourgeois?" Nicole asks. So much for a private conversation.

"Maybe," I say hesitantly.

She laughs bitterly. "Who hasn't slept with Blake Bourgeois is probably a better question."

"Pretty sure she hasn't," I retort, hitching my thumb at Tenley.

Tenley looks upset as well, and her hands go back to her hips. "Right, since he *is* my brother-in-law," she reminds Nicole.

"Well, honey, hope you're not counting on wearing this dress too far out in the future. Everyone knows he has a three-date limit," she proclaims bitterly.

This will be our third date. Well, our third time going out, anyway. But I don't volunteer that information. Instead, I cross my arms and glare at Nicole, remembering how she mentioned dating Blake the last time we were here.

"We've been seeing each other for a while," I finally say. "But we mostly just hang out at home."

"I'm not surprised to hear he makes excuses to stay at your place," she mumbles under her breath. "I've heard he doesn't invite women into his home very often, either."

"That's weird, because he usually insists I come over to his house," I declare with a shrug. I note the way Tenley's eyebrows go up.

Nicole straightens, blinking in surprise. "Well, take it from someone who's gone out with him before: The man's gorgeous, but he's after only one thing."

"Was he a jerk to you or something?"

"Not ... totally."

"Oh. So he tried to get you to take him back to your place?"

She lifts her chin. "No, but I'm sure it's because I gave off the vibe that it wasn't going to happen."

"Right. Good for you, then." I press my lips together, trying to stifle a smile. "It's too bad you judged him based on what you've heard from everyone else, though. I'd say he's the most respectful and thoughtful guy I've ever been with. In fact, he's the one that wanted us to date exclusively."

"Hmm," Nicole squeaks. "I guess you can't believe everything you hear."

Tenley snorts beside me. "And now that we've gotten that straight, why don't we get you out of that dress?" She leads me back to the dressing room, glancing around to make sure we're alone.

"I'm so sorry I blurted that out just now. What happens between you and Blake is none of my business. I only meant to remind you that it takes a while for hormonal birth control to successfully prevent ovulation and that condoms aren't as effective if you're within your window of fertility ... just in case," she explains, looking remorseful.

"Yeah, of course. It was—I mean, we were ..." But my eyes begin to water.

"Oh. Oh, no, Lo. I really am sorry," she says, wrapping her arms around me and pulling me up against her chest. It's honestly kind of nice. I can see why JD enjoys this.

"Please don't think I'd ever judge you about this stuff," she says, her voice cracking. "You know my stance on sex and contraception, but it's certainly not my place ... I shouldn't have brought it up that way. I'm just worried about you."

"It's okay, Ten," I grunt out, my cheek squished against her bosom. "Really. I know you meant well." She lets me go, and I take a deep breath, debating whether I should come clean. "The truth is ..." I stare up at her, and I can't seem to find my voice again.

She smiles knowingly. "You don't owe me any kind of explanation. Just promise me you're okay with the way things have progressed between you and Blake. Because if you're not, I'm going to beat the crap out of him, then I'll get JD to do it again."

I laugh, sniffling. "Thanks. And for the record, I was telling the truth earlier when I said he's not the guy everyone thinks he is. He hasn't pressured me into anything I didn't want to do, and he never would. Which only makes it that much harder to resist him," I say with a sigh.

"I get it." She pulls away and winks at me. "Sometimes I wish their parents were still alive, you know? I'd like to thank them for doing such a great job with raising both of them. Not to mention their genetics were on point, right?"

I nudge her and laugh again before I turn and let her unzip my top. Tenley begins hanging up the pieces as I bend over to pull on my pants, but the floor suddenly lunges at me, and I get so lightheaded that I have to brace myself against the wall.

"Hey, are you okay?" she asks from behind me.

I blink away the fuzziness. "Yeah, I just got dizzy for a second. I guess I stood up too fast."

"Oh, yeah. I've been having that problem, too, especially since I got preg—" She stops and glares at me, and I swallow hard.

I force a laugh. "My balance has always been terrible," I fib.

"Hmm. You should let me check your vitamin levels," she says before she walks out.

I heave out an exhale as I finish dressing, then I meet her up front to check out. My credit card cries out in pain when I swipe it after not having paid much attention to that price tag, but I tell myself this may be one of the last chances I'll have to splurge—maybe ever.

I don't even mind being on the receiving end of another jealous glower from Nicole as she hands over the garment bag, and I give her a pretty smug look in return.

CHAPTER 15

Loren

"THANKS FOR THAT," I TELL TENLEY ONCE WE'RE BACK IN her car.

She forces a smile and nods, and I can practically see the wheels turning in her head as she pulls out of the parking lot. Just like I can feel my stomach grumbling.

"Would it also be too much to ask if we made a pit stop? I could really use a snack," I ask quietly. "I, um, ended up working through lunch today." Another lie. I've already eaten a handful of times, but I'm no less hungry than on any given day I'd have skipped a meal.

"Sure, just tell me what you're craving," she replies, her eyes still on the road. "My appetite has been pretty screwed up lately, you know."

"Huh. Right. Well, I'm actually fine with anyth—wait, can-we-please-stop-at-that-bakery?" I'm about to press my face to the glass as we pass it.

Tenley regards me suspiciously again as she turns at the next block and pulls up in front of a sign for The Magnolia Bakery. My mouth immediately begins watering as we walk inside and get ambushed by the smell of flour and sugar. I bounce excitedly on my toes as I order enough peanut butter cookies to feed a small party while Tenley lingers behind.

"Don't you want anything?"

"Oh, no, I think I'm good, actually," she mumbles, cringing as if the air is making her sick. "I've gotta go," she blurts out before making a dash to the restroom.

I leave my coveted snacks at the counter to follow her. Thankfully, she's done heaving by the time I make it inside. I realize I'm relatively lucky, since I haven't really felt as sick as I did for the first couple of weeks. Now the baby doesn't seem to stir up any trouble, as long as I keep my belly full.

"Sorry," Tenley apologizes as she dabs a damp paper towel over her neck. "*Morning* sickness, my ass. All it takes is a strong smell these days, and I'm done for."

I pat her arm gently and wet another napkin for her. "I'm sorry I made you come inside. You should have said something."

She blows out a deep breath. "You know, I used to secretly wish I knew what all these pregnancy symptoms felt like. But now that I've gotten the chance to experience the joys of constant nausea for myself, if my husband weren't so ridiculously hot, I'd probably be too afraid to risk getting pregnant ever again." She smirks at me in the mirror. "But I'm sure I'll let it happen anyway."

I laugh nervously. "Blame it all on JD."

She turns and studies me for a second, and I'm afraid she's seeing right through me. "Loren, if there's ever anything you want to tell me, you know you can trust me. But if you're not ready, or if you haven't accepted it yet, that's okay, too. I'll be here when you do."

My chin trembles involuntarily. If I don't give her something, I'm going to end up telling her everything.

"Maybe I do have one small secret I'd like to get off my chest," I begin, fidgeting. She nods for me to continue. "Blake and I ended up going home together after your wedding. It was only supposed to be dinner between friends. But we both drank a little too much, then one thing led to another, and all that chemistry I mentioned just kind of ... exploded. And I was mortified at first, since I'd never slept with someone I wasn't attached to before. It's been different with Blake, though. I thought I knew him. But he's not what I expected. Now I like him a lot more than I probably should, which scares the hell out of me."

There, I'd confessed. Somewhat.

She reaches out to rub my forearm. "It's pretty obvious that he's crazy about you, too. JD swears that Blake's always secretly had a thing for you."

I sniffle. "Well, Blake's a better actor than I am."

She narrows her eyes at me. "Yeah, he is."

I swallow hard. "Ten ..." And then my chest heaves as the real sobbing begins. But she doesn't say anything. She only wraps her arms around me and pulls me up to her chest again, letting me soak her shirt with tears and snot.

"How could I let this happen?" I whisper after a minute.

"Chemistry," she replies plainly. "Hormones, pheromones, feelings, alcohol—they can all gang up on you during peak fertility."

I laugh shortly. Leave it to her to have a valid biological explanation for how I managed to get myself pregnant after thirty years of being nearly celibate.

Tenley pulls back and looks me in the eyes. "Just think of the exact circumstances it took for you to conceive this baby the way you did, Lo. That has to mean something."

I let out another sob, mostly because I'm overcome with relief at hearing her acknowledge my pregnancy aloud. It takes a minute before I can talk again. "You're right. It's just hard to think of it that way right now. It's hard to think about anything when I'm so hungry all the time."

She chuckles and hands me a napkin. "Let's get out of here. I'll make a dash for the car while you grab your cookies. We'll pick this conversation up once you've gotten more carbs in your system, hmm?"

I nod and smile weakly at her, equal parts grateful she figured it out and terrified she'll realize Blake and I are just faking our relationship.

She takes a deep breath and fills her lungs with disgusting

restroom air, making me giggle at the irony, then pushes the door open. Meanwhile, I blow my nose a few times and retrieve my bag of baked sugar before joining her in the car.

I groan as I bite into my third peanut butter cookie. "Why do these taste *so freaking good*?"

Tenley laughs at me. "I'm still waiting to get to that part. But I can't believe you've been keeping this a secret from me. The idea of our babies sharing DNA seems too exciting for you to handle alone."

"I'm sorry. Blake and I promised we wouldn't tell anyone until after my first doctor's appointment."

"I'd probably have figured it out by the time I saw your name on the schedule, anyway." She smirks. "As well as your conception date."

"I guess that means we'll have the same due date too?"

"Hmm," she begins thoughtfully. "Pretend I'm not asking this about Blake, but how good was it for you that night? I promise it's relevant."

I sigh. "It was the best *anything* I've ever had ... apart from these cookies."

"And would you say you were just a willing participant? Or more like an eager one?"

"Oh, I was definitely an eager beaver. I still don't understand how it all happened, if I'm being honest, or why we didn't use protection."

She snorts. "Blame it on the hormones, *cher*. I think it's safe to assume it was peak day for you. And, since I didn't ovulate until a few days after the wedding, your Bourgeois baby should be older than mine. Unless you conceived later, during a different session?"

I cringe and stuff another cookie into my mouth. "Nope. I'm absolutely certain it happened that night. It's kind of amazing how you do that, by the way," I say, attempting to redirect our conversation before I'm tempted to divulge too much again.

"Do what?"

"Science the crap out of baby-making."

She chuckles again. "Yeah, well, you can probably manage the relationship part, unlike me."

"I don't know, Ten. I think you're managing pretty well these days." I wish she were right, because I have no idea what I'm doing with Blake.

"Eh, I just got lucky," she replies, grinning. "Maybe we both did."

CHAPTER 16

Blake

"I'VE GIVEN YOU A GRACE PERIOD, BUT IT'S TIME TO FESS up. I need to know exactly how this thing with Loren started," my brother begins as soon as he climbs into the passenger seat of my truck.

I sigh, but I knew this was coming. I've been brushing over his texts for the past couple of weeks, so it was only a matter of time before he started bothering for details in person.

"We decided to call a truce for yours and Tenley's sake, and I guess things just developed from there."

"So it has nothing to do with making you jealous?" he asks with a smirk.

I shrug as I pull out of his driveway. "Technically, it began in middle school. But that's a longer story."

"We've got time. Mass doesn't start for ten minutes."

"Not sure this story's fit for church," I mumble, and he barks out a laugh.

"Then it's exactly the kind you should be telling. Except God and Father Conrad are the ones who need to hear it."

I roll my eyes. "You would say that."

Truthfully, I can't even remember the last time I participated in the sacrament of reconciliation, at least a decade ago? I'd have to go behind a screen if I confessed now. I can't imagine the look on the priest's face while I subjected him to my comings and goings over the past twelve years or so. Besides, I may not be much of a churchgoer or even a decent Catholic, but my parents made sure JD and I were well catechized. And I know I'd need to actually feel contrite for my sins and vow to avoid committing them again in order to receive absolution, so there's no point in wasting anyone's time. I'm only here now because JD's insisted on us attending and offering a Mass for our parents' birthdays and anniversaries since they've passed away.

"Stop pretending you don't care," he says dryly, bringing me back from my thoughts. "You wouldn't be sneaking off to church at six in the morning if you weren't worried about your soul."

I blink away my surprise, because my brother's attempts at evangelization aren't usually this bold. Persistent, sure—but not confrontational. "I'm not here for my own soul," I retort after a while.

"And I'm not stupid enough to believe you don't think you're at least saving Mom's," he holds as I turn into the parking lot. "Or that a man of your intelligence doesn't recognize the truth for what it is. You're just pretending to live in denial because it's more comfortable there."

I huff, because he's wrong. It's not comfortable here at all.

"If you say so, kid. Then again, maybe I'm just here so I don't get fined," I reply, turning to smirk at him as I put the truck in park.

His lips twitch, but he points a finger at me. "That's borderline sacrilegious. You're lucky it's funny."

I smile to myself as I close my truck door, and we walk into church together. I'm plotting on one of the back pews when JD waltzes up to the front, greeting people along the way as if he owns the place. Naturally, he slides into the third pew from the altar, and I reluctantly genuflect and fall in behind him. He kneels to pray for a minute while I sit back.

"Didn't Tenley want to come this morning?" I whisper once he's done.

"She offered, but the morning sickness makes it tough for her right now. Besides, I thought this was our thing."

Then the bell rings, and everyone stands as the priest walks in, and I'm left to consider those words for the rest of the Mass.

We stop to chat with a few of the older Camellians on our way to the parking lot. Some of them offer prayers on our mom's behalf, and one of her former book club friends mentions how nice it is to see both of the Bourgeois brothers in church today.

"What a perfect birthday gift for your mama," Mrs. Prejean declares. I detect JD's satisfied smile from the corner of my eye.

"All right," he starts once we're back in the truck, "before you tell me the rest of that story, I've got something important to ask you."

"What's that?"

"How do you feel about going to Mass more regularly?"

I cock an eyebrow. "The same as I did before this morning," I fib. "Why?"

"Tenley and I were hoping you'd be willing to be our baby's *Parrain*."

An instant warmth fills my chest. I guess I hadn't expected them to consider me, especially with Ethan in the picture. JD's beaming with pride when I glance over at him.

I clear the unexpected emotion from my throat. "I'd be honored. But I'm not sure I'm fit to be a godfather."

He furrows his brow. "What makes you think that?"

"Probably the constant reminders from you and everyone else that I'm not exactly father material," I blurt out.

His shoulders slump, and he's quiet for a second. "I'm sorry, man. You're right, I have been doing that, but I never meant to make you feel like you're not good enough to be a father or have a family. I guess I thought I was steering you down the right path, although in hindsight, it seems pretty judgmental of me to criticize you and your life choices. Hypocritical, too."

I swallow hard. How the heck am I supposed to respond now? JD's nagging has been one of the only things I could hold against him, and this apology is already turning into another example of how much better he is than me.

"Thanks, I guess," I reply awkwardly.

"I'll try to be better about that," he promises. "As long as you acknowledge me when I say this: I know you'll make a great dad one day, and Tenley and I wouldn't ask you to be our kid's godfather if we didn't trust you and wholeheartedly believe you'd be a good influence."

I nod thoughtfully, still unable to look him in the eyes. It hasn't been easy to ignore my insecurities or convince myself I'm worthy of fatherhood lately, especially when Loren seems so surprised to have my support. I've been relying on my competitive nature for the motivation to prove I'm capable of doing this well.

But now, just hearing my brother say he believes I'd make a decent father is enough to crack open that chest of self-doubt I've tried to keep locked away. It's encouraging at the same time.

"So, you don't think I'm a shitty person?" I ask quietly.

He scoffs. "I don't know anyone who thinks that about you. Hell, even Loren seems to like you now," he says with a smirk.

"Yeah," I agree halfheartedly. "I guess she does."

"You'll do it, then?" His expression is hopeful.

"Of course, man."

"Thank you, *Parrain* Blake." He reaches over to bump his knuckles against my shoulder as I continue driving. "Mom would be really proud, you know. Then again, she'd already be bragging about how great you are at your job and the way you volunteer so much of your time and energy to support Ethan and all these other kids on the field and in court."

I clear my throat again. "I'm sure she'd be more excited about you getting married and having a kid, though."

"Well, yeah, she would be thrilled. But it's not a contest, and she'd be just as happy to see you and Loren together, don't you think?" he fishes as I turn into his driveway.

"Is that your attempt at transitioning back to Loren and me?"

He grins. "Maybe."

And then I'm overcome with guilt, what with the way my brother's looking at me and the idea that my mom might somehow be listening to our conversation. I also realize I'm doing that thing with my lips that tips JD off when I'm lying or hiding something from him.

"Are you gonna tell me what happened or not?" he prompts me again.

"JD, I ..." I cringe, then I curse under my breath as I rub my hand over my face. "Loren's pregnant."

I had no idea how relieved I'd feel once I got that secret off my chest, but it's like a weight has been lifted from my shoulders, and I let out the breath I've been holding for the past month or so. I know I've broken my promise to Loren, but I'm hopeful she'll forgive me since we're headed to the doctor later today and will be presumably ready to share the news with her family soon.

Meanwhile, JD's still staring at me with his mouth hanging open. "Whoa," he remarks after a while.

"Yeah. No one's supposed to know yet."

"Well ... congratulations?"

"Thanks."

"I mean, a baby is pretty cool, even if it's unexpected, right?" He shrugs and forces a smile.

"Sure."

"And we've already established that Loren's awesome."

"Mm-hmm," I reply. Why do I sound so breathless?

"How's she doing? Has she been feeling okay?" he asks, genuinely concerned, and I want to groan because my brother's such a good person that even a surprise pregnancy doesn't warrant a negative reaction from him. "Is she good with everything?"

I sigh. "She's great. She hasn't even been as sick as Tenley."

His smile grows wider, and he nudges me in the shoulder. "You know, I suspected something was up when she barfed in class for the second time this month. I'm really glad it's a baby and not salmonella poisoning." I laugh as he continues. "Wow, so you're really having a baby ... with Loren Reed. I'll be honest, I did not have that on my bingo card."

"Yeah, neither did I."

"But, hey, now we get to be first-time dads at the same time, and our kids are going to grow up together. This is actually pretty awesome when you think about it. What a blessing, you know? Blake, this is ... kind of the best news ever," he rambles, his voice thick, and I admittedly have to swallow the lump in my own throat.

Over the past few months, I've struggled with my feelings as I watched JD become more and more invested in his new family. It hasn't been easy to balance the joys of seeing him so happy with the dread of being left behind. But once I found out I was also becoming a father, my focus shifted to my relationship with Loren and how a baby might affect our future. While a part of me relished in the idea of an accomplishment putting me on par with JD, I hadn't really considered that embracing fatherhood could help me grow closer to him instead of causing us to drift apart.

For once, I think I'm looking forward to sharing something with my little brother.

"Yeah, sure," I choke out, willing my eyes to stop watering because there's no way I could live it down if I cried right now.

We're both quiet for a beat before he clears his throat. "Want to come in for coffee? Ten's already at work, and E's at the gym."

I check the time on the dash and nod before I glare at him strangely. "Since when do you make coffee?"

"Happy wife, happy life, man."

CHAPTER 17
Blake

JD leads me inside and points out a new coffeemaker before he retrieves a carton of eggs from the fridge.

"So, uh, how are you really feeling about all this?" he asks hesitantly as he works at the stove.

"It's not like I can take it back now," I say, laughing sardonically. But I already know I wouldn't take it back, even if I could.

"What about your sworn enemy becoming the mother of your child?"

He cranes his neck to look at me, but I turn away so he can't read my expression. I'm not ready to admit that Loren is probably the reason I am more than okay with things.

"It could be worse."

"Really? *It could be worse*?"

For a second, I forgot he doesn't know about our arrangement. "Okay, so we're obviously not enemies anymore."

"And that's it? Blake, is this not the first real, serious relationship you've had in forever? Or like, at all?"

"Who said anything about a serious relationship?" I feel my blood pressure rising. "And, by the way, surviving the first few months of your quickie marriage doesn't make you some kind of therapist or relationship expert. So you can spare me the condescending lecture."

JD chuckles and points a spatula at me. "I'm obviously not an expert, but knowing you better than anyone else on this planet definitely makes me qualified to call you out. And I do have experience helping Tenley overcome her commitment issues."

I cross my arms and lean back against the counter as the coffeemaker groans. "I don't have commitment issues. I just haven't found a reason to commit. There's a difference."

"A baby isn't a good enough reason?" he asks incredulously.

I scoff. "Loren and I agree that forcing a serious relationship would be a horrible idea. Besides, she knows I'm committed to being a decent father, and I'd like to think I've been very supportive so far."

"You're being supportive?" he clarifies, eyeing me suspiciously again. "So, you're just friends?"

"I guess we're more than friends, but technically, we're not romantically attached. It's more of an open relationship."

"That's the dumbest thing I've ever heard," he deadpans.

I sigh as I pour my coffee. He's like a damn dog with a bone, and he's not going to quit until he's figured me out. "Neither of us wanted to risk our ability to co-parent later. But we couldn't just come out and tell everyone she ended up pregnant after an accidental hookup, so we agreed to make it look like we've been dating for a while before ultimately deciding we work better as friends," I explain. "And you don't know any of this, all right? I really want to save her the embarrassment."

"You're only fake dating, then?"

"More or less."

He scoops scrambled eggs into a pair of plates and walks over. "How does one 'accidentally' hook up with a woman he's never liked or found attractive in the first place?"

"I said she was annoying, not unattractive." I take a seat at the kitchen island. "She's ... tolerable."

"Tolerable?" he repeats, cocking an eyebrow as he joins me. He slides a plate in front of each of us. "Is that how you lured her into bed? You told her she was *tolerable*?"

I take a sip and hide behind my coffee mug when I feel my cheeks warming.

Wait, am I blushing? When did I become shy about sex, especially in front of my brother, who knows more of my secrets than anyone and is less mature than his teenaged kid most of the time?

"I'd rather not talk about it," I say flatly.

He gasps, bringing his hand to his chest in mock surprise. "*You* don't want to talk about your sex life? WHAT?"

"I'm not telling you about the night I got her pregnant."

"You mean, you think it'd be disrespectful to discuss the specifics when it involves Loren? Sort of the way I felt a few months back when you kept pestering me for details about the physical part of my relationship with Tenley?"

I purse my lips in distaste. I hate it when he's right, and he's been right about entirely too much today. "Sure. If you say so."

He stares at me for a second, squinting and reading me like a book. "And there was only the one time, so you can't talk about what ain't happening, even though you've been hanging out constantly and totally want it to happen again. Am I right?"

I growl. I've also been hoping he wouldn't figure out that particular detail, but there it is.

"Hmm. Blake the Snake, exclusive *and* celibate with a woman ... sounds like you're in love with her."

That earns him a dangerous glare from me, and he raises his hands innocently, though he's grinning like the cat that ate the canary.

"How do you know I'm not already seeing someone else?" I retort.

"Are you?"

"Well, no," I huff. "But we've been trying to convince everyone we're a real couple by going out together and having her stay over at my place. I'm not going to risk being seen with another woman and subject Loren to any more gossip than necessary. People are already going to give her a hard time when they find out she's pregnant with my baby."

"Oh, so she's only been spending the night because it's part of your cover story and not because you can't get enough of her, then?"

"Thought you'd be happy to hear I've been keeping it in my pants for once, *Padre*."

"I don't know how you're doing it, man," he says, shaking his head. "I mean, say what you want, but Tenley was right. If we'd have given into temptation and started having sex earlier, we'd never have been able to stop ... or think rationally."

"What are you talking about? Nothing about your relationship is rational to begin with," I reply, scowling.

"I thought I was infatuated with Ten before our wedding night, but it's a million times worse now. I couldn't have just walked away from her after, you know, forming that physical connection, much less if we'd been playing house."

I swallow hard, remembering how empty I felt when Loren walked out on me after I thought we'd formed that same kind of connection. "Then it's a good thing I've got years of experience with casual hookups, right?"

He furrows his brow. "Don't do that to yourself, Blake. It doesn't have to be like that this time."

"Yeah, well, I don't have much say in the matter," I blurt out.

"You do want more with Loren, though," he says, stating it as a fact.

I press my lips together. "I don't know what I want. I only know Loren doesn't want *me*, so considering anything else would be pointless."

"But it's too late, isn't it?"

I realize I've revealed too much again, and JD takes a huge bite as another satisfied smile crosses his face.

"Don't look at me like that. All I'm saying is I don't hate her, and if I absolutely *had* to do this with someone, I'm not disappointed it's her. I mean, she's definitely the smartest of all the women I've been with."

"And the sexiest?"

I ignore the sudden urge to shove him off his stool. "Maybe," I concede and take a bite of my own food.

He laughs. "I bet it was different for you that night, wasn't it? That's why you're so *shook*. You don't think you'll ever find that feeling again with anyone else, so you haven't even been tempted to try. She's ruined you for all other women, hasn't she?"

I shake my head and avoid eye contact. "Look, it's not that simple. I told you, Loren and I have history."

"Go on."

"We hadn't slept together before, but ..." He motions with his hand for me to continue, and I sigh. "We were each other's first kiss. And there were a few close calls over the years, but she always shot me down when I tried to make a move. Nothing big happened until this."

"That's why you got so upset when Lo offered to help me, isn't it? You weren't just jealous—I was encroaching on your territory." He leans over and nudges my shoulder.

"Hey, I'm a grown-ass man. It's not like I've been harboring a crush since I was thirteen."

"Of course not," he placates me. "Because you're Blake Bourgeois. You've pulled some of the hottest, most beautiful women from Baton Rouge to Camellia. There's no way you'd let little, old Loren Reed bring you to your knees, right?"

I grunt in response.

No way, right?

"Although, it'd be okay if you did. No one would think less of you for falling for your pregnant fake girlfriend," he continues. "Speaking of, I know you don't want to talk about that night, but something's not adding up. You've always preached about the importance of using protection, so how exactly did Loren end up pregnant?"

I feel my face flushing again. "There, uh ... there wasn't exactly enough time for that. Not the first round, anyway."

JD rolls his lips in, and his nostrils flare as he tries not to laugh.

"It was—I mean, I tried ..." I don't know how to save face without disrespecting Loren. And then I realize how much trouble

I'm in because I care so damned much. "There was a lot of wine involved, and like, a fifteen-year buildup to that moment, all right?"

He's chuckling out loud now. "You mean, you've been fantasizing about her for fifteen years? I thought she was barely tolerable?"

I growl as I rise to dump my plate and mug in the sink.

"But hey, if the chemistry has lasted this long, it's probably worth betting on," he adds.

"Says the guy who practically ran to the altar because of 'chemistry,' " I grumble.

"Chemistry is a gift," he says simply. "Listen, man. I know you still think I based my marriage on an infatuation, but I'm not crazy enough to believe in love at first sight. There's a reason I felt such an intense and overwhelming pull toward Tenley."

I turn and cross my arms as I lean back against the counter. "Well, yeah. She was fresh meat, and you hadn't gotten laid in, what, a few years?"

He sighs before he continues. "Sure, but I'd also like to think the instant attraction was a nudge from the Holy Spirit. I may have come off as desperate, but the physical desire only made me determined to get to know her and more inclined to fall for her once I saw her other amazing qualities, like her intelligence, her sense of humor, our shared interests, and so on. Not to mention, making the ultimate commitment with someone seems a lot more appealing when you're absolutely burning up for one another."

I blink a few times and shake my head. "Are you trying to tell me that God used Tenley's boobs to speak to your heart?"

I expect him to reprimand me for that one, but he just shrugs thoughtfully. "More or less. Don't you think He accounted for biological urges when He designed us?"

I'm quiet for a while as I consider what he's saying. I'm not exactly a theologian, and neither is my brother, but damn if this doesn't sound like one of the wisest things he's ever come up with.

"And you're suggesting the same thing is happening to me?"

"Hell if I know, Blake. You seem to enjoy staring longingly at

Loren," he replies with a smirk. "Any parts of her been speaking to your heart?"

I snort out a laugh. "All right, fine. Things felt different with Loren—*very* different. But she obviously didn't experience the same connection, or you and I wouldn't be having this conversation right now."

He huffs. "In case you've forgotten, Tenley didn't find me so irresistible in the beginning. Our relationship didn't just fall into my lap. I had to trust that God was leading me in the right direction, and it still took some assistance from you and her family and a lot of effort and patience on my part before she was even willing to give me a shot."

"Right, right," I say with a nod, humoring him. "But she can't get enough of you now."

He grins and flexes his arms, making me roll my eyes. "I could give you a few tips."

"Yeah, like I need your help," I retort, gesturing over my torso.

"Not all women like those, you know."

I frown. "But Loren says my abs are *spicy*."

He guffaws loudly this time, and my frown turns into a scowl. "And you honestly don't think she's into you?"

"Like you said, there's always been chemistry, maybe more on my end than hers, but she doesn't think she can trust me."

"So work on earning her trust."

But I know better. I'll never convince Loren to put her faith in me with everyone constantly bringing up my serial dating history and offering their unsolicited commentary on my inability to commit to one woman. My own brother can't even refrain from reminding me of my lack of serious relationship experience.

"I don't see how that's possible in this situation. So maybe we should just drop it," I say flatly, turning to leave.

"Come on, Blake. You don't have a choice. You can't really think your plan's going to work, that you and Loren will both be satisfied with a platonic friendship and splitting time with your baby?"

"I don't see why not, so long as we keep our relationship civil."

"Bullshit, man. You're a freaking family court lawyer. You know exactly how this is going to end."

He has a point there. I've been wracking my brain to come up with some wording for a custody arrangement that would make sense for us, and nothing has come to mind yet. Not to mention I absolutely hate the idea of my own kid having to grow up in the same split-household situation I see all the time at work.

"Besides, how are you going to feel when some other guy comes along to give Loren all the things you can't? Are you really going to be cool with another man sleeping in her bed and raising your kid?"

I glower at him over my shoulder. He's right again, of course. After running that Rowan guy off, I stupidly assumed Loren wouldn't be dating in her condition. But she won't be pregnant forever, and I don't relish the thought of anyone else even getting close to Loren, *my Loren*.

"I've gotta go," I grumble and move to the door.

"*Mais*, where ya going, bruh?" JD calls, his voice tinged with amusement.

"To be a supportive fake boyfriend," I grunt without turning around.

CHAPTER 18

Loren

"Are you sure it's not too much trouble for you to come with me today? I'm really fine on my own."

Blake clicks his tongue at me from the driver's seat. "I told you I wanted to be here, didn't I?" Then he reaches over and rests his open hand on the center console, gesturing for me to fill it, so I place my much smaller hand in his. "Why do you have such a hard time believing me when I say something like that? Do you really think I'm that heartless and narcissistic?" he asks, intending it to sound like a joke.

I shrug. "You're not so bad, Blake. I just don't want this situation to hold you back."

He furrows his brow. "I know my dating history precedes me, but I hope you don't think I'd dodge my responsibilities or not do my best to be a good father."

"Of course not, and you've been great so far. But you don't have to force yourself to become someone you're not."

"What do you mean?"

"I don't expect you to become a monk. I'm sure you miss ... dating," I explain delicately. I'd been meaning to bring up the topic since we'd somehow skated around it when we set the ground rules, and now seems as good a time as any.

"I'm going to ignore the euphemism and answer the question as if you were being literal. I'm perfectly fine with putting dating on hold for now." His thumb rubs soft circles on my wrist as he continues. "Besides, it's not like I'm lonely."

"And if I weren't being literal?"

"I'm not thrilled about the dry spell, but I'll survive. Or maybe I'm still hoping you'll change your mind about rule number one by the next trimester," he says, flashing a coy smirk at me and awakening a few tummy butterflies.

Okay, so every time he hints about a repeat performance of that night, my stomach flutters. A lot. And sometimes other parts react, too. But I have no choice but to keep ignoring the way his flirting affects me if I want to make it out alive.

I clear my throat. "I'm just saying you don't have to give it all up on my account. We can be friends and successfully co-parent while we maintain separate social lives."

He mulls over my offer for a while, still rubbing my wrist. Then he pulls up in front of the doctor's office and puts his truck in park before turning to face me. "Loren, the truth is that I'm not interested in dating other women, even if that means being celibate for a while. I don't like the idea of spending time with you one night and someone else the next. It doesn't feel right, especially while we're letting everyone believe we're a couple."

"And I don't want you to become resentful of me and our kid later once you realize we've ruined your way of life," I retort, my tone harsher than I intend.

He huffs. "If I'm resentful of anything, it's that you can't trust me to be a decent human being," he mumbles, and I furrow my brow in confusion. "Whether you like it or not, Lo, we're in this situation together. And even though you'll only ever see me as a friend, the least you could do is to stop questioning my loyalty."

"I'm sorry," I whisper softly. "I know it's not fair of me to make those kinds of assumptions about you, especially when you've only shown me the opposite. It's just, I've grown up in the aftermath of the same circumstances, and the last thing I want is to hold you back or get in the way of your happiness."

He lets out a long exhale. "I get it. If it makes you feel any better, I want you to know I'd already been considering an extended break from casual dating before you and I got together. In fact, you're the only woman I've been with in a while. Which was probably evident when ..." He turns his lips to the side and shrugs shyly. "You know, the reason we ended up here in the first place."

I snicker under my breath, and he turns to glare at me.

"Oh, of course. *That's* the detail you remember."

"I'm sorry, I was laughing at the part where you expected me to believe women have suddenly stopped throwing themselves at you. It's not like you've made yourself less desirable by secretly deciding to change your lifestyle, as admirable as it may be," I explain with a smile.

"Is this your way of asking me whether I've gotten any offers?"

My lips part in surprise. I may have brushed over his confession just now in lieu of keeping things light, but it's not easy to ignore him when he spells it out like this.

"It's none of my business," I reply.

"So you'd *really* be okay with me seeing someone else? And you wouldn't be the least bit jealous?" His eyes search mine, and my stomach flips when I actually stop to picture it.

Okay, that's an understatement. I want to cut her, and I don't even know who *she* is, though Blake's hypothetical girlfriend bears a strong resemblance to Nicole from the dress shop.

But I won't do this to him. I'm not going to tell him the truth, that seeing him with another woman would absolutely wreck me. Because the only thing worse than having to pretend I don't want to be with Blake would be allowing myself to hope and having that rug ripped out from under me later. There's no way he, of all people, won't decide I'm not worth his time and energy one day.

"Of course I'd be jealous," I say with a shrug. "But I'd hate for you to waste your spicy abs on me."

He shakes his head, and he almost looks angry. "I'm not sure how many times I'm going to have to explain this to you, Loren, but listen carefully. I really wish you'd quit selling yourself short. I think you're amazing. You're beautiful, smart, funny, and any guy would be lucky to have you. The only reason you're still single is by choice, I'm sure. And I'm sorry if our situation makes you feel like any of that isn't true. I may only have initiated something that night while our inhibitions were lowered, but I want you to understand it's because I've always thought you were out of my league, and not because I had to get drunk to want to sleep with you. It was more like a 'liquid courage' kind of thing, all right?"

I chew on my bottom lip as I sniffle, unable to look him in the eyes after that. Surely he's only feeding me lines because he doesn't want to leave me feeling sorry for myself, but it's sweet, nonetheless. "Dammit, Gus Gus. Thanks for making me cry," I mumble, halfway laughing through my tears.

He shakes his head, his expression softening. "Anytime, babe. It's what I do best." Then he stares at me for a full minute in a way that makes my insides melt, without ever looking away from my face. "I'll make you a deal. I'll go on a date when you do."

"What?" I ask incredulously. "I'm not exactly in any condition to date."

"Then neither am I. Once you decide you're ready, I'll get back out there, too. Make it an amendment to the ground rules."

I narrow my eyes at him. "This feels like one of your lawyerly traps."

"Oh, it's definitely one of those," he replies, his smile growing.

"Fine," I say, reaching out to poke him in the chest. He grasps my hand and holds it against him, and I accidentally sigh when I feel his heart beating steadily beneath my palm.

"But if I never date again, you'll find yourself in a bind." My voice comes out breathier than I mean it to sound.

"We'll see who cracks first, Agnes."

I wipe my eyes with my free hand because he's still holding the other one. In fact, he's bringing it up to his mouth when he stops abruptly.

"You know what, I think I'm going to invoke my rights. Come here," he says, dropping my hand and using his to lift my chin as he leans over and presses his lips to mine.

He keeps to his word, only pausing there for a few seconds to get his point across. Still, I can tell he's holding back every time he kisses me or initiates some kind of physical contact. I believe Blake when he says he's attracted to me and that he cares about me, but I know his true feelings could never really outgrow our friendship or progress beyond a combination of fondness and gratitude for carrying his baby. If there was any chance of that happening, he'd feel the way I do when he kisses me, and he wouldn't be able to stop, regardless of the ground rules.

"Better?" he asks once he breaks away.

No. Maybe we should try it again for a little longer.

Ugh, shut up, stupid subconscious.

"Yeah, thanks," I whisper.

"Come on, let's go check out our little sweet pea," he says, but then he freezes as he turns, and his expression changes. "Well, shit."

"What?" I ask as I twist in my seat to find Tenley standing in front of the truck. Her lips form a knowing smile, and her hands are planted firmly on her hips. "Oh. Fudge."

Then she puckers her lips to mime a kiss, winks, and turns to walk inside.

"I thought you said she wasn't going to be here today," he whines.

"She wasn't supposed to be. I made sure to book my appointment on the same day she told me she'd scheduled herself to see a different doctor." I hesitate before admitting the next part. "But she already knows."

He rears back. "You told Tenley?"

"I'm sorry," I cringe. "She figured it out the other day. But she doesn't know about our arrangement, and I made her promise not to tell—"

"JD knows, too," he blurts out. "I told him this morning. I'm sorry, I couldn't hold it in any longer."

"I can only imagine what he had to say," I reply, secretly relieved.

"Although the amount of times I've vomited in class over the past month or so may have been a clue."

He chuckles. "Yeah, he mentioned that. He's pretty excited though."

"So is Tenley," I admit. "Not nearly as judgmental as I figured, either."

"Same."

"Okay, so this is good, right? Now that they know, we just have to tell my family." I bite my lip and wring my hands. For some reason, seeing Tenley here is making this all too real.

"Hey," he catches my attention before I begin hyperventilating. "Don't worry. We'll tell them together, all right?"

I nod too quickly, but he holds my gaze until I'm feeling calmer.

"Don't make me kiss you again, Reed. I can't make any promises about holding back this time."

I laugh shortly as my face heats up. All I'd need is for him to lose a little of his self-control to completely give up on mine. But he gestures toward the door with his head instead of making a move.

"Thanks. I'm ready," I tell him.

He flashes another smile at me before he walks around the truck and opens my door, then we go inside to check in. I don't see any more signs of Tenley, except for her name on the actual signs, of course.

Blake takes a seat beside me in the large waiting room, and I glance up from my paperwork to see him fidgeting uncomfortably when a well-dressed woman greets him. She's a pharmaceutical rep, judging by the logo on her name tag, and beautiful enough to elicit a trace of jealousy on my part. I expect a more flirtatious response from him, but all he offers her is a polite nod. I smirk at the way he blushes and tries to fasten an extra button on his shirt, as if it'll make him look any less sexy.

"Friend of yours?" I ask, stifling my amusement.

He clears his throat and frowns. I lean over and nudge his shoulder with mine so he can see I'm kidding, and he exhales in relief.

And I can't help but feel a little satisfied by his nerves, especially after our conversation in the truck.

"Loren? Loren Reed?"

I rise as one of the medical assistants calls my name, and Blake follows. "Hi, I'm Mackenzie, and I'll be getting your vitals today." She holds the door open, her eyes following Blake as he shadows me. "And who do we have here? Dare I say a Bourgeois?"

"Blake," he returns, forcing another uncharacteristically awkward smile.

"Nurse Tenley's brother-in-law Blake?"

He cringes as he nods.

"I see," she says, directing me to have a seat. "Since you brought your man candy along, I'm gonna go out on a limb and assume you're here after hitting it big in the pee-stick lottery?"

"You guessed it," I reply, trying not to laugh.

"Congratulations to both of you. Date of your last menstrual cycle? Suspected conception date?"

I supply both, and her eyebrows rise sharply. "Looks like somebody might have partied a little too hard after their brother's wedding," she remarks, cackling to herself. I glance over to find Blake blushing furiously, something I've never seen before.

Mackenzie continues gathering information before she hands me a small, plastic cup. I slip into the attached bathroom to fill 'er up, laughing to myself as I hear Blake warding off another unwanted advance by telling Mackenzie we're *definitely* an item. Once I'm done, we follow her to another room with a huge machine stationed beside an exam table, and Mackenzie graciously provides me with the hospital-style gown that I'll be modeling for the next hour or so—no panty lines allowed, of course.

"The doctor shouldn't be long, honey."

Blake and I both let out a huge breath as soon as she closes the door. "*Mais la,*" I grumble, holding up the gown. "I think we may need to revisit the part about you coming to these appointments."

"But this is the closest I might get to *dating* for a while, remember?" He bounces his eyebrows suggestively, and I roll my eyes. Then I step behind a small screen to change into the gown, hugging my midsection tightly as I waddle back to the exam table.

"So, um, what do you think that one's for?" Blake asks carefully, pointing to the phallic-shaped gadget resting beside the ultrasound monitor.

"I suspect I'm about to find out."

A short knock sounds, and Mackenzie sticks her head inside. "Hi," she drawls. "So Dr. Simms got called out for an emergency C-section, and Nurse Tenley's covering his patients for the rest of the afternoon. Unless you want to reschedule …" She cringes and mouths, "So sorry," before she disappears.

Blake and I exchange panicked glances, and the door swings open to reveal Tenley with a folder in hand.

"Oh. Hey, Ten," I attempt to say, but my voice cracks.

"Good afternoon, Ms. Reed," she returns with fake propriety, walking over to sit on the rolling chair at my side. "What brings you in today?"

"I guess it depends on what it says in that chart," I reply sarcastically.

"And who do we have here? Hi, is this *Dad*?"

Blake looks away and mouths a four-letter word, his face reddening again.

I gulp. "I'm sorry, we thought we'd get Doc Simms, you know, to make this less awkward."

Tenley continues ignoring me, her eyes running over the rest of my chart. "Well, you're definitely pregnant, my friend. And these levels look great so far—in fact, your hCG is notably high. Congratulations," she says, smiling genuinely at both of us.

"Thank you," Blake answers. "I hope you understand why we were trying to keep this quiet at first. We didn't want to cramp your moment."

Her expression softens. "Oh. Well, I wish you wouldn't have thought that. You guys deserve to celebrate this as much as anyone. A baby is always a miracle, right?"

My eyes water as I nod.

"Speaking for myself, I couldn't be more excited if it were my own. I'm looking forward to becoming a *tante* again," she adds, reaching out to pat my hand.

"Ten," I begin. "Please don't make me cry right now."

"Mm-hmm," she squeaks, blinking and scrunching her nose. I cringe and reach out, and she leans forward to envelop me in a hug.

"Would this be a bad time to point out that your gown is totally open in the back?" Blake whispers after a minute.

"Yes," Tenley and I both call out at the same time.

"Okay, but don't fault me for checking out your ass, then."

We pull away, and she leans over to slap Blake on the shoulder. "That's for knocking up my best friend and not having the balls to tell me yourself."

"Sorry, not that sorry," Blake replies, grinning so hard that I think his face might crack.

Ugh.

Proud-daddy Blake is entirely too adorable. I force myself to look away.

"Have you told your brother yet?" Tenley asks.

"Yes," he says with a sigh. "I confessed this morning. He got all mushy and gross."

"Of course he did." Tenley rolls her eyes. Then she rubs her hands together before reaching over to grab a pair of medical gloves. "Okay, let's get this party started, shall we?"

"Hold on, you can't, like, be *her* midwife, can you? Wouldn't that be unethical? Or just plain weird?" Blake wrinkles his nose in disgust.

Tenley shrugs. "Not for me. But if you're uncomfortable, Loren, you can reschedule with Doc Simms. No hard feelings."

"I only asked for Dr. Simms because I didn't want it to be awkward for you or Blake," I tell her. "I actually think it would be cool if you got to deliver the baby later. That is, if you're still working by then."

Blake frowns. "We hadn't exactly discussed that. But I suppose it is *your* choice."

I ignore the tension in his voice. "Let's just go ahead with it today. We're already here, right?"

"Right." He sniffs.

"Okay. Party's back on," Tenley announces, slipping on the gloves. Then she grabs the exact tool that Blake and I have been eyeballing, and I hear him gulp audibly. "You might feel a teensy bit of pressure," she warns me as she directs me to lie back.

"Oh, hell. You're really gonna—wow. Okay." Blake looks horrified as Tenley squirts some type of gel over the tip.

She smirks at him before spreading a drape over my knees. "Don't feel intimidated, bro. It might seem big, but personally, I find it to be a pretty accurate representation of what I'm used to working with. You know, as far as transvaginal ultrasound devices go."

He scoffs and turns to me. "And everyone says I'm the indecent one."

"Never would have taken you for a prude, Blake," she says with fake innocence, staring him down again and making him roll his eyes. Then she waits for my cue before she begins the sonogram.

"Doing okay?" she whispers when I inhale sharply, her tone more serious this time.

I nod, figuring this is just the first on a long list of unpleasant situations brought on by that second pink line.

"Let's see who we have here," she mumbles, shifting the instrument and scrolling around on the monitor. Then she stops abruptly, her expression changing. Her jaw flops open, and she shakes her head slightly in disbelief.

"Holy shit."

"Ten, is everything okay?" Blake asks.

"Oh yeah, it's great," she says, coming back from her trance. "Better than great, actually." She stops and smiles at us, then an incredulous laugh bubbles out of her before she faces the screen again.

"Wanna explain what's going on, then?" he demands.

"Okay. You asked for it. But I think you're just trying to one-up your brother now," she mutters. She turns the monitor to face us and clears her throat before she speaks. "Here's your baby, guys." She stops moving again and points to a wiggly oval with a flickering light inside, and my eyes immediately begin stinging.

I continue staring at the small, quivering spot as the screen freezes and "BABY A" appears above it. Tenley bites her lip, repeating the same process with a different figure, typing "BABY B" this time.

My chest tightens as I stare at the letter "B" on the screen. A + B = twins, doesn't it?

There's no way.

It's not even possible.

Women like me don't hook up with men who look like Blake and get pregnant with twins. They just adopt a couple of cats, right?

Tenley turns her eyes to meet Blake's. "And here's your *other* baby. Still overachievers, I guess."

A smile flickers across his face before the realization hits him. "T-t-two babies?" he stutters, blinking at the screen. If I weren't so busy trying to keep myself alive right now, I'd be enjoying his reaction, because I've certainly never seen him this rattled.

Tenley nods softly. "Two babies."

"It can't be, can it?" I rasp, feeling like my heart is stuck in my throat.

"Most definitely. It also explains the high hCG levels. It's still a little early to tell, but from the looks of things, I'm calling them monochorionic-diamniotic."

"What does that mean?" I ask.

"They share one placenta but have their own amniotic sacs."

"Tenley," Blake growls.

She smirks. "Sorry, all signs point toward identical twins. Would you like to hear their heartbeats?"

He exhales loudly, holding his forehead up as if his neck can no longer handle the job. "Two heartbeats?" His voice is coming out in a wheeze now.

"Yep. Listen." She clicks a button, and a loud sound that reminds me of an old washing machine blares from the speakers. There are two distinct rhythms, one growing louder than the other as she shifts around.

My mind is reeling as I take it all in, and I can't decide whether to focus on the screen or on Blake's face. Well, technically, I can't see much of anything with the way I've started crying.

"Hey, Dad? This would be a good time to pull out your phone," Tenley suggests, and he sighs as he records a first look at our babies, squeezing my hand with his other the entire time.

Blake stares down at me, his eyes glistening and admiration clear in all of his features, and I don't know how I manage to take the next breath.

"We made *two* babies, Lo."

"We did," I reply as tears continue spilling over.

"Now do you believe me when I say you're amazing?"

I laugh through a sob. "Yeah, maybe I am."

Then he leans down and kisses me softly, making me feel like the most special human on the planet. That is, until he pulls away, and I hear the FaceTime ringtone.

JD's voice is loud and clear as he answers. "Hey, what's going on? Everything okay?"

"I'm winning, bro. That's what's happening." Blake turns the phone so Tenley and I are in the shot, despite her hand still resting under the tent over my legs.

"Blake, I'm not sure this is—"

"Oh, hey, Loren!" I hear JD say.

"Hey, JD," I return on a sigh.

"Tell him what you just told us, Ten. Show him," Blake urges. And I groan to myself because I can't handle adorable, proud-daddy Blake again.

"He's right, babe," Tenley admits, trying to downplay her amusement. "While the rest of us have been playing it safe and kicking extra points, Coach Blake is out here going for two-point conversions." She turns the screen and points to both babies, and JD lets out an uncharacteristic string of profanities, making me giggle. Then the screen gets blurry, and the babies flutter around even more.

"And what do you have to say for yourself, Ms. Reed?" JD calls out, and Blake brings the phone closer to my face.

I smirk. "Well, boss, I'm gonna need you to sign off on my maternity leave paperwork when you get a chance."

CHAPTER 19

Blake

"ONE BED, BLAKE? SERIOUSLY?" LOREN GRINS AT ME AS WE walk into our swanky hotel suite.

I smirk and follow with our bags. "I couldn't very well ask for two beds, not in front of everyone in line to check in."

She waltzes over and flops down onto the bed in question. "What a predictable rom-com trope."

"Then it's a good thing you made all those rules." I set everything down before lying beside her. She turns her head to roll her eyes at me, and I reach out to drape my arm over her waist, tugging her closer. "I can always sleep on the pull-out sofa if you're worried about breaking the law," I whisper over her shoulder as I curve my body around hers.

She giggles and squirms at first, but she eventually gives up and melts into me. "I'm sure we'll be fine, especially since I have no choice but to stay sober. I'll be the designated Debbie Downer for the evening."

Gah, she smells *so* good.

I groan into the back of her neck and give her one more good squeeze before letting her go. "No need. I'll be on my best behavior, I promise."

She twists around to glare at me again. "Unless I beg, right?"

"I wouldn't actually make you beg, Reed," I say with a pout. "One 'oh, please, Blake,' and you can have whatever you want from me."

She laughs and shoves me away this time, and I sigh as I watch her get up and sort through her suitcase. "I should start getting ready," she declares, draping a garment bag over her shoulder. She drags it across the floor while she gathers the rest of her things, and I can't help but smile. "I'll be in the bathroom for a while, so you'd better go first."

"Yes, ma'am." I pluck the hanger from her grasp and hang her dress on the back of the bathroom door. Then I grab my shaving case and shut the door behind me, only intending to freshen up before deciding I need a quick shower. It's not until I'm drying off that I remember I didn't bring my clothes in with me. Loren's probably going to have something to say when I walk out, but she'll just have to deal with it.

I wrap the towel around myself and venture into the room. "Bathroom's all yours," I announce. But her reflection in the wall mirror stops me in my tracks.

"I borrowed one of your shirts once I heard you start the shower. Hope you don't mind," she says, glancing up to look at me in the mirror as she continues curling her hair. She falters for a second when she notices the only thing I'm wearing is a damp towel, the one that's currently loosening as I stand frozen, gaping at her and practically drooling over seeing her in my button-down.

"You brought my dress in with you," she reminds me when she sets down the curling iron, and once she stands, I'm forced to plant my hands on my hips to keep the towel in place. "So I needed something that opened in the front to avoid ruining my hair and makeup when I have to change later."

I gulp and nod my head quickly, my eyes running over her as I suppress the urge to ask her if she'll need help with the buttons. "Looks like it works fine."

"What's your excuse?" She gestures to my current condition and smiles.

"I hadn't planned on the shower, but I realized it was necessary once I took off my shirt," I spit out.

She crosses her arms over her waist, making the shirt's hem ride up over her bare thighs, and I bite the inside of my cheek. I could use another, much colder shower at the moment.

"Sure, you did, Gus Gus," she replies sarcastically, but I don't miss the way her gaze drifts down.

"Right, and you can stop pretending you don't like what you see, Agnes," I retort, keeping my hands on my hips as I strut over to the bag containing my tux. All it takes is a second of her checking me out to revive my confidence.

I hang up my tuxedo and unzip my suitcase to retrieve a clean pair of underwear. Then I turn to look at her over my shoulder, making sure I flex my back muscles in the process. "Aren't you going to finish primping in the bathroom now?"

She clears her throat and looks away. "You've made it too steamy. I can't go in without ruining my hair."

"Oh, sorry. I hadn't thought about that."

"I'll wait for it to cool off." Her voice sounds distant, like she's walked off or at least turned away from me.

"I guess we'll both have to get dressed in here, then," I volunteer, unsuccessfully hiding the smile in my tone. "I won't peek if you don't."

She huffs out a laugh. "Deal."

I glance behind me after I slip on my boxers, hoping to catch her looking. But my plan backfires, and watching her unbutton that shirt is nearly too much for me to take. I groan and avert my eyes again, resolving to conduct myself as I promised earlier.

We're both quiet except for the rustling of our clothes when she speaks up again. "Once you're decent, would you mind helping me with this zipper?"

"I'm never decent," I say, whirling around to find her standing close with her back to me. "But I don't mind helping you—if and only if you admit to peeking, at least once."

She shakes her head as she reaches to gather her hair and lift it in one hand while holding up the front of her dress with the other. "I did no such thing."

"So, you walked backward to get over here?"

"Shut up and zip me," she commands over her shoulder.

"You're forgetting something."

"*Please*, Blake."

She laughs at me when I whimper in response, then I carefully place my hands on her back and tug on the zipper. My eyes skim over her dress, which consists of two pieces, a long, fitted skirt and matching cropped top, its deep green color perfectly complementing her soft, creamy skin. Even her short nails are painted to match.

"Thanks," she mumbles, dropping her hair and causing the scent to waft up at the same time she turns and lets her hands fall at her sides. "How do I look?"

I'm struck dumb for a few seconds, fumbling for words with my eyes wide and my mouth hanging open. She's the sexiest thing I've ever seen, especially with her skirt hugging her curves just right. Then she does a half-turn, the movement exposing her waist and lower back and my mouth waters.

"I ... uh, you look ... wow," I breathe, and she blushes.

"I still need to touch up my makeup," she says, although I can tell she's pleased with my reaction.

I blink a few times, trying to recoup, but she reaches up to fasten the last couple of buttons on my shirt, and my stomach flutters. I swallow hard. "You're stunning, Loren," I finally manage.

"You're not so bad yourself," she replies, laying her palms over my chest and smiling up at me. "Looks like I'll need to get my warpaint just right so I can fend off the competition."

I force out an embarrassingly shaky breath as I reach down to cup my hands around her hips. "Don't bother. You have my full attention tonight. In fact, we don't even have to go downstairs and socialize if you'd rather stay in," I tell her, my eyes glued to her mouth. "I wouldn't even make you ask nicely."

She inhales sharply, and I find myself leaning in, unable to help the way I'm drawn to her. But she lowers her chin before our lips meet and pushes off my chest to take a step back.

"Come on, Gus Gus. I'd hate for you to waste all of your good lines on me. I didn't get all dressed up for nothing, either." Her tone isn't as convincing as she thinks, though.

I turn to look for my tie. "Right. You want me to save it for someone who actually likes it when I flirt with her," I mumble under my breath. But it's too late, because she's already scurried away to finish getting ready.

I sigh as I slip on my shoes and adjust my tie in the mirror, and Loren emerges from the bathroom a few minutes later, sporting cherry red lipstick and a pair of shoes tall enough to put her at an average height.

"Gah, these were a terrible idea." She takes a few awkward steps forward, growls, and grabs her bag before plopping down to kick off her shoes and toss them across the room. "You're going to have to settle for my regular heels. I just can't manage the stilettos, despite the way other women have mastered the art."

I walk over and kneel in front of her, taking the shorter heels and sliding them onto her feet. When I glance up, she's biting her lip. "Stop comparing yourself to them," I demand.

She nods softly, and I continue buckling her shoe at the ankle. "Is this tight enough?"

"Yes. Thank you," she whispers, her voice gravelly.

I brush my thumb over her ankle tattoo as I finish with the second clasp. Then I stand and pull her up to meet me.

"Loren?"

"Hmm?"

"Promise me you'll be yourself tonight? I don't want you to feel pressured to act a certain way or think you need to fit in with these people. If I'm being completely honest, I've never fit in with most of them either. It's why I selfishly asked you to come with me, because I knew it'd be the only way I'd enjoy myself."

She stares at me intently. "You're really taking the weird girl to the prom, then?"

"Yes. Because I really, really like weird." I grin and hold out my elbow, and she smiles back as she laces her arm through.

We venture downstairs to the ballroom, which has just started to fill up, and Loren and I pose for a few photos in front of a heavily decorated backdrop. Then I take her over to the table reserved for my law office and introduce her to my partners and their wives.

"This is my girlfriend, Loren," I declare proudly, watching for her reaction. She seems pretty collected as she shakes hands with each of them, immediately making everyone laugh with her witty comebacks to their teasing.

"I would have worn higher heels, but Blake's ego is a little too fragile for that," she replies smoothly when Mr. Mark makes a short joke that sends a jolt of anger through me at first.

I stifle a smile and pull out her chair. "Not to mention, the view's better from up here," I mutter over her shoulder when I slide her chair forward, and she turns to glare at me.

"The famous Ms. Reed, finally," I hear Jada calling out as she approaches. She glances at me knowingly when Loren stands, probably looking for evidence of a baby bump since I finally told her about the twins this week. She'd squealed so loudly that I had to ask her to pipe down before the others came in to check on her.

Jada wraps Loren up in a hug and winks at me over her shoulder while Aaron shakes hands with the men at the table.

"I can't wait to pick your brain all night," Loren returns once they're all seated.

Jada laughs. "And I can't wait to hear your stories of Blake as a kid, since I'm told you two have an interesting history."

It only takes a couple of minutes before they've turned to face one another in their chairs, and I'm entirely too pleased with their budding friendship, even if it's based on their common critiques of me. Aaron gets my attention and gestures toward the bar, and we leave them at the table to get a round of drinks.

"So, the girl from the restaurant, huh?" Aaron asks as he takes a sip. I'm surprised he remembers, since he's not a Camellia native.

I shrug and try to hide the silly grin I'm sporting.

He clears his throat. "Jada told me the news. Congratulations," he offers.

And now it's impossible not to beam at him. "Thanks, man."

"I see why your panties were in such a twist that night."

"Yeah," I say on an exhale.

He chuckles and slaps me on the back fondly. "Here lies ole Blake the Snake."

I shake my head and laugh along with him, though I don't tell him how much I actually like the way that sounds. My phone chimes in my pocket as we begin walking back to the table, so I pull it out for a quick check.

JD

screenshot of Instagram post

That's a good-looking couple.

How's it going so far?

Funny my brother should ask right now, especially since I'm thinking I might need his help for once.

BLAKE

Great. Our hotel room is amazing. There's only one bed.

Loren looks beautiful and sexy af, and she's already got everyone at the law office eating out of the palm of her hand.

The only problem is that my super-hot date doesn't want me to put the moves on her, even though she's already having my babies.

And I'm so into her that the moves are just kind of putting themselves on now.

ETHAN R

somebody get a drink for asst coach thirsty over there

My heart hits the floor, and I curse under my breath. I hadn't realized JD's original message was in our family text group.

"You all right, man?" Aaron asks.

"Uh, yeah, fine," I tell him, my voice cracking as more messages pop up.

"I'll meet you back at the table, then," he says with an amused expression before he leaves me to continue reading.

> TENLEY B
>
> Need me to do some recon with your super-hot date?
>
> ETHAN R
>
> have you tried the stalker stare?
>
> it worked for jd
>
> JD
>
> Damn right it worked.
>
> But I have other moves, tyvm.
>
> ETHAN R
>
> hold up
>
> ms reed's pregnant??

Uh-oh.

Well, the kid was going to find out eventually. And at this point, I'm not above any opportunity to brag about one-upping JD by making two babies at a time.

> BLAKE
>
> You caught that, huh?
>
> ETHAN R
>
> are you guys seriously having a baby together?
>
> also why did you say babies?
>
> like there's more than one?

BLAKE

Uh … JD? Tenley? You guys wanna take this one?

TENLEY B

Well, you see, kid, when a man and a woman are in love …

JD

Remember when I told you that it only takes one time?

ETHAN R

* ethan has left the chat *

JD

What are you even doing in the grown folks' business anyway?

ETHAN R

uhhh you're the boomer who rolled up in the group text bruh

so is anyone going to answer the multiple babies question?

BLAKE

The thing is, Big E, some of us make one baby at a time, and some of us are given special abilities … talents, if you will.

JD

TENLEY B

Mais la. That's not exactly how identical twins work.

And this information better not end up in the class Snapchat group, got it, E?

ETHAN R

* ethan has left the chat *

I snort down at my phone and start walking back to the table before noticing a second thread from JD.

JD

My bad, dude.

I'll spare you further embarrassment and let you beg for my help in this convo instead.

BLAKE

I never said I needed your help.

But I think I might be in deep-deep like with Loren.

JD

I think that's exactly what you're saying. And also,

gif of little girl squealing excitedly

I glance up as I reach the table and see Loren laughing with Jada, and my stomach flips. Then she looks my way and smiles coyly, and it takes me a few deep breaths to settle the attraction ramping up within me.

BLAKE

I've never had this problem before. I don't know if I've ever really been rejected by a woman or felt drawn to anyone like this.

JD

Which part?

BLAKE

What kind of question is that? I like all her parts.

She does have a nice ass, though.

Wait, no, it's her hair. I really love the way her hair smells.

JD

I meant which part of that is a problem for you—
striking out or wanting her so badly?

But LOL, man. This is so very refreshing and
entertaining.

In fact, I hate to ruin the moment …

BLAKE

Then don't.

JD

"The day when I need your help to get a woman
will NEVER come."

BLAKE

Whatever, Coach Thirsty. 🙄

I'm growling under my breath when I feel a hand slide over my shoulder. "Hey, there, Mr. Bourgeois," a sultry voice purrs, way too close to my ear for comfort.

I step aside, trying to put some space between myself and my guest. "Hey, Meghan," I greet the legal secretary currently running her manicured nails down my forearm.

"How's your night panning out?"

"Pretty good," I return, forcing a smile. "But that's probably because I brought my beautiful girlfriend, Loren. Have you had the chance to meet her?"

She straightens and blinks away her surprise. After all, I hadn't turned down her last offer. "Girlfriend?"

"Yeah, the sexy brunette in the green dress over there." My smile becomes more genuine as I gesture in Loren's direction. Then I hold up my phone when it buzzes again. "Sorry, I've gotta take this. But it was nice seeing you."

I leave her with her jaw hanging and shuffle off to find a corner to continue texting my brother.

JD

gif of cartoon wolf with heart eyes

gif of man chugging water

BLAKE

Are you done?

JD

Touchy, are we? Must be the lack of …

BLAKE

Very funny. But it's not even about that.

Okay, it's always about that, but it's not *just* about that. Not this time. I don't want her to think I'm only trying to get her back in bed, but I also don't want her to second guess my attraction, kwim?

JD

Absolutely.

BLAKE

Okay, so how do I make her feel respected and desired at the same time?

JD

You're not gonna like this. But …

KEEP IT IN YOUR PANTS, KID.

BLAKE

* blake has left the chat *

JD

Seriously, man. You just have to articulate your feelings, let her know you're interested in other ways, flirt without going overboard, recognize when she wants you to make a move and when she needs space.

BLAKE

That easy, huh?

JD

If things are so different with Lo, then you need a different approach. Instead of relying on your abs, play up the strengths that she values the most, focus on what you have in common.

BLAKE

You did hear me say that sex is off the table, right?

JD

I know you're baiting me rn. But I'll go ahead and humor you by stating that you have more to offer a woman than sex.

BLAKE

Of course I do.

But for argument's sake, if someone else were asking, what would you say I have to offer?

JD

You're sarcastic—I mean, funny and intelligent. You're loyal. And anyone willing to look past the cocky persona knows you're actually humble and selfless.

BLAKE

I guess I'm smart. And I'm good with people, most of the time. I pay attention to what they say and try to show them I care by remembering stuff about them, which I suppose is what makes me good at my job.

JD

It makes you a great coach, too. Which means you're going to be an awesome father, by the way.

And you've always been able to make women feel good about themselves. Why is it so much harder with Lo?

BLAKE

If I knew, don't you think I'd be too busy unzipping her dress to text you rn?

JD

Okay, see, let's start there. I know you're joking, but have some respect. Her sexuality is something to be treasured and protected.

BLAKE

Says the guy who undressed a stranger with his eyes for three months straight …

JD

I did not.

I was only appreciating her figure and considering which qualities made her fit for procreative purposes.

But she is pretty hot, isn't she?

DON'T ANSWER THAT.

BLAKE

Why does every conversation come back to your wife's boobs? And what happened to respecting her dignity?

JD

You can be complimentary without being crude. It's all about intention.

And I've given you a solid game plan:

1. Keep your arms, hands, and tongue to yourself at all times. (Basically, all appendages.)

2. Figure out how she wants you to show interest and affection.

3. Be yourself. Lean on your best qualities.

(I think Lo likes your intelligence most, btw. She probably appreciates that you're sharp enough to keep up with her, because I don't know anyone else who is.)

4. Treat her sexuality as a gift, preferably one that isn't meant to be (re)opened until the right time.

5. And if all that fails, take off your shirt and flirt with her best friend in front of her.

Wait, hold on ... that last one's not going to work so well.

BLAKE

Yeah, yeah. I've got it, thanks.

JD

Good luck, bro. Keep me posted.

I sigh and put my phone away again, ambling back to our table, only to find Loren missing.

"You snooze, you lose, Blake," Mark tells me, gesturing to the dance floor, where Loren is waltzing around with old Mr. Donald. Her eyes meet mine, and she wiggles her eyebrows, making me laugh. Then I march over to cut in.

CHAPTER 20

Loren

I bite my lip nervously and watch as Blake and a strange woman walk out to the dance floor together. She adjusts her sash and tiara before sliding her arms over Blake's shoulders, and I feel my nostrils flaring.

Blake reaches up to clasp one of her hands in his, putting some distance between them and making me smile. He'd done the opposite each time we danced together tonight. In fact, he'd just gotten done guiding my arms so that my wrists crossed behind his neck and resting his own hands much lower on my back than proper when the emcee interrupted us by calling out his name.

Despite being crowned King of the Krewe des Pas Bon Mardi Gras Ball tonight, he'd kept to his word, giving me his full attention any time he wasn't busy being politely charming. And although I certainly wasn't shocked he was voted prom king again, I was a little floored by the extensive list of accolades and community service activities that accompanied the announcement. It sounds like most of his good deeds stem from his pro-bono work with kids and the various fundraisers he coordinates alongside his brother as assistant football coach at Camellia High, a job I hadn't realized he's been doing on a purely voluntary basis for the past few years. Not that I imagine it pays much, anyway.

To say this man continues to surprise me would be an understatement.

I watch Blake and his queen as they spin and sway around the dance floor, doing my best to keep my jealousy in check. But then she steps closer, and their movements slow as she leans in to whisper something near his ear, lingering and resting her cheek against his before she backs away.

He presses his lips together in a tight smile, his eyes darting over to mine as he says something to her, and she nods in response. The song continues even though he drops his hands and steps back, and there's an awkward pause before the emcee gets the hint and calls for one more round of applause. Blake waves shyly and stuffs his hands in his pockets before he ambles over to meet me at the table.

His friends offer their congratulations, but he ignores them as he plops down in a chair and looks up at me, as if he's awaiting my approval. He snakes an arm around my waist and pulls me into his lap.

I can feel their eyes on us, but with him staring at me like this, it's hard to think of anything else. He leans up at the same time his hand slides over my lower back, and his fingers press into my bare skin, urging me forward.

I know what he wants.

"Congratulations, your grace," I say, adjusting his crown as his gaze lands on my mouth. He doesn't reply, but I see his throat working as he swallows hard. Even the air between us is pulling me in.

I bring my lips to his cheek, intending to reinforce our fake relationship with a chaste kiss for the audience. But I accidentally linger after I realize how good his skin feels and how delicious he smells from here. It takes all I have not to move down to his neck.

He lets out a contented hum as my cheek brushes his, his fingertips digging into my back while his other hand fists the skirt of my dress. "Don't stop," he whispers, just low enough so that I'm the only one who can hear him, and I shiver.

Then he turns his face and presses his lips to mine, and we both settle into the kiss as if it's a relief to get to this point. He doesn't push me, only waits patiently for me to decide how far I want this to go.

The problem is I could do this all night.

I bring my hand up to his jaw as I tilt my head and slip my tongue inside his mouth, and he groans. And, oh man, does it take all of my willpower not to wrap my arms around his neck and ask him to take me upstairs to finish this off.

But we can't. Because that's not how it's going to go for Blake and me.

In the meantime, his velvet tongue brushes over mine, and I nearly moan in front of all these people.

I can vaguely hear the sound of a throat clearing at the same time Blake reluctantly pulls away. But his eyes are trained on mine as we part.

"Yes, congrats, Blake," Jada says in an amused tone.

"Thanks," he returns without looking away.

I bite my lip as I attempt to slow my breathing. But the way Blake is staring at me as if I'm the only woman in the world isn't helping.

"Dance with me one more time?" he asks. And I nod, because it's the only thing I can manage.

I shift in his lap, preparing myself to stand, and a growl rumbles in his chest. He smirks at me, and his eyebrows twitch in a silent message.

Do you see what you do to me?

I'm still in awe of my ability to turn him on. Me? Plain, old Loren? He really wants *me*?

He leads me forward, bringing my hand up to his mouth for a kiss as we approach the dance floor. Then his eyes lock onto mine again as he leans down and wraps his arms around me, and I clasp my hands behind his neck, the way we fit together seeming so natural.

"Gah, Lo," he says after a while, shaking his head softly. "I'm afraid I've made a huge mistake."

"What do you mean?"

He furrows his brow. "I shouldn't have taken you here with me tonight."

I frown as my stomach dips. "Oh."

"I'm never going to survive this," he adds, shaking his head again. "I'm trying so hard to control myself, to remember that this isn't supposed to be real, but you just ..." He squeezes his eyes closed. "You undo me, Loren."

I undo *him*?

He's got to be freaking kidding me right now.

I exhale, trying to collect my bearings. I'm sure it's another one of his lines. This is Blake Bourgeois, after all.

"I know you don't want to hear this kind of stuff from me, but I'm so bad at pretending I don't want you," he continues, making my belly swoop again.

"Don't worry, Gus Gus," I say softly. "I'm still planning on turning back into a pumpkin at midnight."

"I love pumpkins," he replies smoothly. "Especially the spicy ones."

I roll my eyes. "You're pushing your luck again."

"I'm sorry. I can't help myself," he mumbles, pulling me in closer so I can rest my cheek against his chest as he rocks us gently. His thumb sweeps across my lower back, sending another round of chills through my body.

"You're not thinking about violating the rules, are you?"

"*Violate* is a strong word, Agnes. I'm a man of the law." Then he leans down, his lips brushing my ear as he adds, "Although, I'm not opposed to bending the rules in certain situations." And I temporarily lose feeling in my legs when his teeth graze my earlobe.

"Whoa, you okay?" he asks, holding me up when my knees buckle.

I clear my throat, feeling my face flush. "Um, yeah, I'm fine. Just tired."

His hands rest on my hips while he steps back to examine me. "Are you ready to go upstairs?"

"Well, now that you mention it ..." I lift one of my shoulders in a shrug, unsure of whether I want him to think I'm flirting or not. "But

I can go up on my own, you know, if you want to grace your subjects with your presence for a while longer."

He glares at me strangely. "Loren, all you have to do is say the word, and I'm happy to take you to bed."

I nearly choke on my spit. I'm in way over my head, and I can't tell if he realizes how suggestive he sounds. Then I see the slightest twitch in his lips. I sigh and slap him playfully in the chest, and his face breaks into a grin so wide that his eyes crinkle on the sides. And I'm half-tempted to take him up on that offer.

"I just need to stop by the restroom, and I'll meet you back at the table. That'll give you a few minutes to say good night to your friends," I tell him before I even notice what I'm doing.

Am I really doing this? Do I actually want to break the rules with Blake?

His eyes darken as he leans in and lifts my chin for a short kiss. "I'll walk you to the ladies' room. But after that, I'm carrying you upstairs," he says, his eyes glued to my mouth.

That fifty percent may have just shot up to a solid seventy-five.

"I don't know if I can manage a piggy-back ride in this dress," I retort, but the trembling in my voice threatens to betray me.

He shrugs and smirks before he turns and leads me on with a hand on my lower back. "We'll just have to lose the dress then, won't we?"

I nudge him with my elbow, and I hear him snickering quietly as I dart into the restroom.

I blow out a loud exhale and find the cleanest stall at the end. I shut the door behind me and press my hands to my cheeks to cool myself off before I pull my phone out to text Tenley.

LOREN

Halp. Please.

Then I slip it into my purse to attend to my business, but it begins ringing a second later.

"Hello?" I answer quietly.

"Hey, what's wrong? Are you okay?" Tenley asks in a panic-stricken voice.

"Oh no, everything's fine. Sorry to worry you," I say, balancing the phone on my shoulder as I adjust my skirt. "I just need you to talk me out of jumping Blake's bones again."

She snorts on the other end of the line. "And how the heck am I supposed to do that?"

"I don't know, remind me of some of the stuff I told you when you were ovulating and stuck in a hotel room with JD."

"Right. So, um, if you want to build a lasting relationship with the guy who's already gotten you pregnant, then you should totally not have sex with him tonight."

"That's not as convincing as I'd hoped."

"To be honest, Lo, I'm gonna need a little more context before I know where to begin my chastity sermon."

"A sermon—yes, that's what I need. Or just talk to me like I'm one of your patients. Technically, I am, right?"

"Loren, what's going on?"

I cringe. "Blake and I are only faking it. We haven't actually been dating. It's just a cover-up to make the pregnancy seem less scandalous."

She's quiet for a second. "But I thought you said you really liked him?"

"I do. That's the problem. And even though I banned him from initiating any funny business when we made this agreement, he didn't see fit to apply those rules to me."

"Ah, I see. You're afraid you're about to take advantage of that loophole?"

"Yes. He's so sexy that he literally made me weak in the knees just now. I mean, how am I supposed to combat that?"

She chuckles. "Sorry, my friend. I wish I could tell you he's only after one thing, but I honestly think he's just that into you."

I whine.

"I don't get it, though," she continues. "You like him, he likes you, so why aren't you together for real?"

I open my mouth to answer, but the words get caught. "It's a long story," I spit out. "I'll fill you in later."

"Fine. Then all I can say is that sleeping together before obviously left you both in a weird place. And, the whole miraculous conception aside, if you think you're confused about your feelings now, just remember that acting on your attraction could change everything—again."

"Yes. You're right. Now give me the sermon."

She laughs again. "That whole thing about sex being intended for marriage—huge fan. Ten out of ten, highly recommend."

"Okay. Thanks for that."

"Sure, but I think you already know what you should and shouldn't do, right? You wouldn't have called me to talk you off a ledge if you didn't."

Then I hear the outer door swinging open, followed by drunken laughter.

"Um, gotta go, but thanks again. Love you, bye," I whisper over the sound of feet shuffling into the bathroom.

"I can't believe you propositioned Blake Bourgeois and got turned down." My ears perk up. "What exactly did you say?"

The second voice groans. "Some crap about it being fate that we were crowned together and that we should meet up in my hotel room to celebrate."

I lean forward, peeking at the group of three women primping in front of the mirror. "At least he let me down gently," continues the queen of the ball, readjusting her sash. "He told me he was flattered but only interested in spending the night with one woman."

"That girl he brought as his date?" the third chimes in, wrinkling her nose in distaste.

"He actually called her his girlfriend, so things must be pretty serious. I heard she's a teacher at the same high school where he coaches," the queen says sarcastically as she wipes mascara from beneath her eyes.

"Are you sure he didn't just say 'she's in school'? She looks more like a student than a teacher," Thing One retorts. And though I'd be lying if I said it didn't bother me at all, it's not the first time I've over-heard a dig about my size or looking young. I'm hopeful it'll start feeling more like a compliment in a few years.

Queenie laughs sardonically. "Judging by the way his eyes never left her, I doubt the hookup would have been worth it, anyway."

The third one scoffs. "I don't get it. The man's hot as hell. He could have any woman he wants, married or not, and he passes on you for, what, that weirdo from *New Girl*?"

I guess that's not the worst roast, either. I *am* basically Jess on a good day. But they're right—there's only so long cute and quirky can hold the attention of a man like him.

"Yeah, I guess she's pretty. But Blake deserves *sexy*, and she's just not—"

The main door creaks open again, and the three musketeers are struck silent. I continue watching through the door jamb as Jada moves to stand beside them, a tube of lipstick in hand. "Congratula-tions, Morgan," she declares after she applies a fresh coat of lipstick, then saves it in a small clutch. "It's very deserving. You look amazing, and I really admire the work you've been doing with the Children's Miracle Network."

"Thanks, Jada," Morgan returns quietly.

Then Jada turns and grins at the three of them. "Some advice, ladies: It's not going to happen. My boy's pretty smitten."

"Who is she, anyway?" Morgan asks, crossing her arms and looking dejected.

"They grew up together," Jada replies.

"It's not like him to date down," the first woman says bitterly. "What, is she a charity case? Is she blackmailing him?"

Jada purses her lips, and I worry for a second that she'll tell them about the babies. "Hmm. Jealousy isn't your color, Bailey. It doesn't look good on you."

She scoffs, but Morgan continues the line of questioning. "Is he just using her to fix his reputation, then? I heard he's trying to get that ADA position. Does he think the rest of us aren't wholesome enough for him?"

"If he's doing anything to clean up his image, it's to win Loren over, not the other way around. And, frankly, I don't think Blake would care much for the way you're talking about his girlfriend. Neither do I, for the record."

Morgan looks away. "Sounds like you like her, Jada."

"I do," Jada says, her eyes darting over to the mirror, and I swear her reflection zeroes in on me. "Because I like seeing Blake happy, and she definitely makes him happy. Besides, I never thought the 'Blake the Snake' persona really suited him. 'Blake the Family Man' seems to be a better fit." She caps it off with a wink directed at my stall, and I bite my lip to keep myself from snorting.

"Enjoy the rest of your night, ladies," Jada offers as she walks out of the bathroom, and the three women finish their mirror-checks in silence before they follow.

I emerge from the stall and stare at my own appearance as I wash my hands, still wondering what Blake might see in me that no one else ever has. I guess I've always thought of myself as generically attractive, but nothing special. The only things my looks have ever earned me are short jokes, anyway. Until the night Blake told me I was beautiful, I don't think I'd ever heard it before. And even if it's true, the fact that the one person who bothered to notice is also a connoisseur of beautiful women confuses me on so many different levels. It certainly doesn't make it any easier to believe he would be interested in me were I not having his babies, especially after hearing the other women confirm my suspicions. They may not know I'm pregnant, but they're not wrong to assume I've got something to hold over his head.

I let out a shaky breath before I venture out to meet Blake at the table. His face lights up the second he sees me, and my stomach does another one of those funny flips.

"There she is," he says aloud, standing and reaching out to pull me in by the waist. "Ready to call it a night?"

I swallow hard as he stares at me, noticing the way Jada's smirking at us in the background. "Only if you are," I reply.

He nods. "Still want a ride?"

I shake my head and press my lips together to stifle a reaction.

Then he bids his colleagues good night, and they all smile and titter as we walk out of the ballroom hand in hand.

He pulls me along, and we end up alone on the elevator. I lean back against the wall across from him, afraid he can hear me struggling to breathe with the air so thick and stifling between us. When I bring my gaze up to his, he's already staring intently at me with his jaw clenched. I watch the muscles in his cheek flexing, the heat becoming unbearable by the time we reach our floor.

The elevator dings as the doors finally open. Then Blake's eyes twinkle mischievously as he lunges forward and scoops me up in his arms, making me giggle while he carries me to the door of our hotel suite. He pretends to object when I snatch the crown from his head and toss it on the desk inside our room. I have to scold myself for wanting to keep my arms around his neck after he sets me back down on my feet.

Blake sticks his hands in his pockets once I let him go. It's his tell-tale nervous tick, I've decided, and seeing him with his confidence lowered only makes him that much more irresistible. So I move to dig in my suitcase, distracting myself by fishing for my pajamas and toiletry bag.

He clears his throat as I stand. "Need any help with your dress? I'm good with zippers, remember?"

Oh, I remember.

"Would you mind?" I ask shyly, turning my back to him. His knuckles brush my neck as he moves my hair to the side, and I feel his warm breath on my shoulder before his lips graze my back. I whisper my thanks in an effort to hide the shiver that goes through me as he slowly drags the zipper down, then I shuffle off to the bathroom, pressing my things to my chest to hold up my top.

I avoid the mirror this time, figuring it's for the best. By the time I return in my modest pajamas, he's still removing the final layers of his tux. I avert my eyes as he steps into a pair of athletic shorts. "Sorry, I stopped to answer a text from my brother," he says quietly. "But I should have changed faster."

"You're fine," I reply, slipping under the covers.

He spends a minute in the bathroom, hesitating at the edge of the large bed when he returns. "I can take the couch if you want."

I roll my eyes and pat the empty space beside me. He smiles softly before he slides in and turns on his side to face me.

"Thank you again for being my date tonight. This was ... the best."

I laugh. "Of course you'd think so. You came away with an actual crown."

"I couldn't care less about that," he tells me, his mouth turning up on one side. "It was all about the company."

"I'm sure it was," I say sarcastically.

"I mean it. I know you didn't enjoy having to be my trophy girlfriend for the night, but you were amazing. Everyone thinks you're beautiful and charming ... and that you're good for me," he explains and scoots closer.

"They do?"

"Yes, they do." He clasps my hand beneath the sheets. "And I wholeheartedly agree. Though I think I'd add 'unbelievably sexy' to the list." Then he brings our hands up to his lips and presses a kiss over my knuckles. He turns my wrist over and kisses me there, too, lingering and staring me down the whole time.

And my ego says, *eat that, mean girls*, because the way he's looking at me right now makes it hard to believe he doesn't mean what he's saying.

However, my heart counters with, *Tenley's right. I can't risk being this vulnerable with him again.*

I try to speak, but the words catch in my throat at first. "Blake, this is getting so confusing for me. I don't ... What are we doing?" I finally get out, my voice barely a whisper at the end.

He blinks and loosens his grip on my hand. "We're sticking to the ground rules," he says after a second, his tone different now. "I'm sorry I keep crossing the line. But I'll be more respectful of your boundaries from now on. I promise." He gives me a sad smile before he rolls over and turns off the lamp on his side, then leans down to kiss the top of my head.

"Good night, Loren."

My face falls, and I'm grateful he can't see my expression in the dark. For the first time, I'm kicking myself for being the kind of girl that makes safe decisions and instills stupid rules, because every bit of me wants everything he has to offer.

"Good night, Blake," I return, not even bothering to hide the disappointment in my voice. I can't help but wonder whether he'd be so respectful of my boundaries if I looked like a Mardi Gras ball queen. Then I turn to face the wall and pray he won't hear me crying myself to sleep.

CHAPTER 21

Blake

THOSE ROSES GET ME EVERY TIME.

I inhale deeply, letting Loren's intoxicating scent fill my lungs. She's still asleep, so I'm getting my stalker-sniffing in while I can.

Goosebumps line my skin as I stare at her. She's so beautiful that it hurts right now. She fidgets a little, making some of her hair fall into her face. I reach over to move it. But it feels so soft between my fingers, like silk, and I can't let it go. Her dark eyelashes curl up from her cheeks, and she purses her lips. All I can think about is how badly I want to kiss her without having to hold back for once.

My date with Loren last night was incredible. She was unbelievably sexy, not to mention altogether charming, witty, and funny. Everyone in my work family had fallen in love with her by the end of the night. She'd made it easy to keep my promise to forget about all the other women in the room, and knowing she's having my babies only made her even more desirable, if that's even possible.

Her eyes finally flutter open, and she smiles and blushes adorably when she notices the way I'm staring at her.

"Morning," she rasps.

"Morning, beautiful," I return, and her cheeks grow red.

"Were you watching me sleep?"

Now I'm blushing. I drop the lock of hair I've been holding. "Maybe."

"Why?"

Because I want you more than I've ever wanted anyone in my entire life.

That's when it hits me—I don't just *want* Loren. She's the *only* woman I want, possibly ever again. Sure, I've probably been thinking it on a subconscious level for a couple of weeks now, but it's the first time I recognize this for what it is. I still don't understand why her touch feels so good, but every other physical encounter before her seems empty and pointless now. I'll never be able to recreate that connection with anyone else. And the mere idea of having her in my arms again is driving me crazy.

"I was sort of cataloging your features, I guess. Trying to imagine what our babies might look like," I lie, reaching over to palm her stomach. Because I'm not allowed to say what I'm really thinking.

She smirks. "I've been trying to picture that, too. We're so different. It ought to be interesting."

"I can't wait," I whisper, to my own surprise.

Her brow goes up sharply. "Yeah, me, too."

My thumb rubs circles over her belly. "Loren," I begin without even knowing what I'm going to say next. "I had an amazing time last night."

"So did I. Thanks again for taking me to your ball, your highness."

I chuckle shortly. "I'd actually forgotten about that part. I meant that I really enjoyed your company."

"Oh," she says softly, her lips forming a perfect oval. "Well, um, ditto."

I let my hand drift over to her side and gently draw her in closer. "I like spending time with you. Maybe more than I've ever liked it with anyone else before."

Whoa.

Where did that come from?

I guess I'm doing that "be yourself" thing now? Or have I just reached a whole new level of awkwardness?

She gulps and blinks a few times. "I suppose that's a good thing, since we're sort of stuck together now."

I nod. "But just as friends and co-parents, right?"

"Right," she says, and her voice is so low that I can tell she doesn't believe it.

"And what if ... what if I proposed an amendment to the ground rules?"

"What kind of amendment?"

It's getting harder to breathe by the second, but I manage to pull her in so that her body is nearly flush with mine. "Maybe we could give this a real try before we resolve to stay friends?"

"Oh," she says again, even more breathless than I am.

I lick my lips, my mouth suddenly feeling unnaturally dry. "I can't help how much I like you, Loren." She shivers when I run my hands down her back. "I don't think you understand how badly I want you," I add, my voice sounding deeper.

"I see." Her eyes are wide, and she's almost panting, but she still seems hesitant.

"I know relationships haven't been my thing in the past, but I could be different for you. I ... I want to be different when I'm with you."

I have no idea who's talking for me anymore. But I'll let this guy have free rein if it gets me a shot.

"Oh," she repeats a third time, and her chest is heaving now. It also looks like she might cry.

And, yep—there she goes.

"Hey, are you okay? Did I say something wrong?"

She cringes and stiffens in my arms. "I'm sorry. I can't do this, Blake. We aren't built the same."

"What do you mean?" I ask as I bring my hands up to swipe the moisture from her face.

"I know you're not used to going this long without connecting *physically* with someone. And it's not that I'm not attracted to you. I mean, I wish I weren't, if I'm being honest. This would all be so much easier," she rambles.

I frown. "Slow down. I don't understand what you're talking about."

She sniffles. "You … you said you *want* me," she replies, barely audible. "But I made those rules for a reason. I can't just give that part of myself away again. I don't think I'll be able to bounce back this time, and the last thing we need is to build resentment between us."

I nod softly, but my chest feels like it's just been hit with a sledge-hammer. "You think I only want sex from you."

"Maybe you think you want more now, but the novelty will eventually wear off, and you'll get bored with me and the whole relationship thing. And I can't afford the risk, especially not in my condition."

There it is. I was right before. She doesn't trust me. She has no good reason to believe I'm capable of doing this, after all. And although I hadn't even planned to make my move until I started this conversation, I think I might be kind of … devastated.

I roll onto my back and stare up at the ceiling. "I understand," I mumble after a while. "I guess I forgot for a second that I'm not built for anything real. But thanks for reminding me."

"Blake, that's not what I meant," she says, her voice cracking.

I huff. "Sure it isn't."

"I'm sorry," she whispers after a while, reaching over to place a comforting hand on my chest. I want to push it away, mostly because even the slightest touch from her is making my insides melt, but I can't.

"This has a lot less to do with you and your dating history than it does with my shitty self-esteem and trust issues," she continues.

"It's fine," I reply dryly, slipping out from beneath her hand and leaving her alone in the bed. "It's about time for us to break up, anyway, isn't it?"

"Break up?" She has the nerve to look hurt.

"We agreed to a few dates. This was our third public outing. I think it's safe to say we convinced everyone we're sleeping together, especially after last night. Hopefully they'll assume the babies are early or just not bother to do the math, right?" I explain as I sift through my suitcase for my clothes.

"You don't want to pretend we're dating anymore?" she asks quietly, sitting up in bed.

I shrug. "It's probably best if we end it now, don't you think? Especially if you want to keep our relationship completely platonic. Things have obviously started getting hazy on my end, and I wouldn't want to do or say anything else that might compromise our friendship."

"Right," she agrees, nodding quickly. But I can see she doesn't like being on the receiving end of my rejection. "Shouldn't we just ease into it, though? I'd rather not stage a fight or come off too over-dramatic."

"Yeah, of course. We'll stick to the original plan and tell everyone we're better off as friends. You could even say it was your decision, if you'd like to keep our story closer to the truth."

She bites her lip as she stares back at me with those big, brown eyes and her chin trembling.

"Don't look so upset, Reed. This is what you wanted. And you'll be safe now, since you'll only have to interact with me as a co-parent from here on out." I flash her a scornful smile before escaping to the bathroom to get dressed.

I try not to think as I change my clothes and brush my teeth. She's perched at the edge of the bed when I return, her eyes red-rimmed as if she's been crying again.

"Bathroom's all yours," I announce. She stomps out and closes the door behind her without another word.

I finish packing and consider going downstairs for a cup of coffee, but I don't think I could stop myself from getting one for her, too. Even though my chest still stings from earlier.

I'm pathetic.

I'm sitting here, pining over a woman who doesn't want me, just like my brother. No, scratch that—I might be worse than JD. I'm infatuated with a woman who doesn't even think I'm capable of a real relationship. And I'm pissed at myself because I called her bluff, and she still won't cave.

But I can't dive into all that right now, not when I still have to endure the ride home with her. I settle for mindlessly scrolling on my phone until Loren's done. She emerges about twenty minutes later and begins gathering her things, which she's somehow managed to spread over the entire room in less than twenty-four hours. It takes all I have to stay angry and not smirk at her because it's so freaking cute when she tosses everything into a messy pile and has to sit on top of her suitcase to zip it. I instinctively reach for her bag once she's done, but she shoots me an angry glare.

"I've got it, thanks," she murmurs.

I cock an eyebrow at her and gesture for her to go first, stifling my laughter when she struggles to open the door and get past the threshold with all of her stuff. I consider taking the stairs for a second, because I enjoy antagonizing her almost as much as I do making her feel good. But I don't want to give her the chance to overexert herself.

I exhale loudly as I press the "down" button, annoyed at myself for being such a simp and at her for being so stubborn. She glances up at me questioningly, just as the elevator doors open to reveal the assistant district attorney and his wife.

They offer a friendly greeting as they make room for us. This time I don't give Loren the chance to object when I snatch her suitcase and wheel it in behind her. She scowls at me again, and I tip my head toward the others, hopefully signaling that I need her to play along for one final act.

"Sleep well, lovebirds?" Mrs. Moreau asks, batting her eyelashes suggestively.

Loren bites her lip and blushes as she looks up at me. I clear my throat before letting go of her suitcase to wrap an arm around her waist. "I always sleep better with Loren beside me."

She swallows hard when I stare her down. "Yeah. Me, too," she says, faintly. Then she catches herself and turns away. "How about you? I seem to remember you saying you were getting up early for Mass this morning, Mrs. Moreau. I suppose your plans changed?"

Loren's expression shifts into one of admiration as the older couple chuckles and looks lovingly at one another.

"Oh, well, you know," Mr. Moreau says. "We may have stayed up a tad too late last night. We had to make a little *paresseux* this morning."

"Hmm, I wonder how many other couples used that excuse? Maybe we'll see a few Mardi Gras ball babies in about nine months," Loren returns, her eyes twinkling.

They laugh again as the elevator stops, charmed again, of course. Then they both stop to hug Loren as they say goodbye, and Mr. Moreau holds out his hand in front of me, despite the way he usually ignores me altogether.

"It was a pleasure, Blake. You know, I've been looking for someone like you to endorse as my successor. We should schedule a tee time at the country club to talk it over once it warms up outside. I'm sure our lovely ladies would enjoy getting together for brunch and mimosas at the clubhouse while you and I play a round of golf."

"Yes, sir," I reply, not even a little bitter about Loren winning over the Moreaus within a couple of hours when I never could. "Sounds like a date."

"Oh, and I'll be expecting a wedding invitation in the mail soon," Mrs. Moreau adds with a wink.

I force one of my trademark fake grins before placing my hand on Loren's back. "If I'm a smart man, you'll get one."

Loren squirms uncomfortably beside me as we wave goodbye again.

A few more of my acquaintances stop to greet us as I check out of the hotel before we finally make it to my truck. The valet offers to load our bags, but I tell him I can manage since there are so many others waiting behind us. By the time I turn back from handing him a tip, Loren's adjusting the handle on her suitcase as if she's preparing to lift it herself.

"What the hell do you think you're doing?" I ask.

"Taking care of myself," she replies without missing a beat.

"It would be nice if you started doing a better job of that, you know, since you're carrying two babies." I rip the luggage from her hands and heave it into my truck.

She rocks back on her heels and lifts her chin defiantly. "I've been perfectly fine without you for the last thirty years, and I'm sure I can manage without your help now, thank you."

Her bottom lip quivers as she crosses her arms over her chest and stares me down. Then she lunges forward and reaches into the back seat for her suitcase, but I grab her shoulder and flip her around to face me.

"Listen here, Reed," I begin, smiling at her. "Like it or not, I care about your well-being more than I care about your pride. And I certainly don't have any of that left myself. So if you don't get your adorable, stubborn, pregnant-hangry ass in the truck right now, I'm going to pick *you* up and toss you in, too."

She gapes at me incredulously, her mouth hanging open. "I'm not going anywhere with you," she declares once she catches her bearings. "Give me my things. I'll get an Uber. Or I'll call Tenley or JD to come pick me *uhhp*—DAMMIT, BLAKE! Put me *down*!"

I scoop her up into my arms and round my truck, calmly ignoring her protests as she alternates swatting and clutching at me. I shift her weight to one side and use my free hand to open the passenger door before setting her down gently on the seat, and my smile turns more genuine when she keeps her hand on the back of my neck. Her chest heaves as I lean in to whisper to her.

"You're making a scene, Agnes. And you're the one who didn't want a public breakup. So I recommend you prepare yourself, because I'm going to have to pull another one of those moves you pretend to hate so much when I kiss you so hard that everyone watching from the lobby will assume this fight was just foreplay. Got it?"

Her tongue darts out to lick her lips, and her eyes move down to my mouth. She gives me a short nod, and I close in the space between us in an instant, trying desperately not to devour her the way I really want to. But when *she* slips her tongue into my mouth first and deepens the kiss, I lose control, at least for a while.

Before I know it, my hands are tangled in her silky hair, and her body is turned so that I'm leaning into her while her legs wrap around me. And as hot as this is, and *damn* is it hot, I know I've got to stop now if I ever want her to take me seriously. Even though I'd give my left arm and a good chunk of my 401k to sleep with Loren again, I won't prove her right and allow her to continue believing I only want something physical with her. I don't know if I'll ever understand what it is about her that makes me act this way, but I'd rather leave her with a healthy self-esteem than risk hurting her more, even if it means that she'll never see me as anything more than a friend and co-parent.

Her eyes are still shut and her lips swollen when I pull away, and I take a second to commit this image of her to memory. I rest my forearm against the door frame and clear my throat, and her eyelashes flutter as she awakens from a trance.

"I, uh, I think it worked," I say gruffly. "I'm also pretty sure if we break up any time soon, half of my friends and colleagues will disown me," I add, smirking and tilting my head in the direction of the crowd waiting at the valet podium.

She nods absently, still looking flustered. "Yeah. See, you need me more than I need you, Gus Gus."

I chuckle at her, but I don't deny her claim. Instead, I lean in and kiss her forehead, hoping to convey that I want things to go back to the way they were earlier this morning, before I made it awkward by bringing up my stupid, mostly unrequited feelings. She sighs when I linger for a second, and I reach over her to open the center console and pluck out a bag of Reese's hearts, dropping them in her lap as I back away. Then I shut the door between us and go around to the other side.

She watches me carefully as she unwraps one of the candies and pops the entire heart into her mouth. "This doesn't change anything," she mumbles around a mouthful of peanut butter.

"Course it doesn't," I agree, pulling out of the parking lot and smiling to myself when she hums contentedly.

"Wait, where are we going? Home is that way." She hitches her thumb in the opposite direction.

"I'm going to feed and caffeinate you before I bring you back. I know you better than you think."

She scowls at me while she continues smacking. "Your babies do want coffee. Preferably something with lots of syrupy-sweet, fake flavoring." Then she bites into another heart. "Just don't tell my midwife about that last part."

CHAPTER 22

Loren

"Welcome back, Coach JD," I grumble and open the door to my classroom. The rest of the class is split between amused snickers and annoyed groans.

"Just here for a walk-through, Ms. Reed," he returns with a *canaille* grin.

"Only the third one today," I add under my breath.

"Pretend I'm not even here." He feigns an inspection of the slides on my SmartBoard as he sneaks over to my desk and stuffs one of his huge hands in the box of peanut butter cookies I left hanging around.

I snort as I return to my lesson. JD may be many things, but subtle he is not.

"So, now that we've read a little more, can anyone tell me what's bothering our boy Young Hamlet? Do you think his attitude toward King Claudius and Queen Gertrude is fair?"

My eyes scan the classroom until they land on Ethan, who's leaning back in his seat and wearing a very Hamlet-esque sneer of his own. I haven't called on him in a while, but that's probably because I'm afraid he's going to make some underhanded reference to Blake or the pregnancy. He's just witty enough to pull it off, and from the knowing looks he's been giving me since he heard what's going on, he's dying to say something. And I'd rather have a little more time before I have to start fielding questions from the entire class.

"His mom rushed into marriage, and now his *n'oncle*-daddy is in charge, and you're asking whether Hamlet has the right to be in his feelings?" Ethan mutters, causing the rest of the class to break out into hysterics, myself included.

JD stands there, biting into a cookie and tapping on an iPad as if he's actually conducting a classroom observation, though we both know better.

"I think," I begin, stopping to laugh again and secretly relieved JD's such an easy target. "I think a shot has been fired, Coach."

He furrows his brow and looks around the classroom, noticing his own nephew/foster son in the corner. "Oh, yeah?"

Ethan smirks. "You tell me, King Claudius."

Caidence backhands him softly on the shoulder. "He's not at all a Claudius. If anything, he's a Fortinbras."

"Nice one, Caidence. Anyone want to tell me why that was super insightful? Bonus points if you use the right literary terms."

"Because Fortinbras is a foil," Ethan answers, still staring JD down. "He's the good prince. He's a better leader than Claudius, and he's not as emo as Hamlet. He's basically there to make the other guys look mid in comparison."

I watch as JD's jaw flexes. The rest of the class must be at the edge of their seats as well.

"But then again, I'd say Coach is probably more of a Polonius," Ethan continues. "He talks a big game, but at the end of the day, he doesn't scare anyone."

His friends chuckle again, and this time, JD smiles along with them. "You're lucky I haven't read *Hamlet* since I was in high school, kid."

I clear my throat. "You guys don't wanna know what Hamlet does to Polonius later," I mumble to myself, just before the bell rings. The students shove their books into their bags and file out, and JD makes sure to stick out his foot to trip Ethan as he passes. Ethan stumbles, and they trade amused looks before Ethan manages to escape unharmed.

"Well, this is awkward," JD begins once we're alone, suppressing a grin. I should have known he'd be dying to discuss the whole pregnancy thing.

"Um, yeah, because *you're* making it awkward," I retort as I busy myself with straightening a stack of books.

"Ah, no, I think *you* made things awkward when you let my brother impregnate you with twins. Yeah, pretty sure that was the turning point."

My lip twitches as I try not to smile. "You're right. It was a very climactic night."

He wags a finger at me. "Ooh, I'm telling him you said that."

"Great." I roll my eyes. "As if he's not cocky enough as it is."

"I thought you liked that crap, though," he replies, regarding me suspiciously.

"I do," I say too quickly. "But you know Blake. Sometimes he takes it too far."

"Loren, if he—"

"Don't worry," I assure him. "He's actually been really, really great, especially about the baby stuff. And after all those years of hostility, I suppose he's earned the right to tease me when I show him any kind of affection."

"You guys *have* been looking pretty cozy."

"We are. Maybe I'm just a bit more guarded than Blake."

JD attempts to sit in one of the student desks, and it's hard not to laugh when he sings "Fat Guy in a Little Coat" as he contorts his body to fit. "Seriously, though. You're having *two* babies together. That's a pretty big freaking deal. Are you sure you're okay with that?"

I exhale as I take a seat behind my desk. "Yeah. I mean, the timing isn't ideal, but it's not like we can undo what we've done, right?"

"Not the way you've done it, apparently," he offers with a cocked eyebrow. "But you didn't answer my question, Lo."

I look down at my hands as I formulate a response. "I obviously never imagined myself in this predicament, much less with Blake. But, now that it's actually happening, I can't say that I have any regrets, and I doubt I could've found a better partner. He's going to be an amazing dad."

He smiles softly. "I know he will. But is that all that matters to you?"

I shrug. It's so hard lying to JD like this, and the last thing I want is to paint Blake in a negative light or to give anyone an excuse to misjudge him. That happens enough without my help. But I can't go around gushing about him, either, not if I want our forthcoming amicable breakup to look natural.

"I guess the romantic element of our relationship doesn't seem as important as the co-parenting part now. I wouldn't be a good mother if I weren't willing to put my own feelings aside and make decisions based on everyone's best interest in the long run."

"And you don't think raising your kids in a loving, two-parent household is in their best interest?" he asks, narrowing his eyes at me.

"I do, but there's a lot more at stake now. And I won't risk subjecting them to the same shitty situation I grew up in," I reply defensively.

"Right," he says, nodding. "So what happens if it doesn't work out between you and Blake?"

"We'll go back to being friends while we co-parent," I answer cheerfully.

But he's not buying it. "Yeah. Okay, then."

"What?"

"You'll be best buddies, just like before, and neither of you will have any hard feelings?"

"I don't see why not," I lie.

The bell rings again, and JD pins me with a rueful smile as he unfolds himself from the desk. "As long as you're absolutely sure you're not using your 'predicament' as an excuse to lead my brother on and break his heart or anything like that."

I furrow my brow as he walks over to pick up his iPad, and I slap the back of his hand when he attempts to sneak another cookie off my desk.

"Get your own damned cookies, Coach Thirsty," I tell him with a scowl. Then I reach down to pluck one from the box for myself.

"Better get on those maternity-leave lesson plans, Ms. Reed," he mocks me.

I pull a face at the back of his head as he waltzes out of my classroom, then I grab an Uncrustables sandwich from my mini-fridge. I only have a few minutes left before lunch duty begins, thanks to my boss. And I'm not going to spend it thinking about his totally unfair and false accusations.

I pick up my phone with the intention of scrolling through my Bookstagram feed when a message pops up.

LANDO

LOREN AGNES REED

WTH IS THIS?

I bite my lip and whine as I stare down at a screenshot of Blake's latest Instagram post. He's tagged me in the photos from the Mardi Gras ball last weekend.

Well, well, well. If it isn't the bridge I said I'd cross when I got there.

I know I'll eventually have to put on my big girl panties and break the news to my family that I'm not only dating but also carrying the twins of my former archenemy. It's really the part about my brother subsequently ruining whatever it is that Blake and I have going for us that I've been dreading the most. Yes, we may be settling for friendly co-parents with benefits—and by benefits, I mean mostly PDA-appropriate kisses, suggestive flirty banter, and fully clothed snuggles —but it's working, despite what JD implied earlier. And Landry has this way of wrecking every relationship I've ever been in, friendships included.

As kids, he'd issued an open threat to castrate any boy in the Camellia city limits who tried to come anywhere near me. (Ironically enough, Blake had been the only boy not to heed that warning, but that's something to unpack on a different day.)

Then there was the time he stole Tenley from me in middle

school. I was able to win her back with the help of Ethan and JD, but still.

Even though we'd gone to different colleges, Landry continued to scare off every boyfriend I brought home or talked me into dumping them over some silly beige flags. And by "scare off," I don't mean he used his intimidation techniques the way he did in junior high. Over the years, his methods have evolved to include bringing up embarrassing moments from the past, acting totally gross and weird over dinner, asking inappropriate questions about my sex life, and even coming on too strong to his "new best bro."

I can't allow him to sabotage things with Blake, not when we have a lifetime of raising our twins together on the line.

Still, there's no hiding the truth at this point—or most of the truth, anyway. My condition is only going to get more obvious, especially since there are two goldfish in this tiny tank, and Blake and I have been diligently laying the groundwork for our fake romance.

I look down at the picture again. I can't help but snicker to myself when I imagine my brother's face as he scrolled through his feed and unsuspectingly stumbled upon the visual evidence of Blake Bourgeois getting awfully cozy with his baby sister. Especially since Blake's hand is basically resting on my butt. I snort when Landry's next text pops up.

LANDO

I DEMAND AN EXPLANATION.

LILLEY

Whoa, hello, handsome! 👀

And you look amazing, Lo! 🔥

Calm your tits, Lando. Baby sis doesn't owe you anything.

LANDO

She does when she's posing with this dirtbag.

I smile, grateful to my sister for softening the blow. Sadly, I sort of wish Blake was here with me for moral support, even for a text convo. But becoming even more codependent on him isn't going to help matters, so I take a deep breath and force myself to move ahead.

LOREN

I went to my first Mardi Gras ball last weekend. And I had a great time, thanks for asking.

LANDO

And you just happened to meet up with this asshat while you were there?

LOREN

I mean, sure, if that's what you'd like to tell yourself.

What's it to you, anyway?

LANDO

You know how much I can't stand the Bougie Bros. They're total douche canoes.

LOREN

Takes one to know one, Dr. Dickhead.

LANDO

Real mature, Loren.

LILLEY

Omg, Lo-Lo, do you have a BOYFRIEND?

LOREN

Okay, you caught me. I've been seeing someone, even though I forgot to ask Landry's permission first. 😌

LANDO

Not just anyone. BLAKE FREAKING BOURGEOIS? Seriously?

LILLEY

Holy cow, you're really dating The Other Bourgeois? I honestly didn't see that one coming, but I am totally HERE. FOR. IT.

I curl my lip up in disgust when my sister's last comment comes through. I know she's just kidding, but I hate the way everyone continues to judge Blake. And as one of his worst critics over the years, I feel obligated to fix that.

LOREN

Surprise!

But he prefers when people address him as "The Hotter Bourgeois," fyi.

LILLEY

heart react

LANDO

You're kidding right?

I went through the trouble of setting you up with a great guy—a doctor—and this is how you repay me?

LOREN

Rowan was nice, but Blake is a catch, too, you know. He's handsome and witty. He graduated at the top of his class in law school. He's financially stable, and he's always volunteering in the community. He's good with kids.

What's not to love?

"Yeah, Lo, what's not to love?" I mumble, mocking myself aloud.

LILLEY

He almost sounds too good to be true. Are you sure he doesn't have any skeletons in the closet? No illegitimate kids of his own?

LOREN

No kids from previous relationships, but he does have a really nice set of abs.

LANDO

You cannot be serious.

LOREN

Actually …

gif of Kip from Napoleon Dynamite saying "I guess you could say things are getting pretty serious"

The best thing about him is that Landry can't scare him off.

LANDO

THE HELL I CAN'T.

LOREN

I think he might be the only person on the planet that's not bothered by you, which makes him even sexier.

LANDO

So you're actually claiming him? This is really a thing?

LOREN

Maybe it is.

Why don't you ask him yourself at dinner this Sunday?

Okay, so maybe that wasn't so smart. I *was* planning on asking Blake to come to dinner with my family this weekend to make "the announcement." However, inciting my brother against him before we even get there wasn't part of the whole scheme.

LANDO

NO. I FORBID IT, DAMMIT.

LILLEY

I sure as hell wouldn't turn down a proposition from Blake Bourgeois.

If I were Loren, I mean, and not an already happily married woman. 😌

LANDO

Do you have any idea where that guy's been?

LOREN

I know the last place he's been, and that's all that matters.

I know it's wrong to imply something this crude, but now I'm pissed. And it's not technically a lie.

LILLEY

gif of "Well that escalated quickly" from Anchorman

I mean, good for you, sis!

LANDO

Idk how you could even trust him.

LOREN

He did punch you in the face in my honor that one time back in 8th grade.

LANDO

"In your honor?" What's that supposed to mean?

LOREN

Remember that time you found us in the pool house at Trent Manuel's party?

LANDO

Yeah, and?

LOREN

We'd been making out. I asked him to lie about it, and when you embarrassed me, he tried to fix things, but you kept making it worse. So he just slugged you instead.

LANDO

Come on, Lo. You can't tell me that forgiving him for a misunderstanding when you were 13 makes him fit for a real relationship.

LOREN

I'm—wait a minute, let me check. Let's see, front facing camera *on*—Oh, yeah. It looks like I'M A GROWN ASS WOMAN, LANDRY. And I'll date whomever I damn well please. And Blake pleases me.

Take that last remark as you will.

See you all on Sunday. I'm bringing the man candy—I mean, dessert.

LILLEY

gif of mic drop

Wait, do I get to have some of that candy with my cake? I am the birthday girl, after all! 😇

LANDO

Looking forward to it.

Then my phone lights up with a new alert, letting me know someone's commented on a photo I was tagged in on Instagram.

@big.doc.lando See you this Sunday, @theblakebourgeois. Can't wait to hear about your weekend with @lolo_reads.

The next comment appears before I can even send another threat to Landry.

@theblakebourgeois @big.doc.lando Awesome. @lolo_reads and I have plenty to share, don't we, babe?

CHAPTER 23

Loren

TWELVE YEARS AGO

I TURN AWAY FROM MY CLASSMATES AS I WRING MY HANDS together nervously. I'm doing my best not to panic, but in just a few minutes I'll be standing on the stage in front of everyone—well, almost everyone—to deliver the valedictory address I've been practicing for weeks.

I hear a throat clearing quietly behind me, and a gentle hand curves around my arm.

"Hey, you okay?" Blake murmurs near my ear, standing a little too close for comfort.

I ignore the impulse to jerk my shoulder away. He's probably just trying to be nice, for once.

There's also the urge to lean into him and let him continue whispering against my neck, but I stifle that one immediately.

"Yeah," I breathe, stepping forward to put some space between us. "I'm fine."

"You don't look fine, Reed," he replies, and I twist around to glare at him. But he's smiling at me in a way that seems less *I hope you fall on your face* and more *I want you to be okay.*

"There's just a lot of people out there," I say, gesturing to the audience, even though the one person I wanted to see the most couldn't bother to make the effort.

He shrugs. "At least they're all here because they're proud of us. There's nothing to be nervous about."

I furrow my brow at him. "What do you mean?"

"Those people showed up to celebrate our achievements. And you've accomplished the most, so that makes you the most important person. When you think about it, they basically came just to hear you speak."

I roll my eyes, trying not to smile. If nothing else, he'll make an amazing lawyer one day. "Your logic may not be as sound as you think."

He grins at me. "Work with me, for once." Then he leans forward again to speak against my ear. "Besides, I heard your speech at practice. It's great. You'll wow everyone with your witty jokes, and they'll think it's adorable when you have to pull out the little step stool you've got hiding behind the podium just to reach the mic."

I shiver against my will. "Adorable? Are you sure that's the right word?" I return, crossing my arms and trying to hide the way my voice is trembling. Hopefully he'll just chalk it up to my public-speaking nerves.

"Positive," he says, still smiling as he holds out a hand. I stare down at it blankly as he continues. "I never congratulated you, Loren. I'm sorry for all the times I let my competitive nature get the best of me, but no one deserves this more than you."

I blink in surprise before I finally slide my palm over his, and he shakes it slowly, gazing at me the whole time and making my insides feel all warm and mushy. He stops moving but holds onto my hand until I tug it away. And my eyes just happen to dart down in time to see the way his fingers curl in and stretch out as he brings his arm down to his side.

Was that ... a freaking Darcy hand-flex?

No, there's no way Blake Bourgeois is in any way affected by me. Right? He was probably just struggling to swallow his pride long enough to congratulate me on beating him out.

"Thanks," I mumble. "Congratulations to you, too. And thanks for being just a little dumber than me."

He chuckles, smiling so widely that it reaches his eyes. "Don't give yourself too much credit. I'm sure it's a result of our genetic makeup. You'll probably live longer, too."

"Right." I smirk back at him. "It was my duty as a female to beat you. After all, we can't have the good people of Camellia lamenting over that Bourgeois kid putting the *dick* in *valedictorian*."

He laughs again. "You should have included that one in your address. I bet it would have brought the house down."

"I suppose there's still time. I'm sure I can come up with an equally clever roast for our historian over there." I lift my chin toward the class president. She's watching us carefully, probably because she's jealous and still delusional in thinking she ever had a chance of passing up both Blake and me.

"Oh, I've got Allison covered," he says conspiratorially. "I left all the good lines out of my speech at rehearsals."

"The good lines?" I ask, my eyebrows shooting up.

"Figured I might as well piss everyone off on my way out, since I'm never coming back here anyway," he replies with a shrug.

"I can't believe you're leaving your loyal following behind just to become a small fish in a big pond," I retort without thinking.

He purses his lips and looks away. "I think you might be confusing me with that other Bourgeois kid. Don't worry—happens all the time."

I lean around him to peer at the front row where our families are seated. Both of his parents are there, as well as his younger brother. Lilley and her new husband sit in the empty chairs beside my dad and Landry.

"You may be The Other Bourgeois, but at least your parents care enough to show up," I mumble.

He glances over to the same spot and sighs. "Damn, Lo. I'm sorry."

"It is what it is, right?" I shrug, my eyes watering against my will.

"Did she ... were you expecting your mom to be here?"

"She called last week and said she was hoping to get out of rehab any day now. She also swore that she wouldn't miss this for the world and claimed that she was so incredibly proud of me," I say sarcastically. "But I guess the chance to watch her baby graduate and deliver the valedictory address wasn't enough of an incentive to complete a twenty-eight-day program in forty days."

Blake shakes his head. Then he surprises me by grabbing my wrist and gently pulling me in so he can wrap his arms around me. I bite my lip, trying my best to hold in a sob, and he presses me tightly against his chest.

"I really am sorry," he says quietly. "You deserve better. You know that, right?"

He backs away after a second, regarding me carefully as I sniffle and wipe the moisture from beneath my eyes.

"Uh, yeah, thanks." Then I reach out to smack his arm lightly. "And thanks for making me cry, you jerk."

He chuckles. "I was hoping we'd get in one last interaction that ended with me making an ass of myself and you in tears, just for old time's sake."

I laugh. "Of course. Classic Blake and Loren, right?"

He continues smiling at me, and my stomach dips in a way that makes me more anxious than before. Then the rest of our class begins shuffling around, and everyone sorts themselves into the right order again. I take my place at the end of the line, and the "Pomp and Circumstance March" plays in the background. I inhale deeply and lift my chin high as I follow Blake down the aisle, gulping when I notice how nice his shoulders look from behind despite the frumpy graduation gown he's wearing.

We take our seats at the edge of the stage, where I tune out most of the first half of the ceremony in lieu of practicing my speech in my mind. But then I realize Blake is speaking, so I give him my attention for a second, only to catch him delivering a line that makes the audience laugh.

"... And sometimes life happens, and our plans change. Maybe we don't accomplish every one of our goals, or maybe the outcome doesn't look exactly the way we think it should, but I believe there's always an opportunity to learn and grow from our experiences. In fact, I wish you were all lucky enough to get repeatedly bested by Loren Reed, since it's always been such an effective reminder to keep my pride in check," he says, beaming. Then he turns and aims that perfect grin at me, and I swallow hard and squirm in my seat. "Thank God she was there, you know, to stop me from putting the *dick* in *valedictorian*."

I press my lips together, stifling a smile of my own. He turns back to the audience, but I'm unable to focus on anything but his useless shoulder muscles for the rest of his speech.

The next thing I know, he's thanking everyone and ignoring the crowd's standing ovation as he struts over to take his seat beside me. Allison rises for my introduction, but she has to wait for the crowd to finish murmuring their approval of Blake's charming, self-deprecating address before she can speak. My eyes dart to him when he leans back in his chair, and he's already staring back at me.

He winks secretively and whispers, "Your turn, Reed. Got 'em all warmed up for you."

And I nod curtly, trying to hide my blush before I amble over to the podium. I hear a few good-natured laughs when I pull out my step stool, and then I begin.

CHAPTER 24

Blake

"Landry knows," Loren blurts out as soon as I open the passenger door. We're parked in the driveway at her dad's house.

My eyebrows shoot up. "He knows you're pregnant?"

"No. He and Lilley just think we're dating ... and sleeping together."

"Oh," I reply. "He didn't give you too much of a hard time, did he?" I can already feel my blood pressure rising.

She shrugs coyly. "He received the news as well as I thought he might, but I probably made it worse by oversharing and cracking a few suggestive jokes. By the way, if Lilley is overly flirty with you, it's probably because I've been talking you up a bit, mostly just to mess with Landry. I hope that doesn't make you feel too uncomfortable."

I shake my head and smile. "Gossip doesn't bother me anymore. And I'm not afraid of Landry Reed, babe."

"Good, because I also implied that I find your propensity to not give a rat's behind about what my brother thinks to be the most attractive of your desirable qualities and the one which ultimately induced me to fall for you." I nearly choke on my spit, but she corrects herself quickly. "I mean, you know, because faux-Lo would totally be into the one guy who would piss off Landry the most, right? And I figured it would make things simpler if I just embraced my alter ego for the duration of this fake relationship, at least when I'm in front of my family."

"Uh, right." I hate the way I've started blushing since this whole thing with Loren began, and I scramble to hide my face. My cheeks feel warm after hearing her talk about falling for me, even though I know she's not serious. I just wish I could say my reaction is purely due to discomfort and not because I liked the way it sounds entirely too much.

"Blake," she calls, bringing me back.

"Yeah?" I hope my face has cleared up by now or that she'll at least assume I'm nervous about telling her family we're having two babies together.

"Thanks for doing this, for being here with me today," she says, her voice low. Then she looks up at me with an expression that has me wanting to pull her in for a hug if not a kiss.

I settle for reaching out to interlace our fingers before I bring her hand up to my lips. "You don't have to thank me. We made these babies together, and I fully intend for us to go through the rest of this together, too."

She nods. "Okay."

I swallow hard and turn away before I say or do something else too mushy.

She knocks when we reach the front door before letting us both in, though it appears that most of her family is outside in the back-yard. We pass through the house, stopping to put her sister's birthday cake down in the kitchen before we meet them on the patio, and we're ambushed by Lilley's two kids first.

I assume her brother has already forewarned her dad about me, because he barely bats an eye when I greet him with a firm handshake. "Coach Reed," I begin. "Thanks for having me over today."

He nods, mumbling something in return. Loren's dad has never been a man of many words, unless he's explaining something on the football field. And even though I'd once considered myself to be one of his favorites, back when he'd given me his attention and made me the starting quarterback as a freshman, his favor was short-lived. I'd been just as easily replaced by a shiny, new toy with the same last name, and after that I was only as good as the passes I completed to JD.

"Blake Bourgeois," Landry drawls, waiting patiently to receive me next. "What a pleasure."

"Ditto, Landry," I retort with only a hint of sarcasm, since I figure he's having the same thoughts about me after I booted him out of that QB1 position in high school. "Or should I say Dr. Reed?" I correct myself as I shake his hand. Still, it takes all I have not to start a thumb war or squeeze harder than necessary.

"Dr. Landry is fine," he replies with a smug grin. "I suppose lawyers don't get a special title, though, do they?"

"No, we don't. Although, we only have to pay back half as much in student loans."

Landry surprises me by laughing, and it almost seems genuine.

"And happy birthday to you, Dr. Lilley," I say, pulling Loren's sister in for a friendly hug. Well, I intended it to be a friendly hug, but I'm pretty sure she's making suggestive faces at Loren over my shoulder while she gropes my back.

"Hmm, you smell delicious," she mumbles when I attempt to extricate myself. "And call me Dr. Colbert."

But she's winking at me and squeezing my bicep when I pull away, so I shoot her the smile I reserve for harmless flirting with older women as I shake hands with her husband, Emmett.

"Mom couldn't make it?" Loren asks behind me, and everyone goes quiet.

"Ah, no. She wasn't feeling well, and when I went to check on her this morning, she had a fever. So I told her it would be better if she stayed behind," Landry explains.

Loren rolls her eyes, and I step in closer to wrap an arm around her waist. "Of course," she mutters. I lean down to press a kiss over her temple, hoping to comfort her a little, and she gives me a sad smile in return.

I help Emmett man the grill while Landry shows his dad how to find a college baseball game on the smart TV. Eventually, one of the kids comes over to help, since the adults can't seem to manage technology as well as the preteens. Loren sits off to the side and chats with her sister, but I notice her glancing my way every so often and looking genuinely pleased. It makes me feel warm and fuzzy inside each time she does it.

Then it hits me—this is the first time I've done this. I've never been the type of guy that gets invited to Sunday dinner with the family. I've been the blind-date guy, the wedding-date guy, and especially the party-date guy. But I don't remember ever having been the family-dinner guy. Some of these moments with Loren are turning out to be much more significant than we planned, regardless of our intentions.

I try to ignore the way my feelings keep bubbling up and getting in the way when I hear Landry calling me back to consciousness. "How about a game of washerboards? The Reeds versus the sons-in-law," he poses, watching my expression carefully.

I grin. "You're on."

Though my partner turns out to be the worst (Emmett's excuse was that he's better at cornhole than washerboards), I still manage to beat Landry in the second round. He continues listing the reasons why my last few points shouldn't count when Loren surprises me by bounding over and bouncing up to her tiptoes to place a lingering kiss on my cheek.

And I'm pretty sure I'm blushing again. I don't know how to stop this train anymore. Hell, I don't know if I want to.

"Come on, best two out of three?" Landry poses, still butthurt about losing.

I glance around, noticing how everyone looks annoyed. "Maybe next time, huh?" I offer.

"Yeah, right. Next time," he grumbles, turning away.

"Hey," Loren calls, reaching out and grabbing his arm. "What the hell is that supposed to mean?"

He rolls his eyes. "Oh, come on. We're not really doing this, are we?"

"Doing what?" she asks.

He scrunches his face in disgust. "Pretending that this *thing* between the two of you is actually serious and that he won't have moved on to the next woman by Easter."

I clench my jaw tightly, willing myself to remain calm. It's amazing how quickly this guy manages to get under my skin. It must be his superpower. But I know this is his plan, and I can't just slug him in the face like I did when we were teenagers. I have to keep it together for Loren, at least.

"That's not going to happen, Landry," Loren speaks up, her chin lifted. "In fact, Blake's pretty much going to be a permanent fixture in my life from this point on, so you might as well learn to get along."

I reach over and grab her hand, partially because I need her help to keep myself from murdering her brother, and partially because I want to convey how proud I am of her for not backing down.

Landry huffs. "Oh, is that so? And what makes you think you can trust him to stick around?"

She swallows hard and squeezes my hand, and her eyes flash over to mine before she opens her mouth again. "Well, because ... I'm pregnant."

"Uh, come again?" Landry spits out.

"That's what she said, apparently," I hear Lilley mumble from behind me, and I bite back a laugh.

Loren nudges me. But I honestly can't stop grinning. I know I was just angry beyond belief and that I'm supposed to feel embarrassed or even uncomfortable in this moment. Loren's dad and brother are without a doubt contemplating my murder as we speak.

Yet, every time I get to claim Loren and our babies, I feel proud. Elated?

Have I ever felt *elated* before? I don't think so. The closest I've come to a feeling like that was hearing the results of Ethan's custody hearing, getting asked to be a godfather, or maybe taking part in JD's wedding. There was also the part after the wedding that I spent with Loren that made me feel pretty elated, but I can't go there right now.

"She's trying to tell you that she's having my baby," I clarify smugly for Landry as I pull Loren in closer to my side. "Actually, two babies."

He narrows his eyes as he glances back and forth between us, then he breaks out into a loud guffaw. "You really had me going for a second," he says, wiping his eyes. Then he comes over and pats me on the shoulder while everyone else looks on uncomfortably. "Okay, how long were you planning on keeping this up?"

"Keeping what up?" Loren asks, glaring at him. "Landry, this isn't a joke." Then she reaches down with her free hand and flattens her dress over her small bump. At this point, it could easily be mistaken for a food baby, but excitement still flutters in my stomach at the sight of it. "I'm pregnant with twins."

He chuckles again. "Yeah, and so am I."

Loren turns to me for backup. "Would anyone like to see the ultrasound?" I call out, and Lilley replies with an, "Ooh, me!" right away. I pull up the video from my favorites album, and I think I see Loren smirking when she notices.

Lilley glances at me with a knowing smile as she watches, probably because she can hear my voice in the background.

"We made two babies, Lo ... now do you believe me when I say that you're amazing?"

She squeezes my arm after she hands my phone back, then she turns to Loren. "My baby sister is going to be a mama? And you're having *twins*? Where the hell are you going to put two babies, Lo-Lo?" Lilley cries out incredulously, and Loren's smile grows wider when Lilley wraps her up in a hug.

Landry clicks his tongue. "How do you even know that's really her ultrasound?"

"Because they always put the mother's name and the date on the top of the screen, Dr. Dipshit," Lilley retorts as she pulls away.

Landry blinks a few times, then his mouth opens and closes without a sound, sort of like a fish. "Dad, don't you have anything to say about this?" he mutters after a while.

I turn to my old coach, awaiting his reaction. He shakes his head. "Your sister is grown enough to make her own decisions, even if they aren't the smartest ones. And I'm sure Blake will do right by her."

I clear my throat. "Absolutely."

"For the record, that does not include a shotgun wedding," Loren adds. I shoot her a *say less* look, but she continues. "Although we've already decided to come to a friendly arrangement if things don't work out between us. Because the last thing we want is a custody battle, right?"

I force a smile. Of course, she's mortified. She's just admitted to her family that she's not only dating a guy like me, but that she was naive enough to let me get her pregnant. I imagine Landry's comments are starting to wear her down, and she feels like a fool for trying to convince them that we're in a committed relationship.

In other words, she's less ashamed of what she's done and more embarrassed to admit she's done it with *me*. It's another harsh reminder that I'm not good enough for her, and I never will be. But this isn't the time for me to dwell on feeling sorry for myself, not when her family is still gaping at her and her cheeks are still flushed.

Dammit. Why does she have to look so cute when she's *honte*?

And if my thoughts are all over the place right now, I can't imagine what it must be like inside her head. Her eyes meet mine again, and I can tell she's spiraling, too. So, I do what I do best—I antagonize her.

"We have a back-up plan if things don't go as intended," I begin again. "But it's not going to be necessary, because we're already so happy together that I can't imagine us ever breaking up. Right, pumpkin?"

Her nostrils flare, and I shoot her a cocky smirk. "Right ... babe," she answers dryly.

"And you never know, sugar britches," I continue, noting the way her neck is turning red. "I could surprise you with a proposal when you least expect it and make an honest woman outta you."

"You could," she says through her teeth. "But we've already agreed that there's plenty of time for that, darling."

"That's true. You know how much I adore you. I'm not going

anywhere anytime soon ... lover," I say, puckering my lips and going in for an exaggeratedly awkward kiss. She groans but plays along, and I sigh inwardly because I still enjoy every time our lips make contact.

"Good grief, you're disgusting," Landry grumbles, crossing his arms and grimacing. "You're going to make me lose my appetite."

Then I see a flash of gratitude in Loren's eyes and a sense of smug satisfaction when the corners of her mouth turn up, and I can't help but grin back at her. She spins around in my arms and leans back against me, and my breathy exhale is audible this time.

"Oh, somehow I doubt that," Lilley mutters. "By the way, where's my birthday cake? What are we waiting for?"

"We haven't even had lunch yet," Landry objects, still pouting.

"Let the woman have her cake first. It's her birthday," Loren pipes up.

I take advantage of our position and sweep her hair to the side before I lean down to press my lips on her neck. "You're just saying that because you want cake."

She bites her lip and tilts her head to the side, and I can't tell whether she's shrugging or inviting me back for more. "Now, later, it doesn't matter. I'm getting a piece of that cake, one way or another."

"I'll buy you a whole cake later, Agnes. A peanut butter one," I say with a chuckle. Then I place one more kiss just below her ear, because I'm fully aware that this woman has become my weakness, and I'm not above seizing an opportunity when I can. I pull away and watch Loren's throat working when she swallows hard. A flush returns to her cheeks, and I hope it's my kisses and not that peanut butter cake that are making her so flustered.

"Ugh, I'm going inside to eat," Landry declares, wrinkling his nose and scowling at us.

"Wow, *someone* needs to get a girlfriend," we're all surprised to hear Emmett mumbling, and everyone laughs at Landry's expense as we follow him in for lunch.

By the time dinner is over, Landry seems to have softened up a little, though not much. He's already making plans to move back to Camellia and raise our kids on our behalf—I mean, to make sure they have a decent pediatrician. Loren's dad gives me a slightly firmer handshake and a warning nod when it's time to go, and Lilley whispers congratulations again when she hugs me goodbye. Then she makes Loren protest when she smacks my butt and says, "Way to go, Tiger!"

"That wasn't so bad, right?" I ask once we're back in the truck.

She heaves out an exhale. "Not if you don't mind getting groped by my sister."

"You did grant me permission to see other women," I reply, unable to stifle my laughter.

She scoffs and shoves my shoulder from across the cab. "I was going to crack a joke about you attracting cougars and married women, but I'm afraid I don't want to know the answer."

My laughter dies down as that empty feeling settles in my chest again. I crank the truck and pull out of the driveway, looking for a distraction. But then I decide that it's time I start defending myself. If I want people to know the truth about me, then I have to start setting the record straight, right?

"I'm not that brand of asshole, by the way. I've never been someone's side piece. At least, not as far as I know."

"I'm sorry," she says quietly. "It wasn't funny. And I should have learned my lesson about bringing up your dating history by now, since it apparently bothers you more than you let on."

"It's fine. I'm usually the first to make fun of myself, and it's not like I don't deserve worse after the way I've behaved over the years. I'd just rather not be that guy anymore if I don't have to."

She's quiet for a while before she speaks again. "Is that what you meant before?" I panic, thinking she's referring to my offer to marry her an hour earlier. "When you said you hadn't been going on as many dates," she clarifies, and I breathe a sigh of relief.

"Yeah, I guess. I mean, at thirty-one, isn't it past time for me to start taking myself more seriously? Shouldn't I be looking for something like JD has now, especially with two babies on the way?"

"So you do want to settle down ... to get married and all that?" she asks, her voice catching.

"I don't know. Maybe. I guess I never had a good reason to consider marriage and family before now. But it seems more important lately, and it certainly wouldn't hurt my career if I had any political aspirations. Don't you think?" My heart rate quickens as I await her response.

"Well, yeah, sure. That makes sense," she agrees, maybe a little too eagerly.

"What about you?" I ask.

"I never imagined I'd be a single parent, so I guess I'd need to revisit my stance on marriage altogether."

"But you've always wanted a family, right? Isn't that why you went out with that doctor?"

"To be honest, I only agreed to that date to make my brother happy," she says shyly. "And hey, I may have given up on getting married or having kids a while back, but look at me now. One out of two ain't bad."

I frown. "That just sounds like your way of saying 'I'm afraid to admit I want all those things because I don't think I'll ever have them.'"

"And that sounds like your way of saying you know the feeling."

I shoot her a side-eyed glare. "How do you always manage to do that?"

"Do what?"

"Turn everything back around on me. Can't you just let one of my lines ride every once in a while?"

She smirks. "I thought you said the smartass thing was a turn on?"

I blow out a breath. "It is. That's the problem."

CHAPTER 25

Blake

I'M AWAITING THE JUDGE'S RULING ON MY LAST CASE WHEN one of the district's legal secretaries comes over to whisper a message.

"Mr. Bourgeois, I'm sorry, but we just got a phone call from a Loren Reed? She asked us to let you know that she wasn't feeling well so she was going to drive herself to the hospital."

My heart drops to my toes as soon as I hear Loren's name. I know it must be something serious for her to have a message delivered. "Is, uh—is that all she said?" I ask, finding it harder to breathe by the second.

"I think she mentioned something about meeting your sister there," the secretary adds, giving me a sad smile.

I take a measured breath, willing myself not to panic. Hopefully she's with Tenley now, who I know will take good care of her. "Okay, thanks for letting me know."

"Is everything all right, Mr. Bourgeois?" asks the judge a second later.

"Um, no, your honor. Actually, my girlfriend is pregnant, and I just got a message that she had a medical emergency."

"By all means, then, please go," he excuses me. "We can finish up without you." I apologize to my clients, grab my things, and scurry out of the courtroom as fast as possible. Our courthouse has a no-cell-phones policy, so I call Loren as soon as I get to my truck.

"Hey," she answers quietly. "I'm sorry to bother you in court."

"What? No, I don't care about that. Are you okay?"

"I think so. I just ... well, I'll spare you the gory details, but I started having some scary symptoms at school earlier. I called Tenley, and she told me to meet her at the hospital. I'm feeling okay now, but they just hooked me up to a few monitors, and I think she's coming to check on us."

"Okay. Um, I'm on my way."

"Blake, you don't have to rush over here. I didn't mean for you to leave work. I just thought you'd want to know something was up."

I sigh, because it's super annoying when she tries to downplay stuff like this, especially when she feeds me the "you don't have to trouble yourself" line. "No, I'm glad you called, because I care about you, and I want to be there for you."

"Okay. If you insist," she says after a second, sniffling.

"I do. I'll be there in a few minutes."

I look down after we hang up and notice I've been going nearly twenty miles over the speed limit. I shrug it off and hope my work connections will get me out of a ticket if I get caught. I don't know why I'm in such a hurry, since it's not like I can do anything to help if Loren and the babies are actually in danger. I just can't bear to think of her being alone and afraid. I know she's a capable adult, yet I find myself wanting to be there to hold her hand, and maybe even liking the idea that she needs my support.

And then I make the huge mistake of letting my mind wander into what-if territory.

What if Loren loses the babies? Would she be relieved? Would I? I cringe, my face mimicking the way my stomach clenches at the thought. I can't imagine a world in which either of us wouldn't want our babies to be safe and healthy, much less to exist. Sure, having kids outside of marriage or even a serious relationship is inconvenient, but that's our own fault.

Then I'm off on another tangent, thinking about whether she'd want to have anything to do with me if not for the pregnancy. Sadly, I know the answer to that after reflecting on the morning after our babies' conception.

Finally, I wonder about the statistical chances that we'd ever get together and make not one but two babies in the first place. I suddenly feel very lucky and grateful that things happened the way they did, though I don't understand the reasons yet. And I desperately hope that all three of them are okay ... maybe even pray for it.

It's not that I never pray or that I don't believe in God, but less so in His interest in our mundane lives, especially when it pertains to intervening in the consequences of our own actions. Then again, maybe it's worse that Loren and our unborn children might suffer because of the mistakes I've made over the years, since this whole situation is technically my fault.

I'm definitely above bartering with God. But I still make Him a promise about continuing to clean up my act on the off chance it might save them from bearing the brunt of some of my wrongdoings. It'll probably make me a better father, anyway.

My mind finally slows down by the time I drive up to the hospital. I toss my suit jacket into the back seat before rushing into the building.

"I'm looking for my girlfriend, Loren Reed," I tell the ER receptionist. "Cute little brunette, pregnant with twins?"

She smiles. "The midwife just took her back for some tests. If you want to hang out in the waiting room—"

"I need to see her. Please?"

"Oh, well, we don't usually let anyone back there unless they're family."

"I'm her fiancé," I blurt out before I turn on my most charming smile.

The receptionist narrows her eyes at me, but I can tell she's going to give in. They always do. "I'll have to ask the midwife if it's okay."

"I'm sure Nurse Tenley will be fine with it. We can give her a call if you want," I offer, unlocking my phone and pulling up Tenley's name in my contacts.

"Hey," Tenley's voice rings out over the speakerphone when she answers. "Where are you?"

"I'm in the ER. The very lovely and very capable professional at the front desk just wanted to get your permission before I join you." I raise my brow encouragingly.

"Hi, Nurse Tenley. Just making sure it's okay for me to send your patient's fiancé on back," she says aloud.

I hold my confident expression as best I can and pray my face isn't as flushed as it feels.

"Oh, yes. Please allow my dear brother-in-law to join us. We're heading to radiology for an ultrasound right now," Tenley replies cheerfully. "And damn, don't I wish I'd answered this call on speakerphone."

I clear my throat as I slip my phone into my pocket, and the receptionist smirks knowingly as she leads me through a hallway to meet Tenley and Loren.

"Hey," I greet them, genuinely glad to see Loren smiling back at me from the hospital bed. I reach over and clasp a hand around hers. "How are you?"

"I'm fine. We're just going to check on the babies now."

Tenley wheels the bed forward again, so I continue walking beside Loren and holding her hand. "So, what's going on?"

Loren scrunches up her nose. "I started feeling this pressure during class, and later I noticed some bleeding." I frown out of concern, but she must assume she's made me uncomfortable. "I'm sorry, TMI, I know."

I shake my head quickly. "No, of course not. I mean, if you're living through it, the least I could do is listen to you talk about it."

She smirks. "It seems like whatever was going on has slowed down since I've been resting in the ER."

I glance back at Tenley, looking for a signal or a gesture as to whether I should worry.

"Bleeding is a pretty common symptom, and it can indicate so many things, some minor and others more serious," she says, pressing her lips in a hard line. "But I'm hopeful we'll know more after the ultrasound."

We turn to pass through a wide set of double doors, and Tenley deftly maneuvers the bed into a smaller exam room with an even bigger sonogram machine than the one at her clinic. She gets started right away, and I'm relieved when she lifts Loren's shirt instead of making her take off her pants this time.

"Okay," Tenley begins, shifting around on the screen and taking measurements. Her face is hard to read as she drags the wand over Lo's belly, and her silence makes me even more anxious.

"The babies look fine," she announces a few minutes in, and I let out the breath I've been holding as I give Loren's hand a gentle squeeze. "But I think I've found the problem."

"What kind of problem?" I ask.

Tenley sighs. "Lo, it looks like you have a condition called placenta previa."

"And that's …" I gesture impatiently for her to continue.

"It's when the placenta, which is the organ that attaches to the uterine wall and transports oxygen, blood, and nutrients to the babies, is sitting over the cervix and blocking the opening to the uterus."

"Is that bad?" I consider myself to be a pretty intelligent man, but they weren't exactly teaching me this stuff in law school.

"We'll have to keep a close eye on all three of them, and Loren will need to take some precautions to ensure that the placenta isn't damaged, or else a very dangerous amount of bleeding could occur."

"How dangerous are we talking here?"

"Life-threatening, for her and the babies," she replies, her tone serious. "But, so long as she's careful, there shouldn't be any complications. And there's still a chance that the previa could correct itself later." She reaches down and pats Loren's arm affectionately before she continues the ultrasound. "It's common to see this in multiples. Two fish in a tiny tank means less room. You're actually relatively lucky that they're sharing one placenta, because that frees up a little more space."

"Oh. So what do we need to do? Will she be bedridden or whatever?"

"I don't think complete bed rest is necessary at this point, but I doubt she'll get through the rest of the school year. She'll definitely need to avoid overexertion, standing too long, lifting heavy stuff, and anything else like that. And pelvic rest is very important for the duration of the pregnancy, unless we can verify that the problem has been resolved," she explains, rolling her lips in as if she's privy to a joke that the rest of us haven't gotten yet.

"What's the difference between pelvic rest and bed rest?" I ask like the idiot I am.

"From the looks of her expression, we're probably better off waiting until she leaves and Googling it ourselves," Loren finally speaks up.

But Tenley is grinning from ear to ear. "Too late, he already asked," she says in a sing-song voice, batting her eyelashes at me. "Pelvic rest means complete abstinence from sexual intercourse."

I gulp. Looks like my newfound celibate lifestyle is here to stay, at least for a while. "Right. Got it," I say awkwardly. I turn to Loren and notice her cheeks darkening, and I somehow think I'll lighten the situation by continuing the conversation. "Because she shouldn't overexert herself, right?"

Tenley holds back a full snort. "That's part of it, but there's more to it. Semen is a prostaglandin, which naturally ripens the cervix. And with the placenta in the way, any chance of opening the cervix would be dangerous. Additionally, orgasms prompt the release of oxytocin, the love hormone. Oxytocin triggers uterine contractions, and the last thing we'd need is for one of the babies to get pushed down onto the placenta and cause a rupture or hemorrhaging."

"Okay, then. No more orgasms," I remark, making Tenley laugh.

"Oh, same goes for nipple stimulation," she adds, and I sigh inwardly.

"Well, there go my plans for the evening," I quip.

"Ignore him, please," Loren mumbles, backhanding my arm, but I can tell she's trying not to smile.

"Seriously, though," Tenley begins again. "You'll need to take it easy in general. If work gets to be too much, just say the word and we'll put you on early maternity leave."

She cringes. "I don't think I'd like that."

"Then you'll see to it that she behaves, right?" Tenley says, turning to me.

"Absolutely." I look at Loren, already queuing up another one of those verbal diarrhea moments that I seem to keep having whenever I'm around her. "In fact, I think you should move in with me. At least until after the babies are born."

"WHAT?" she chokes out.

"Why not? There's plenty of room, and I can take care of you and make sure you don't overdo it."

Maybe this will be part of my penance. I'll work off some of my wrongs by going above and beyond for Loren and the babies.

"I don't need anyone to take care of me," she says after a while, crossing her arms and pouting in a way that suggests otherwise.

I twist my body to sit at the edge of the narrow bed, facing her and grabbing her hand. "I know you don't need my help, but I'd really like it if you'd let me. You can even think of it as a favor to me, because as long as you're living across town, I'll be up all night worrying about you and our babies. Besides ... my bathtub is better for reading than yours." I dangle the bait in front of her, and my heart races as I wait for her answer. "Don't make me bribe you with peanut butter, Reed," I add.

She purses her lips as she thinks it over. "Fine. But we have to stick to the ground rules."

"Deal," I say, grinning.

Did I just make Loren my roommate? With no chance of anything physical happening? I've basically locked myself in the friend zone, indefinitely. Yet, I'm still happy about it?

"What rules?" Tenley perks up. I almost forgot she was in the room.

"Not that it's any of your business, Mrs. Thirsty, but some of us prefer to develop our relationships within set parameters and don't leap from a first date to the altar."

She rolls her eyes. "You realize how hypocritical that sounds given your current situation, don't you?"

"Fair enough," I concede, making Loren laugh.

Tenley smiles before she starts again. "There's one more thing I found in the ultrasound. I'm not sure what your plans are for a gender reveal, but … one of your kiddos is a bit of an exhibitionist."

"Really?" Loren asks eagerly, her eyes lighting up. "So you can tell us right now?"

"If that's what you both want," Tenley replies hesitantly.

"I don't think we're planning any kind of big gender reveal, right?" Loren turns to me for reinforcement.

I shrug. "Um, should we? Are you guys having one of those?" I ask Tenley.

"Eh, it's not my style," she says. "We'll do a baby shower later on, so JD can still get his moment," she adds in a joking tone.

I glance back at Loren to find her wide, pleading eyes staring back at me. She basically looks like one of those cartoon puppies, and I've never seen anything more adorable. "Whatever you want, babe, I'm good for it," I tell her, as if I could deny her anything at this point.

She actually squeals, and Tenley laughs as she moves the wand over her stomach again.

"All right, you guys. This is Baby B," Tenley begins, pointing to the monitor screen. "My neh … my neeh …"

She drags the sound out, and Loren sits up in bed and crushes my hand in anticipation.

"My beautiful niece."

Loren gasps and covers her mouth with her free hand. "Girls?" she squeaks.

Tenley nods and grins. "Here's her sister, Little Miss Baby A. And I was almost certain they'd be boys, what with the timing of the conception date in correlation to peak ovulation. Another unlikely coincidence or small miracle, I'd say."

"Are we really having two baby girls?" she asks Tenley meekly.

"Yep. Congratulations to both of you. Hope you don't mind the color pink."

Loren turns to me with tears streaming down her face, and I'm fighting back the urge to join her. "Blake?"

"I don't hate it. After all, they say I'm pretty good with women," I declare with a flirty wink.

"I'd call you out for that, but the truth is, I don't know what I'd have done with a pair of boys," Loren replies.

"I'm sure you'd have made a great football mom. But this is probably for the best."

"You can always give it another go later," Tenley adds, smirking to herself.

Loren rolls her eyes. "Very funny."

Truthfully, I haven't even considered having more kids before now. It's hard to wrap my mind around the idea when I haven't gotten to see what life with two babies is like yet. But what I do note is the way I automatically picture Loren as the mother of any additional children, as if my subconscious is already making plans.

"Just putting it out there, but I'm more than willing to take one for the team if you ever change your mind. Even if you just need the practice," I lean in and whisper beside her ear.

She turns her lips to the side and suppresses a smile. "I think I'll be satisfied after this round."

"I can make sure of that, too," I promise her, my voice deepening.

Tenley snorts without looking away from the screen. "The rizz on this kid," she mutters under her breath, darting her eyes over to let me know she's disappointed in me for wasting her setup.

I frown at her. My lines can't actually be worse than JD's, can they?

"Now that we've gotten that out of the way, let's get you set up in a room," Tenley says.

"A room?" Loren pouts.

"I'm keeping you in tonight for observation," Tenley declares, eliciting a whimper from Loren. "Everything is most likely fine, but

I'd rather leave you on a monitor overnight to make sure the babies are still comfy."

"Do I have to?"

"Yep," Tenley responds without hesitation. She begins shifting the rails on Loren's bed and preparing to wheel her away again. "I'm also going to send you to a maternal-fetal-medicine specialist as soon as possible. They have better equipment and more experience with multiples than I do, and I'd rather be safe than sorry."

Loren's frown deepens, but I grab her hand again. "I'll take you, okay?" I assure her, and she nods.

"So, when can I bust her outta here?" I ask Tenley, following them down the hall and into a regular room.

"Barring any problems, late tomorrow morning."

And the wheels are already turning in my head. "Listen, I've got some work to take care of. I'll be back later to keep you company. I'll bring my Ninja Turtle jammies."

Loren frowns. "I don't want you to have to sleep on that doll-house sofa."

"Too bad. I'm staying until they kick me out. Besides, I've been looking for the perfect opportunity to use my new Ironman sleeping bag," I say softly then lean in for a quick kiss, though I let my lips rest against hers a second longer than I should, mostly because I'm so relieved she's safe.

Tenley looks amused once I pull away. "I've actually got to check on another patient. I'll walk you out." Then we both bid a whiny Loren goodbye.

"What on earth are you plotting?" Tenley asks as soon as the door shuts behind us.

"What makes you think I'm plotting something?" I ask, already pulling out my phone. She narrows her eyes at me. "Fine, I'm calling in reinforcements. I don't want her worrying about having to move her things into my place, and I also need to have some control over what she brings, because the woman is an absolute book hoarder."

She chuckles as we turn down the hall. "That's a pretty nice gesture for a fake boyfriend. So is insisting on staying the night with her."

My brow shoots up. "I don't know what you're talking about."

"Save it. Lo's already fessed up."

"Oh."

"I also suspect *you* are *not* faking it. Not as well as you think you are, anyway."

I scoff. "Please. Blake the Snake doesn't do relationships, remember?"

She stops me with a hand on my arm, frowning at my sarcasm. "You sure about that? I heard he was recently engaged."

"Come on, Ten. You know I only said that so the receptionist would let me in."

"You could have just pulled the 'I'm with the midwife' card and you know it."

I exhale loudly. "What do you want me to say? I panicked, all right."

"Blake," she begins, her expression softening. "The last thing I want is for either of you to get hurt, especially when there are two babies involved. But you really ought to come clean. Trust me, these feelings aren't just going away."

I brush her hand off my arm. "Why is everyone so sure I'm going to break her heart?"

"Oh, I think you're the one that's about to get his heart stomped on, if I'm being honest," she replies dryly. "If you keep playing this game, Loren's never going to trust you by the time you finally tell her how you really feel."

"And maybe you're advising the wrong patient," I return, a bit too harshly.

Tenley frowns as she reaches down to scratch her belly over the top of her scrubs, making her small bump visible. "I'm sorry. I guess she hasn't told me everything."

I shrug, feeling guilty for snapping at her a second ago. "Yeah, well, I guess I shouldn't be surprised to hear that she's confessed to fake dating me but not to actually caring about me."

She smiles ruefully. "You know I can't repeat what Loren's confided in me. But I won't leave you thinking she doesn't care."

An inkling of hope springs within my chest, and I bite back a smile of my own.

"Don't give up yet. And don't be afraid to go after her if she runs scared. I let her go once, and it was one of my biggest regrets," Tenley continues.

"So I'm just supposed to keep chasing her, even if she tells me she doesn't want me?" I ask incredulously.

"I thought you'd have figured this out by now, but, yeah—women are weird. Anyone who claims we aren't influenced by our hormones doesn't believe in science," she says with a short laugh.

"I'm starting to grasp that, yes," I say on an exhale.

She bites her lip. "Although I'm not surprised by the way you've stepped up and prioritized your little family, I am proud of you, Blake."

My little family?

"Loren and those girls are very lucky to have you—we all are," she continues. "And I'm really grateful you've been willing to add *N'oncle* and *Parrain* to your plate, as full as it is."

I furrow my brow and swallow hard. "Thanks."

"All right, that's enough of that," she declares, spinning on her heels and waving over her shoulder. "I'll meet you and the guys at Lo's with a few pizzas later. I'm sure she'd prefer it if I were the one packing her unmentionables, since you're just faking it."

CHAPTER 26

Loren

"Are you sure you'll be okay alone?" Blake asks, standing over my hospital bed.

"For the hundredth time, yes. I'm fine. I drove myself here, and I can drive myself home."

He narrows his eyes at me. "Home?"

"I don't have to move in today, do I?"

He shrugs and stuffs his hands in his pockets. "I sort of thought that was the plan, but if you need more time …"

Who am I kidding? Blake has an amazing house with a huge TV, a really nice pool, a bomb-ass bathtub, and, well … Blake. For a guy with a reputation such as his, I hadn't expected him to be an expert cuddler, but add it to the list of his best qualities, which is already starting to look like a CVS receipt.

"How about I run to my place to grab just enough of my things to last a few days, and then we can pack up the rest over the weekend?"

"We?" he asks, an eyebrow raised. "You're actually going to let me help?"

I sigh. "Only because Nurse Tenley said so, and to be honest, she kind of scares the you-know-what outta me."

He chuckles. "Don't tell anyone this, but …" His eyes dart around before he cups his hand around his mouth and whispers loudly, "She scares the hell out of me, too."

I smile, and he bends over to grab the overnight duffle bag he'd shown up with late last night. He'd apologized for not getting here earlier, but the pizza and junk food he brought served to soften the blow. Honestly, the fact that he bothered to stay with me in the hospital was enough to melt my heart all on its own. Then, he'd woken up early this morning, gone home to shower, and returned with iced coffee and donuts, all before leaving for work.

The man certainly gives good fake boyfriend.

I clear my throat as an awkward thought occurs to me. "Hey, Blake?"

"Hmm?"

"I was just thinking ... with me moving into your house and all, um, what are we going to tell everyone? They all still think we're dating, well, except for ..."

Oops. I forgot he doesn't know that Tenley knows about our fake-dating arrangement. Damn pregnancy brain.

But he only smirks at me. "JD figured it out, too."

"I guess we aren't as good at acting as we think."

"I'm sure we can work on that since we'll be spending plenty of time together," he says with a laugh.

"So, we're just going to keep pretending to date?"

He shrugs. "I don't really know what other choice we have at this point. It wouldn't exactly make sense for us to move in together unless we were a couple, right?"

"My point exactly."

He purses his lips. "I don't like it when you use my own words against me, Reed. One would swear you've been to law school." Then he leans down to kiss me on the cheek, leaving me with a nice lungful of his cologne. "I'll see you this afternoon. Don't go overboard with the packing, all right?"

"Fine."

I watch him leave, reminding myself that I shouldn't be drooling over the way he looks in a suit.

A nurse comes in shortly after with a stack of papers for me to sign before I can go, and I drive home, my mind already reeling with packing lists. I barely make it in time to dash to the bathroom and relieve my poor, cramped bladder. The lack of space is already concerning since I still have a long way to go.

I wash my hands, noticing that the counter is oddly bare and my go-to toiletries are missing. Then I hear a text come through.

GUS GUS

I'm sure you're freaking out by now. But don't worry, you haven't been robbed.

Well, except for your panty drawer. Some creep may have raided your dresser before anyone could stop him. 😊

LOREN

Then where's all my stuff?

GUS GUS

At my house, duh. Aren't you supposed to be the smart one?

LOREN

You moved everything without me?

GUS GUS

Before you get upset, remember that this was for your own good. I knew you'd end up overdoing it, so a few of us went over and grabbed the essentials for now.

I stare down at the phone in shock. I can't believe he went through this much trouble. Hell, I don't even understand how he managed to pack and move all of my things and still spend the night with me in the hospital.

LOREN

So, what? Am I just supposed to show up at your place and make myself at home now?

GUS GUS

That's exactly what you're supposed to do. I'll see you later, roomie. 💀

I put the phone down and make a round through the house, realizing he's actually taken nearly everything important. Then I reluctantly head over to Blake's.

Using the code he gave me a while back, I unlock the door and let myself in. I don't see any changes in the main living area, so I poke my head into the guest room I occupied the last couple of times I stayed over, expecting to find a stack of boxes. Instead, I open the door to unveil a tidier version of my own bedroom back home. My favorite pillow is perched on the bed, right beside a nightstand holding the book I'd set down before going to sleep a couple nights ago. I bite my lip as tears well up in my eyes. Then I dart over to the closet to find my things arranged neatly and the rest of my clothes folded within the dresser.

There's even a note in the top drawer that reads:

Sorry, I tried to keep your panty drawer sacred, but your pervy "boyfriend" got there first. I figured I'd let him have this, since it's the closest he'll get for a while.

Love,
Ten

P.S. This is not fake-dating behavior ... js.

I roll my watery eyes and replace the note before going around and inventorying most of my things until Blake texts again.

GUS GUS

Btw, I took the liberty of putting your toiletries in the master bath, since I figured you'd want to use the tub. And I don't mind swapping bedrooms if you'd rather have the bigger bathroom to yourself.

LOREN

No, it's all perfect. Thank you.

GUS GUS

Good. I don't want to smother you, Lo. But I want to take care of you. It's important to me, and I like doing it. Okay?

LOREN

Okay.

GUS GUS

I'd Facetime you if I weren't in public right now, just so you could see how big I'm smiling after that "okay."

He thinks *his* smile is telling right now? Thank goodness he can't see my face. I laugh as I wipe my nose on the back of my sleeve.

GUS GUS

Anyway, I think you should take that book from your nightstand and introduce it to your new soaking tub until I get back.

Text me if the mood strikes and you feel like sending me a sexy bath selfie.

But only of your face, bc we can't break the nudity clause already. 😉

"Ugh. Why me?" I stomp my way over to grab my tablet and a change of clothes before I run myself a bubble bath, pouting and sniffling the whole time. If I thought being friends with Blake and fake dating him were dangerous, what the hell am I supposed to do now?

I take in a deep breath as I collect my thoughts. Maybe I just need to relax with a good book to clear my head. Reading has always been my escape, especially when I was younger. Immersing myself within another world was the only way I could avoid dwelling on the boredom and loneliness I felt in real life, and I still find it easier to connect with imaginary characters than actual people most of the time. Not to mention, bookish communities have the best social media content, hands down.

I stop to check out my growing bump in the mirror after getting undressed. It never ceases to amaze me. Then I pick up my tablet and settle into a warm bath before queuing up a cute new rom-com. Although I'm never going to stop rereading *Pride and Prejudice*, and I'm admittedly a sucker for a well-developed fantasy series, there are days when I don't have the energy to read anything complicated. Give me all the well-written easy and cheesy—I can appreciate the classics while still enjoying a lighthearted romantic comedy with a guaranteed HEA, especially when life makes none of the same promises.

I sigh as I sink into the water and flip the first page. Before I know it, I'm a third of the way through my book and my bathwater has gotten cold. I reluctantly step out of the tub and put on a pair of comfy leggings and an oversized T-shirt with one of my favorite book quotes. I settle in a cozy spot in the corner of the sectional in the living room, and Blake opens the door a few minutes later.

"Honey, I'm home," he calls out.

"Hi." I smile as he drops his briefcase before plopping down beside me with a groan.

"Rough day?" I ask hesitantly, setting my book down on the coffee table.

He only grunts in response, his eyes closing as his head lolls back.

"Is everything okay?"

He wipes his hand over his unshaven face, and I take a second just to appreciate him. His hair is a little longer than usual, and his shirt sleeves are rolled up over his forearms. I continue staring as he removes his tie and undoes the top buttons of his shirt, but I have to avert my eyes before I end up asking him to keep it going.

Gah. He's so hot.

STFU, pregnancy hormones.

All of my reasons for avoiding an actual romantic relationship with Blake suddenly seem so trivial. My subconscious isn't making it any easier to stick to the ground rules, either. At this rate, I'm not sure how much longer I can resist crawling into his lap and asking him if he'd mind letting me stay there forever.

"Yeah, I'm good, just glad to be home," he says after a while, turning to shoot me an exhausted smile. "How are you feeling?"

I blink a few times to keep my eyes from wandering down to check out the bit of his chest he's exposed. "Like I'm in love ... with your bathtub."

He laughs lightly then cringes as he rubs one side of his neck.

"What's wrong?" I ask.

"My neck's just a little stiff, probably from the hospital couch. I'm sure it'll be better by tomorrow." But he continues to turn his head as if it's causing him more pain than he's letting on.

"Well, here, let me help," I say as I instinctively move to kneel behind him.

"I'm fine, Lo, you don't have to ... hmm." He lets out a deep, throaty groan as I press my tiny fingers into the sore spot. "Oh, man. That's *really* nice."

I clamp my mouth shut as I continue working my hands over the tight muscles of his neck and shoulders, and he moans again.

"I had no idea you were so good at this."

I huff, trying to cover up the way he makes me shiver. "What kind of underhanded compliment is that?"

He laughs softly. "You've been holding out on me."

"It's not like you give me much of a chance to do anything nice for you. You're always too busy trying to take care of me."

"Eh, you know how much I get off on one-upping you," he replies with a smile and his eyes still closed.

"Ha ha," I retort.

"Seriously, though. You're literally risking your life for me and our girls. Moving a few boxes seemed like the least I could do."

"Well, thank you," I say after a while, my voice thick. "I really do appreciate everything, Blake. And I'm sorry if I haven't always been so gracious about it." I sense his muscles are finally loosening up, so I slide my hands up the back of his head.

He sighs contentedly. "I'll do all the dishes and satisfy every one of your late-night *envies*, if only you promise to do this to me every once in a while."

I bite my lip so hard it might bleed. He tilts his head back so I can run my fingers through the rest of his dark blond hair, and he emits a low hum this time. Then he opens his eyes and cranes his neck to look at me.

"I know it's against the rules for me to say it out loud, but this feels so damned good."

I furrow my brow but continue, because I secretly love playing in his hair.

"I'm only telling you in case you need to bribe me later. Because this is my Klondike bar, my kryptonite," he continues.

My breathing quickens. "You mean, the shoulder massage or the hair thing?"

His head shakes slightly as he turns his body to face mine, leaving my fingers entwined. "The hair is my favorite, but it's the same every time you touch me ... wherever you touch me."

I watch his Adam's apple dip and his chest rise and fall. And I can't bring myself to remove my hands.

"Blake ..." I begin. But he shuts his eyes again and slides a hand up over mine.

"I'm sorry," he whispers, then he drags my palm down to his scruffy cheek. It makes a scratchy sound, and I can't help but fantasize about the feeling of his face against mine. I've never kissed a man with this much facial hair before, but I don't think I'd mind the beard burn. I sit back on my heels as he opens his eyes, his hand still holding mine over his jaw.

I'm not sure what comes over me, but I tilt his face up and press my lips to his, just for a second, though I could certainly stay longer. I pull away quickly and drop my hand, and he stares back at me with widened eyes.

"What was that for?"

I roll my lips in, trying to stop the tingling sensation. "I don't know. I just felt like you needed it," I say after a while, stealing his favorite line.

He nods and swallows hard, his eyes darting down to my mouth, and for a second, I think he might pull me back in.

I sure as heck wouldn't stop him right now.

Instead, he clears his throat and stands abruptly. "Thanks," he says awkwardly. "For the massage, I mean. My neck feels much better."

"Yeah. No problem." I frown and sink further into the couch.

But he doesn't move away. Instead, he stuffs his hands in his pockets and keeps his eyes trained on the ground. I know him well enough by now to recognize his signature nervous stance. "So, um, I think there's still pizza in the fridge from last night. You know, if you're hungry."

"That sounds great," I reply quietly.

He nods shyly. "Loren, are you sure you're okay with everything? I realize this is a lot at once, and the last thing we need is for you to feel stressed."

"It is a lot, but I think I'm okay. Thanks to you."

His smile widens again. "Good. All I want is to make you comfortable ... and happy."

"I will be, so long as you stock enough peanut butter for the foreseeable future. And you don't mind sharing your tub."

He chuckles. "It's all yours. And I wasn't kidding before. If you want my bedroom—"

"No, I'm fine in the room next door. I'll just use the hall bathroom in the middle of the night and bathe in yours, if that's all right with you."

"And if I said we could share my king-sized bed so you could be closer to the en suite?" he ventures with a hopeful look.

I scrunch my nose. "I think that might be pushing our luck, don't you?"

He lifts a shoulder in a shrug. "It was worth a shot."

I look away and try to hide my smile. Why would he want me in his bed so badly, especially now that he knows there's no chance he'll get lucky?

"Speaking of getting naked, I'm going to take a quick shower before we eat. I smell terrible."

"You smell great," I blurt out before I can help myself, and his lips twitch. "I mean, I'm starving, so I'd rather just eat now. I'm used to eating lunch in a cloud of teenage boy B.O., anyway."

He continues staring at me, and the butterflies in my stomach take note. "Only if you're sure I smell *great*, Reed."

"Did I say 'great'? I meant to say, 'good enough,' " I retort, rolling my eyes.

He nods, pursing his lips as he regards me skeptically. "Sure you did."

"Fine. See if I give you a pity kiss again," I grumble.

"Is that what you're calling it?"

"Well, I—I ..." I stutter, unsure of how to answer that. "It was a kiss between friends, like all the other times."

"Not *all* other times."

I scoff. "Those were just for show."

"Hmm. If you say so," he begins with a sexy smirk. "You kiss all your friends the way you kiss me?" His voice is deep and his brow cocked.

I shift on the couch, trying to disguise the way his question makes me squirm. "Only the ones I pretend to date."

He immediately straightens up and narrows his eyes. "What do you mean by that? What exactly constitutes a pretend date?"

"Wouldn't you like to know?" I answer, pressing my lips together and stifling a grin.

"Agnes, you'd better answer that question if you want my brother to live to see another day."

"Relax, dude. No need for the fratricidal threats. You'd know if

JD and I had been willing to take it that far, because Tenley would have gotten to me first," I say, giggling. He rolls his shoulders back and forces a small smile as I continue. "I made that same joke in front of your sister-in-law once, and I swear my life flashed before my eyes."

"Who needs to worry about Landry Reed with her around?"

"Yeah." I laugh again, and we stare at one another for a second before I speak up. "You'd better go shower. I'll be hangry before you know it."

"Sure you don't want to give me a friendly kiss goodbye first?"

I rake my teeth over my bottom lip when it starts tingling again. "I told you, no more pity kisses from me."

"For the record, Lo. I've never kissed you out of pity. Not when you were desperate to get your first kiss out of the way, and not yesterday at the hospital when we made plans to move in together. And it certainly wasn't a kiss between friends that led to you having my babies." His eyes run down my body and up again.

I inhale sharply. "You're breaking a whole mess of rules right now, Gus Gus," I manage, my voice shaky and a suspicious warmth creeping up my throat.

"I figured it wouldn't matter since none of it ever meant anything to you." He crosses his arms, but his lips tilt upward.

I grimace. "Okay, I'm only going to say this once. You know I only used that excuse the next morning because I'd never been more mortified in my life. And because I'm ... weird. I just couldn't bear the thought of watching you pretend to care."

His expression softens, and he shakes his head. "Lo," he begins, stepping toward me, but I hold a hand out to stop him.

And I'm not sure whether I'm fueled by the look on his face or the guilt I've been harboring for the past few months, but I start rambling again. "Look, Blake, I should have apologized sooner. But I am sorry about the way I left. I'm sorry for making those assumptions about you and for hurting your feelings. I'm sorry I was such a jerk, but that's as much as I can say about it if you want me to continue living here. I can't ..." My voice cracks, and I shake my head.

"Thank you for that," he mumbles. "It means a lot more to me than you might think."

I turn around before he can see the tears forming in my eyes and attempt to clear the emotion from my throat. "You'd better hurry up in the shower. I'm about to eat these pillows."

"Yeah, sorry, I'll be right out."

By the time I turn, he's gone.

CHAPTER 27

Blake

"THEY WON'T HAVE TO USE THAT BIG WAND THINGY THIS time, right?" I ask carefully, glancing around the perinatologist's exam room.

"I hope the heck not," Loren replies. "But if so, I'd like to at least find out the good doctor's name before I get violated again."

I chuckle and point to the wall. "Athanasius? That's about the only name more Catholic than Augustine or Agnes. I bet he's the youngest of ten and already has a handful of his own kids at home, right?"

She leans up on the exam table to squint at one of the diplomas on display. "Oh, yeah. Dr. Athanasius sounds like a loving father of five homeschooled daughters who make their own goat's milk soap. I bet his wife is a total doll and breastfeeds her babies for like, three years, minimum."

"Hey, for the record, I only expect you to nurse our twins for the first two years," I say, smiling. She rolls her eyes and smirks back, and the doctor knocks on the door and walks inside.

"Hi, I'm Dr. LaFleur," he greets us, staring down at the chart he's holding in one hand as he extends the other to Loren. But his jaw and his hand both fall as soon as he looks up. "Loren?"

"Huh. Hey, doc. Small world, right?" I volunteer, standing up and grinning as I offer my hand instead.

Rowan tilts his head to the side and glances back and forth between Loren and me, probably counting backward in his head. Eventually, he forces a smile and shakes my hand. "Yeah. It's good to see you both." But he doesn't sound like he means it.

"You, too," Loren replies in a small voice. "And ... I'm sorry. We didn't realize—I mean, I just saw Athanasius and ..."

He shrugs as he walks around to sit beside the ultrasound machine. "I go by my middle name. My parents are uber Catholic."

She glares at me, and I wink. I may be enjoying this *entirely* too much.

Meanwhile, Loren's probably stressing over having to explain to her brother's best friend that she didn't know she was already pregnant when she agreed to go out with him. Which means Landry's also going to hear about this.

"So," Rowan begins, his eyes trained on Loren's chart again. "Uh, congratulations?"

"Thanks," we both answer.

"I see your midwife diagnosed you with placenta previa? And you are about sixteen weeks into your—wow—monochorionic-diamniotic twin pregnancy. That's ... *wow*."

Loren sighs. "I think 'unexpected' is the word you're looking for."

He laughs softly and finally looks up. "I guess I should have picked up on that vibe a little sooner," he says, nodding his head in my direction.

"About that ... I owe you an apology," Loren begins. "I promise I didn't know about this when we went out. I wouldn't have let Landry set us up if—"

"It's my fault," I interrupt her to explain. "I've never been Landry's favorite, so even though Loren and I had been dating on and off for a while, she had to make sure it was worth the trouble of telling him we were an item. Even if that meant dating other guys until she knew for certain." She exhales and reaches out to clasp my hand in hers, squeezing it gently to convey her gratitude.

Rowan shrugs, looking more amused than offended. "Hey, you don't owe me any kind of explanation. These things happen, right? Although, I have to say, this is a first for me."

"Understandable," she says, smiling now.

"All that aside, let's check on your babies, hmm?"

How is this guy friends with Landry, anyway?

"Quick question—do we know the babies' sex yet?" he asks as he reaches for the ultrasound tools. I feel my blood pressure spike when his hand hovers over the longest option, but he eventually picks out one of the flat-ended instruments and squirts some of that weird jelly over it as Loren pulls up her shirt.

"Yes. Blake's sister-in-law is my midwife, and she told us we were having girls."

"Gotcha. Just wanted to make sure in case I slip up and use a gender-specific pronoun," he says with a chuckle. He moves the wand around, locating the babies' heartbeats within a few seconds, and that anxious feeling I've been harboring for the past week is slightly alleviated.

Dr. Rowan actually turns out to be somewhat cool, explaining things as he continues the ultrasound and addressing both Loren and me equally. He basically reiterates Tenley's advice from before, except he adds modified bed rest to his recommendations. He also mentions that Baby A is measuring smaller than her sister and that we'll need to keep a close eye on her growth from here on out, which includes weekly visits with Tenley and Dr. Simms and monthly ones here.

"I'll let you go back to work," he barters with Loren. "But only light duty, and just long enough for you to get things squared away, and then you'll have to work from home. I don't think you can afford to take any chances with this, Loren. Your frame is so small, and you're going to get uncomfortable pretty soon, anyway. You should also prepare for the likelihood of an early cesarean delivery. I don't foresee anything changing for the better, especially since the babies are going to run out of room and block the placenta from moving out of the way."

"Okay," she replies quietly, and I can hear the disappointment in her voice.

"Hey, this is why you moved in, right? It'll be fine, Lo. I promise," I reassure her. She nods, but I can see her chin trembling. "You'll just have to let me drive you to your appointments and make all of your middle-of-the-night Reese's runs, okay?"

"Thank you," she says after a while, staring intently. And I can't help myself when I lean down for a short kiss.

All three of us are blushing when I pull away.

Then there's another knock at the door, and the room instantly seems crowded when Dr. Landry Reed walks in.

"Hey, Lo-Lo," he greets her sardonically. "What did your asshat boyfriend do to you this time?"

I run my tongue over my teeth and count to ten in my mind. Loren rolls her eyes but leans up for Landry to kiss her on the cheek.

"The lady is popular," Rowan quips, smiling to himself. And I think I kind of like Dr. Red Flag.

"Sorry about this whole situation." Landry turns to Rowan now. "I didn't realize my baby sister was dumb enough to go there, but—"

"Landry," she starts. "Shut the hell up."

He grunts but turns to shoot me a cocky smirk. "What, aren't you going to defend yourself, Blake the Snake?"

I shrug. "Why would I care what either of you think? I'm the one sleeping with your sister, remember?"

Rowan clears his throat. "Eh, not exactly, dude. She's still on pelvic rest indefinitely."

Okay, then. I take all that stuff about liking him back.

"Gee, thanks for clarifying that, doc," I retort while Landry snickers on the other side of the room. "While we're at it, let me remind you that I'm also the guy who cockblocked you on your date."

"Blake?"

"Yes?" I turn to Loren.

"Can you also kindly shut the hell up?"

I puff out my cheeks and nod. "Yeah, sorry."

"Wait a minute, are you—does she already have you whipped?" Landry asks, crossing his arms and smiling knowingly. "And you're not even getting laid at this point?"

I glance at Loren, who fumbles with her lip and pretends she's not listening for my answer.

A few years ago, I'd probably have decked Landry or any other man who dared to call Blake Bourgeois whipped. Six months ago, I'd at least have offered a crude yet witty rebuttal. But now, it feels like everything I could ever want is lying on that exam table beside me. I'm beginning to think that Loren and these babies are all I really need, and I've just been too stupid and scared to realize this could be better than any of the other empty accomplishments I've been striving for all these years.

"Maybe I've always been whipped," I say, staring down at her and watching her cheeks flush. Then I pull her hand up to my mouth for another kiss.

"Whoa, not in front of the kids, man," Landry tells me, gesturing at the sonogram monitor and making us all laugh. "So, Lo, have you told Mom yet?" he asks, effectively changing both the subject and the mood again.

Rowan's still quiet as he continues the ultrasound, tapping on a keyboard and taking measurements.

"No," Loren admits after a while.

"You really should—"

"I'll tell her if and when I'm ready."

He huffs. "Your plan is to just let her figure it out when she sees you, then?"

"She'd have to show up for something in order for that to happen, though, wouldn't she?" Loren fires back, and I give her hand a gentle squeeze.

"Right," Landry mumbles. Then he steps over and picks up Loren's chart.

"Hey, I never said you could look in there," she protests, but it's too late.

He raises his brow and glares at me. "Guess you two really have been dating for longer than I thought." Loren's face flushes again, but she stays quiet. He gazes up at the monitor for a while. "Baby A's smaller."

"Row—Dr. LaFleur already told us that," Loren says sarcastically.

"And what about your regular OB-GYN? Didn't he notice?"

"My midwife—her name's Tenley, maybe you know her? Anyway, my midwife is the one who diagnosed the placenta previa and sent me here."

"Wait, Tenley Robin's back?" he asks quickly.

"Yeah, she's a DNP now, too," Loren adds, smirking at me.

"Nice. Maybe I'll look her up next time I'm in town."

I snort, and Loren chokes back a laugh. "Heads-up—Nurse Tenley goes by a different name these days," I tell Landry.

"What, did she get married or something?"

I clear my throat. "Yeah. Or something."

Landry looks confused, and Loren laughs out loud this time. "She's Mrs. JD Bourgeois now. She's also pregnant, for the record."

He grimaces and glares at me again. "You guys aren't afraid to date up, are you?"

I grin at him in return. "No, we are not."

Landry scoffs and mumbles something about my brother and I ruining everything while Loren wipes the gel off her belly. Rowan directs us to stop in the lobby for more information and paperwork, and I thank him again as we shake hands.

"Of course. I'll see you both next month," he says with a genuine smile.

I guess he's all right, as long as he keeps my girls safe.

"So, you guys still want to grab lunch together?" Landry asks, following us out.

"Sure," Loren replies with a sigh. "Just text us an address."

"Actually, I was thinking of a place Loren would really like," I venture. "If that's cool with you, Landry."

He frowns. "Well, Mom's already ..."

Loren's eyes narrow as he trails off. "You invited Mom? After I told you I didn't want to see her?"

"You owe it to her—"

"I don't owe her anything," Loren retorts, crossing her arms over her middle, and I step forward and drape my arm across her lower back. "She lost her rights when she stopped showing up for me."

"Come on, Lo. I know she's done a shit job, but she's still your mother. Don't you think you'll regret keeping her away from your kids? Isn't that a little selfish?"

"Hold on, now," I interrupt, stepping forward and lifting my hand in front of Landry's face. "If anyone's working on regrets, it's you, Reed. Say another word to upset my girlfriend and you won't feel like talking again for a while."

I hold Landry's gaze for a few more seconds until I feel Loren's fingers fumbling for mine behind me, and the red tint clears from my line of vision once I clasp her hand.

"Yeah, fine. I'm sorry. I overstepped," Landry mutters dryly.

Loren sighs. "It's okay. I know you meant well."

I turn to face her, standing with my back to Landry. "We don't have to go anywhere you don't want to, babe. Like you said, you don't owe your family anything."

She forces a sad smile. "As much as I hate to admit it, he's partially right. Maybe we should just get this over with while we're in town." Then she squeezes my hand, and I realize what she's trying to tell me, that she wants me with her.

"Okay, if you're sure. I'll take you wherever you want to go."

She nods. "I know." She leans around me and looks at Landry. "We'll text you the address of the restaurant Blake mentioned. Mom can come if she wants."

He clears his throat. "We'll meet you there."

I lead Loren out to the parking lot, only letting go of her hand once I've helped her into my truck.

"Blake," she begins, staring at me and looking more vulnerable than I'm used to seeing her. "Thank you. You don't have to …"

"I can't help it," I reply, and it's like there's a magnet drawing me in closer. I lean in to press my lips to hers for the second time today, and it's getting harder and harder to pull away.

Her eyelashes flutter, and she licks her lips as I close the door and walk around to the other side. But Landry stops me before I open the door.

"Hold on," he calls out. "You and I need to talk first."

I run my eyes over him before I nod, reaching in my pocket to remote start my truck so that Loren won't hear what we're about to say. "Go ahead, Landry. Talk."

"I don't know what kind of hold you think you have on my sister, but I'm not going to let you hurt her."

"You think I'm the one hurting her?" I stare incredulously. "Loren just found out that she has to choose between her job, which she loves, and the safety of herself and her babies. Not to mention, on top of the life-threatening condition, she was just told that one of the twins isn't growing properly and to prepare for a premature cesarean delivery. Your sister is freaking terrified right now, and you've got the nerve to barge in and pester her about your mom's feelings. What about Loren's feelings? Don't you think she's already torn up about not having her mother by her side throughout all of this?"

He scoffs. "You're the one who put her in danger in the first place."

"Maybe I did. Maybe I am selfish. But I've liked Loren for so long that I didn't hesitate when she finally gave me a shot. And I plan to spend the rest of my life taking care of her and our daughters, whether you like it or not."

"Come on, man. Stop acting like you know what's best for her or that you understand anything about our family."

I shake my head. "You still don't get it, do you? She doesn't need you to fight her battles. Your sister is actually pretty good at holding her own, at least when you're not bullying her around. So why don't you get your head out of your ass long enough to ask her what she really wants and try supporting her for once?"

"And if I ask, you think she'll say she wants *you*?" He laughs.

I look away, and my eyes meet Loren's through the window. She's watching with concern, so I attempt to soften my expression. "I think she'd say she's overwhelmed. But she's also learning that taking care of herself is the only way to keep her babies safe and healthy. She's going to say that she wants to see your mom another time, when she's ready." Then I turn back to face Landry. "And since it's my job to protect my family, I'm taking her home."

He cocks an eyebrow at me. "*Your* family?"

I think about the way Tenley called Loren and the girls my family before. Nothing has ever felt so right. "You heard me."

"I'm not letting you kidnap my sister and tell her what—"

I ignore him as I turn to open the door this time, looking up at Loren.

"Hey, how are you feeling right now?"

She inhales raggedly. "Honestly? Very overwhelmed. A little terrified. Somewhat angry, and mostly hungry."

I grin at her. "Okay. I told you I'd take you wherever you wanted to go. And I will."

She nods.

"And I agree that you should see your mom, but on your terms and no one else's."

She shakes her head. "I'm not ready today."

"So can I take you home?"

"Well, I—"

"I'll feed you on the way, Agnes."

Her smile stretches wide, and she relaxes her shoulders. "Then take me home, Gus Gus."

I wink at her before turning back to Landry. He's standing with his arms crossed, glaring daggers at my head.

"Sorry, Lando. You heard your sister. We'll catch you next time we're in town. Give my regards to your mama."

Then I hop in the truck and leave him pouting in the parking lot while I reach over and lace Loren's fingers through mine.

"Blake?"

"Yeah?"

"Will you still come with me, once I'm ready?"

My heart skips a beat. "Of course, Lo. Anything for you."

CHAPTER 28

Loren

EIGHT MONTHS AGO

I DUCK DOWN IN A HURRY WHEN I SEE BLAKE APPROACHING the concession stand. He's the last person I want to see after our interaction earlier today, when he basically declared me too unattractive to make anyone jealous.

I'm not even sure why I'm letting it bother me so much, but I am. I've never had trouble ignoring his insults in the past.

Well, maybe that's not completely true. But even though it's been a long time since I cared what Blake Bourgeois thought of me, for some reason his words cut a little deeper today than I expected, and I couldn't bear letting him see that.

"Hey, Mrs. Kelli," he greets my co-teacher at the window beside me, and she smiles widely, batting her eyelashes as they make small talk.

"What's Jeff up to these days? You know, he still owes me a morning in that fancy duck blind of his," he inquires about her husband, making me roll my eyes.

"So, what can I get for you, Coach Blake?" she asks after a while, her eyes flickering down to me. She's probably wondering why I'm watching from the ground. I look away quickly and pretend to dig around in my purse for my phone.

Then I make the mistake of glancing up again, only to see Blake's muscular forearms resting on the counter. "Oh, I'll just take a Gatorade. And how about some of those Reese's footballs?"

"Coming right up," she replies before she goes to retrieve his order.

I keep my eyes trained on my phone this time, knowing I'll just get angrier if I look up because he's entirely too handsome. I listen when Kelli returns to exchange cash for candy and to wish him good luck. Then she shoots me another skeptical glare as she moves away from the window, as if she knows I'm hiding.

"A-hem," comes the sound of Blake clearing his voice above me. "You know I can see you, right, Reed?"

I cringe inwardly. "I'm just checking my phone."

He sighs. "Can you please stand up? I came over to talk to you."

"No, thanks. I'm good down here."

"Fine. But you should know I have a clear view down your shirt from this angle."

I press a hand to my chest, and he chuckles lightly. "So, what? It's not like I've got anything worth seeing, anyway."

But I regret the show of vulnerability as soon as the words leave my mouth.

"Don't ... Look, I'm here to give you a real apology, okay?" He sounds surprisingly remorseful.

I stand and lift my eyes to his. "What for?"

"I don't know what happened earlier today. But I didn't mean to insinuate that you aren't ... you know." He lowers his voice and swallows hard.

To my astonishment, he actually seems a little nervous.

"Why, I have no idea what you mean, Blake." I press my lips into a line, trying not to smile at the way he's squirming and avoiding eye contact.

"You're going to milk this, aren't you?" he asks, finally allowing his eyes to meet mine.

"Maybe."

His lips turn up at the corners as he leans in closer. "Fine. I'm sorry for implying you aren't sexy, Reed. I definitely didn't mean it."

I gulp. "Then why'd you say it?" I blurt out.

"It was supposed to be a joke. I only meant to lighten things up, the way we always do when it gets awkward."

"Oh, is that what we've been doing all these years?"

He scoffs. "What do you want from me, Loren?" His voice is tinged with annoyance now. "I just—I don't know what happened, okay? You blindsided me when you forced me to picture you and JD together. It didn't seem right, and my knee-jerk reaction was to discourage both of you from going through with your plan."

I blink a few times at his confession. "Oh," I repeat.

"And I still don't care for the idea of him using you or leading you on."

I laugh, and he furrows his brow. "First of all, despite the way this looks, I *am* a big girl. I don't need anyone to protect me, least of all you, Blake." I can see his jaw clenching after that. "Secondly, I'm the one who offered to help JD. I knew what I was getting myself into. And, even though it's absolutely none of your business, you don't need to worry. I'm not in any danger of falling for your brother."

I know JD obviously has it bad for Tenley, but I'm still a little disappointed about feeling next to nothing earlier when I wrapped my hands around his rather large biceps. Even when he'd spilled his guts about his crush, I should have at least been slightly disheartened by his complete lack of romantic interest in me. Instead, I was simply envious of Tenley's ability to get a man to fall for her in the first place. JD Bourgeois really is a catch, yet there were no sparks or chemistry between us at all. And it's not that I wanted something with JD, specifically, but I *was* holding onto the smallest bit of hope for something with someone … someday.

Blake turns his gaze back to me as a small smirk forms. Then he looks up at me from beneath his lashes, and his tone changes. "So, you're not into oversized golden retrievers, then?"

I laugh in spite of myself. Is he flirting with me?

"Even if I were, what's it to you?"

He shakes his head and smiles wider. "You're going to make me say it out loud, aren't you?"

"I guess I am, because I still don't understand why seeing me with JD would bother you so much when you and I have barely managed to acknowledge one another since high school."

"I told you, it just felt wrong." His voice sounds thick.

"Why? Because you gave me a purely transactional pity kiss nearly two decades ago?"

His eyebrows go up. "A purely transactional ... is that all you thought it was, even after I explained myself?"

"I'm certainly not stupid enough to think an awkward first kiss meant anything to you, especially after all this time." I cross my arms over my chest.

"Even if you really believed that, you should know exactly why I can't stand the idea of you and my brother together. If anyone would get that, it's you," he explains.

He's right. Although we were never *really* friends, and we've barely spoken over the years, we're probably the only ones who truly understand the complicated dynamic we share with our respective brothers. But that doesn't excuse him from acting like an ass.

"Right. Just like you ought to know that I wouldn't appreciate the overbearing-big-bro act."

He hisses and clutches his chest playfully. "Did you just bro-zone me, Reed?" He's grinning now.

I roll my eyes. I'm not up for this. I don't need him to patronize me with his sympathy flirting just so he can make himself feel better.

"Look, my feelings are fine, and all is forgiven, okay?" I return, my tone harsh. "You should go. The game's about to start."

"Wait. Just tell me one more thing, please?" He leans in until he's basically inside the concession stand with me. "How far are you willing to take this plan of yours? I need to know, to prepare myself," he whispers, staring at my mouth.

My lips part, and I'm momentarily flustered. "As far as it takes to get Tenley good and jealous, I guess," I spit out once I've recovered.

"Just Tenley, right?"

I draw back in surprise. "Well, yeah. Who else is there?"

He nods silently and slides a pack of Reese's Peanut Butter footballs toward me. "Good, then. See you around, Loren." Then he winks at me before turning and strutting over to the sidelines, leaving me with my jaw open.

CHAPTER 29

Blake

EIGHT MONTHS AGO (CONTINUED)

JD AND I ARE CLOSING UP THE LOCKER ROOM WHEN ETHAN comes over to ask for help with a flat tire. JD glances at me apologetically, but I tell him it's a lucky coincidence, since his plan for making Tenley jealous hinges on Ethan getting her to hang around long enough to see JD and Loren walking out together.

He motions for Ethan to lead the way, and I follow closely behind. JD's more than capable of loosening a few lug nuts without my help, but he looks like he could use the emotional support.

Then again, maybe I shouldn't bother. I'm not sure I want to be subjected to Loren clinging to JD again, even if it's just for show. Since this afternoon's pep rally, I haven't been able to stop picturing the way her long, dark hair looks hanging down her lower back and how well it highlights her petite, curvy form. Aside from finding Loren Reed much sexier than I care to admit, I'm also feeling guilty after hurting her feelings earlier today. And seeing her go out on a limb for my brother might have softened my previous assertion about her being an annoying know-it-all in general.

It seems like it's always gone the same way with Loren and me, though, ever since middle school. Any time the two of us are alone, my brain misfires, and I end up oversharing or taking it too far. And, sure enough, even though I'd rehearsed my apology ahead of time and

261

gone in with my secret weapon—Reese's—I walked away feeling like a loser again.

I clear my throat as I continue following the others through the gate and try not to stare after Loren comes out from the concession stand to join us. JD stops when we reach the parking lot and makes an awkward showing of walking Loren to her car, and I peel my eyes away from them for a second to check Tenley's reaction. She's absolutely bothered. In fact, it looks as though she's hiding because she can't even bear to watch.

"What's going on with them?" Ethan asks me after a second.

Then I see my brother's hand brush over Loren's lower back as he urges her forward, and I'm pretty sure I let out an audible growl.

I try to save face by turning it into a hum, but it's too late. "Not sure. Must be new," I spit out before I steal a move from Tenley's playbook and excuse myself to take a fake phone call at my truck.

I shake my head quickly, realizing this is ridiculous. Besides the fact that this is supposed to be about helping my brother get with the girl he's been pining over for the past couple of months, I'm not even *that* attracted to Loren Reed.

I redirect my efforts, pulling up Facebook on my phone and searching for her name in the Messenger app. Ironically, I don't even have Loren's phone number, despite being able to boast a longer list of female contacts than any other man in Camellia.

BLAKE BOURGEOIS

It's definitely working.

Your girl's totally flustered over there. I think she might be turning green and everything.

LOREN REED

I narrow my eyes at her response, trying to remember whether that emoji still means "okay," or if the kids have turned it into something more insulting or inappropriate by now.

I wave it off and continue watching against my better judgment as my brother leans in and brushes a strand of hair away from Loren's face. And I don't even need to look Tenley's way to know exactly how she's feeling right now.

Loren must have conveyed my message to JD, because he backs away to aim a cocky grin at Tenley before he closes the car door. But Loren keeps their act going by rolling down the window and reaching out for his hand, and I can't help but stare at the spot on her wrist where he's rubbing his thumb over her smooth, creamy skin.

My mind is instantly overtaken by a concerning amount of violent thoughts, all of them of the Cain and Abel nature.

I avert my eyes before I'm tempted to pick up a rock and lob it at my brother's head—for the record, I'd totally hit my target, since I've still got a decent arm and JD's *gros tête* is hard to miss—and I notice Tenley and Ethan seem to be in the midst of a heated discussion.

At least I can rest assured that JD has successfully grabbed Tenley's attention, if the look on her face is any indication. Which means there's no reason to dwell on my reaction to seeing JD and Loren together.

I bring up the thread with Loren again.

BLAKE BOURGEOIS

I think she's good and jealous.

You can probably stop now.

I know how unpleasant this must be for you, especially since JD gets gassy under pressure.

I venture a glance at Loren again, just in time to catch her looking down at her phone and stifling a laugh. Then she says something to JD, and he glares angrily in my direction before walking off toward Tenley and Ethan.

LOREN REED

It's actually no worse than his brother's tendency to put his foot in his mouth every time he's challenged.

BLAKE BOURGEOIS

You mean you're not a fan of my peanut butter and chocolate apologies? After all this time?

LOREN REED

I'm always a fan of Reese's.

It's my feelings for the brother in question that have wavered over the years.

BLAKE BOURGEOIS

And here I was, thinking you'd admire the kind of man who isn't afraid to admit when he's wrong.

Especially since you've always been so good at making me look like an ass.

LOREN REED

Now, Blake, we both know that's not true.

You don't need my help for that.

I'm still smiling down at the screen when the sound of gravel crunching beneath JD's feet brings me back. He stomps over to Tenley's car, shaking his head and clenching his jaw. I reluctantly put my phone away and walk over to assess the situation, just as Ethan comes around with Tenley trailing behind him. She looks guilty as she stares down at her feet.

What the heck did I miss?

I don't know what she's done, but the way JD's making it a point to ignore her tells me I'm supposed to be mad at her, too. I don't usually take kindly to anyone who makes my brother feel bad, anyway. That's *my* job.

I stand across from them and continue staring Tenley down as JD squats in front of the tire and begins loosening the lug nuts. Her eyes are heavy-lidded and glued to his arms, and I nearly laugh out loud when she swallows so hard that it looks like she's choking on her own desperation.

"You okay, Tenley? You seem ... thirsty," I ask, amused. But JD shoots me a look that says he's abandoned the original plan, so I leave it at that.

"I'm fine," she replies defensively as Ethan tries to stifle his laughter.

JD finishes up, and Ethan and Tenley both thank him, though I can tell he's still upset by the way he avoids eye contact as she apologizes for bothering him. Then he makes a quick retreat, and I follow him back to the field to help him lock up the home gate.

"Did you see that, kid? It actually worked. She's totally into you," I remark as he fixes the lock.

He huffs. "Whatever. She doesn't want *me*, only my help, as usual."

I grab him by the arm. "I'm serious, JD. I wish you could have caught the look on her face while she watched you change that tire. You flipped that switch when you came out with someone else. Make no mistake—Tenley Robin absolutely wants to jump your bones, man."

But he only frowns harder. "Then why does she keep saying the opposite? If she liked me half as much as I liked her, she'd already have given in."

"Maybe she's just stubborn, I don't know. But you can't give up now. You're finally wearing her down."

He shakes his head. "No, you were right before. I can't keep doing this to myself. If all she wants is a friend, then that's all I'll be. The last thing I want is to force something that isn't there." He sighs, lifting his ball cap and scratching his head. "If I were able to do that, then I wouldn't be pursuing Tenley in the first place."

I furrow my brow when I realize he's referring to Loren. But my chest floods with relief once I grasp his meaning, despite knowing I should be sharing in my brother's pain right now.

"I'm sorry, bro," I say after a while, and we turn back to the parking lot together. "Maybe you just need to sleep on it and see how you feel about everything in a day or two."

"Yeah," he agrees halfheartedly. "And I guess it wouldn't hurt to pray about it."

"You do that," I mumble before climbing into my truck and immediately taking out my phone.

BLAKE BOURGEOIS

Listen, thanks for doing this, Reed. It was really cool of you to help him.

LOREN REED

No worries.

Your brother is a good guy. I'm sure he'd do the same for me.

Or any of his friends.

BLAKE BOURGEOIS

Yeah, sure.

But ftr, if you ever need help making a guy jealous, I don't mind taking one for the team.

LOREN REED

Right. I'll keep that in mind.

Good night, Blake.

BLAKE BOURGEOIS

Good night, Loren.

CHAPTER 30

Blake

Loren texts me that she needs my help with some paperwork for school when I have time.

What she doesn't understand is that I can't concentrate on anything else until I figure out what she needs and how to fix it for her. A few months ago, I was afraid of what that feeling might signify. Now, I find myself welcoming it with open arms.

"Hey, I'm really sorry to bother you at work. This can wait," she says, trying to disguise her sniffling when she answers the phone.

"Are you okay?"

"Of course. I'm fine."

"You're crying, aren't you?"

"No." She barely manages to get it out before it turns into a sob.

"Loren, tell me who's making you cry."

"No one," she lies.

"I swear, if my brother is bothering you, I'm going to—"

But she cuts me off. "It's not JD. I'm actually hiding from him right now, because I can't be held responsible when he loses his job for telling off the wrong person."

"What in the hell's going on, Lo?" I growl, already grabbing my keys and heading for the door.

She sighs. "I'm just upset about this maternity leave paperwork.

The lady from HR is so unpleasant. You'd swear they were making her pay for my time off from her own pocket. I mean, it's not like I asked to be put on bed rest."

Another rumble escapes from my chest. "What's her name?"

"I wasn't messaging you to tattle, Blake, only to vent. I can take care of myself."

I stop just before shifting my truck into drive. "I'm sorry. I know you can. I just ... I can't help it." It's become my favorite excuse lately.

She's quiet for a second before she starts again. "I think I'm also feeling guilty about leaving before the end of the year and missing the beginning of the next one."

"But you've got to prioritize your health. Teaching may be your day job, but taking care of your babies is your vocation, now, right?"

"Yes."

"And your students will understand. I'm sure they'll miss you, because you're irreplaceable, but I doubt they'll mind the easier work-load while you're out."

She laughs and sniffs again. "You're right. Thank you."

"You're welcome," I say, my chest warming.

"Maybe you could help me look over this paperwork later?" she asks.

"Of course."

"I'll email you a copy. I'm still confused about whether I'm filing for extended sick leave or maternity leave. And I've got to figure it out before the next time we see Dr. Rowan, since he'll be the one signing off on it."

"Send it over. I'll read through it. And I promise I won't rub it in when I understand it better than you can."

"Kiss my ass, Gus Gus."

"I love it when you talk dirty to me, Agnes." I can practically hear her smiling through the phone, though she's definitely trying not to give me the satisfaction of hearing her laugh. And then I'm hit with the sudden urge to see her, maybe even to touch her.

"Have you had lunch yet?" I ask as I switch my phone over to my truck's audio system and drive out of the parking lot.

"I've eaten. I'll probably eat again," she says, her voice tinged with humor. "Food's just about the only thing on my mind these days."

"Hmm. That's funny. The more you eat, and the bigger your belly gets, the less room there is for anything but you in my daily thought rotation."

"Blake," she chides me, and I hear her smile again.

"Fine," I say with a sigh. "I should get back to work. Don't forget to forward that paperwork to me."

"Okay. Thanks again."

"Anything for you."

"Mm-hmm. Bye."

I'm grinning stupidly when she ends the call, and I pull up to the closest grocery store and run inside for a box of Strawberry Uncrustables. I pull out a bag of Reese's Easter Eggs from the secret stash I keep in my truck, then I head over to Camellia High School.

"Hey, Ms. Sam," I say when I walk into the front office.

"Coach Blake," the school secretary returns with a knowing smile. "Are you here to see your brother or ...?"

I clear my throat and turn on the charm. "Well, I was actually here to see you, but I suppose my girlfriend might get a little jealous."

She cackles loudly before hitting the button under her desk that unlocks the door into the hallway. "She's probably at lunch duty, over by the girls' restrooms."

"Thanks," I return with a wink before passing through the doors and down the hall. I stop to reply to a text from Jada asking me if everything's okay since I left in a hurry, and I tell her that Loren needed my help with some paperwork. She sends me back a "cool story, bro" and a winking emoji, making me blush. I'm still getting used to that.

I step outside, and I'm immediately met with dozens of glares from the student body. But I continue on, giving a few of my football players the nod as I approach Loren. Her eyes widen when she spots me, and a coy smile takes over her face.

Gah, she's adorable.

Her Ophelia T-shirt stretches across her baby bump, which I

swear has grown overnight. The outline of her belly button pokes out, making me want to pull her shirt up and brush my lips over her skin.

"What are you doing here?" she whispers when I approach.

I cup a hand around her belly and lean in to kiss her cheek, lingering a few seconds for a hit of roses. Her face reddens before my eyes, and my self-control absorbs another blow.

"I was in the neighborhood."

"You're full of it, Coach Blake," she says, narrowing her eyes.

I lick my lips. "Maybe I just needed to see you."

Her chest expands, and I can tell I'm affecting her. "I told you I was fine."

"Don't make me kiss you for real, Agnes. Not in front of the kids," I tip my head down to murmur beside her ear, making her shiver.

She clears her throat, signaling that she's deliberately ignoring that last line. "So, what's in the bag?"

"Second—" Her eyebrows shoot up, and I correct myself. "Third lunch? Fifth breakfast?" I hand her the box of Uncrustables, and when she moans aloud, my knees threaten to buckle beneath me.

"Ugh, I love you for this," she proclaims, frantically unwrapping the box. And I know she's just kidding, but the rest of my body can't seem to get the memo.

I shake my head before adding, "But wait, there's more." Her eyes light up when I pull out a bag of Reese's Eggs. She instantly tucks the Uncrustables under her arm and reaches for the candy. "Uh-uh," I tease her, lifting the bag out of reach. "You know you have to earn these, right?"

She glares angrily. "You've made your point. This'll be the biggest scandal of the week, as it is," she spits out, and I glance around to find she's not exaggerating. More students have gathered around and are now shamelessly watching our exchange. I think it's also safe to assume they'll take that cheek kiss as confirmation of my involvement in their teacher's recent extracurricular activities.

Good.

"For propriety's sake, I'll accept verbal proclamations in lieu of PDA, but only this time," I concede after a while.

She squints at me. "Fine. Thank you, Mr. Golden Ratio."

"My pleasure, Ms. Reed," I drawl with a crooked grin, and I'm pretty sure I hear a few squeals from a pack of girls stationed around the corner, including Ethan's girlfriend. I bring the bag down and open it for her, then I hand her one of the peanut butter eggs.

She shoves the entire egg into her mouth, then groans even more loudly as she chews, forcing me to look away and bite my lip when her eyes roll back.

I can't decide whether it's better this way, with her still somewhat oblivious to the extent of her power over me, or if it's even more tortuous because she won't acknowledge the way she's able to turn me into putty in her hands so easily, without even trying.

"Don't do that," she mumbles through a mouthful of peanut butter.

"Do what?"

"Make Reese's sexy," she says after she swallows. "Don't ruin my favorite candy."

"Ruin?" I cock an eyebrow.

"You can't satisfy one of my cravings and trigger a different one at the same time," she breathes, her eyes darkening. "It wouldn't be fair, Blake."

So, she's not *that* oblivious. Duly noted.

I run my tongue over my teeth as I attempt to collect myself. "I guess you're right. It wouldn't be very fair to either of us, would it?"

The bell rings loudly, somewhat breaking the spell, and JD rounds the corner, ushering Ethan and his friends back inside. He raises his brow in approval when he notices us talking and continues herding students toward the building. Ethan comes over to offer a silent fist bump, and his expression looks suspiciously like Mrs. T's "I told you so" look. Then Caidence walks by and flashes us a knowing smile before she grabs Ethan's hand and tugs him along.

"I've gotta get back to class," Loren says shyly. "But thanks for the snack. I feel better already."

I think for a second about how differently things might have gone if we'd have been a couple in high school. And I'm suddenly filled with regret for not listening to my mom when she advised me to go after Loren that day when we fought about prom.

"Anything for you," I vow. Then I notice a bit of chocolate on the corner of her lips and reach up to wipe it with my thumb. She watches carefully when I instinctively bring my finger to my mouth, her eyelashes fluttering as I hum my approval at the taste.

I stretch my left hand over her belly one more time. I won't embarrass her with another kiss, despite the fact that it takes everything I have not to plant one on her in front of everyone, but the way I'm tenderly caressing our babies through her tight T-shirt ought to convey the same sentiment.

"Ugh, get a room," I hear my brother bark out over my shoulder. But when I turn to shoot him a glare, he's grinning widely at me. "Need me to watch your class, Ms. Reed?" he offers, bouncing his eyebrows suggestively.

She licks her lips, and I drop my hand. "Uh, no, I'm on my way." Then she gathers her treats in her arms and steps forward to follow JD inside.

"See you at home?" I call out after her. She nods before she disappears into the hallway, leaving me alone in front of the girls' restrooms. I figure it's not the most appropriate place for me to hang out, so I hustle into the building, stopping by the assistant principal's office.

"What brings you here, Coach?" I hear JD asking from behind me when I raise my fist to knock.

I shrug. "Lo forgot her lunch," I lie.

He huffs out a laugh as he moves past me to unlock the door. "Yeah, right. Like I haven't seen her eating at least three times today." Then he gestures for me to join him in his office.

"I don't think I've been in here since you took over," I remark, my eyes scanning the room and landing on the "Assistant Principal Bourgeois" plaque on his desk. "But it's actually pretty cool. Proud of you, bro."

"Wow, how much did that one cost you?" he asks in amusement.

I roll my eyes. Truth be told, I *have* been giving him a hard time since ... well, since he was born. "Fine. Go ahead and tell me I've gone soft. This conversation's been coming for a while, anyway," I reply, leaning back in the chair across from him and propping my feet up on his desk.

"Nah, that would imply you weren't a big softie to begin with," he says without missing a beat. But then he leans forward and studies me carefully. "You can't blame your sensitive side on Loren or the babies if it's been there all along. But I have noticed something different about you lately."

I press my lips together to avoid the cheesy grin that threatens to take over. "I don't know what you're talking about."

He shakes his head. "Nope, you're lying to me. You always do that weird thing with your mouth when you're not telling the truth."

"What thing?" I ask in protest, realizing I'm rolling my lips in as I say it.

"Yep. I can see it right there. You've got 'whipped' and 'simp' written across your face. Well, that and the way you made me move all of Loren's stuff into your house, not to mention the fact that you haven't left her side for anything besides work in months."

I scoff. "As if you have any room to talk, Coach Thirsty."

He shrugs. "I've never cared. You, however, have a rep to uphold."

"I'm pretty sure my reputation's already been damaged beyond repair."

"In other words, you don't care anymore."

I can't help it when the corners of my mouth turn up this time. "I really don't."

"Then I'm proud of you, too, man." He grins back at me.

I look away. "This is getting uncomfortable. I can see why Ethan's always complaining about the level of cringe."

"I am what I am," he says, lifting his hands. "I'm also your girlfriend's boss," he begins, and I growl under my breath. "And as much as the entire staff and student body seemed to enjoy watching your make-out session in front of the restrooms, I'm obligated to tell you that lunch recess isn't the appropriate time to drop by just to say I love you. Save that mushy crap for when you get home, bruh."

"It was a kiss on the cheek," I mumble, bringing my feet down.

JD stares at me thoughtfully. "She still hasn't given in, has she?"

"I honestly don't know what's going on anymore," I say, rubbing the back of my head. "We act like a real couple most of the time, except for the physical stuff. But we haven't really discussed our relationship status in a while."

He frowns. "Why not?"

"I guess I got a little tired of being rejected," I retort. He opens his mouth to respond, but I cut him off. "So help me, JD, if you call me Roy Kent or tell me to 'be a goldfish' right now ..."

He holds up his hands apologetically, and I take a deep breath before I begin again. "Look, I know I'll never be good enough for her, for them. I just want her to see how hard I'm trying and to know that she's the reason I want to be better. But the stronger my feelings become, the less I'm able to risk getting shut down."

"Blake, there's nothing wrong with falling in love with the mother of your children and growing as a person. In fact, that sounds like a whole lot of right."

I allow my head to roll back as I let out a loud groan. "Can we just skip the sermon and go straight to the part where you tell me the secret to making her go from tolerance to white dress overnight?"

He beams at me, and I feel my face flushing again. "You know, a wise man once told me that it's important to actually *make a move*, because there's only so much hinting around a guy can do if his girl's afraid of commitment for one reason or another. You've been doing a great job of laying all the groundwork for your relationship, and she obviously wants to be with you, too. Now you just need to help her figure out what's holding her back, so you can resolve it together. And that starts with being honest about your feelings."

"Dude, I haven't used the L-word, but I've done everything I can over the past few months to show her I want something real. I have no idea how to be any clearer without scaring the hell out of her."

"Hmm. 'I love you, will you marry me?' is pretty clear."

I huff. "You would say that."

"And you said 'white dress.' "

But I can't help it as the corners of my mouth begin turning up at the thought of Loren meeting me at the altar … one day. "It was a figure of speech."

He grins at me again. "You know who could help you with this?"

"One of your patron saints?" I ask, rolling my eyes.

"Well, yes. But I was going to recommend talking to a good priest —and I just happen to know one. In fact, he's been asking to get together with you and Loren to discuss the baptismal stuff, anyway."

"And how's Father Conrad going to help my situation?"

"For starters, he's an ordained minister and can preside over a wedding ceremony."

"You're getting ahead of yourself again."

"I meant that you'd be surprised at how good he is with couples' counseling. Not to mention, he can help you lift some of that burden you've been unnecessarily carrying around for the past few years."

"What's that supposed to mean?" I ask defensively.

"Forgiveness from your sins does wonders for your confidence," he replies matter-of-factly. "And it's a lot easier to love someone else properly once you're able to love yourself."

"You do realize there's a good chance Father Conrad won't allow us to be godparents, right? I probably can't even receive absolution, so long as Loren and I are living together."

"Look, not that it's any of my business—"

"It's not," I cut him off, since I already know what he's going to ask next. "But we're not stupid enough to risk anything with her condition. Not that it's even like that with us right now. We still sleep in separate rooms."

"Then explain your situation. I'm not saying he won't recommend or maybe even require a few lifestyle changes, but I think you'd be surprised at how easy this could be."

"Lifestyle changes? Wait, is that why you asked me to be a godfather?" I squint at him.

"Of course not." His expression changes. "Tenley and I both love you, and we sincerely want you and Loren to be our baby's godparents. We also love you enough to risk pissing you off by nudging you in a positive direction. Although at this point, we're just supporting you as you continue down the path you've chosen on your own."

I groan. "Fine. I guess we have to meet with him either way."

"Perfect. I'll set it up."

I glance down at my watch before I stand. "I've gotta get back to work," I start. "But I need you to keep a closer eye on Lo and make sure she doesn't overdo it. She's really not supposed to be working this much, and now she's stressing over her maternity leave paperwork."

"Hey, don't tell me how to do my job, man," he replies, sitting up straight and gesturing to the assistant principal sign on his desk.

"Coach JD, are you available? We have an altercation in the gym," a voice crackles over the walkie-talkie he's wearing on his hip.

"Yeah, I'm on my way," he says into the radio. Then he sighs and steps out from behind his desk. "I guess that means I should get back to work, too."

I huff out a laugh. "Have fun, kid."

"Have fun, *boss*," he corrects me with a smirk before he darts down the hall.

CHAPTER 31
Blake

I shuffle into the kitchen, my bare feet sticking to the hardwood floors. Even though the AC thermostat displays sixty-eight degrees, the humidity in Louisiana at this time of year is unavoidable. And I've been tossing and turning for so long that I figure stretching my restless legs can't hurt.

I yawn as I open a cabinet to retrieve a glass and set it beneath the tap in the fridge door. It beeps loudly when I push the fill button, and I cringe, hoping it doesn't wake Loren. She's gotten to the point where sleep seems to evade her every night, and the last thing I want is to wake that adorably grumpy bear.

And *damn* is she adorable. She's also the funniest and cutest and smartest and prettiest and sexiest ...

With a loud sigh, I take a seat at the kitchen island and rest my elbows on the cold quartz countertops. I glance around, noticing the small piles of books and junk littering nearly every surface, courtesy of Loren. And I smile to myself, because I've grown overly fond of her clutter. Even the dirty laundry she leaves on the floor and the ridiculous amount of skincare products surrounding my bathroom sink have become endearing, because they're all reminders of her.

I certainly don't mind the lingering smell of her rose-scented shampoo around the house, either.

My brother was right—again. I'm definitely in love with Loren, have been for a while, and am ready to make some serious moves. It's past time I start amending or even abolishing the ground rules we set months ago. I'm tired of pretending I don't want a romantic relationship with her—a permanent one—even though I'm not sure what that might look like for us just yet.

I think back on my parents' marriage for a minute. They were a little older than I am now by the time they had kids. My mom once told me they struggled to get pregnant for more than a decade before they had me and were pleasantly surprised when she found out she was expecting again, shortly after my first birthday. It must have made them more grateful to be parents, and although my dad and I often butted heads, I know I'm really lucky to have had them. My only grievance comes from losing both of my parents before I'd even turned thirty, my mom developing Alzheimer's in her early sixties and lasting only a couple of years after her diagnosis, and my dad passing away from a heart attack not long after. I think he was happy to go, because I've never seen a shell of a man as sad as my father without my mother by his side. For all the size and big, booming voice that characterized Drake Bourgeois, he was equally gentle and loving, at least when it came to my mom. It's no secret that JD inherited his borderline sickeningly sweet romantic tendencies. My dad looked at my mom with the same dumb, goofy expression I've been seeing on my brother's face since Tenley came around.

Then Loren pops into my mind again, and I close my eyes and swallow hard. Because I think I might be just as love drunk as those two idiots.

What the hell am I going to do when I have two baby girls to dote on in addition to her?

I laugh incredulously at myself as I sit alone in the dark, thinking I might as well throw in the towel and take my lick now, because I'm never going to manage any semblance of my old self after this. And for the first time, the prospect of owning up to my softer side seems so much more enticing and rewarding than putting on that old, worn-out asshole mask.

The sound of the door creaking shakes me from my thoughts, and my heart begins beating faster, just from the anticipation of seeing Loren. She pads out of her room with her eyes closed and gropes her way into the kitchen. I smile, watching her carefully in her cropped T-shirt and sleep shorts, her belly obscuring the elastic waistband.

She scratches her left butt cheek as she reaches out for the counter on her right, seemingly oblivious to my presence. One of her eyes cracks open for a second, but the night light over the stove must be too bright, because she moans and shuts it quickly. Then she continues feeling her way around the island until her hands land on my biceps. Her face contorts, and she stops abruptly, squeezing my arm a second time.

I flex the muscles beneath her hand, and she lets out a frightened squeak. "Feel something you like, Agnes?" I quip.

Her eyes pop open in surprise, and she reaches out to shove me. "You scared the crap out of me. What are you even doing in here?"

I chuckle at her. "Couldn't sleep. You?"

"Same. Well, technically, I did fall asleep earlier, but my empty stomach woke me up."

I laugh again, automatically standing and guiding her to take my spot at the counter. "What are my girls hungry for this time?"

She sighs wistfully. "I'll give you one good guess."

"How do you want it?"

"Mm, jam me, Gus Gus. Jam me *real* good."

I snort as I turn to the fridge and look for the jar, smiling when I find the right one. I don't have to go far to find the peanut butter, since it rarely makes it back into the pantry these days.

"Is it weird that all of my spicy dreams include peanut butter lately?" she asks through a yawn.

My brow lifts. "I think it depends on the rest of the dream and the amount and usage of the peanut butter. But my gut says *yes*."

"I'm not going to answer that, but just know this whole scene is giving me an overwhelming sense of déjà vu," she replies, her voice thick and making her sound drunk. I force myself to take a slow, deep breath before I read too much into it.

This woman is going to kill me. I'm going to need to up my life insurance policy before I can convince her to become my beneficiary.

I blink and shake my head quickly. Since when do I rate my attraction based on the urge to name someone in my will?

I turn and slide the plate in front of her, telling myself I need to step up my game. I am Blake the Snake, after all.

"The crazy thing is, it's giving me the same vibe ... except I feel like you're supposed to be topless by now," I say with a cocked brow.

But she's too busy lusting over the food to notice my flirting.

"Gah, I just ... I need you to fill me up so badly ..."

My eyes nearly bug out of my head. "You do?" I sputter. If I wasn't fully awake before, I certainly am now.

"Shh, I was talking to my sandwich," she deadpans before picking it up and taking a huge bite. She moans, and I smile, trying to ignore the way my body's reacting to the sounds she's making.

"Hmm," I hum. "You're taking this surprisingly well."

"Whah?" she asks as she chews.

"That pickle you just put in your mouth."

Her eyes widen the way mine did a second before, then she drops the peanut butter and dill pickle sandwich before she begins whining and frantically searching for a napkin. I guffaw loudly before I hand her a paper towel to spit into, and she bats at my chest with the back of her free hand as she gags and steals a long gulp from my glass.

"Ugh. I hate you so much, Gus Gus," she says breathlessly.

"That's what you get for teasing me," I tell her, already going back to retrieve the strawberry jelly.

"What do you mean?" she protests. "You're the only tease around here, walking around shirtless and doing sexy stuff right in front of me."

I stop mid-peanut butter swipe when she says it. "Excuse me? What have I been doing, now?"

"You know, *sexy stuff*," she repeats, waving her hands for emphasis. "Working out in your stupid hoochie-daddy shorts, asking me to rewatch the extended editions of *The Lord of the Rings* while you rub my feet, calling it the 'University of Louisiana' and not 'Louisiana-Lafayette,' taking all those showers ..."

My brow lifts in surprise when she admits her voyeuristic tendencies. While I haven't been relying on all of my usual methods of seduction, I have been attempting to lay a honey trap for the past few months. I've just been taking a more subtle, wholesome approach. But maybe I was wrong to assume some of my old faithful techniques wouldn't work.

"So you think I'm sexy?" I venture.

She scoffs. "Your selective hearing is acting up."

"Oh, I heard you loud and clear. To be fair, I don't think you could stand to live with me if I quit showering. And you're the one who barged in on *me* in the bathroom earlier. How exactly was I supposed to stop you from checking me out while I was already so wet and lathered up and ... naked?" I pause to watch her eyes glaze over, and it makes me ridiculously happy to think she liked what she saw.

"Nobody told you to spy on me while I lift weights in the garage either," I add, pointing an accusatory butter knife at her, and she stares at it so hard that I worry for a second that she might actually lick it. I scold myself for the thoughts that cross my mind and return to sandwich duty.

"I had no choice but to barge in. I told you, I was already on the way to the bathroom before I realized it was occupied, but then I sneezed, and the nearest toilet became my only option if I wanted to avoid peeing on myself. And stop trying to change the subject!"

"Oh, so you *want* to break the nudity clause and talk about me doing sexy stuff now?" I ask, a smile spreading across my face faster than I can cover the bread with jelly.

"Yes. It's become a legitimate problem. One that begs to be addressed."

"Begs? Really?"

"Okay, that was poor word choice."

I turn and slide the fresh sandwich in front of her, trying not to smirk. "Fine. Just tell me which direction to go with this." She narrows her eyes at me before I continue. "Am I supposed to be more or less sexy from here on out? Because, I gotta tell ya, babe, I'm just getting started. All you have to do is say the word, and I can lay it on thicker than that jam."

She ignores me and picks up the sandwich. "If there's anything wrong with this one, the only thing getting jammed around here is that butter knife in your neck."

I purse my lips. "That took an unexpectedly violent turn. Good thing I decided not to use the jalapeño pepper jelly."

"Dah ack-sh-lee shoundsh shorta good," she says while chewing. Then she swallows, and I gulp along with her. "Maybe I'll try it in my next inappropriate kitchen dream."

She sighs blissfully before she takes a second bite, and my eyes are glued to her mouth. When she licks her lips, I do the same.

"Only if I can come, too," I mumble, staring hard.

Then she grunts and tries to articulate a muffled, "That's what she said," making me smile.

"Thirsty?" I ask, grabbing the empty glass on the counter as she replies, "You have no idea," and I turn quickly to the fridge before I say or do something else embarrassing.

"Thank you," she says once I set the milk down in front of her.

"My pleasure, Agnes."

"I mean it." Her expression transforms into something more sincere. "For all of this."

And the way she's staring at me with that look of gratitude and adoration for making her a freaking sandwich while she's literally growing my babies makes my stomach swirl with a dangerous combination of guilt and desire.

"And I mean it when I say I'd do anything for you."

"You're already spoiling me too much. I don't know how I'll survive on my own after this."

"Maybe that's the idea," I say under my breath, and she frowns.

Then she chugs the milk and slams the glass on the counter when she's done. "You haven't shaved. Are you growing a beard?" she blurts out before she rolls her lips in, as if she's embarrassed she asked.

I shrug as I rub my jaw. "Why? Do you think I should?"

"It's probably a little warm outside for that," she begins. "But I suppose it would look okay on you."

"Good to know." My eyes search hers until she scrambles to her feet and turns to rinse her dishes in the sink.

And I'm not sure what comes over me, maybe some false sense of confidence or plain old desperation, but I find myself walking over to stand behind her. I brush her sides as I stretch my arms to brace myself against the sink before I lean down to whisper in her ear.

"Tell me, Agnes. Does your spicy-dream boyfriend have a beard?"

She drops the glass in the sink, making a loud thud, and I watch as her chest heaves. She swallows hard before she answers.

"He might."

"Hmm." I tilt my head down and brush my cheek against hers, my stubble making a rustling sound over her smooth skin. "And in your dreams, does it feel this coarse? Or is it softer?"

She shivers. "It's um ... not quite that scratchy. I guess because the beard's a little longer."

"I see," I reply, turning slightly so my breath fans over her neck. Then I step in and press my chest to her back, just firmly enough not to crush her belly against the sink. "You like it rough like this, though, don't you?"

"Maybe," she sighs.

"Don't you want to know what it's like?"

"Wha-what?"

"My beard burn on your face." I move my left hand to cradle her hip, just as my lips brush her earlobe and my chin scrapes her jawline.

"I ... it was just a silly dream," she says breathlessly.

"Was it really a dream, Loren? Or have you been fantasizing about me?"

I move back as I tug on her hips, spinning her around to face me. Her lips part in surprise as she stares up at me, and I cup my hands around her lower back and pull her in closer.

"I wouldn't mind if you have, you know," I mumble, staring down at her mouth. "It's only fair, since you've starred in all of my dreams for some time. In fact, I'm definitely imagining what it'd be like to kiss you right now."

"And what's stopping you from making it come true?" she asks, panting, and her forwardness catches me off guard.

"Only the ground rules," I spit out awkwardly. "But there's nothing saying you can't kiss me first."

She gulps and fists her hands in my T-shirt before she yanks me down to meet her, urgently pressing her lips to mine. I moan as I sweep my tongue over hers, so relieved and impatient for more at the same time. Then I grasp her backside and hoist her up over my hips so I can turn her and set her down on the counter.

But she pulls away as soon as her butt hits the cool stone. "Um, what's happening here?"

"I don't know," I breathe, gripping the corners of the island in an attempt to restrain myself. "But I *really* need it to continue happening."

I move my mouth down to her neck before she has the chance to clear her head, and she tilts her chin back for me. "I'm willing to just let this unfold if you are," she mutters, and I laugh against her skin.

We kiss for a while longer, both of us seemingly lost in the act. Then I notice my hands venturing beneath her shirt, so I reluctantly pull away. Because somewhere in the farthest recesses of my brain, I remember that I need her to understand how I feel about her. And her current mood suggests I should start with the physical part, for once.

"Loren," I begin, gazing into her half-lidded eyes. "You are the sexiest woman I've ever seen. I know we can't go any further right now, but one day, after the babies are born ... and you're ready ... I would do anything to have you again." I grind my hips into her, demonstrating my desperation, and she whimpers. "Anything," I repeat.

"What if we ... maybe I could just ..." She reaches down between us to cup me, and I nearly sink my teeth into her shoulder as I groan at the feeling. She turns her head to look at me. "There's no rule against me touching you, right?"

My hips seem to be involuntarily bucking up to meet her now. "Gah, Lo ... I ..." I squeeze my eyes closed and bite my lip, and I think I might combust when I hear her moan softly.

"You can add these damned gray sweatpants to the sexy ban," she whispers, sliding her hand up and slipping her fingertips beneath the waistband.

My stomach flutters in anticipation. But then I remember everything I've been telling myself, the way I've been working so hard to build that trust with her. "I've never wanted anything more in my entire life. But I can't," I barely manage to choke out.

She stops, her body immediately stiffening with the sting of rejection. "It certainly feels like you can," she says quietly.

"I don't want anything one-sided. It could never be about gratification for me, especially not with you."

"But I know it must be—"

"Don't you dare," I cut her off. "My past doesn't matter—nothing before you does. Wanting you so badly is what makes this difficult, Loren. Especially because I want *all* of you."

She yanks me back in and shoves her tongue down my throat before I can continue, and I'm not sure whether I'm disappointed that she interrupted the big emotional proclamation I was working up to or just ridiculously turned on by the way she's kissing me so desperately now.

I resolve not to push my luck when she surprises me by giggling into my mouth. Then she breaks away again and laughs harder.

"What's wrong?" I ask, trying to catch my breath.

But her eyes are filled with amusement when she smiles at me. "The babies are going crazy right now. They've never moved this much before."

"Oh. Do you think it's the, um, kissing?"

She smirks at me. "Probably the peanut butter and pickle sandwich."

Then I watch as she reaches down to grab my wrists and drags them to her hips. "I wish you could feel them. It really is the coolest thing ever."

I lean in and rest my forehead against hers as I stare down at my hands. They're splayed over her stomach now, a dark contrast against her porcelain skin. "I never thought I'd get to do any of this stuff, you know," I say quietly. "But I'm loving every second of it. I hope you get that, Loren, how happy you've made me by allowing me to be a part of this with you."

She's silent as I slowly move down to my knees, my hands sliding back to her sides as I press my cheek against her bellybutton. She sighs and runs her fingers through my hair, and I swear this is the most amazing moment of my life.

Nothing could compare to this feeling, I think as my heart swells in my chest and my eyes start to sting. But I don't even bother to hide my tears this time.

I contemplate telling her the rest, but I know she isn't ready for these enormous feelings I've been having. For now, my job is to help her figure out what she needs to get to this point with me, however long that takes.

Her hands are still cradling my head against her stomach when I notice a light tick against my cheek. I make myself as still as possible, focusing my attention on the same spot, and it happens again, this time against my temple.

"Was that ... was that one of them?" I ask.

She straightens up. "You felt it?"

I pull away and stand again, using her shirt to wipe the moisture I left behind on her skin. Then I cup my palms over the same spot, and my eyes dart up to hers when I feel another flicker. "Right there?"

She nods and moves one of my hands across to the other side. "Here, too."

There's an immediate flutter beneath the surface, and I let out a surprised laugh as I glance up at her, my expression probably filled with awe. She doesn't say anything as she stretches her shirt and uses it to dab at my eyes, which have grown watery again.

"Thank you, Lo," I whisper. "You're amazing." She sniffles, her own eyes shining, and I lean down to press a kiss over her forehead. "I hope you know this is going to be my new favorite pastime."

She laughs. "I'm sure I can find some time in my busy schedule to lie around and let you grope my huge belly. As long as you keep the PB&Js coming," she says, yawning as soon as she's done.

I smirk at her. "Ready to go back to bed?"

"Yeah. Although, that's not exactly how you worded that question in my spicy dream," she replies in a wistful tone. "And we made more use of this kitchen island first."

I groan and turn around for her to cling to my back, mostly to avoid having to show her my body's involuntary reaction to her. "You're killing me, Agnes."

She giggles as she scoots forward and wraps her arms and legs around me, and I walk down the hall and set her down on her bed.

"Blake?"

"Yeah?" I twist around to look at her.

"I, um, I'm sorry about all that just now. It's probably not very fair to you."

"What do you mean?"

"I shouldn't have let things go that far. I just ... I'm not exactly in control of my hormones right now. But that's not an excuse to spring a midnight make-out session on you."

My mouth turns up at the corner. "You think I minded?"

She looks down at her hands. "But it feels wrong to use you for that stuff, especially since I'm the one who made the rules. I promise, it won't happen again."

That tight feeling in my chest returns. Not the one from a few minutes before, when my heart was so full I thought it might burst. This is the one I get every time she shoots me down, the one that resembles both an aching emptiness and a crushing weight at the same time.

"Right," I answer her after a while. And I'm tempted to say something sarcastic, to make a passive-aggressive comment that lets her know she's hurt me again, but I also just vowed to do whatever it takes to get her to love me back.

So, nice guy it is.

I shove my hands into the pockets of my sweats before I continue.

"Well, uh, thank you for that, for considering my feelings. And I'm sorry being pregnant makes you so ..." I clear my throat, trying to choose my words wisely. "Uncomfortable. Just know I don't mind helping out in any way I can. Good night, Lo."

"Yeah. Good night, Blake," she returns softly, looking surprisingly disappointed.

Then I shuffle back to my own bedroom.

CHAPTER 32

Loren

"This ought to be interesting," I mumble as we drive up in front of the church office.

Blake sighs when JD and Tenley pull up beside us, and we turn and watch as he walks around his truck to open the door for her. As per the norm, JD stops to kiss Tenley's hand, which leads to them staring at one another with a silly look, and eventually them making out in the parking lot.

I smirk as I turn away, slightly embarrassed. Then my eyes meet Blake's, and I worry he can read the longing in my expression. I hope he isn't able to figure out whether I'm pining over him or just for the chance to be loved that passionately before I can sort it out myself.

He clears his throat after a second. "Ready?"

I shoot him a panicked look. "What's our game plan again? Are we together? Are we friends? I'm so confused these days."

"You're not the only one," he mutters to himself. Then he looks away thoughtfully.

"Blake?" I ask, bringing him back.

"Sorry," he says, and I can't help but wonder what he's thinking. "What do you want to tell Father?"

"I certainly don't want to lie to a priest," I return. "Maybe he won't notice I'm pregnant?"

He laughs and reaches over to cup his hand over my belly. "I think that ship has sailed."

"Right. But I can't imagine he'll want to hear that we're cohabitating *and* pregnant, much less that we're not even in a committed relationship."

He frowns and pulls his hand back. "At least we can tell him we're not sleeping together. I'm sure that's all that matters."

"I don't know." I shrug. "Don't you think he'll say playing house has the potential to develop into more? That there's too much temptation?"

"Yes," he replies after a while, his voice thick. And that one word is so loaded with emotion that it makes my stomach flutter.

"Let's not volunteer that information, then," I offer, trying to lighten things up.

He nods. "Okay. We'll tell Father Conrad the truth, but on a need-to-know basis. If he asks, we'll be honest."

"The problem is that I'm not even sure I know the truth at this point."

Blake groans and shakes his head, seemingly frustrated with me. "It's a good thing I'm heartless, Reed. Or you'd have formed a habit of ripping it out and tap dancing on it every day."

I gape at him, unsure of how to respond to his uncharacteristically emotional outburst.

"I'm kidding," he says, looking embarrassed. "It's just so impressive, your ability to draw out the kind of information I've spent a lifetime suppressing from myself. You would have made an amazing interrogator."

I swallow, my eyebrows still drawn together in concern. "Blake ..."

"Please stop looking at me like that," he begs quietly. "I can't tell whether you love or pity me when you do."

My breath catches in my throat when I try to answer. "I don't—"

"Look, we're going to go in and act like our situation is perfectly normal, and if he asks questions, we'll tell him the same thing we plan to tell everyone else, that we're better off as friends. It's not completely true, but it's not a lie, right?"

It takes me a second to answer, mostly because something about the way *he's* looking at *me* today has me totally flustered. "Isn't it, though?" I venture after a while. "A lie?"

His breathing quickens as he continues staring back at me. He opens his mouth to say more when there's a loud knock, making us both flinch.

"Seriously?" Blake yells through the driver's side window.

JD and Tenley stand back, cackling at our expense. Blake turns to me one more time, but I panic and reach over to open my door. I hear him cursing under his breath before he hurries around the truck to help me out, glaring at his brother as he goes.

"Sorry. I didn't realize I'd be interrupting something important," JD says, looking remorseful.

"Just a discussion of how we're going to face the priest in our current predicament," I reply softly.

JD turns his mouth to the side before glancing over at Tenley. They have some kind of silent brainwave exchange, and she places her hands on my shoulders to lead me on.

"Let's go inside. I don't know about you, but it's been five minutes since we left home, and I've already gotta pee."

I look back at Blake before reluctantly following Tenley into the rectory for a potty break, probably my tenth of the day, and the guys join us in the front office a couple minutes later.

Father Conrad comes out to greet us, his eyes darting down to my belly as he declares remembering us from the wedding a few months back. "Well, it looks like I'm in for a two-for-one special," he says cheerfully.

"Three-for-one," Tenley corrects him. "Loren's expecting twins, Father."

"What a blessing," he declares, and he sounds like he genuinely means it. "Congratulations."

"Thanks," I say quietly, somewhat relieved. Blake only nods and gulps.

"So, are we all here for the same thing?"

Blake glances at me. We haven't discussed whether we want to baptize the girls, I think because we're both afraid of being denied the option with our current situation.

"We're just here as potential godparents for now," Blake finally returns. "But I was hoping to ask about our babies, too."

I'm surprised to hear him bring it up for the first time, but I chalk it up to convenience.

"Great. The two of you can come on back for a short interview. It's all part of the process," Father assures us. He gestures toward an open door down the hall, and Blake waits for me to stand before he clasps my hand. I'm not sure whether he's overcompensating in front of the priest or trying to calm me, but I feel better knowing we're going in together.

We sit in a pair of chairs across from Father's desk, and Blake hesitates before dropping my hand. Father watches carefully before he dons a pair of reading glasses.

He shuffles a stack of papers on his desk. "Let's see ... have you been confirmed?"

"Yes, but I'm not sure either of us would be considered practicing Catholics," Blake volunteers.

It's a fair statement. I made my confirmation back in high school, alongside Blake and Tenley, and I've always based most of my moral code on my Catholic upbringing. I just haven't been so great about keeping up with some of the particulars since then, such as regular attendance at Mass. But my parents hadn't exactly made our faith a priority when I was growing up. They sent my siblings and me to catechism, took us to church on a rare Sunday between Christmas and Easter, and made sure we'd received a few of the sacraments. And that was that. I'm pretty sure I remember Blake's household being more devout than mine, though.

"Oh? What makes you say that?" Father asks.

"Lack of effort, I suppose," Blake says.

"Would either of you have any problems renewing your own baptismal vows?" He hands us each a sheet of paper with a list of questions, most of them pretty simple and direct.

Blake glances at me again. "I don't think so," I answer this time.

"Then, we'll just settle the rest. There's still time for you to get back into practice, isn't there?" Father smirks at both of us.

"Yeah, sure," Blake admits reluctantly.

"Do you mind if I address the elephant in the room?" Father begins again, and my stomach turns. "Hmm, sorry, that was a poor choice of words," he crawfishes, laughing softly and making me smile. "I probably should have said, 'your current situation.' "

Blake and I trade nervous looks before he speaks up. "We, uh ... well, we're having these babies together, and we aren't married, if that's what you mean."

"Do you have any intentions on changing that last part?"

I fidget in my chair, and Blake clears his throat. "We haven't spoken about it explicitly."

I'm taken aback for a second. He could have just said *no*.

"May I ask why not?"

This time Blake looks directly at me as he replies, "I don't actually know."

Okay, what the heck is that supposed to mean?

"But you're *together*?" Father ventures.

"Our relationship is ... unconventional," Blake explains while he continues staring at me. "We've known each other all of our lives, and one night things got physical, obviously. But we agreed that being good parents was more important than acting on that attraction again, so we started back at square one. We've been working on a friendship and sort of ... lightly courting since then."

Courting?

Is that what Blake thinks he's doing when he makes me like him so hard that I second guess my ability to function as a reasonable adult? When kissing him makes me forget my middle name until the next time he calls me "Agnes" again?

"Mm-hmm, and where do you see this going?" the priest continues, despite the way my face must look right now.

Blake shrugs. "I suspect we both want more, but we can't seem to get on the same page. I think she's too afraid to jeopardize our friendship for the sake of our kids, and I'm just trying to respect her wishes."

Whoa.

Why is he just saying all of this now?

Or maybe ... is this the stuff he's been trying to tell me when I've been "ripping out his heart"?

"I see. What do you think, Loren? You've been awfully quiet."

I nearly choke on my spit. "I, um ... I guess I would agree with most of that."

"So, you're okay with remaining friends with Blake indefinitely? Living separately, splitting time with your kids, pursuing other relationships?"

"We're not exactly living separately," I admit meekly. "Blake invited me to move into one of his guest bedrooms after I developed a medical condition. At least while I'm on bed rest."

His eyebrows shoot up. "Oh. So you're roommates?"

"We're not having sex, if that's what you're worried about," Blake volunteers after a second.

Father's lips twitch, as if he's trying to hold back a smile. "But you'd like to be?"

"I guess it depends on which of us you ask on any given day," Blake retorts.

Holy shit, he's totally throwing me under the bus in front of the priest! Well, if he's airing out his true feelings, I'm allowed to be brutally honest, too, right?

"Blake has been very attentive and taken great care of me throughout the pregnancy," I blurt out. "But it's hard to differentiate between his fondness for me as a co-parent and any romantic feelings he might be harboring."

He licks his lips and looks away. "Yeah. Same here."

"And you don't think those feelings could coincide or even overlap?" I had no idea we'd be walking into relationship counseling when we started this, but Father looks pretty invested now.

"I guess it's possible, but I can't figure out what he's thinking most of the time," I reply.

Blake scoffs, to my surprise. "Is it really that hard for you, Lo?"

"What?"

"You honestly can't tell how I feel about you by now?" he asks, shaking his head. He's talking to me like we're alone in the room.

I twist my lips to the side as I contemplate my answer. "The problem is that I'm not sure I can trust you."

He starts to protest, but I continue. "I know you believe your feelings for me are genuine, but I think you're just confused. You love the way I accept you for who you really are and that you don't feel lonely when I'm around, and maybe you even love me for carrying your babies, but you're not *in love* with me."

He runs his tongue over his teeth, brooding silently as Father speaks up. "I'm not sure there's a difference for him, Loren. What if the qualities you named are the ones he values most in a partner?"

I laugh shortly. "Yeah, sure. Blake Bourgeois has been secretly longing for a family all this time and was simply test driving every attractive woman in South Louisiana until he found the right one to bear his children." And then I cringe as soon as the words leave my mouth. "I—I'm sorry. That wasn't very nice. I didn't mean it like that."

Blake still looks wounded, though, and I'm kicking myself for being such a jerk. Why can't I stop bringing up his past? I say I don't care, and I think I mean it each time.

Maybe I'm the one who's confused? Maybe I'm ... jealous?

We sit in tense silence for what feels like a full minute. "If I'm being honest, your extensive dating history does bother me," I admit after a while. "Not that it makes me think any less of you, but because it makes it impossible to imagine that out of all the women you've been with before and all the women you could have now, you would really choose *me.*"

Blake's face is still downcast. "Why?"

"No one else ever has." I sniffle, and he reaches over to grab a tissue box from a side table. "Thanks," I mumble before drying my nose.

"Lo, I'm sorry, but you are so much more worthy of love than your shitty parents and your misguided brother have let you believe."

I furrow my brow. "And so are you," I return. "Only you've convinced yourself otherwise."

He lets out a sarcastic laugh. "Maybe you were right, though."

"About what?"

"All the others, my history of casual dating and meaningless sex. I think I was just looking for something I'd only ever found with you."

"What?" My mind is reeling now.

"It started with our first kiss. I was having such a hard time with my self-worth that night, and once I got that rush, as soon as I realized how much I enjoyed making you feel good, I was hooked. It's all I ever wanted to do after that, and I've been chasing that same high for years. But it's never been the same with anyone else. And I'd take it all back in a heartbeat if it'd make it easier for you to trust me."

My breath catches in my throat at his confession, and I shudder. I had no idea he could possibly feel this way. And yet, the way he's looking at me right now, pouring his heart out, it's so hard not to believe him.

He shakes his head. "You're doubting me again, aren't you?"

"I want it to be true," I reply, swiping at my cheeks. "But you're telling me you enjoyed one silly kiss more than sex with other women, women who are far more experienced, interesting, beautiful, and desirable than me. It doesn't make sense."

"Do you really want it to be true?" he asks, his voice even. "Is it just because of your insecurities that you can't believe me, or is it that you don't feel the same? Because none of those other women have ever come close to being as interesting or beautiful as you, and I've never found anyone more desirable—*never*."

That one nearly knocks the wind out of me, but I continue on, doing my best to seem unaffected. "Blake, I don't know what to say. You terrify me. You always have. You're good at every damn thing you try, and you make it look easy. Every time I think I have you pegged, you reveal another layer, and it makes me want to fall even harder. Because I know what you are at the core: kind, sensitive, generous, selfless, humble. You put on a good show, but I know your heart by now. And it's so *good*."

His shoulders rise and fall as he exhales, and I notice his eyes are misty now.

"It's also why I can't afford another risk, not when it's too late to prove your feelings for me are real and not just a side effect of watching me have your babies. There are two tiny humans depending on me now, and I refuse to subject them to the same childhood I had, with parents who kept going through the motions and self-medicating because they were too chicken to admit that they felt nothing for one another."

There's another uncomfortable stretch of silence before Father clears his throat, making me wince. I'd forgotten he was there.

"Loren, have you spoken to anyone about this before?" he asks carefully.

I nod and wipe my nose. "I saw a therapist for a while, back in college. Believe it or not, I'm better than I used to be," I answer with a sardonic laugh, and Blake reaches out to clutch my hand again.

"Have you thought about forgiving your parents, even if they don't deserve it, as a gift to yourself and to God?" the priest continues.

"I thought I *had* forgiven them, but apparently my therapist and I both underestimated my ability to hold onto a grudge."

"Duly noted," Blake says, though he's smiling.

"And you, Blake, are you ready to forgive yourself?"

He frowns. "But I'd have to admit I was wrong in order to do that, wouldn't I?"

Father shrugs. "We all heard you say it a minute ago, so you can drop the act. No one in this room believes you're really as horrible as you pretend to be."

My eyes grow wide, and Blake presses his lips together and stifles a smirk. "You also heard her say I was sensitive, Father. How come I get the bad-cop treatment while she gets the sugarcoating?"

"I grew up as the oldest son in a large family. Which is a nice way of saying that my mother taught me to tread lightly around pregnant women."

We chuckle as Father leans back in his seat. "It's also my job to remind you about the sacraments. I find reconciliation to be particularly helpful in situations when you need to drop some of the weight you've been carrying around for too long."

Neither of us says anything, so he continues. "But I think you've given yourselves enough to prayerfully consider for one day. Why don't we plan to meet again in a couple of weeks for the rest of the baptismal prep, hmm?"

"What about the others? Don't you need to see them?" Blake inquires as he stands and helps me up.

"Oh no, your brother and his wife are long gone," Father replies matter-of-factly, waving his hand. "This was just a setup."

I snort as we walk to the door, but Blake grins. "He does owe me a few of these set-up deals."

"Speaking of your family," Father Conrad begins. "I noticed the two of you were present for Ethan's confirmation last month, and I've seen you in church a few more times since then. I hope you'll both make it a habit to attend Mass regularly from here on out, you know, to better prepare for your new roles as godparents-slash-actual-parents. And possibly even marriage one day, right?"

"I guess that's doable," Blake answers, to my surprise. Then he stops short, glancing at me with an apologetic look before he calls out, "Actually, Father, do you think I could bend your ear for another minute?"

"Of course."

I furrow my brow, and Blake opens the door to lead me out to the front office. "I'm sorry to make you wait, but this won't take long. I promise," he whispers before he kisses my cheek and heads back inside.

I pull out my phone and spend the next five minutes or so trying and failing to concentrate on a book until Blake returns.

"Ready?" He's smiling, and even though it's not a full-face grin, it reaches his eyes in a way I'm not used to seeing from him.

"Yeah, sure."

He holds out a trembling hand to help me up again, and I stare at him before I move to take it. There's something different about his posture. Even his shoulders seem more relaxed.

"Everything okay?"

He nods quickly. "Yeah. Nothing to worry about."

"Blake, you asked to speak to a priest alone, but you're telling me not to worry?"

He shrugs and offers another shy smile in return, then he leads me out to his truck. And I swear, his steps are lighter.

Great, I think to myself as I climb inside with his help. *Now I can add "floating" to the list of ways Blake makes walking look good.*

"You're really not going to tell me what happened back there, even after I shared my most embarrassing secrets today?" I prompt, nudging him gently as he cranks the truck.

"I took my brother's advice for once, okay?"

"About what?" My curiosity is killing me now.

He sighs and gives me a side-eyed glance before he pulls out of the parking lot. "I asked Father to hear my confession," he admits. "For the first time in … I don't know, at least twelve years."

"Oh," I breathe, not expecting that answer or the way it makes my heart quicken. "That's … that's amazing, Blake."

"I'm not sure yet, but it kind of feels like it," he says softly, still smiling, and my chest warms. I reach over the center console and hold out my hand, and he doesn't hesitate to interlace our fingers.

"Loren, while I'm clearing my conscience and everything, there's something else I want to say."

"Hmm?" I squeak.

"I haven't been honest with you. I've been … cheating, in a way. And that ends now."

I inhale sharply. "What?"

He pulls up at the one traffic light in town and turns to me. "The only thing I've faked is being okay with our arrangement. These past few months have been the best, and I've enjoyed every second of being your boyfriend, even if you were only pretending. It all felt very real to me."

"It did?"

"Yes," he replies, swallowing hard. "And I don't want to pretend anymore."

The light turns green, but he doesn't move.

"What does that mean?" I ask quietly.

"It means I'm done lying about us. I want the chance to prove I'm worth the risk, to show you how great we could be together. I'm open to whatever level of commitment you want, and I promise not to pressure you into anything physical." He pauses for a second before he adds, "I'm yours, Loren, whether you want me or not. But I really want to mean it when I say you're mine, too."

He squeezes my hand and brings it up to his mouth for a kiss, and I let out a shaky exhale.

"Okay," I breathe. After today's turn of events, I don't know how to keep acting like I don't want him, regardless of my fears.

His eyes meet mine. "Yeah?"

I nod. "I'm all yours. Just promise you'll be patient with me, okay?"

He leans over and cups my face before he brings his lips to mine for the sweetest kiss I've ever had.

"I promise."

CHAPTER 33

Loren

"Hey," I greet Blake from my favorite reading spot in the corner of the sectional. I'm not sure whether it's a result of being stuck at home all day without adult interaction or the fact that I'm genuinely this happy to see him, but there's a flurry of butterflies in my stomach.

"Hi, babe," he returns, coming over to give me a short kiss, and I'm tempted to latch onto his tie and hold him there a bit longer.

Between our accidental midnight make-out session in the kitchen and the declarations he made during our meeting with Father Conrad, things have been growing increasingly tense between us over the past few weeks—but like, the sexy kind of tense. It's the type of tension that results from a combination of pelvic rest and a crazy gorgeous and incredibly witty boyfriend doing and saying all the right things while he walks around the house looking like a total snack. And that's not including the way he's been openly declaring his feelings for me since we agreed to date for real.

I'm still glad we're taking things slow. But when I'd asked Blake to be patient with me, I sure as heck didn't think I'd be the one exercising all the patience.

I allow my eyes to run over his profile again, noting the sharp perfection of his jawline beneath the short beard he's started keeping.

I wonder for a second whether he'd let me slather him in peanut butter and ...

Nope. No, ma'am. Not going there.

But I'm so hungry. And I like snacks.

I clear my throat. "How was your day?"

"Good, court just ran long," he says after a while, turning to shoot me an exhausted smile. "How are you?"

"I'm still pregnant, so that's a loaded question."

He laughs and scrapes his fingertips over his cheek, making a rustling sound, and I don't miss the way his shirt sleeves are rolled up to expose his forearms.

"Hungry yet?" he asks, sitting down beside me.

"Mm-hmm," I return, trying to keep my thoughts from veering off into dangerous territory again. "Always."

"What are you craving?" He reaches over and cups his hands over my belly.

"Peanut butter."

He chuckles softly. "And I was going to offer to get takeout."

"I was actually hoping you wouldn't mind bringing me to pick up a new book this weekend. Unless you're too tired to go tonight?"

He smiles wider when he feels a kick under his hands and lifts my shirt. "Of course not. We can grab dinner while we're out."

"Okay," I squeak as he leans down and begins kissing his way around my belly button. I shiver when his chin tickles my skin.

"Blake," I begin, my voice breathy. "Why did you grow out the beard?"

"You know why," he looks up and says with a smirk, and I make him laugh when I accidentally whimper.

"I don't like that you feel the need to change anything about your-self for me. I shouldn't have that much influence."

"So you don't like it?" he asks, sounding disappointed.

"Oh no, I freaking love it," I blurt out. "I'm just trying to be a good girlfriend."

He chuckles again and sits up, leaning in to plant a kiss on my forehead this time. "You're already the best girlfriend I've ever had."

I roll my eyes. "That's not saying much, is it?"

"I'm going to freshen up," he says with a smile, ignoring my dig. "I'll meet you in the truck in a few minutes?"

"Okay," I reply quietly before I watch him walk away. I go into my own bedroom to throw on a comfortable dress. It's one of my favorites because of the Elvish pattern, and I put on a pair of wedged sandals. But once I make it to the garage, I'm confused to find Blake's truck missing. My phone chimes at the same time I glance around.

GUS GUS

I'm here to pick you up for our date, ma'am.

I narrow my eyes at the message and turn to the road. Sure enough, Blake is standing at the curb, leaning against the open passenger door of his truck.

LOREN

Who said anything about a date?

GUS GUS

Get your sweet ass in the truck, Agnes. I'm starving.

Better?

LOREN

Much.

I try not to smirk at him as I slip my phone into my purse and walk over. He wordlessly reaches down to help me climb inside, then shuts my door and comes around to the driver's side.

He taps on the screen and switches the bluetooth input to my phone, and I put on an old playlist from the year we graduated high school as a nice compromise.

"So, ah, what new book are you just dying to pick up today?" he asks, breaking the silence.

"It's actually just a special edition of one of my favorites, and I could use another copy because I sort of read my old one to death," I admit sheepishly.

"Oh. Does this book have a title?"

"*Outlander*."

His eyebrows go up. "Isn't that …?"

"Yes, it's also a TV series." He nods and keeps his eyes trained on the road, but I can tell the wheels are turning in his mind. "What? Have you seen it?"

He shrugs. "It's sort of a chick-show, isn't it?"

"It's not just a romance series. There's time travel, battle scenes, historical context …"

"Boobs."

I snort. "So, you *have* seen it."

"Maybe." I reach over to pinch his arm, and he fakes a wince. "You know, I'm more than just a pretty face, Reed," he adds after a few seconds.

"Are you trying to say you've read the *Outlander* books?"

"I wanted to see what all the fuss was about," he confirms with another shrug.

He turns into the parking lot of my favorite Chinese restaurant, just as I remember that I'd been rereading the series a few months back, right around the time I found out I was pregnant. And it's likely that my well-loved copy of *Outlander* had been hanging out on my nightstand when he'd started coming over to my house.

"But, *dinna fash*. I can keep pretending I don't know about all the spicy romances you read if you want me to," he continues, interrupting my thoughts. "*Sassenach*."

My jaw drops slightly, and Blake winks at me before getting out of the truck.

Down, girl.

"I thought we were just getting takeout?" I ask when he comes around and opens my door.

"I told you I was starving. I wasn't kidding about being stuck in court all day, and I suspect I'll never be able to drag you out once I let you loose inside of a bookstore."

"I see your point."

He leads me inside and gives the waitress our regular order once we're seated. "Anything else?" he asks me.

"Uh, no," I return, swallowing hard. "That's … good."

I'm not sure when watching Blake perform normal, everyday tasks became such a turn on for me, but here we are.

The waitress leaves, and I feel my cheeks darken as he stares at me from across the table. "I'm so glad to hear you're dating again, Lo. I was having a really hard time holding out on our deal," he says, his hand venturing over to mine.

Butterflies flutter around in my stomach, in addition to the hungry babies doing acrobats, and it takes me a while to respond.

"I knew you'd crack first," I finally manage.

He laughs. "The thing is, I've been saving my first real date in months for this one woman. In fact, it feels like I've had a crush on her for half of my life. And after practically throwing myself at her for years, she's finally agreed to give me a shot. But I'm so pathetic that I overreact every time she shows me the least bit of affection, even though I can't stop thinking about her lips and plotting on how to get her to kiss me again."

I bite my lip and stifle a smile. "You are a piece of work, Blake Bourgeois."

He gives me a smoldering stare from across the table, rubbing his thumb over the back of my hand. "My mama used to say that about me all the time."

"Your mom *was* the best," I offer, effectively changing the subject.

"She was, wasn't she?" He leans over as if he's imparting an important secret. "And I don't care what my brother says—I was her favorite."

I chuckle. "I could see that. You were a cute kid."

He sits back, keeping his hand over mine. "Who do you think our babies will look like?"

"I certainly hope they get your eyes and hair. And some of your height."

"Mm, I think they'll be beautiful like their mama, with your fair skin and dark hair. And smart like you."

"They'd better be clever, for their own sakes. Surely, they won't survive having us for parents if they can't get sarcasm," I say, trying to ignore the way he's still staring at me.

"Speaking of the babies, there's something I've been meaning to ask, something I probably should have brought up a long time ago." He pauses for a breath. "I know you already have your heart set on their first names, and I love Penelope and Charlotte. But would it be okay if we gave them my last name?"

I see his throat working as he swallows hard. "Of course, Blake. They're just as much your daughters as they are mine. Besides, Bourgeois is a much cooler surname, and I've never really been all that attached to Reed, anyway," I reply with a smirk, and he grins back at me.

"I'm glad to hear you think so," he returns, his tone deepening and making my stomach swoop.

"Were you really worried I wouldn't want them to have your name?" I ask quietly, brushing over his advances again.

"A little," he says on an exhale. "It's really important to me, and I guess I got nervous and built it up in my mind."

"Sort of like me and childbirth right about now." I scrunch up my nose, and he laughs.

"Then you should probably pray the girls do end up taking after you. I hate to sound insensitive, but at least there's a chance they'll be smaller with your genes and having to split their peanut butter sandwiches. My sister-in-law, on the other hand, is probably in more trouble than she'd like to think."

"Wait, were you guys big babies?"

He shrugs apologetically. "I was nine pounds. JD was nearly ten."

"*Nine* pounds? Holy hell, man. You should really lead with that the next time you have unprotected sex," I exclaim a little too loudly.

He snorts. "Sorry I didn't make it a point to mention my birth weight up front. Besides, at the time I was a little busy with a mouthful of—"

I clear my throat as the waitress approaches with our food, thinking I'm safe. But a second later, my phone vibrates, and I open the notification to find a text from Blake with an emoji that fills in the blank. He bats his eyelashes innocently at the waitress and thanks her, and I try to hide my blush and pelt him with a fortune cookie as soon as we're left alone again.

"Hey, now, I know you're pregnant, but no tossing your cookies at the table," he protests as he pushes a plate of noodles my way.

I boo his terrible dad joke as I begin shoveling in lo mien as if I haven't eaten in ages. That's the thing about being pregnant: Hungry is the hungriest I've ever been, thirsty is the thirstiest I've ever been, and so on. It doesn't bode well for all my other growing urges.

We finish dinner, and I crack open one of the cookies to read my fortune.

"What does it say?"

I lift a brow. "I didn't take you for the kind of guy who buys into fortune cookies."

"Maybe I just wanted you to read it aloud so I could add 'in bed' or something else at the end that makes it sound dirty."

I smirk and look down at the slip of paper, then I click my tongue. "'Our brightest blazes of happiness are often triggered by unexpected sparks.' Ugh. Too easy."

He licks his lips and tries his best not to laugh as he reads his. "'People may doubt what you say, but they will believe what you do ...' *in bed*."

"I think you planted these ahead of time, you nerd."

He winks at me before standing and gesturing for me to go ahead, and I get another text as I wait at his side while he pays for our meal. Now he's just sending me random suggestive emojis. I put my phone away and elbow him in the ribs as he accepts the receipt. He responds by pinning me with a sexy glare, his mouth turning up slightly on one side.

We leave the restaurant and head over to the bookstore, and I ask him more about his reading habits on the way. Truthfully, his answers surprise me. I might have thought I knew Blake better than most, but the more I learn about him, the more I like.

"Wait," he says as he reaches over and pulls my door closed. "I just remembered. It's the markings on the inside of the ring, right? Those letters on your dress?"

Oh, come on. This isn't even fair anymore!

I blink at him as my brain malfunctions, eventually finding the wherewithal to nod.

"I like it. It's one of my favorites on you. And it goes well with your little tattoo."

"You don't think it's weird?"

"I told you, Reed. I thoroughly enjoy your particular brand of weird," he says, leaning in to plant a short kiss on my lips. Then he comes around to the other side to help me out.

Just as I'm getting my bearings again, Blake reaches down and laces his fingers through mine as if it were the most natural thing in the world for us to be walking into the bookstore hand in hand. Meanwhile, my inner twelve-year-old girl is squealing so loudly that I can't even hear myself think anymore.

"Lead the way." He gestures with his free hand once we're inside.

I can barely contain my giddiness. We head over to the fiction section first, and I reluctantly let go of him to pick up the book I came in for, plus a couple more that look interesting. He reaches over to pluck the books from my hands and stacks them in his capable arms. I pay a second glance to his forearms since his sleeves are still rolled up, and they look even sexier as they support my reading habit.

It takes me a few seconds to peel my eyes away, and I look up to find him staring at me expectantly. "Oh, um, that's it," I say quietly.

"I was thinking we could check out the baby section before we go? I'd like to educate myself so I can avoid both the scary Google rabbit holes and having to text my sister-in-law a dozen questions per day."

I furrow my brow. "You've been asking Tenley pregnancy questions?"

"What? No—who me? Pfft. I would never," he says with exaggerated disgust, making me giggle.

I attempt to school my reaction as we cross the store and make it to the *What to Expect* corner, and he adds a few titles relating to pregnancy, childbirth, and breastfeeding to the stack in his arms.

"I'm not making any assumptions," he clarifies as I eye up a nursing mother's guide. "Only grabbing a little of everything, just in case."

"Oh, man, I haven't even really started thinking about that stuff," I mutter, more to myself than anything. "I'd always figured I'd breastfeed the babies I never thought I'd actually have, but I don't know the first thing about tandem nursing."

He smiles ruefully. "We'll read the books together. And once you make your decision, I'll be ready with whatever you need. You know, nipple cream or bottle warmers, whatever it takes."

"Blake, do you realize that we'll need *two of everything*? Two car seats, two cribs, two wardrobes? And then once I go back to my own place, that's like *four* sets of everything!"

He lifts his free hand to my arm to soothe me. "Hang on, Lo. Let's not worry about all the logistics yet. I'll make sure we have everything we need, I promise. You and the babies will never go without, okay?"

I look down and nod. "I know, I just hate the idea of you spending your 401k on us."

He lets out a short laugh. "I can afford a couple of cribs, babe. I do all right financially, and I haven't exactly had anything worthwhile to spend my money on before this. Don't worry about it."

"Right, but ... shit, I'm gonna need a new car, and I—don't you dare think you're buying me a car!"

His eyes widen with feigned innocence. "I was thinking no such thing," he lies and tries to disguise a smile. "But what I *am* thinking about is why you would want to move out so soon after the babies are born."

"I just figured once I wasn't in this placenta-previa predicament anymore that I'd go back to my own place," I explain, my heartbeat drumming loudly in my ears. "You weren't expecting us to continue living together after this, right?"

He has the nerve to look hurt. "Well, yeah, at least for a while."

He clenches his jaw as I stare at him. "Hell, Loren, you didn't think I'd just drop you off on the way back from the hospital and leave you on your own with our newborn twins, did you?"

I sniffle, my eyes watering on their own accord. "I ... I don't ..."

Then his expression softens, and he places the stack of books down on the nearest table before pulling me into his arms. "Come here," he begins, placing a kiss on top of my head as I cry into his dress shirt. "I'm sorry."

Ugh. Of course, he smells amazing.

"No, *I'm* sorry, because I honestly have no freaking clue why I'm crying right now."

"Maybe we could find the answer in one of those books," he offers, making me laugh.

"Maybe." My voice cracks again before I pull away.

He brings his hands up to wipe my cheeks. "I've overwhelmed you again. Let's table that other stuff until you're ready, okay? In the meantime, you'll just have to compromise by letting me buy you a certified pre-owned minivan."

I snort, and he drops his hands.

"Come on," he says, piling our stack of books in the crook of his left elbow—*hello again, tasty forearm*—and clasping my hand in his on the right. "I want to show you something I spotted on the way in."

I follow him to the children's book section, where he points out a set of classics for babies. "Your favorite, right?" he asks, picking up the illustrated copy of *Pride and Prejudice.*

Well, shit.

My nod is barely visible as my chin begins to tremble again. The more room I give Blake to be himself, the better he gets. It's becoming harder and harder not to completely fall for this man as the seconds tick by.

I reach out to grab the book, but he pulls it back and places it in the middle of the stack. "Nope, it doesn't exist if it makes you cry. I'll bring it back out at home."

I press my lips together. "Mm-hmm."

"Any other titles up here that might make you particularly sentimental?"

"Just grab one of each."

He smirks and follows orders. "As you wish. Anything else?"

"Uh-uh," I squeak out, hoping I'm not telepathically projecting all of my wishes, or the good people of the B&N children's section are about to get a show. "I'm done," I announce, and after hearing him deliver that *Princess Bride* line, I mean it.

CHAPTER 34

Loren

"Let's get you home, then." Blake leans over to address the books directly, and I audibly groan.

"You all right, Reed?" he asks, looking at me strangely.

"Fine, I just ... need to pee."

"Want me to wait here for you or just meet you in the front?"

He's willing to wait outside the bathrooms for me?

"I'll find you when I'm done, unless you're going to let me pay for my own books?"

"Not in actual currency, no," he returns. "But perhaps we can work out an arrangement later."

I shake my head and walk away, leaving him there to laugh at his own joke. As soon as I round the corner, I scurry off to the bathroom to empty my poor, inept bladder. Then I attempt to freshen up in the mirror, reminding myself that I'm not supposed to be doing this. I may have agreed to give Blake a chance to prove we could work romantically, but I'm not sure I'll ever be convinced that going all-in is the right thing to do. There's got to be some safer middle ground where I can hang out for now, right? Somewhere in between like and love—that's where I need to set up camp.

I do a few rounds of deep breathing before rejoining him. I can see him waiting near the entrance as soon as I emerge from the restroom, but I stop to check my phone along the way when it vibrates within my purse. It's another cheeky emoji from him. I bite my lip and send a response this time, then watch his face from afar as he reads my message.

His eyelids look heavy, and his chest rises and falls as he stares down at his phone. He types something out, smiling to himself, then shakes his head quickly. And, dammit if he doesn't look *smitten*? I don't know. But I'd be an idiot not to see that he's really into it … into *me*, at least for now.

Don't do it, Loren.

Then he looks up and sees me, and a huge grin splits his face, as if I'm his favorite person on earth, as if he adores me … as if he's in love with me.

Shit. It's too late.

I think I may already be in love with *him*.

I force myself to glance down at my phone again when my limbs get all tingly.

GUS GUS

Now THAT'S the kind of currency I accept. 😉

My face heats up against my will, and I force myself to continue on, slapping him lightly in the chest once I reach him. And he's still looking enamored with me as he grabs my hand and leads me back to the truck without a word.

Blake's fingers brush the back of my neck when he braces himself on my seat and turns to back out of the parking lot, making me shiver. There's something about the way he does everything so confidently and capably. It's a quick reminder of his masculinity each time he accomplishes a small, mundane task, even something as simple as one-handing the steering wheel, carrying my books, or ordering dinner, and although I've never thought *capable masculinity* would be my thing, I find myself *very* attracted to these qualities in Blake.

Who am I kidding?

He's the sexiest man in existence, and I'd pay good money to watch him chop firewood or fix something right now.

Can we get a flat tire over here?

Hell, I'd settle for watching him open a jar at the moment.

We ride home in silence while I contemplate whether Blake is really a Legolas or actually an Aragorn—for the record, I'm fine with either—and that spicy tension returns, lingering between us when his hand slides over to cradle my belly. I find it odd that he parks his truck in the front instead of pulling into the garage as usual, but I keep my thoughts to myself while he helps me out.

"Can I walk you to your door?" he asks as he leads me into the house.

I laugh, still confused, but he sets our book haul down in the living room and follows me to the guest bedroom. I stare at him curiously as he glances up at me with his hands in his pockets.

"I had a really nice time tonight, Lo."

"So did I," I reply cautiously.

"And I'd really like to take you out again sometime soon, if it's not too forward of me to ask."

I snort and cross my arms as I lean back against the wall. "You mean, you're not interested in coming in?" I say sarcastically and gesture to my bedroom door.

He shakes his head slowly and blows out a breath. "Wow, as much as I'd love that, and I mean, really, *really* love that, I feel like we should take things slow, don't you?"

I narrow my eyes at him. "What are you playing at, Gus Gus?"

He steps forward, stretching his arms over my head and staring down at me in a way that leaves me breathless. "Just trying to convince my girl to give me a good night kiss."

My eyebrows shoot up. "Your girl?"

He's doing it again—the kind of crap that makes me roll my eyes when I read it in a romance novel. Except it makes me weak in the knees when Blake aims it my way.

"You heard me," he whispers. Then he leans in, rubbing the tip of his nose against mine. "So, how about that kiss?"

My eyes flutter closed as I tilt my chin up instinctively. "I suppose

I do owe you for the books," I mumble, and our lips meet a second later.

But this instantly feels different. It's not a ground-rules sanctioned kiss, it's not a middle-of-the-night accident, and it's not forced PDA. This is a *real* kiss.

His mouth parts, and he slowly slips his tongue between my lips. I clutch at his sides, then my fingers hook his belt loops and I pull him closer, arching my back up from the wall to meet him. He moans and deepens the kiss again as one of his hands curls around the back of my neck, and my head is absolutely swimming. I can't think of anything but Blake right now, how good he is at this, how totally and completely gone I am for him, how I don't care about the consequences when he's kissing me this way, how badly I want this to go on forever.

I'm just about to climb him like a tree when he pulls away abruptly, untangling his hand from my hair as his chest heaves over me. "Okay, then," he begins, swallowing hard. "Good night, Agnes." He leans down once more to kiss my forehead before he pushes himself away from the wall. Then I watch as he saunters down the hall to his own bedroom, closing the door behind him.

"What the actual heck?" I mutter aloud, and I think I hear him chuckling from his room.

I pull out my phone as soon as I turn and dart into my own bedroom, ready to send him an angry text or at least demand an explanation. But he beats me to the punch.

GUS GUS

I know I'm supposed to wait longer before I text, but when can I see you again?

LOREN

I'm not sure I want to go on another date with you after the way you ended things just now.

I glare down at the phone, my anger already dissipating. I can't be mad at him for respecting my wishes, can I? And then I'm disappointed when I get no response for a full seven minutes. I sit on my bed, staring and willing those three dots to appear again.

Instead, I hear a soft knock before the door opens to reveal Blake looking fresh from the shower in a pair of gym shorts and a white tee. "You're upset. Did I do something wrong?" he asks, his bottom lip sticking out in a sexy pout.

Actually, no, scratch that. It's a totally stupid, unsexy pout.

"Yes. And no."

He furrows his brow and steps into the room, and I bring my legs up to cross them in front of me when he sits beside me on the bed.

"I'm sorry. I wasn't trying to make you feel bad. I'm just trying to keep things light," he explains, and I notice he seems to be holding his breath as if he's genuinely concerned about my reaction.

"I don't like being the butt of your jokes, Blake. I thought we'd established that."

"Lo, look at me."

I obey, like the glutton for punishment that I am.

"You were never a joke to me. And you never could be," he declares.

I feel my eyes watering again. "Then why do I feel so stupid right now?" I whisper, my voice cracking. "And why did you stop kissing me?"

He shakes his head and brings a hand up to my cheek. "First of all, it took everything I had to stop kissing you. In fact, we're still making out in my head right now."

I snort out a laugh, and he smiles as he continues.

"But you're not stupid. I just keep going about this the wrong way."

"No, you're … great. Tonight was great. It was actually one of the best nights I've ever had, besides all the crying. I just … I'm still so scared."

"Hey, I'm not going anywhere, all right? If anything, you're going to have a hard time getting rid of me," he says softly.

I bite my lip as I feel my chin trembling. "Yeah, well, sometimes sticking around after you've stopped caring is even worse than leaving."

Immediately, I realize I wasn't supposed to say that thought aloud.

He drops his hand and looks away, his expression forlorn. "It's late. I should let you get some sleep." He leans over and kisses my temple before he stands. "Good night," he bids me quietly, stepping out and closing the door behind him.

I sniffle a few times, deciding that he's right and that I'm entirely too exhausted to give the topic any more thought. Then I change into my pajamas and look down at my unmade bed.

"Oh, hell," I mutter to myself before slipping out of the guest bedroom and into Blake's.

I crawl into his bed, and he smiles ruefully as if he's equally sad and relieved to see me. "Let me get my shirt," he offers, but I shake my head and curl into his bare chest.

"I'm sorry," I whisper as he wraps his arms around me. "I know it's not an excuse, but I swear I'm only saying these mean things to you because I'm full of stupid baby-growing hormones. And because I'm not used to anyone caring this much about me. I know I still have so much shit of my own to work out, and you've been entirely too good to me, Blake."

"It's okay. I'm probably taking some of it too personally, anyway."

"No, I should really think before I blurt out my biggest fears and scare you away."

He chuckles softly and presses a kiss on my head. "You didn't scare me away just now. It just feels like I keep pushing you too far."

"But I hurt you again, and I really am sorry. I didn't mean to imply that you aren't capable of all that long-term, big L-word stuff. Everything you've shown me says the opposite."

He hums thoughtfully. "Lo, have you ever been in love?"

I blink and pull back in surprise, and my stomach cuts a flip, though it's not the babies' fault this time. "Well, yeah, at least I think I have. But it was a few years ago, and I'm probably a different person now, so who knows?" He nods without looking at me. "How about you?" I ask, trying to hide the way my voice is trembling.

He shakes his head. "I *have* been in a few relationships, contrary to what everyone might think." And I wince, because I'm guilty of making that girlfriend joke earlier. "But I've never said 'I love you' to anyone outside my family."

"Oh," I reply. "Does that ... bother you?"

He brings his shoulders up as best he can to shrug. "Maybe."

I reach up to cup his cheek. "Hey, any woman would be lucky to hear those three words from you."

"And what if I finally worked up the courage to tell her, and she didn't feel the same? Or, worse, she couldn't trust me enough to believe I really meant it?"

My chest tightens when he stares into my eyes. "I know you. You'd make it so that she had no choice but to believe you."

He huffs and looks away. "I suspect I'm not as smooth as my reputation led you to believe."

"If anything, the real Blake is even better," I say with a smile.

"Hmm." His tone shifts, and he raises his brow as he turns back to me. "So what I'm hearing is, if I'm consistently honest and vulnerable with her, she'll eventually have no choice but to reciprocate?"

Breathe, Loren.

I'd forgotten how to do that for a second.

"It's been working pretty well for you so far," I whisper.

He smirks, and I watch as his confidence visibly returns. He's like a video game character that just ate a weird plant and developed a flirty superpower. "Has it?"

"For the past few months, actually," I confess, surprising myself.

He pins me with one of those smoldering looks again, and I suspect my pajamas may be melting away by now. "Are you admitting that you've fallen for me?"

"I mean, hypothetically speaking, if your goal *was* to get me to fall in love with you, then I guess I'd have to say you've been doing a damn good job."

"Oh? How so?" he asks, running a finger down my arm and giving me the chills.

I gulp. "Uh, you know. Besides being yourself, I'd probably cite all the compliments, the chivalry, showing an interest in my interests, making me feel important and ... desired."

"Then—and this is still purely hypothetical, of course—would you venture to admit that you actually like being taken care of?" He continues stroking my skin softly, growing more and more cocky as he garners a different reaction from me. And my heart and my body are both providing feedback at the moment.

"Under the right conditions, I suppose there's some truth to that."

"And that maybe, just maybe, if I keep at it long enough, I might convince you that you're worthy of love? And that I'm capable of it?"

I'm basically a container of hot soup at this point.

Sorry, babies, but it's your daddy's fault that you're cooking in there now.

"Maybe you already have," I rasp.

He stares at me for a while, and it looks like he's not sure whether to go on. "Lo," he finally begins, his poise slipping just long enough for his nerves to resurface. "There are so many things I haven't been able to tell you, because I promised I'd abide by your rules, and I've been afraid to overwhelm you."

I nod, because I don't trust myself with words anymore, and he continues.

"But every time we're together, I find myself thinking, *This has to be it. I can't imagine ever feeling this way with anyone else.*"

Now I'm having trouble *not* breathing too quickly.

"You really think that?"

"I think maybe you're it for me. I think ..." He stops to lick his lips as he stares down at me. "I think this must be what real love feels like. And I know you probably don't—"

"Dammit, Blake. I do love you," I blurt out. "I tried *so* hard not to fall for you, I did. But I couldn't help it, and I want to be angry with you, but I can't manage that either. Because I'm too far gone, and everything you do and say makes it impossible to feel any other way about you."

He cocks an eyebrow at me, though he's smiling. "Reed, did you really just interrupt my heartfelt speech so you could one-up me and say you love me first?"

I bite my lip and shrug shyly. "Maybe. What are you gonna do about it?"

He scoffs. "I'm going to one-up you back," he declares, "and tell you I love you better."

My heart and lungs are having to work overtime now. "I'd like to hear you try," I barely get out.

He leans in for a short kiss. "Loren, it's been months since I've been able to think about anything but you. You're on my mind all day, and I can't wait to come home to you every afternoon before I dream about you all night. So, yeah, I'm pretty sure that means I'm in love with you, too."

"Oh," I reply. "That's—"

He holds up a hand. "I'm not done. Did it sound like I was done?"

I can't help but smile when he grins at me. "By all means, continue."

"Thank you. Now, where was I? Oh, yeah. I love you for being my best friend," he starts again, adding another kiss. "I love you because you're already an amazing mother to our children." The next kiss is a second longer, and I'm tempted to grab his face and hold him there.

"I love you for never backing down from an argument. I love you for teaching me that I *do* have the capacity to love someone. I love you for being the sexiest, smartest, funniest woman I've ever known."

I sigh when he pulls away from the kiss that follows, which was much less chaste than the first few.

"But not just because you are all of those things to me, Lo. Mostly, I love you just ... *because*."

"Wow," I say through the tears I should have seen coming. "I think you won."

He laughs softly and brings his hand up to swipe the moisture from my cheek. "I didn't realize how relieved I'd feel after I finally got that out."

"You mean you've been feeling this way for a while?" I sniffle again.

He nods. "I'm sorry it took so long for me to figure it out and to work up the courage to tell you, but I can't even remember a time when I didn't feel this way about you."

"And before, when you said I might be *it*, you meant ..."

"I think you know exactly what I meant," he replies, his deep voice making me shiver before he closes in the distance again. He kisses me slowly and tenderly for a minute, then pulls away to whisper, "I love you, Agnes."

"I love you, too, Gus Gus," I return. "But do we—"

"We can decide what the rest of our lives will look like later. Let's just enjoy this for now."

"Okay," I agree, sliding my hand down his bare chest. "But I was actually going to ask if we could throw out the ground rules for good, because I'm absolutely dying to make out with you and maybe even grope your spicy abs for a bit."

He grins so widely that it reaches his eyes this time. "To hell with the ground rules," he proclaims, pulling me in again.

CHAPTER 35

Blake

THREE YEARS AGO

"Good thing our teachers weren't this hot back when we were in high school," I lean in and say over Loren's shoulder after letting myself into the Camellia High teachers' lounge. "I'd never have graduated second in the class with a distraction like you. Then again, maybe that's how you managed to secure that valedictorian spot."

She whips her head around, curling her upper lip in distaste as soon as she recognizes me. "What are *you* doing here?"

I pull back and cross my arms over my chest. "I work here. Didn't anyone tell you?"

"Blake Bourgeois, teaching?" she asks, cocking an eyebrow.

"That's *Coach Blake* to you, Miss Loren. But I'll only be moonlighting in my Camellia High polo. I'll still be sporting a suit and tie until four in the afternoon."

"Right, you're a lawyer now. How original. And that's *Ms. Reed* to you."

I shoot her my sexiest smirk, and she barely falters as her eyes skim over me in a way that reminds me she's immune to my brand of charm. "My apologies, Ms. Reed. I'll be sure to get it right the next time we run into one another."

"Don't worry, it shouldn't happen often, since I assume you'll only be gracing us with your presence for the duration of football season," she retorts, lifting her chin and crossing her own arms.

"We could always plan to meet up after hours, you know, for a little extracurricular activity," I flirt, bouncing my eyebrows at her until she scoffs.

"I see you haven't left your ego behind in Baton Rouge."

"And you seem to be keeping tabs on me," I point out, smiling wider now.

She frowns in return. "Doesn't it bother you to hear that you've earned a reputation for having a cocky attitude and loose morals? Especially since it's followed you home?"

"*Loose morals*?" I continue grinning, though her question most definitely hits harder than I expect. "You haven't changed a bit, have you, Reed? Still single and walking around with your nose in a Jane Austen book?"

She flinches, and I realize I'm being overly harsh. Then I watch as she visibly musters up the courage to respond. "While you've been preoccupied with sleeping your way around LSU's campus, I've been busy working on a double major in education and English lit, so, yeah. Call me a spinster, but I'll take a good Regency romance over flailing around in this dating pool any day," she says, her tone acerbic. "Especially now that *you're* back to pollute the waters."

I roll my shoulders back before I reach up to adjust the collar of my polo. If I were wearing my usual dress shirt, this is the point where I'd start loosening my tie or unbuttoning the cuffs and rolling my sleeves just to watch her drool. As if that kind of crap would work on Loren, anyway.

"That's funny, because in my experience, the ladies of Camellia have been more than happy to welcome Blake the Snake back with open hearts and open arms. Well, and open—"

"Ugh, spare me." She blocks me with her palm.

And I'm grateful for the interruption once I hear how disgusting I sound. She was right before. I could stand to tone down the frat-boy talk. To be honest, I hadn't even planned on bringing that douche back home in the first place. But once I returned to Camellia, the only thing that made me interesting was my reputation for having such "loose morals" throughout my stint in college.

Sure, I've done my fair share of partying and bedding eager sorority girls over the years, but I never set out to be *that* guy. It's not like I misled any of them into thinking we were in a relationship, and the few times I did venture into monogamous territory were just that —monogamous. I'd never cheat on a woman, and since I didn't commit to anyone unless I liked her enough to make the relationship part come easily, I didn't make any frivolous commitments.

Still, I liked women, and I especially enjoyed making them feel good about themselves when we were together, even if I wasn't after anything serious. So I began relying only on reputation to screen my prospects. Girls didn't approach me unless they understood what I was and wasn't looking for. Everyone seemed happy with the arrangement, and no one got hurt. But the rumors continued to escalate over the years, and by the time my persona had grown larger than life, it'd also become too difficult to correct all the misconceptions without leaving myself too vulnerable.

Then I moved back, and people only acknowledged me as Blake the Snake or JD's brother. It wasn't a hard choice between which one of those titles I was more apt to lean into. Although the joke's on me, because I can't seem to shake either of them.

"I'm sure your mother would have been real proud to hear you say that," Loren's voice rings out bitterly, bringing me back from my thoughts.

My stomach churns as anger bubbles to the surface. How dare she bring my mom into this? Especially since it's barely been a year since her passing, and Loren knows as well as anyone that my mom and I were close.

"And how the hell would you know what my mom would have thought?" I fire back, narrowing my eyes at her.

"The same way I know more than I care to of your whereabouts in general—Mrs. Monica told me herself. We were in a book club together for the last few years before she died. She worried about you more than you think, by the way. Nearly every character in every plot reminded her of her boys, though she related all of the handsome but wayward and confused male leads to you."

I grimace. "A book club, Reed? That's where you get your gossip? What are you, sixty?"

"Only at heart," she retorts.

"No wonder you're still single."

She sniffs indignantly. "What I'm hearing is, 'Wow, Loren, you're so mature and classy, must be the wise company you keep.' "

"Oh, I get it now. You're so busy trying to find someone else's mom to latch onto that you haven't had time to hunt for a man."

Her lips part in a quiet gasp, and she blinks at me in disbelief. "I—I can't believe you just said that."

"Yeah, well, I'm already a disappointment to my dead parents, so ..." I stuff my hands in my pockets, then I look away and shrug. "I guess it doesn't matter."

"For the record, I never said you were a disappointment to your mother. I just wanted you to know how much she loved you and worried about you, how she talked about you all the time, and that her last wish was to see you happy and settled," she mumbles.

"I don't hear the difference," I lie.

"Then it's probably because your life has been so charming that you don't actually know what feeling unloved or unsupported looks like," she replies, her voice cracking at the end.

And the full weight of what I've just said to her hits me as soon as I see her rolling her lips in to disguise the way she's started crying. She turns around, but I watch as her shoulders shake lightly, and I know she's only stifling her sobs.

I blow out a breath and step forward, reaching a hand toward her. "Loren, I'm so—"

"Don't you dare touch me, Blake," she grinds out before I can get my apology out.

"Yeah, okay," I say, jerking my hand back and shaking my head. "Sorry."

"Just go away. You aren't supposed to be in here, anyway."

"Yeah," I repeat, swallowing hard. I only thought I felt sick to my stomach before, but it's nothing compared to the way I feel now.

"Hey, is everything okay?"

I turn to find my former history teacher in the doorway. I clear my throat as I turn to offer her a smile. "Hey, Mrs. Rachel. It's good to see you."

"Hi, Blake. Glad to have you back, baby," she returns, eyeing me suspiciously. "Are you all right, Loren?"

Loren sniffles again and turns to face her. "Yeah, all good. Blake and I were just catching up."

Mrs. Rachel places a protective hand on Loren's shoulder. "Then why do you look upset?"

"Oh, you know us," I start, trying to lighten the situation. "We've never been able to manage a conversation without turning it into an argument."

"Yeah. Turns out I'm more sensitive than I thought about the whole UL-LSU rivalry."

"UL-*L*," I correct her. "You're not a flagship school."

"Then you should know you graduated from LSU A&M, the Louisiana State University Agricultural and Mechanical College, you ass," she retorts, making Mrs. Rachel laugh.

"I guess college hasn't changed either of you. Maybe you should have gone to McNeese instead," Mrs. Rachel says, winking and giving Loren's arm a squeeze before letting it go. "Come on, Blake. I'm going out for cheer practice. I'll walk you to the field, where you belong."

"Yes, ma'am." I nod and force another smile, because Mrs. Rachel isn't one to be contested. "I'll see you around, Ms. Reed," I add, shooting her a remorseful look.

"Not if I can help it," she mutters. And for some reason, that tightness in my chest is replaced by a few flutters.

CHAPTER 36

Loren

"This might be the best Fourth of July barbecue I've ever been to, girls," Mrs. T comments from her kitchen sink, nudging Tenley and nodding her head toward the back yard.

We both move in closer to gaze out the window, and I watch Blake peel his button-down shirt off of his arms and toss it on one of the deck chairs outside.

"Well, shit," Tenley curses under her breath as JD's polo flies over and lands on top of Blake's discarded shirt.

I stifle a laugh until Blake's eyes dart to mine while he jogs over and catches the football Ethan tosses his way. Then he winks at me before he stretches his arms.

"Hot damn," I say a little too loudly. "I mean, go sports!" The other ladies laugh at me.

Now, one would think I'd have at least a basic understanding of football, given my family history, but I've never cared enough to pay attention ... until now. I look back to my boyfriend as he picks up the football and shuffles his feet, then launches it forward while JD runs out to make a leaping catch. JD comes back around to initiate a brotherly celebration handshake, and both Tenley and I are rendered speechless.

"It really isn't fair that he looks like that, and he's still good at everything," I mutter to myself.

"Isn't it annoying?" Tenley adds.

"The worst." I watch Blake's back muscles flex as he steps back and hands the ball off to Ethan this time. "Dang, Ten. What have you been feeding that kid? I just realized how much he's grown since school let out."

"The better question is what *doesn't* he eat. I'm pretty sure I had to stop him from devouring a paper plate at lunch. You don't want to see my grocery bill, between those two bottomless pits out there and the feral animal I've been growing in here," she says, pointing to her belly, which is now the same size as mine, though I've got double the baby.

"I'm pretty sure Blake feels the same about me. I think I've been going through a jar of peanut butter every other day."

Blake stops then, calling Ethan over to give him a mini lesson with the football and ending it with an affectionate slap on the back.

Mrs. T leans in and wraps an arm around me. "Tell me, Loren, are you going to lock that down, or what? Because if not, I might need to throw my hat in the ring."

"You were right, you know," I whisper quietly, smirking at her. "He is a good man."

"Of course I was right," she retorts, pursing her lips. Then she lets go of me to move to the coffeemaker. "I'm always right about these things. Just ask Tenley."

"Huh?" Tenley says, blinking and shaking her head. "I'm sorry, it's just, uh, well, I'm honestly having a hard time not going out there and tackling JD myself."

The rest of us cackle at her as she stares dreamily at her husband through the window while he circles around the others and catches the ball again. Then he jogs back toward us and tosses the football to Blake before tapping on the glass.

"Hey, babe," he says through the window, adjusting the backward cap on his head.

"Hi," she drawls, fluttering her eyelashes and making me snort.

"Don't be mad, but, uh, I'm pretty sure I just ripped my new shorts back there." Then he lifts one leg to show the hole in the seam of his crotch. "Okay, love you, bye." He mimes a kiss before he runs off.

"He's lucky he's hot. I just bought those."

Mrs. T laughs as she turns to hand her a mug of coffee.

"Thanks, Mom." They trade genuine smiles, and my heart constricts slightly.

"Yes, thank you," I say when Mrs. T offers the next cup to me, and I realize how badly I wish my mom was capable of being there for me the way that Tenley's is for her. But I do have a family that loves me, even if it looks different than I expected.

I stare out the window again, drifting while I continue watching Blake. He laughs and shrugs after he deliberately hits his brother in the back of the head with a football.

"He reminds me of Jude sometimes, you know," Mrs. T says wistfully. "Blake, I mean."

Tenley glares at her strangely. "I thought you said JD reminded you of Daddy?"

"Oh yes, but that was after I reformed him." Mrs. T smiles ruefully, and Tenley cringes. "Though it seems like Loren's doing a pretty good job on that front, too." I blush as I take a sip from my mug.

"I agree," Tenley begins, eyeing me carefully. "He's gone from Blake the Snake to passing the collection basket at Sunday Mass within the past few months. That's pretty impressive."

To be honest, watching Blake step up as a spiritual leader and having him ask me to attend church with him has become another example of that capable masculinity I admire so much. All the more reason for me to fall more deeply in love with him.

"I wish I could take the credit for the changes he's made, but I haven't done anything," I say after a while. "He's actually the good influence."

"But he seems to be the best version of himself when he's with you," Tenley maintains.

I look down at the table. "I think he's always been the same amazing person, but he felt pressured to be that other guy in public. And he just needed someone besides JD to reassure him it was okay to be himself all the time. If anything, I'm guilty of making him feel like the real Blake wasn't good enough for too long."

I glance up, expecting them to laugh, but all I find are wide eyes. Mrs. T reaches over to pat the back of my hand softly, and I swallow hard.

"Then again, he might have decided to turn himself around just to spite me or to one-up his brother, right?" I add with a forced smile.

"Maybe he's always wanted to play tennis, but he was so good at being a quarterback that he was too embarrassed to admit it," Tenley ventures after a while. "And now that he has you for a doubles partner, he's given up on hiding how much he loves tennis."

My smile softens into a real one when she references the metaphor she once used to tell me she'd fallen in love with JD. "Yeah, maybe."

"Sounds like you're pretty invested in your tennis game, too."

"Blake's a natural athlete. It was getting too hard to keep pretending I didn't want to play tennis with him, so I finally gave in."

Tenley bites her lip and tries to hide her excitement as Mrs. T glances back and forth between us. "Is this some kind of code talk for stuff you think I'm too old to know about?"

"Sorry to disappoint you, Ma, but we're only talking about feelings. Loren's still on pelvic rest."

Mrs. T shoots me a sympathetic look, and we all laugh again.

"And it's probably for the best, to be honest. Do you have any idea how difficult it is to navigate a new relationship while simultaneously juggling all of these ridiculously gross pregnancy symptoms?" I offer.

"I hate to sound insensitive, but it's probably inconvenient for a reason. And to answer your original question, yes, I do, even though I'm lucky enough to have a better understanding of what to expect than most first-time moms and a husband who's literally stuck with me. I imagine it's been even harder for you." Tenley lifts her mug in my honor, and I feel slightly better.

"That all tracks, Ten. But your husband is also notoriously gassy and would, therefore, not be as shocked by surprise pregnancy toots," I reply dryly.

Tenley scoffs. "That's exactly why I can't ever fart in front of him. Don't you realize he'd never let me live it down? He'd be beside himself if I let one rip, especially if it was an accident."

I giggle. "You're right. He would enjoy that way too much."

"He and Ethan would totally gang up on me, like they always do," she adds, rolling her eyes. But I can see the fondness behind her griping. "Although, it was actually kind of sweet when JD cheered me up with his Billy Madison impression after I didn't make it to the bathroom in time last week. We ended up having an Adam Sandler movie marathon so Ethan could get the 'you're not cool unless you pee ya pants' reference."

I cringe at the reminder. "We've had one of those moments, too. Nothing says 'new level in the relationship' like sneezing and having to rush in to use the toilet while your boyfriend's still in the shower, right? We've skipped right over most of the normal stages of development and gone straight into peeing in front of one another."

"You both know men are wired differently. I'd be willing to bet that stuff is bothering you more than it bothers them," Mrs. T volunteers with a laugh. "They're probably just excited to catch a glimpse of you, even if it's because you have to change your pee-soaked pants."

Tenley sighs. "According to JD, she's not wrong."

"Well then, I've got an even better story for you. Blake has since returned the favor by accidentally interrupting me during a very unsuccessful waxing attempt."

Mrs. T fakes a serious nod while Tenley bites her lip and stifles her laughter.

My face heats up as I relive the moment. "I can't exactly see what's going on down there, and I thought I'd try to clean things up, since I figure I'll have to start getting checks pretty soon."

Tenley shrugs, still struggling to hold it in.

"But it wasn't going smoothly to begin with when he barged into the bathroom, unannounced, making me flinch and spread hot wax everywhere. Which meant I eventually had to get that wax off, if you know what I mean. Let's just say it was equally traumatizing for both of us."

Tenley finally snorts loudly and laughs until she tears up, Mrs. T and I joining in after a while. "Though I appreciate the gesture," she begins breathlessly, "it's not necessary. We've pretty much seen it all."

I pout. "It's too late. My downstairs is all patchy now."

"Why didn't you just ask your boyfriend for help, you know, since he was already in the room?" Mrs. T asks as she brings her mug up. "It's nothing he hasn't seen before."

"We, uh, well ... he did offer, but ..." I glance at Tenley for backup.

"He didn't get much of an opportunity to map out the terrain before he got banned," she explains for me.

"Oh." Mrs. T's brow lifts. "Still, he's probably got enough experience to know his way around, in general," she mumbles, and I frown. It seems like no matter what he does right, Blake can't seem to escape his old reputation.

But then I realize that I'm upset for a good reason this time, because Blake really has managed to change, and I don't feel the need to wonder whether I measure up to the women he's been with in the past anymore.

Tenley notices my reaction and glares at her mom, and Mrs. T offers a quiet apology.

I shrug. "You're not wrong. I'm just choosing to see his dating history as practice now."

"Preseason games don't actually count, anyway," Tenley says with a smirk, just as my phone chimes, and I groan out loud when I see Landry's name on the screen.

"What's wrong, baby?" Mrs. T asks.

"Landry's been driving me bananas lately. He's fallen back into his old overbearing habits since finding out about the problems with my pregnancy," I explain with a sigh. "He texts or calls at least once per day, and he's even been talking about moving back home to be closer to the girls."

"Give your brother a break, Loren. He loves you more than you know," Mrs. T replies.

"What do you mean?"

She looks at me carefully, as if she's unsure whether she should say more. "Besides having to tend to your mom, that boy had a bigger hand in raising you than your parents ever did. And look how well you turned out."

I glare at her in confusion. "He did?"

"You probably thought he was just bossing you around, but he really tried to take good care of you. I bet he spared you from more unpleasant experiences than you realize."

"Oh." I look down at my hands. "I guess I was too young to see it that way."

"I'm sure you were. And although Landry's always had a tendency to be ... *brute*, I believe he means well, especially when it comes to you."

My expression must seem odd as I consider everything she's saying, because Blake looks concerned when he and the others walk into the kitchen, using their shirts as sweat towels.

"Hey, you all right?" he asks, coming over to me.

I force a smile. "Yeah, I'm great. I was just complaining about my brother," I say, holding up my phone.

Blake smiles back and leans down to give me a short kiss. "He's just worried about you, babe. It's hard on him, you know, being a doctor and unable to help you."

Tenley and her mom trade looks across the table before they both purse their lips at me in Mrs. T's signature told-you-so glare, making me laugh.

"Yeah, I'm sure you're right," I tell Blake after a while.

"Speaking of brotherly love, JD and I have a special favor to ask you guys," Tenley begins. JD clears his throat and prepares to speak as he stands behind Tenley's chair, but she wrinkles her nose. "Wow, you smell terrible."

JD rolls his eyes. "*Mais*, we were playing outside, and *ça fait chaud*. Of course I smell like a *chien*," he says in his defense while she pulls her shirt over her nose as a filter. "As I was about to say before, Tenley and I are thinking about having a co-ed baby shower, and we were wondering if you guys would want to partner up for it."

Blake and I look at one another questioningly. "To be honest, I assumed we wouldn't be having a shower because of our situation," I say on our behalf.

"Mom and I were planning on teaming up with Lilley and throwing you one either way," Tenley declares. "So we can either kill two birds—well, three birds—I guess, or we'd be just as glad to give you your own party."

Blake smiles and shrugs. "Whatever you want, Lo. It's your shower. Although, you do seem to like intruding on others' showers lately ..."

I slap his chest playfully while Mrs. T and Tenley snicker quietly. "Ignore him. If you really insist on giving us baby shower, it does make more sense to combine everything. Especially because I know you'd rather not be the center of attention all on your own, Ten."

She grins and nods gratefully. "You know me too well."

"We could host it at our house," Blake offers. "Since we have a bigger outdoor kitchen, and when Loren gets too tired, she can go inside to rest."

"I figured you'd say that," JD returns with a smirk.

I swallow hard, my chest feeling heavy. Between figuring out more of my feelings for Blake, finding out about my brother's dedication to me, and now listening to my found family's offer to throw me a baby shower while my boyfriend calls his house "our" home, I'm not sure how much more my hormonal little heart can take.

"You know I'm right," Blake fires back with a cocky smile. Then he uses his shirt to wipe the sweat from the back of his neck, and I cover my mouth with my hand to avoid letting out a squeak.

"Okay, then. We'll pick a date for next month," Tenley announces. Then she turns to JD. "Hey, can you do that thing that he just did so I can watch?"

Ethan groans and moves to dig inside the fridge when JD obliges and flexes his arms for his wife, making the rest of us laugh. Blake glances down at me and cocks an eyebrow, wordlessly asking me if I'd noticed him a second ago.

"I must have missed it," I lie. "Maybe you should do it again."

"I agree," Mrs. T adds with a wink.

CHAPTER 37

Blake

"Do you still want to do this?" I ask Loren.

She nods softly. "Yeah. I do. But thank you for making sure."

I pull up at the restaurant in our brand-new minivan. Loren finally caved and allowed me to drive her old Toyota to Baton Rouge for our appointment with Dr. Rowan today, then we stopped at a dealership for a quick swap. I think she only agreed to it because it was getting too difficult and dangerous for her to climb in and out of my truck, but she seems happy with her decision, having already named it after one of the horses from *The Lord of the Rings*. I'm also hopeful it's a sign of her growing trust in me.

Today feels big, even though neither of us have acknowledged it. But it's all giving me that same buzz I always get from being with Loren.

I turn to face her and pull her in for a kiss, then I rest my forehead against hers for a second. "I love you, Lo," I say on a sigh. "And I'm so proud of you."

She draws in a ragged breath. "I love you, too."

A smile spreads across my face, because I still haven't gotten tired of hearing her say that, and I don't think I ever will.

I walk Loren inside, where her mother and brother are already waiting at a table. Her mom covers her mouth in shock when she sees

Loren's belly, then comes around to hug her tightly, waiting to give me a hug, too. Lunch goes better than I expected, with Loren soaking up some well-deserved attention, and after a while, I ask Landry if he'd like to check out her new ride.

"You should take Shadowfax for a spin," Loren says with a soft smile, acknowledging my attempt at giving her some alone time with her mother.

I motion for Landry to lead the way, and we walk out to the parking lot.

"I have to say, a minivan might just be the craziest sign of commitment I've ever seen," he remarks as we sit in the front seats and watch Loren and her mom through the restaurant window.

I chuckle softly. "Yeah, I guess twins will do that to you."

"Hmm. Is this your way of asking my permission to marry my baby sister after you've already knocked her up?" He cocks an eyebrow at me, but he's also smirking.

Is that what I'm doing?

I blink at him, and it takes me a second to find my voice again. "I obviously don't need your permission, Reed. I'm looking for your blessing. There's a difference."

"Do you have a ring, or were you just using this van as a gesture?"

I snort. "There's a ring. I just need to get it sized."

I think of my mother's old engagement ring, sitting in a box inside my nightstand. I know it's there because I've taken it out and looked at it more often in the past month than I have over the last few years combined.

"When are you planning to propose?"

I clear my throat. "I guess I need to make sure she actually wants to marry me, first."

"You mean to tell me that Blake the Snake is afraid to get shut down?" He glares at me strangely. "You're the cockiest guy in history, and she's been obsessed with romance novels since she was a little girl. All you'd need is a big, cheesy proposal. I don't see a problem."

I stare out the window for a second before I respond. "Loren doesn't usually put much stock into what other people think, the only exception being your family. And whether you realize it or not, you've all had a hand in convincing your sister that we couldn't possibly work."

He huffs. "What's that supposed to mean?"

"I know you're just trying to protect her, and it's not your fault that your parents' shitty marriage messed you guys up, but you've been sabotaging her and screwing with her self-worth for years. Between that and the constant reminders of my embarrassing track record, I haven't had the easiest time getting Loren to buy into the idea of making our relationship a permanent thing."

"Who the hell are you to talk about my parents' marriage?" Landry fires back.

"Hey, I'm sorry," I say, lifting my hands. "You and your sisters deserved better. But I want to do this right for Loren and our daughters, so if you really love Lo and want to see her happy, you'll show her it's okay to believe in me."

"Maybe you've changed, and I can respect the way you stood up for Loren the last time we talked. But I still don't know if I can trust you."

"Landry, do you remember that party when we were kids, the one where I sucker punched you in front of everyone after you accused me of messing around with Loren in the pool house?"

"Yeah, I guess."

"She gave me my first kiss that night. And it was hot." He scoffs, and I smile as I continue. "Anyway, I'm pretty sure I've been in love with her since then on some deep, subconscious level, even though I spent the better part of the past seventeen years in denial while I unsuccessfully searched for another woman that could measure up to her."

Landry stares blankly at me. "Um. All right."

"But all those years of trying to fill that void in my heart with empty, meaningless sex only ended up serving to highlight my feelings for Loren. And now that I know what real love feels like, I'm never going to be able to settle for anything less again. I mean, I bought her a freaking minivan."

He blows out a breath and sits quietly for a minute. "Fine. I'll be more supportive," he says after a while. "But I want to be the twins' godfather."

I cringe. "Too late, man. We've already done a clean swap with JD and Ten."

He frowns. "That dude gets everything."

"Tell me about it."

"What about the next kid?"

"If I can convince your sister to sleep with me again after this, you're on."

He wrinkles his nose in distaste. "And you've gotta quit being gross in front of me."

"I'll try, but I can't make any promises," I say with a smirk.

"What *can* you promise, then?"

"To ... love, honor, and respect Loren. To give her my loyalty and fidelity for the rest of our lives, in sickness and health. You know, the usual?"

He waves his hand in annoyance. "Oh, I've got it. Can you convince her to let me stay in her old house?"

I furrow my brow as I consider it. Loren's never going to want to move back into her place if Landry's there.

"As long as you don't crowd us once the babies are born or make a pass at my sister-in-law, you've got a deal." We shake on it and head back inside, joining Loren and her mom again as a waitress brings out dessert.

"What's this?" Loren asks curiously when a slice of cheesecake appears in front of her.

"Your emotional-support peanut butter," I tell her.

She beams at me and offers a kiss before digging in, sighing and doing a happy dance at the first bite. I watch as she interacts with her brother when he asks her a question, then while she takes another forkful of peanut butter cheesecake into her mouth and pulls the fork out slowly and seductively.

Wait, no—I'm sure that's just my fault for staring too hard. Except she turns to me with a knowing smirk.

"What's wrong? Do I have something on my face?" she asks, batting her eyelashes innocently.

I smile as I reach up and wipe an imaginary bit of food from her bottom lip, and she squirms in her chair. I bring my thumb up to my mouth and she licks her lips.

"Ugh, I'd say 'get a room' but we all know you're not allowed," Landry chimes in after a second, and I shoot him a dirty look. "I mean, you guys are adorable. You should totally get hitched," he adds dryly.

Loren glares at him before she gets up from her seat and plops down in my lap, her belly bumping the table. Then she leans in for another kiss that's just long enough to elicit a groan from Landry and a laugh from her mother.

And that's all the confirmation I need. I want to marry this woman, more than anything I've ever wanted before.

As soon as she moves back to her seat to finish her dessert, I slip my phone from my pocket and pull up a text thread with my brother.

BLAKE

How would you feel if I gave away Mom's ring?

I grin to myself and set my phone down, but it begins buzzing right away.

ETHAN R

you're proposing to ms. reed??

TENLEY B

gif of little girl squealing excitedly

JD

gif of little girl squealing excitedly

I curse under my breath, and everyone at the table glares at me. "Uh, sorry, just ... my brother." They all shrug and continue their conversation, and JD sends another text in a private thread.

JD

Are you for real?

Don't play with me like this, man. My little heart can't take it. 😶

BLAKE

Yes, I want to marry Loren. I don't know if I've ever been more sure of anything.

It's just the part about Loren feeling the same way that's still up in the air.

JD

I thought you said she'd finally cracked?

BLAKE

You may not be aware of this, but there is a pretty wide canyon btw "ily" and "I do."

JD

You can fill it with all your baby crap.

Ask. Her.

gif of Ben Stiller saying "Do It"

I smile again and pull up another thread with Jada.

BLAKE

Lo's checkup went well. She and the twins are all good.

We also got the keys to the new whip and are enjoying lunch with her mom as we speak.

photo of Blake and Loren in front of a white minivan

JADA C

All great news! 😊

Thanks for the updates. ADA Moreau called for you this morning, by the way.

BLAKE

Thanks, I'll swing by the office and give him a call when I get back. I also need your help with a very important task.

JADA C

Whatcha got?

BLAKE

Know any good jewelers?

JADA C

gif of little girl squealing excitedly

CHAPTER 38

Blake

"Are you doing it today?" Ethan asks.

I furrow my brow. "Always in the grown folks' business, aren't you, kid?"

"I wouldn't have to be if y'all didn't need my help all the damn time," he retorts.

"Hey, watch your language," JD says, reaching over to backhand Ethan in the chest. Then he turns back to me. "*Are* you doing it today?"

I shove my hands in my pockets. "I don't know if she's ready."

"It's never going to be the right time," JD reminds me. "You'll just have to go for it, man."

"I've also been having a recurring nightmare in which I barely get down on my knee before she runs away screaming 'no,' so forgive me for being a little gun-shy," I say sarcastically.

JD scoffs. "As if she can run in her condition. Look at her, she's already waddling."

My eyes scan the crowd at our co-ed, joint baby shower to find Loren sitting in a circle between Tenley, Jada, Mrs. T, her mom, and her sister. She sees me watching her after a while, and she stops talking to one of her coworkers to pucker her lips and blow me a kiss.

"Gah, what a freaking simp," Ethan mumbles, taking the opportunity to snatch my cup and sneak a sip of my drink.

"And we all know you're not man enough to handle your liquor, kid," JD says evenly, holding out his hand.

Ethan groans and mumbles some unintelligible insult under his breath before he walks off and pulls out his phone.

"He and Caidence are on the outs again," JD explains Ethan's mood. "But you really should think about popping the question today. It's the perfect opportunity, and she's less likely to turn you down in front of everyone, right?"

I scratch the back of my neck. "I don't know. My gut says she won't take it seriously as long as she's still pregnant. I think a part of her is still worried I'm going to lose interest in her once the babies are born. Not to mention, she deserves a big, romantic, grand gesture. And I haven't figured out the perfect proposal yet."

JD puts his hand on my shoulder. "You won't know until you ask. And if you wait for the perfect time, you'll never ask."

I exhale deeply and let JD lead me on to a crowd of our oldest friends, most of them Camellia natives.

"I still can't believe this, man," Jase says. "I mean, JD's corny ass? Sure. But Blake the Snake, a father?" He chuckles and shakes his head before taking another sip of his beer.

I force a smile, regretting my decision to invite him. "Yeah, well, it was just as much of a surprise to me."

"Look at yourself, man. You're driving around in a damned minivan, and out of all the women in the world, you managed to knock up Coach Reed's daughter." He snorts. "It's almost like a bad movie."

I furrow my brow and take a swig from my own drink. "What's that supposed to mean?"

Before Jase can answer, my brother steps forward and puts one of his massive hands on Jase's normal-sized shoulder. "Tread carefully, bruh," JD says with a smile. But we can all sense the warning hidden behind his playful tone.

"Come on, Blake," another one of my former classmates starts. "Loren Reed doesn't exactly seem like your type, and it's not like you've been dating her since high school. I mean, who would have thought after so many years of playing the field, you'd get *her* pregnant?" Brock asks.

I huff out a laugh. "You do realize that Loren and I *are* together, right? And for what it's worth, I made a few moves on her back then, but she shot me down because I was still a cocky little jerk."

"*She* turned *you* down? You're shitting me." Jase chuckles, and I see JD and the others staring uneasily. "I don't remember you asking her out."

"That doesn't mean it didn't happen," I retort. "There's a lot of stuff you don't know about Loren and me. About me in general."

He crosses his arms. "If you say so, man."

JD pats him on the back, more gently this time. "I think what my brother's trying to say is that he's not the same guy he used to be."

"Yeah," Brock agrees. "You're both whipped now and don't care what any of us think anymore."

I roll my eyes when they all laugh, but I still feel myself smirking.

"All right, I get it," Jase says after a while. "I guess it's not easy convincing everyone you're settling down after so many years of being *that* guy."

I frown again. "You could say that."

"You probably would've had an easier time of it if you'd picked a more likely candidate, though. Like I was saying before, it's a little harder to take you seriously after hearing you've quit partying to screw around with Landry Reed's baby sister. I thought it was a joke at first. I mean, no offense, but I couldn't help but wonder if you were just trying to settle an old grudge or something." He's grinning as he says it, nudging some of the other guys and trying to get them to agree.

I swallow hard, my blood starting to boil. "No offense, huh?" I mutter.

Jase shrugs. "Don't get me wrong, she's hot, even if she dresses like my weird *Tante* Fay. But wasn't she the last virgin in our class? Unless you're trying to tell us you were secretly hitting that in high school the whole time?"

By now I'm clenching my jaw so hard that I'm starting to worry my teeth might crumble. If I allow myself to move, I'm afraid I'll end up choking him.

"That's enough, Jase," JD tells him.

Jase coughs out a laugh. "Aw, come on, Blake. When did you start letting Junior fight your battles for you? You really have gone soft, bro."

"Not *that* soft," I growl.

The rest of them are all quiet, and JD's eyes flash to mine. He's trying to convey that it's not worth it, but it's taking all I have not to knock this asshole out right here and now.

"Hey, what's going on?" Loren asks, glancing at me as she approaches. "Everything okay?"

"Your boyfriend's gone off the deep end," Jase mumbles.

"Maybe I have," I say under my breath. She furrows her brow in confusion, so I continue. "I just ... I need you and everyone else to understand how lucky I am, because you are ... so incredible in your own right. You're beautiful, smart, funny, sexy as hell, and literally the most interesting woman I've ever known. You're my favorite person in the whole world."

Her expression softens slightly. "Um, thank you?"

"I love you, Lo, and I can't bear the idea of anyone making you question my loyalty to you or how I feel about you."

She blushes, and her eyes lock onto mine, though I can tell she's mostly trying to avoid having to acknowledge the way everyone is staring at her. "I love you, too, Blake," she replies, her voice barely above a whisper.

And the mere fact that she's willing to say it in front of all these people is enough to fuel me on. My heart starts drumming loudly in my ears, and my focus shifts to JD's face behind her. He smirks and nods encouragingly, and I exhale slowly. Then I see the way his hand curls around Tenley's side when she joins him, and I know, without a doubt, that I want that, too. I don't care if my brother did it first. I just know I want my own family, with Loren.

I mouth the words, "In my nightstand" to him, and he nods

quickly before darting off into the house. Then I clear my throat and reach for Loren's hand. She takes a step closer, still staring at me carefully.

"I know you're still worried our relationship wouldn't have progressed this far if you hadn't gotten pregnant. But to be honest, I'm grateful it happened, because I don't know how else I would have tricked you into falling for me." I lean in and kiss her softly, and her cheeks are bright red.

"A generally unwise man once told me that only a lucky few get to experience this once-in-a-lifetime, undeniable chemistry with another person. It's an attraction so strong that it might even seem wrong or inconvenient at first, until you recognize it as a nudge from the Holy Spirit. Because this person is meant for you, and your desire is just a gift that makes it easier to commit to spending forever together."

She's quiet for a while as she considers it. Meanwhile, my heart feels like it's beating out of my chest as I wait for her to acknowledge that I've just confessed to thinking she's my soulmate. She's got to sense my desperation if I'm spouting all these mushy lines in front of everyone, especially since I obviously borrowed them from my brother.

"And ... you believe that's what's happening here, with us?" she asks hesitantly.

"I do. Except, I think it's always been that way for us, but we were too stubborn to see it before. So God must have figured it was time to step it up," I add, sliding my hand over her belly.

She laughs. "I guess I could see that."

"Loren," I begin, closing my eyes and leaning down to catch her rose scent on the next inhale. Then I open my eyes again and stare into hers, imagining we're all alone and not standing in the midst of all these people. "Stay with me, please. I know you may not be convinced yet, but I don't have any doubts. I want ... I want to marry you. I want to spend the rest of my life making you happy, making you feel loved, and trying to get you to see yourself the way I see you. I don't want to miss a minute of watching you with our girls, because I know you're going to be an amazing mom. I want a family with you."

Her breathing grows ragged again, and I bring my hand up to wipe a tear when it collects on her cheek. "You want to get married?"

I nod, and then I notice my own vision getting blurry, just as JD returns and taps me on the shoulder. And I have to use the back of my arm to clear my eyes before I open my hand behind me. He drops something into my palm before he pats my back affectionately. Then I take a deep breath before I get down on one knee and hold the ring up in front of Loren.

"Loren Agnes Reed," I drag out her name, smirking at her. But she looks more alarmed than touched now. Still, I push on. "Will you please marry me?"

It feels like five minutes pass with the only sound being Loren's sniffling. Her mouth opens and closes a couple of times, as if she's trying to form words, but it takes a while before I get an answer.

"Blake, I—I'm not sure what to say," she breathes. "I didn't realize you ..."

I lick my lips and look down. "Yeah, well, apparently I'm not so good at conveying my feelings most of the time." She's quiet again, and I hear a couple of whispers behind me. "So ... ah, will you? Marry me?" I prompt her again, this time with only a smidgeon of the confidence I had before.

"Oh, uh, yeah. Sure."

"Sure?" I ask, standing.

"I mean, of course I will," she adds nervously, blinking at me and forcing her mouth into a horribly fake smile.

My stomach turns, because I can see the panic and uncertainty on her face. Her hand trembles when she holds it out for me to slide the ring onto her finger, and she doesn't bother looking down at it as she slips her arms around my waist and buries her face in my chest. She's mortified, hiding her face from the crowd.

I lean down and kiss the top of her head to the sound of applause and shouts of congratulations. "Come on," I whisper so that only she can hear. "Let's go inside."

"It's fine," she says, her voice muffled. She pulls back, leaving a wet spot on my shirt. "We'll talk later."

I flash her my pushy-lawyer grin. "We'll talk now."

She lets out a shaky exhale and nods, and I ignore the rest of the reassuring shoulder pats and cat calls as I lead her by the hand into the house. I practically drag her into my bedroom, only letting go to shut the door behind me. I'm silent as I cross my arms over my chest, still unable to look at her.

"I, um, I'm sorry if that wasn't the reaction you hoped to get from me," she begins softly. "But the whole thing was really unexpected."

"Was it really?" I finally glance her way, but I'm afraid it's with more of an angry glare than a loving gaze. I don't even know why I'm so upset, since I fully expected her to freak out this way. I guess I'm just mad at myself for being dumb enough to hope the others were right.

"I didn't mean to embarrass you. I'm just shocked."

I scoff. "You can't seriously tell me you had no clue this was coming."

She stares down at her feet, finding the ring with her thumb and fidgeting nervously. "I certainly didn't think you'd propose in front of everyone today without ever having brought up the idea of marriage in private."

"We may not have discussed it in detail. But I've been dropping hints for a while, so forgive me for thinking you'd appreciate a spontaneous, romantic gesture."

"I did—I mean, I do," she replies, her voice sounding small.

"Then it's just as I thought. You still don't trust me."

She sighs and closes in the space between us, grabbing my hand. "Of course I trust you. When I said I wasn't worried about your past or what anyone else thinks of our relationship, I meant it."

I lick my lips and look away again. "I guess you don't feel the same, then. You don't want to be married to me."

"Hey, don't do that, please," she says, turning my head back to face her. "I never said I didn't want to marry you, and the last thing I intended was to make you feel bad. But I can't help the way I reacted when you put me on the spot."

"Loren, I told you I wanted to spend the rest of my life with you, I bared my freaking soul with both of our families standing right there, and when I asked you to marry me, you said, *sure* ... like I asked if you wanted me to make you a snack! *Sure, why not, I could go for a peanut butter sandwich*," I rant, waving my hands and mimicking her at the end. She rolls her lips in, making my nostrils flare.

"Don't you dare laugh at me right now, Reed."

"Sorry."

I take a deep breath in and exhale before starting again, trying to garner the last bit of my patience.

"I really am sorry, okay," she continues. "If I could do it again, I would—"

"What? Fake it better?"

"Well, no, but ..."

"You shouldn't have needed time to think about it," I blurt out. "My proposal should have been a surprise, not a shock. And if you feel anything close to what I feel for you, you wouldn't have thought twice about saying yes."

She opens her mouth to defend herself again, but nothing comes out.

"I've seen the way you look at JD and Tenley. I've watched you watch couples fall in love in the movies, listened to you gush about the characters in all your favorite books. You claim you want true love and romance and a happily ever after, yet you keep pushing me away."

"I know, but ..." she starts again, but her voice breaks off.

"You say I'm confused. But it's starting to feel like you're the one who's stringing me along. Maybe you're not in love with me, just with the idea of love. And you've been using my past and this pregnancy as an excuse to avoid a real commitment. After all, you can't be expected to bother with all that painful self-reflection and risk putting yourself out there when you've got to protect yourself and your babies from a heartless man like me, right?"

"You're not heartless, Blake," she chokes out, her chest heaving. "And I do love you."

Shit. I've really done it now. I'll never get her to stop crying.

I sigh and pull her in for a hug. "Come here. I'm sorry. That came out harsher than I intended," I mumble as I tighten my arms around her.

She relaxes in my embrace for a while, waiting for her breathing to settle before she speaks again. "So, you don't hate me?"

I pull away and lock eyes with her, and my chest tightens. "I could never hate you. But I'm not sure whether I want to shake you or kiss you at any given time. I suspect it's always a good bit of both."

She chuckles quietly. "I get it."

"I just don't know what to do with you," I say softly. "I never have."

I still can't help myself, and I want her so badly that I doubt I'll ever learn.

CHAPTER 39
Loren

Blake swallows hard and curses under his breath before he cups my face and pulls me in to crush his lips against mine, kissing me so hard that he knocks the wind out of me. One of his hands slips behind my head and tangles in my hair as the other travels down to rest beneath my butt, nudging until I lift my legs and wrap them around his hips. He walks us over to the wall and rests my back against it as he continues exploring my mouth hungrily, and I could kick myself for questioning whether I want to do this with him for the rest of my life. He pushes himself into me roughly, and I moan into his mouth as I tighten my grip on him, fisting my hand in his hair and making him growl.

His hair—that's it, right? It's his kryptonite.

I run my fingers over his scalp again, and this time he breaks away and whimpers. "Shit," he says breathlessly. "I—we can't."

"I know," I reply, my lips finding his jawline. He grinds his hips against me again, and my eyes nearly roll back at the mere thought of what it'd feel like to give in to our need right now. "I just want … more," I murmur against his skin. I don't know when I became this forward, but I'm pretty sure the hormones are speaking for me now.

I bring my hand down between us, and his lips part with a gasp.

His jaw is slack, and his eyelids look heavy as he stares down at me reverently. "Please—"

I interrupt him with another kiss. "Blake," I speak into his mouth again, using my teeth to tug on his bottom lip. "Let me down."

He moans in response, following my orders and backing away to let me slide down the wall to my feet. I sigh when I wrap my hand around him again, and he slams his palm against the wall over my head, clenching his teeth as he spits out another curse.

I use my free hand to fumble with his belt, but he reaches down and stills me. "Don't."

"Okay," I say, pulling my hand away reluctantly and relishing in the way he whines. Then I bite my lip as I move to unbutton his shirt.

But Blake stops me and shakes his head again. "No, Loren."

"No, what?" I ask, confused.

He clears his throat and pushes off from the wall before he buttons his shirt again, and my expression falls. "I'm sorry, I should have stopped us sooner."

"But I just need a little more of you this time," I protest, though I'm feeling the sting of his rejection.

"And I told you a while back that I don't want anything to be one-sided with us," he retorts, his tone harsh. "Besides, that kind of stuff isn't going to help right now. We're both already confused enough as it is."

My chin trembles as I struggle to rein in my disappointment, once again.

He doesn't want me?

I don't understand. Why would he want to marry me if he's not even interested in letting me do sexy stuff to him? Is he only proposing because I'm pregnant? Or is he worried I'm not experienced enough to make it worth his while?

I cross my arms, feeling more vulnerable than ever. "I'm sorry if that wasn't up to your standards."

He takes a step back and glares at me incredulously. "You think I stopped you because it wasn't good enough? How many times do I have to tell you how amazing it feels when you touch me before you'll believe it?"

"Enough times that you'd actually lose control and let something happen again, I guess," I yell, waving my hands in the air.

"So you want me to risk yours and our babies' lives?"

"Of course not. All I wanted was to make you feel good. And just once, I wanted to be the one to pull the emergency fire alarm and put a stop to it. If all those other women were sexy enough to make you give in, don't you think I need you to show me the same courtesy every now and again?"

He growls. "You still don't get it, do you? It's different with us. I've never wanted anyone the way I want you."

"If that's true, then why does it seem like you're still holding back?"

"Because you asked me to, Loren," he begins, raising his voice. "Because it's the only way I could prove I want you for more than sex and earn your trust. Because I've been trying to protect both of us." He gulps as he continues staring at me. "Despite what you might think, I couldn't risk seeing that look in your eyes again, the way you pitied me in the morning after I shared more of myself with you than anyone before, my heart and my body. You gave me my first taste of real intimacy that night, just so you could continue rejecting me every day since then. So, yeah, I've been holding back. I've had to."

"And you don't think I've been feeling rejected? It hasn't been easy for me either," I croak out, trying to ignore the heat that flashes through me.

"*Easy*? I just expended the last pitiful shreds of my willpower to stop you after vowing never to use you that way—a promise I made to you, to myself, and to God, more recently. But you ..." He groans and runs his hands through his hair before he begins again. "This has got to be my penance for the past dozen years, right?" He shakes his head, blowing a breath out of his lips. "I've been *killing myself* to change. And now you're upset with me for surprising you with a marriage proposal and stopping you from taking off my pants?"

"Okay, I get how this could be confusing. But I can't help that

I'm full of irrational hormones right now. And can we stop with the morning-after bit, already? I said I was sorry, and you said you'd forgiven me," I remind him quietly.

"I *have* forgiven you, but it's still hard for me to forget how worthless I felt after you left, especially when I'm constantly worried about you running scared again."

"Yeah? Then why the hell didn't you man up and tell me how you felt that morning, Blake? Why didn't you speak up to say I was wrong, that spending the night together did mean something to you? Why didn't you stop me from leaving so we could have talked about it like rational adults?" I realize I'm yelling, and I stand there with my chest heaving as Blake frowns at me. But now that I've finally started this, I don't think I can stop.

"If one night with me was really all that enlightening for you, the least you could have done was called me the next day or even the following week and told me how wrong I was to assume you didn't care," I continue, trying not to choke over my tears. "I waited for weeks to hear from you. I probably fantasized a hundred times about seeing your name pop up on my phone and hearing you say, 'It absolutely meant something, Lo—it meant *everything*.' Shit, I only forced myself to go on that date with Rowan because I was so desperate to get you out of my head, and you showed up and sabotaged that, too!" He runs his tongue over his teeth and drops his eyes to the ground while I finish my rant.

"You've done this to me so many times. You build me up and make me think I'm special enough to hold your attention, but the second I hesitate, you let me go. You did it the night of our first kiss, then again every time we were alone in high school. And you wonder why I'm terrified to admit how much I need you and how hard I've fallen for you? If you weren't willing to fight for me before you knew about the babies, then how can I be sure you'll care as much later, once I've trapped you in a miserable marriage that you'll undoubtedly want out of in a few years? You want to know why I'm afraid to acknowledge how badly I want to marry you? It's because it feels like I'm damned either way, whether I drive you away now or I give in and wait for you to realize you're sick of me later."

I'm out of breath by the time I'm done, but *gah* does it feel amazing to get that off my chest! I don't even think I've been conscious of some of those ideas until saying them aloud just now But if there was ever a time to win an argument with Blake, I'm pretty sure this is it.

"Loren ... I'm sorry," he replies after a while, stopping to clear his throat when his voice cracks. "I guess I thought I was being a martyr, but I've actually been too busy nursing my own wounds to realize how much I've hurt you. You're right, though. I've been a coward." He frowns and shakes his head. "And I was about to do the same thing all over again, wasn't I?"

I shrug. "It feels a lot like that, yeah."

He scratches his head and curses under his breath before he begins again. "Thank you for being brave enough to admit all that. I'll never be good enough to deserve you." He laughs sardonically. "What the hell was I even thinking with that proposal?"

I sniffle, fighting back the tears again. Hearing that he already regrets asking me to marry him sort of takes all the fun out of winning an argument.

"Do you want this back, then?" I ask, holding up my left hand. I glance at the ring he put there only minutes ago for the first time. It looks ... familiar. And pretty, very pretty. "Or am I leaving it on so we can go back to faking it, at least until we figure things out?"

"Neither," he mutters, just as a knock sounds on the door. And his cryptic answer reminds me of what he said before about not being sure whether he wants to shake me or kiss me most of the time.

"Uh, hey, everything all right in there?" JD calls from the other side.

"Depends on what you mean by *all right*," I reply dryly, glancing in the mirror and swiping at the mascara pooling beneath my eyes.

"I hate to interrupt, but everyone's getting a little worried, and you haven't been answering your texts."

"Sorry. We'll be out in a second," Blake says.

"Okay, then." It's quiet for a moment, but I can tell JD hasn't moved. "Mind if I ask what the vibe's gonna be when you emerge from your cave? You know, so I can prepare everyone else?"

Blake shakes his head and calls JD a not-so-nice name under his breath, and I can't help but snort.

"It's definitely giving moody preggo at the moment," I yell, and I think I hear Tenley giggle on the other side. "With a side of happily engaged couple."

Blake's still silent.

"I'm not sure if that's the answer you wanted me to give them," I say, taking a step forward. "But you can correct me if you want."

Blake grabs my arm and stops me. "We're not done with this conversation."

"Everyone's waiting," I remind him.

"You're not leaving this room until you at least hear me say this: I love you, Loren. I'm truly sorry for not going after you that morning and for all the other times I've screwed up. For the record, not a minute has gone by in which I don't regret letting you go without telling you how I felt or insisting that we date for real from the beginning. And regardless of whether you want to marry me or not, I still plan to spend the rest of my life trying to make the last couple of decades of stupidity up to you."

I nod and focus on not crying again long enough to whisper, "I love you, too."

He heaves out an exhale before he opens the door. And JD's expression falls as soon as he sees our faces.

"I took the liberty of telling a few people I ordered you to put your feet up for a while, since you're supposed to be on bed rest," Tenley begins, her toned concerned. "In fact, I think it's time for the 'thanks for coming but hit the road' speech."

My eyes dart over to Blake's, and he stuffs his hands in his pockets, looking nervous. "I certainly don't feel like facing everyone again."

I sigh. "Same. I'm actually pretty tired, now that you mention it."

I rub the underside of my belly. "And I'm feeling a bit more pressure than usual."

Tenley glances between us carefully. "You two didn't sneak away to celebrate, did you?"

"Nope," I declare while Blake stares at his feet. "No hanky panky here. My fiancé's been *very* diligent about making sure we uphold those rules."

"Then why is his belt undone?" JD whispers loudly, raising his eyebrows.

"Why would you even notice that is the better question," Blake grumbles before he turns and refastens the buckle.

My face flushes, and Tenley steps in line behind me to run her hand over my hair, presumably to smooth it down. "You sure you're okay?" she whispers. "You're starting to worry me. Maybe you should just lie down now."

"I'm fine," I say, probably unconvincingly. Because I'm not fine at all.

We reach the doors to the backyard and step outside anyway. JD addresses everyone first, thanking them for their presence and their presents before declaring his love for Tenley and reminding them about how much he's looking forward to watching Ethan become a big brother-cousin while having the great honor of becoming a first-time father alongside his best friend, i.e., his brother, and yada-yada. It's the classic JD cheese we've all grown to both love and barely tolerate.

Blake's eyes meet mine for a second and he rolls them. I stifle a laugh. Then he reaches over and clasps my hand in his as he picks up the opening his brother leaves after congratulating the "happily engaged couple with a side of tired preggo lady."

"Yeah, um, thanks again everyone. JD said it best, but I just want to add how much we love all of you and appreciate your support, especially since Loren's had to endure so much throughout this high-risk pregnancy. And we hope you'll keep us in your prayers now that she'll be getting closer to delivering the twins." He squeezes my hand, and it feels like he's forcing the air out of my lungs. "I just need the three of them to be safe, more than anything. We'll worry about the rest later."

Then he lifts my hand and kisses it, looking over to make sure I understand he was talking to me. I sigh and nod, adding my own wary line or two of thanks and good night.

Everyone begins clearing out then, coming over to embrace and congratulate us before they leave. By the time most of them are gone, I walk into the kitchen to find Mrs. T, Lilley, and my mother wiping down the counters and setting the dishes on the drying rack.

"You should be resting," my brother says when he joins me. "You're looking pale."

"I'm fine," I repeat.

"If you say so." He nods and wraps me up in an unexpected hug. "And congratulations. I love you, Lo. Be safe, and call me if anything changes. I want to be here when my girls arrive and check them out myself."

"Yeah, yeah, we get it. You're a doctor," I say, rolling my eyes.

Lilley, Emmett, and my parents come over next, each of them congratulating me. I look to the side and find Blake watching carefully when my mom approaches, and I give him a small smile to let him know I'm okay before she embraces me. He walks over and stands beside me anyway, shaking my dad's hand, who looks surprisingly happy about our engagement. My father pulls me in for a hug and a cheek kiss for the first time in as long as I can remember. Maybe I should have started dating the quarterback a lot sooner.

Blake's arm drops from my waist as soon as they shut the door behind them, and we're left with JD, Tenley, and their family.

"Go, put your feet up, please?" he asks me quietly, kissing me on the temple.

"Yeah, I'm going."

"Let me help you with that," Blake mumbles when he sees Ethan and Mrs. T carrying the last of the baby boy gifts out.

I sigh longingly once I'm alone, rubbing my tightening stomach again.

"I think it's past time for you to sit your adorable ass down, Ms.

Reed." I jump when I hear JD's command, thinking he was still outside. "Or should I say, Mrs. Bourgeois-to-be?"

"I'm fine," I say again as I make my way to the couch.

"Hmm. I don't think you are," he replies, helping me lift my feet, and I press my lips together to stop myself from tearing up again. He must notice it, because he plops down beside me and reaches over to grab my left hand. "She would have absolutely loved seeing this on you," he says wistfully, holding my hand up in front of us.

I furrow my brow in confusion, and he smirks. "Mom always liked you. He doesn't seem to remember it, but she used to tease him about you all the time. She must have known about his crush."

I stare down at the ring. "This was Mrs. Monica's?"

"Oh, I'm sorry, I thought you knew."

I shake my head slowly as the panic returns. "JD ... I've ruined everything. Even if Blake says he still wants to marry me after this, he's going to wake up one day and regret giving me your mother's ring," I ramble, reaching down to tug the ring off my finger. "This belongs to Tenley, not me."

"Hey, slow down," he says, putting his hand on mine. "You're scaring yourself out of this right now. Do you really think he's going to change his mind, or are you just afraid of saying yes?" Then he pulls me closer when the only answer I offer is a loud sniffle.

"We can't get married, though," I wail. "I can't let us end up like my parents."

"It's not fair to compare yourselves to them," he says softly as I continue sobbing in his arms. "Besides, your parents got hitched in high school. You and Blake are two of the most intelligent, mature people I know. If you can't make this work, who can?"

"It's too risky to give in."

"It's too risky *not* to give in," he corrects me. "You can't ignore your feelings and expect not to build resentment this way. I promise you there is something worse out there than being sad, and that's being alone *and* being sad."

Ugh. He's right. But I can't tell him that right now.

"Wait a minute. You're quoting *Ted Lasso* again, aren't you?"

"Coach Theodore Lasso is the wisest prophet of our time," he says, making me laugh. "But, seriously, Lo. What's stopping you? Do you really think there's someone else out there meant for each of you? Do you doubt how much he loves you? Are you not sure how you feel about him?"

"No," I say, sitting up again. "No one tolerates me as well as he does. And I'll never love anyone else the way I love him, will I?"

"You probably won't," he admits ruefully. "But the truth is you'll still have to make the choice to keep loving him every day. So if you don't think you can do that, then you shouldn't keep leading him on, either."

I frown, not expecting JD to say that. "We're talking about spending forever with the man I probably wouldn't even consider a friend if I hadn't gotten pregnant."

"So what? You *did* get pregnant, and you *did* fall in love. Who cares about what probably could have happened? Identical twins and a surprise proposal are way better than a sad and lonely existence."

I tilt my head back and groan. "Gah, JD. Why are you making so much sense today?"

"I may not be a smart man, but I know what love is," he says in his best Forrest Gump impression, making me snort.

I hold my hand up again, and he smiles as he stares at the ring with me. "You and my mom were friends, right?"

"Yeah, I guess we were. We had book club together."

"I bet your taste in books was about the only thing the two of you had in common, though, besides your ability to secure my brother's unconditional love and all that."

I roll my eyes. "I mean, yeah. Your mom was lovely. She was so tall and ..."

I look down at the ring again, swallowing hard. Monica Bourgeois wasn't a tiny woman. I am. (Well, I used to be, anyway.)

"He already had her ring resized to fit me," I whisper, more to myself than to JD. "He was just waiting for the right time, wasn't he?"

"Yep." He smiles again.

"Okay, so what now?" I ask, wiping my nose on the back of my sleeve. "What if he wants it back? I've already embarrassed him in front of our closest friends and family."

"Oh, please. We all know you were just making out for most of that 'fight' you had back there," he declares, using his fingers to make air quotes. "You both came out half-dressed and ruffled."

I blush. "So what if we were?"

"He's too far gone to care whether you embarrassed him or not. There's no way he's taking that ring back. If he could resist you, he wouldn't have thrown you up against the wall earlier."

My eyes widen. "How long were you listening at the door?"

He purses his lips and looks away. "Long enough to overhear what kind of consolation prize you were offering."

"JD," I growl.

"You should also know that I'm the one who's been encouraging him to keep your love life rated PG. I thought it was good advice at the time, but I had no idea you were so thirsty. My bad," he adds, stifling a smirk.

"You—"

But just then, my stomach tightens in a way that feels different than before. This time, it hurts, and I flinch and hiss through my teeth.

"Are you okay?" JD asks, concerned.

"I don't know. Something's not right." Then I move to shift my position on the couch, and there's an uncomfortable gush.

"Don't move," he says carefully. "I'm going to get Tenley, okay?"

I inhale sharply when another contraction begins. "Okay," I breathe.

JD glances down, and the look on his face makes me realize the weight of the situation. "I'll be right back. I promise."

"Wait, I'm scared. Don't leave me. I need ..." But I can't finish before another sharp pain shoots through me, this one worse than the last.

"Want me to call your mom? Your sister?" I cringe and shake my head. "Landry?"

"No, I just need *him*. Bring him to me, please."

JD nods, then I close my eyes, feeling sleepy and heavy, despite the pain. I think he must be squeezing my hand, but I might be dreaming. "You're gonna be okay, Lo. Just hang on, all right?"

"Mm-hmm." I struggle just to get it out, and JD makes me cringe when he calls out for someone.

Then I hear what sounds like Ethan's voice in the distance as he yells for help. There's a commotion, and I vaguely sense Blake coming to my side and whispering to me before I'm lifted up, and everything fades away.

CHAPTER 40
Loren

"Thanks," I mumble to Blake when he takes the breast pump from me. He brings it into the kitchen, and I watch as he goes through the process of bagging and labeling the milk while I stuff my sad excuse for mammary glands back into my nursing bra. Then I shuffle to the bathroom to finish getting ready, which basically means I brush my teeth and wash my face before twisting my unwashed hair up and securing it with a clip. I avoid looking at my reflection for too long. It's easier to pretend the dark circles under my eyes don't exist than to bother trying to cover them up.

"Ready?" Blake asks from the doorway, and I nod before I stop to grab the two mugs of coffee he fixed from the counter.

He carries the ice chest of milk and sets it carefully in the back seat of my new minivan. I move slowly, buckling my seat belt and gingerly pushing the strap away from my incision, and he reaches out to clasp my hand in between taking sips of coffee as he drives us to the hospital.

We both clip our special NICU-parent IDs onto our shirts before walking hand in hand through the maternity wing. The NICU's automatic doors swing open after Blake scans his ID badge, and we're immediately greeted by smiling, familiar faces and a cacophony of steady machine beeps on our way to the hand-wash station.

We scrub our hands meticulously, and one of the nurses takes the cooler of milk before we rush over to a pair of plastic bassinets, each of them displaying a pink "Baby Bourgeois" tag. Both babies are snuggled together in the same bed, clad only in diapers and wires. I reach down to stroke their tiny, fuzzy heads, and they begin squirming and grunting beneath the heat lamp. Blake leans in to pick up the smaller of the two while I sit in a nearby rocker and wait for him to place her on my chest.

"There you are, Princess Pen," he murmurs as he helps me unbutton my shirt and settle her against my skin. Then I watch carefully while he undoes the top half of his own button-down and tucks the second baby beneath the fabric. "And how are you today, Queen Charlotte?"

My mouth curls up on the right as I continue staring. He uses one hand to secure Charley and the other to drag the nearest rocking chair beside mine before he sits with a loud sigh.

"Penny's got the hiccups again," I announce, and he laughs softly.

We rock in silence along with the bustling NICU soundtrack. The nurse brings us a set of bottles and we attempt a feeding, but only Charley gets it right this time. She's already got a few ounces on her sister, weighing in at almost four pounds. Penelope has been hovering just above the three-pound mark.

Tenley walks in a minute later, and I stifle my protest when she accidentally bumps into the back of my rocker with her belly while she asks about Penny's progress.

"Ope, sorry," she apologizes when I hiss quietly after the second time she knocks me forward.

"You're fine," I reply, reaching up to pat her baby bump. "Jake just wants to remind us he's here, right?"

She laughs. "As if my blood sugar would let me forget."

"Damn. You look like you've grown since the weekend, Ten," Blake comments. But his expression falls when Tenley shoots him a dirty look. "You're totally glowing, though."

"It's the gestational diabetes. And if I didn't know you were so sleep deprived, I'd tell you to kiss my increasingly large ass, Blake," Tenley grumbles. Then she turns to me. "Ready?"

I nod before unclipping my nursing bra, and Tenley guides me as we try and fail to get Penny to latch on for a nursing session. I clear my throat and look away, trying to hide my sniffling when Tenley finally takes the baby from my arms long enough for me to redress. I don't have time for an emotional breakdown right now, I remind myself.

Blake reaches over and wordlessly strokes the back of my neck while I get myself together, then he stands and puts Charley on my chest, taking Penny for a quick snuggle before placing her beside her sister and covering the three of us with a blanket.

"I'll see you at lunch," he says, leaning down to kiss my temple before buttoning his shirt and vowing to return with a peace offering for Tenley.

She comes around to give each of the babies a loving squeeze before she follows him out, but she says she'll be back soon to help with the next feeding. She manages to walk away without adding yet another apology for convincing me to participate in our joint baby shower and not noticing I'd gone into preterm labor until it was almost too late. She's been beating herself up over the situation for the past couple of weeks, despite my reassurances. Not only had I previously ignored doctor's orders on numerous occasions, but I hadn't even realized I'd been having contractions, and I was the one having them. And she seems to have completely forgotten how many times Dr. Rowan proclaimed that if it weren't for Tenley and Dr. Simms's quick actions, the twins and I might not have survived.

I sigh as I lean back in the chair, closing my eyes and trying to ignore the way my brain wants to replay the traumatic events of that evening. It's better to live in the here and now, with my babies out and mostly safe, slowly but surely growing bigger and healthier each day. Except that it feels like we'll never make it out of the here and now.

I drift off and end up napping until Tenley's return. We change the girls' diapers and repeat the feeding process, except this time I get Charley to nurse for a few minutes while Tenley struggles with Penny to take her bottle. Eventually, Tenley gives up on the bottle and squeezes a couple of drops of milk into Penny's tiny mouth, and Penny smacks her lips. Then Tenley immediately puts Pen on one breast as Charley continues nursing on the other, and I bite my lip to keep myself from crying out when my uterus contracts.

"The pain is a good sign, I promise. It's natural," Tenley reassures me. But I think this hurts more than the actual labor did. "Look— she's getting it!"

I glance down to find that Tenley's right. Penny finally latches and proceeds to gulp awkwardly.

"You're doing it, Lo," Tenley announces proudly, her eyes shining. "You're such a baddie."

"Thank you," I whisper, trying to turn my grimace into a smile. Then one of the nurses comes around to take a picture of our first successful tandem nursing session, even though Tenley's still technically assisting by holding Penny in place.

Blake walks in just then, and he grins and leans down to kiss me, repeating the same congratulations. Penny chokes a second later, and Blake takes her away to burp her, but the staff all declare it a major victory. I decide to play along, mostly because I'm afraid of what might happen if I give myself the chance to feel anything right now.

Once the girls are nice and milk drunk, we place them in their incubators for a nap. Tenley goes back to work, waddling away with her new bag of sugar-free cinnamon candy in hand, and Blake and I go down to the cafeteria together.

We fill our plates and sit at a table, automatically swapping out some of the food on our trays and digging in. Blake adds more of his French fries to my stash once he sees how ravenous I am. Though I'm not producing as much milk as we hoped, working as a dairy cow has kept me just as hungry as being a double incubator did.

After lunch, he leads me back to the NICU, where we repeat the same scrupulous hand-washing routine for what seems like the millionth time. Landry is already there, talking to one of the nurses. He praises us for getting Penny to nurse today while Blake picks her up. I reach over and unbutton his shirt for their skin-to-skin contact, and his eyes lock onto mine for a few seconds when my fingers brush his bare chest. I look away quickly when my stomach flutters.

Landry helps me settle in with Charley before he leaves for an interview with a local pediatrician's office. Now that Mom's finally doing well on her own, he's decided to stick around Camellia to be closer to the girls.

Blake stays through the next feeding, but Penny's still tired from her big accomplishment, and we have trouble waking her to take a bottle. Meanwhile, Charley gobbles hers down in no time and has a little left boob for dessert, and the nurse tells me she's probably starting a cluster-feeding cycle. I know I've heard it before, but my brain still isn't functioning properly so I just nod and resolve to look it up in one of the baby books when we get home. Blake must sense my confusion, and he leans over to whisper that newborns often go on a feeding spree before they have a growth spurt. I sigh, because my nipples are already sore.

After another changing, Blake gets ready for a couple more hours at work. "I guess I'll make a quick stop at football practice this afternoon, if you're okay with that." He forces a smile, but it's overshadowed by the set of under-eye circles he's sporting, which are only slightly lighter than mine. He's still just as handsome, though, as most of the nurses like to remind me when he's not around. I reassure him that we'll be fine until he returns.

We're lucky that Camellia's hospital is the best in the area, despite the rural location. I can't imagine how we'd be getting on without the small NICU in our hometown.

Nothing changes for the rest of the day, except that Charley has transformed into a greedy piglet. Tenley stops by for another visit and uses her magic touch to get Penny to eat again. She also explains that Charley's cluster-feeding cycle is another good sign but adds a caveat about preparing myself in case Charley's ready to go home without her sister.

Blake comes back with Reese's pumpkins and an iced coffee, and Tenley groans before announcing that she's going home to demand a foot rub from JD. It looks like her feet are barely fitting in her sneakers at this point.

I nearly devour the whole bag of peanut butter pumpkins while he leans back and rests both girls on his broad chest. I didn't think my favorite candy would be out this early, but I shouldn't be surprised that he's managed to find it for me.

"I can't take all the credit," he admits. "I did send Jada to track the pumpkins down. But it's the thought that counts, right?"

I guess I wouldn't know. I haven't been allowing myself too many thoughts lately. So I nod and offer him a half-smile before he looks away with a hint of disappointment in his expression.

He's murmuring to the babies about how proud he is of their big-girl appetites when he catches me staring at him a few minutes later. "You'd better stop looking at me like that, Agnes," he says quietly, his voice deep. "You're making Reese's sexy again."

"Okay, Daddy," I reply in an unexpectedly sultry tone.

He smirks and winks at me this time, and my stomach dips again.

I rock my chair in sync with the beeping monitors, and Blake and I spend the next few hours in the same routine—feeding, changing, and snuggling. We're rewarded with squeaky grunts, newborn scrunches, finger squeezes, big stretches, and short glimpses of their tiny blue eyes peering back at us. And it feels like we're holding the pieces of my heart outside of my chest.

"It's probably time to go home and get some rest, Mama," Dana, one of the older nurses tells me after a while. "You need sleep and real food. With both the princess and the queen getting their fill today, I wouldn't be surprised if your supply ramps up in a day or two. You'll want to hydrate, too. I expect to see you come in with one of those super-tall, insulated cups tomorrow."

"I've been telling her she's not drinking enough water," Blake tattles.

I roll my eyes at both of them. "I'm trying, people. But it's not easy balancing coming back from the dead with tandem nursing."

"Hey, I'm just kidding, babe. You're doing an amazing job," he says more softly, lifting my left hand to place a kiss over the ring I've been wearing but whose significance we haven't found the time or energy to discuss since he slipped it on a couple of weeks ago.

"Listen to your husband," Dana says. "And take care of yourself, *cher*."

I glance over to catch the fake smile he flashes her. "Don't worry. I'll make sure she brings her big cup tomorrow, Mrs. Dana. And she'll actually have water in it this time, not coffee."

I narrow my eyes at him. "For the record, you've been the one supplying all of my coffee, *hubby*."

His smile fades as he drops my hand. "I guess I still can't say no to you."

I huff before I turn to kiss the girls good night, trying to disguise my sniffles. Those darn postpartum hormones must be flaring up again.

Blake and I are both silent as we leave the hospital and drive home. I don't miss the way he gazes longingly at his truck in the garage. He's been taxiing me around in Shadowfax until I get cleared to drive myself, and I can barely walk, much less climb into his lifted truck in my current state.

As soon as we make it inside, he goes straight into the kitchen to warm some of the leftovers that Mrs. T has been stocking in our fridge. Then I hear him start a load of laundry before he puts my sanitized breast pump back together and brings my supper to me in the living room.

I frown as he sighs over his plate of chicken and sausage *sauce piquante*. It doesn't take me long to inhale mine, yet he's barely touched his plate of rice by the time he gets up to tend to the dishes.

"I'm going to take a shower," I announce, and he darts back into the living room.

"Do you need my help?" he asks, a mixture of exhaustion and concern lining his face. And those aren't exactly the emotions one would hope to elicit when she mentions getting undressed in front of her fiancé.

"I think I'll be fine, thanks. I'll leave the door open and call for you if I do."

"I'll be in right behind you." He goes off to finish his chores.

I allow myself a good five minutes of sobbing in the shower before I hear the bathroom door opening. By the time I step out and wrap a towel around myself, Blake's already there, waiting for his turn. He doesn't seem to notice the way my eyes are glued to him while he undresses.

Then I look down at my Frankensteined stomach and the rest of my postpartum body. And my eyes start to sting again.

I swipe at my cheeks, reminding myself that tears are the least of my worries as I add padding to all of my undergarments, since I seem to be leaking from every nook and cranny these days. I try not to stare at the immaculate specimen in front of me when he steps into the spray to rinse himself, but another sob threatens to bubble up when he turns off the water and leans back against the shower wall with his eyes closed, as if he can't go on anymore.

I cover my mouth and scamper out of the bathroom before he can catch me crying over ruining his life.

A few minutes later, Blake joins me on the couch, plopping down beside me and pulling out his phone while I set up for another pumping session.

Dammit, can't a woman get any privacy these days? Don't I deserve to bawl my eyes out until I start to hyperventilate in peace?

I watch as he scrolls down his TikTok feed, stopping to chuckle at a video with a baby giggling at a puppy, suspiciously skipping over one about married life, watching the next clip about being a girl-dad, and landing on a list of tips for "boosting your milk supply."

And even though I still want to be alone, I'm also grateful he's sitting next to me, because I'd started missing him already. It's like I'm desperate for him to wrap me up in a hug but simultaneously loathe the idea of being touched right now. These hormones really are the worst.

"Hey, Lo, maybe they're onto something. I think I read that stuff about oatmeal in one of the baby books, too. I'll make a grocery run in the morning so you can have some for breakfast, hmm?"

My expression softens when he looks at me earnestly. "I think your algorithm is confused," I tell him.

"Are you referring to my FYP or my life?" he asks, smirking.

"Blake," I begin, my voice already cracking. "How miserable are you right now?"

He frowns. "What makes you think I'm miserable?"

"You must be. You haven't had a break in weeks. You're driving around in a freaking white minivan, for goodness sake!"

He reaches over and interlaces his fingers with mine. "I'm exhausted, not miserable. Sure, I'd much rather have our girls home with us by now, but the three of you have made my heart so full that I'd give up sleep forever to do this with you."

I sigh, melting into the couch. "Are you sure?"

"Of course I'm sure. I'm sorry this experience has been so scary for you, and I can't imagine what you must be going through, both physically and emotionally. Tenley explained that it's probably a million times harder for you to leave them behind at night, especially while you're dealing with the postpartum hormones. So don't be afraid to tell me if there's anything else I can do to help you."

I look down at our clasped hands. "Is this really the life you wanted?"

"I wish this last part had been a little easier, but yes, it is, because of you. Although, I really do miss my truck."

I snort out a laugh as he strokes the side of my hand with his thumb. "And you still ...?"

The rhythmic noise from the breast pump is killing the vibe, so I reach down to switch it off. Blake watches me carefully as I remove the flanges and tuck myself back into my clothes, and I swear he's got the same longing in his eyes as I did when I stared at him before. And I'm so relieved by the notion of him checking me out that I could cry again.

"If you're going to ask me whether I still want you, the answer is *always*," he declares, his voice deepening in a way that makes my body take note.

"I don't even feel like a whole human right now. I'm ... broken.

Like Humpty Dumpty, except they managed to put me back together, and none of the seams line up. But, you—you're still so perfect. You're only getting better looking and more handsome every day. How could you want me now?"

He shakes his head. "First of all, I'm pretty sure I look like I've aged twenty years overnight, but if you've got a thing for older men, then I don't hate it. A compliment from you means more than one from anyone else. Secondly, you're not broken, babe, you've just changed. And you might feel terrible right now, but you're still sexy as hell to me," he affirms, reaching out to run a finger down my arm.

"But the first time you saw me, the night we slept together, you said I was perfect," I say, sniffling. "And I'll never be perfect again."

"You don't need to worry," he begins with a short laugh. "If anything, you've reached a whole new level of perfection in my eyes, because you're so strong and amazing. Look at what you've been doing—growing two tiny humans at once, surviving a crazy dangerous delivery, and now feeding and caring for them. I'm just a lousy cheerleader. All I've done is supply a little DNA and a few jars of peanut butter. The fact that you're continuing to do all of this miraculous stuff with your body only makes me more eager for the day when I get to make love to you again, to catalog every bit of you that's new, because it's a reminder of how lucky I am to have you."

I wipe my nose on the inside of my shirt. "Gah, you really are a piece of work. You could have just said I was tolerable."

He smirks. "Loren, when I say that I'm proud of you, that I'm in awe of what you've done for me and our babies, I mean it. And I've never found you more beautiful than I do now."

There's a tingling in my chest as he continues gazing at me adoringly, and it's not just a let-down sensation. "You know, I never could have survived all this without you. When I wasn't sure what was happening, whether or not we were going to be okay, you are the only person I wanted by my side. And I'd never choose to go back to a life without you now." His smile softens as I continue. "I'm sorry it's taken me so long to realize that I never needed anyone as much as I need you. I just want to make sure this is still what you want, too."

"You are all I've ever wanted," he replies evenly. "And that's never going to change."

I turn my body to face him, reaching around with my free hand to cup his cheek and pull him in for a kiss. He sighs and draws me in closer while his lips seem to melt into mine.

"I love you so much," he whispers when I back away. And the way he follows me like he's not ready to stop kissing me yet makes it all the more believable.

"I love you, too," I breathe. "But there *is* something I really want from you." I reach up and run my fingers through his hair, and he hums appreciatively, his eyelids growing heavy.

"Anything."

I smile and bring up my left hand, which is still intertwined with his. "I want to keep this ring ... forever."

He blinks at me in surprise. "Yeah?"

"Yes, please, and I'd like to request a matching band. I could even get one for you to wear, too, if you think you'd be into that sort of thing."

His chest rises and falls as the words settle. "And how soon would you like to schedule this exchange?"

I shrug. "Right around the time I get cleared by the doctor to resume all regular physical activity would be ideal."

He chuckles loudly, then he brings my hand up to his mouth for a kiss. "Is that so?"

"It is," I reply, turning and hitching my leg over his so that I'm sitting in his lap. Then I kiss him again.

"Blake Augustine Bourgeois ...." He moans when I enunciate his name. "You are my Darcy, my Wentworth, my Jamie Fraser, the Aragorn to my Arwen. And I'm desperate to marry you, if you'll still have me, because I really want to spend the rest of our lives making up for lost time." By the time I'm finished, I'm crying again.

He swallows hard and stares at me for a while before he says, "*Sure*, I guess we can do that."

I swat him playfully in the chest, and he grins before he leans in for another long, tender kiss.

"So, how long before you think Doc will give you the all clear?" he asks when I finally pull away so I can catch my breath.

"At least not for another month or two." But I'm already staring at his mouth again.

"Hmm," he begins, running his hands down my back and making me shiver. "I think I'll give Father Conrad a call early tomorrow morning, just to get his input on all this. Maybe he'll be able to help with your request."

"You do that, Gus Gus."

He tilts his head down to kiss me again, but he stops just short of my lips, teasing me. "You know, once we get married, I won't be able to call you 'Reed' anymore."

"You've got enough nicknames to choose from," I mumble, willing him to close in the space.

"And after the new ones you gave me tonight, it looks like I've got some catching up to do," he whispers, brushing his lips over mine before he backs away again. His mouth curls up to form a satisfied smirk when I whimper. "But, you know, Agnes, out of all the names you've called me so far, I have to say 'Daddy' is my favorite."

Epilogue

A FEW MONTHS LATER

LOREN

This is it.

It's really happening.

I lift my eyes to Blake's face, and his expression knocks the wind out of me. He's staring at me with his eyebrows drawn together and his chin trembling. The emotion in his eyes is enough to reassure me that I'm doing the right thing, because there's no way this man would be looking at me the way he is right now unless he was seriously in love with me. Then he brings his hand up to swipe at his cheeks, and I lose it. A sob wracks my chest against my will, making Blake shake his head at me in an unspoken apology.

But it's okay, because as far as "first looks" go, I can't imagine a more amazing reaction than this. It's also classic Blake behavior, because only he could manage to make being a big sap look so good.

I continue watching through teary eyes as JD nudges Blake, making him smile. My groom blows out a breath, his shoulders rising and falling with the exertion. Meanwhile, I'm biting my lip to keep myself from ugly crying the rest of the way to him.

"Hey, Dad? Can we pick this up?" I venture after I regain control of my lungs.

He laughs quietly and quickens our pace, stopping at the altar to shake Blake's hand and pat him affectionately on the arm (well, as affectionately as my father ever gets) before shuffling off to the front pew.

"Hi," Blake whispers, turning his attention to me. "You look … *perfect*."

I swallow hard. "You're pretty freaking hot, too."

He leans in, chuckling softly. "I still can't believe you agreed to marry me when you wouldn't even let me take you to the senior prom. But I feel like the luckiest man in the world."

"Ditto," is all I can choke out.

He takes my hand to lead us up the altar, but not before gently pressing his lips to my knuckles. My knees threaten to buckle beneath me. Maybe I should just ask him to carry me up the steps?

Tenley walks over and winks as she collects my bouquet. I inhale deeply, trying to calm myself as Blake and I turn to face the priest, although the way his thumb rubs soft circles on the back of my hand only makes me anxious for an entirely different reason.

Father Conrad greets us warmly and begins with the sign of the cross, and I do my best to listen intently. But my eyes admittedly wander off to the side when a baby cries out. It sounds like Charley, though I can't tell from this angle which baby Mrs. T is lifting over her shoulder. She pats the diapered bottom softly and bounces, quieting what must be Charley, since Penny would never calm that easily without her pacifier. My mom stands beside them, slowly rocking an identical swaddle from side to side. Both of the babies are dressed in the frilly white gowns we recycled from last week's triple baptism.

I turn my attention back to the priest, since this stuff is probably pretty important. A few minutes pass before another cry echoes throughout the church, but this time I instinctively know it's not one of mine. I glance at Tenley, who cringes and shoots JD a panicked look before she crosses her arms over her chest, I imagine to prevent a lactation malfunction.

Baby Jake continues to fuss, and Father pauses for Tenley to pass our bouquets to my sister so she can take the baby from Ethan. My godson's new agenda quickly changes once he smells his mother, and he begins rooting around and snorting greedily.

Tenley groans and turns to mouth a "sorry" to me before she flings a blanket over her shoulder and pacifies the *petit cochon* with yet another snack. I smile inwardly when I remember how she never thought she'd be able to handle motherhood a year ago, and now she's seamlessly nursing a baby during a wedding—*my* wedding.

Because I'm getting married. To Blake freaking Bourgeois.

Pay attention, Lo.

Blake laughs quietly when Father begins again and has to raise his voice to cover up the smacking and grunting sounds emanating from beneath that blanket. My eyes drift over to JD, whose elbow nudges my brother's side when he catches Landry watching Tenley too carefully, and I can't help but giggle.

We make it halfway through our vows before Penny begins screeching—her trademark, high-pitched shriek is unmistakable—but, thankfully, her pacifier does its job.

"Pen, of course," Blake whispers, grinning at me.

I smile warmly in return, because I'm so lucky to be marrying the kind of man who recognizes his three-month-old identical twins by their cries. It's such a good thought that I say it aloud, and he bites his lip while his eyes water again.

Father Conrad finishes up and pronounces us man and wife, inviting Blake to kiss his bride (that's *me*, y'all—the bride, aka Mrs. Blake Bourgeois). And I imagine each of our guests is waiting with bated breath for him to do something inappropriate. But before he can move, I grasp the lapels of my husband's jacket and drag him down as I lift to my tiptoes and plant my mouth on his. I feel a rumble of approval in his chest, and he cups his hands around my waist to tug my body closer.

"Hey, now. That's not church tongue," I hear JD calling out in the distance, followed by a chuckle from the crowd.

Blake reluctantly pulls away, a cocky smirk plastered across his face. "I hope you realize this new contract renders the original ground rules completely null and void, Mrs. Bourgeois," he murmurs, staring at me with a sexy, smoldering look and making my stomach swoop the way that only he can.

I lick my lips before I answer. "And how do you know this wasn't my plan all along, Counselor?"

"Gah, I love you." He sighs and shakes his head.

I shrug and bat my eyelashes at him. "Prove it, Gus Gus."

He cocks an eyebrow and makes me squeal when he leans down to lift me into his capable arms, and I crook my elbow behind his neck and beam at him as he walks us out of the church.

Nope, I take that back—Blake never simply *walks*. This time, I think he *floats*, despite the extra weight in his arms.

"Does this mean we can go home and take care of some pressing business before the reception?" he asks and sets me down just outside the doors of the church.

"Unfortunately not," I say with a sigh, directing him to go around so we can reenter the church on the other side. "At least, not yet. We've got pictures."

He groans but stops us and kisses me softly anyway. "I *was* hoping to get a small taste of cake first. I've been such a good boy, after all."

"There'll be some—*oh*," I giggle when I finally catch on. "Well, here's the thing. You didn't really give me a budget when I was dress shopping, and I just happened to fall in love with two dresses. So, per Tenley's recommendation, I bought both," I tell him with a shrug.

"Yeah?" he asks, pulling me in again.

"Yep. One for the ceremony, one for the reception."

The truth is that I really did find two dresses I absolutely loved, and I'd have felt entirely too guilty buying more than one dress had it not been a total flex on Nicole at the dress shop. I'm not usually a mean girl, but she fired the first shot when she picked on my man.

"What I'm hearing is, you're going to need some help to get changed?" Blake asks, his voice deep and velvety and his lips warm against my skin.

I tilt my head to the side for him to continue kissing and nipping at my neck. "My matron of honor was originally assigned to those duties, but I suppose you'll do in a pinch."

"You can assure my sister-in-law that she'll be leaving you in very, *very* capable hands," he mutters, emphasizing his offer by running his palms down to my butt and grazing his teeth over my earlobe. He hums in approval when I shiver.

But we're interrupted a second later by the rest of the wedding party, and my sister ushers everyone back to the altar for the most chaotic group photo session in history with all of the squabbling infants involved. And I have to spend the next thirty minutes pretending I'm not thinking so hard about doing spicy things with my husband that my toes are curling inside my fancy shoes.

"I know I'm supposed to assist you with your wardrobe change now," Tenley begins with a smirk, "but I'm afraid your godson is prepping for his first big growth spurt, so it's probably best if your husband goes in my place. Can you forgive me for abandoning you in your time of need?"

I stifle a grin. "See you at the reception in a few minutes?"

She lifts a shoulder. "Take your time. If you rush, your zipper might get stuck, which could delay you for a while. But, I mean, if such an unfortunate event were to occur, I'd probably just create a diversion by asking the caterers to start serving the food a little early. I'm sure no one will mind, if they even notice."

Blake waltzes over with one of the girls in his arms. "Are we heading out?"

"Yep, I'll take that," Tenley replies, extricating Charley. "You've been reassigned to wardrobe-change duty."

Blake's eyes meet mine, and his lips curl into a sly smile as he salutes her. "Aye-aye, Nurse Tenley."

I assume the position as my husband lifts me again, just as JD and Landry approach. "You don't have to actually carry her to the truck, you know," JD snickers. "Wouldn't want you to hurt yourself there, bro."

"Wait, where are you two going?" Landry asks, eyeing us suspiciously.

"Wardrobe malfunction," Tenley answers for us. "She needs to swap dresses, but this one's got a tricky zipper. It may take a while, so we should probably just go on and get the reception started without them."

"We'll, uh ... we'll be there in a few," Blake assures them when Landry frowns.

JD pats Landry on the back. "Don't worry, that zipper's been stuck for close to a year. It'll only take a couple of tugs to loosen it up."

"Oh, but I'm good with zippers." Blake smirks at me, and I shiver again. "Because I take my time."

"Yeah, but this is your favorite zipper," JD continues, waving his hand. "Prior zipping experience doesn't apply when you're this overeager. I bet it'll be over much faster than you think."

Blake tilts his head to the side. "He's got a point."

"I'll need a couple more rounds of zipping, anyway," I offer. "Since I have to put on the second dress and take it off later tonight. But we won't need to rush the last one."

JD chuckles loudly as Landry wrinkles his nose in disgust. "I hate it here," he announces.

Then my friend Daisy passes by, offering a quick "congratulations" before she turns to ask Landry for a ride, and I watch as his expression softens.

"Eh, you'll learn to love it," I tell him.

～

Acknowledgements

Mais, gardez donc. Another Camellia book!

This story was written with the intention of bringing glory to God and highlighting His greatest gifts—His infinite love and mercy—and to provide a reminder that, though we are human and we make mistakes (especially when hormones and emotions are involved), we can always strive to do better next time. Let us remember to ask for His grace and to treasure the sacraments on our own paths to holiness.

To my husband—Thank you again for everything. I could (and would) never have done this without you. I am so grateful for your confidence in me, especially when I had none, for picking up the slack on my behalf, for your inspirational growth in holiness, and for stepping up as the spiritual leader of our family. I am so proud of you, and I love you more with each day.

To my amazing children, A, E, C, and R, my parents, and my (large) extended family—thank you for your patience and your encouragement. You are my greatest blessings, and your support means the world to me. I love you all so much.

To Kait—There are so many reasons why this book would not have been possible without you, and you know it. Thank you for all of it—the constant planning convos, counseling sessions, meme sharing, inspo pics, proofing and edits, "Things JD/Blake Says … " text threads. Here's the Bougie Bro MMC I promised you. I hope you love Blake as much as I do. And tell Jojo I said thank you, too.

To my awesome cover designer and alpha reader, Cindy R—thank you for your support, your input, and your encouragement. Your friendship is truly a blessing and one of the best parts of this experience. Thank you for sharing your amazing talents with me and keeping me (and Blake) in line.

To my friends and coworkers—especially RG (my constant sounding board), Laura N (my other Lo inspo), Emily C (my title genius), Elizabeth V (my writer's-vent pal), Claire M (by biggest cheerleader), Kira W, Jahn, Kate L, Shaley, ST, and KJ, thank you for your input and your support and for not letting me give up. I am so grateful to you all for your guidance, your friendship, and your prayers.

To my alpha and beta readers—especially my mom (L) and sister (A), Kelly, Mel, my Tantes Bibby and Ellen, and anyone else I may have missed—I can't tell you how much I appreciate the time and energy you wasted on me and my silly stories. I love you all.

To my editors, Pauline H and Kait F—thanks for helping my crazy ideas make more sense.

Shout out to the @bookrackacadiana in Laffy! Thanks for your support and for taking a chance on a leauxcal author.

And to all my readers, especially my ARC readers and those from my hometown, the 'Fettes, and the Bookstagram/BookTok Community (@wallflower_m_reads, @abbys.always.reading, @anastasia_layne_author, @klhester_author, @mary.reads.romance, @carolineskindle, @the_krissi, @ntw8925, @bookishbeachbabe, and everyone else!)—thank you *so very much* for your time and energy. I am truly grateful for your support and reviews. I hope you each get something from this, at least a few laughs or a character crush and at most appreciation for the Catholic faith and the sacraments.

About the Author

A former high school literature teacher from South Louisiana, Marie Veillon is still learning to balance her ridiculous accent, Cajun-French—inspired vocabulary, and horrible speaking syntax with writing humorous stories and creating characters and situations relatable enough to make readers forget they aren't real. She enjoys reading books about her Catholic faith and rom coms with guaranteed HEAs, watching football, fangirling, and spending time with her amazing family.

Thank you for reading and reviewing!
marievwrites.com
@marievwrites

instagram.com/marievwrites

threads.com/@marievwrites

marievwrites.substack.com

facebook.com/marievwrites

tiktok.com/@marievwrites

bookbub.com/authors/marie-veillon

goodreads.com/marie_veillon

amazon.com/author/marieveillon

Also by Marie Veillon

THE CAMELLIA ROM-COM SERIES

Third and Ten

Going for Two

Hail Mary Catch

Walking Green Flag

Lagniappe

...A LITTLE SOMETHING EXTRA

Sign up for my newsletter and join the Camellia Crewe Facebook group to receive updates and announcements, including free content and the latest news regarding the next installments in the Camellia Rom-Com Series!

Continue the Camellia Rom-Com series with **Daisy & Landry's story** and read the first chapter of ***Hail Mary Catch*** for FREE!

Need more Blake + Lo?
Get a Bonus Epilogue and more at
marievwrites.com

www.ingramcontent.com/pod-product-compliance
Lightning Source LLC
Chambersburg PA
CBHW021408310726
48971CB00005B/1255